BLANK SLATE

BLANK SLATE

Tiffany Snow

Text copyright © 2013 Tiffany Snow
Originally released as a Kindle Serial, December 2012

Published by Montlake Romance
P.O. Box 400818
Las Vegas, NV 89140

ISBN-13: 9781611099485
ISBN-10: 161109948X

This book is dedicated to Eleni and the phone call that changed everything.

EPISODE ONE

CHAPTER ONE

It had begun to snow.

Special Agent Erik Langston sighed in frustration, his breath fogging up the glass inside the SUV. He hated the cold, and he hated snow, which was why he was particularly irritated that he was stuck in both at the moment. Colorado was a place he might actually enjoy visiting, when the temperature wasn't hovering about ten degrees above zero.

It was getting late, the darkness outside the car windows broken only by the amber glow filtering from the windows on the villa nestled in the side of the mountain. The trees surrounding the luxury residence lent to its artistry. Picking up his high-powered binoculars, Erik could see through the floor-to-ceiling windows to the party going on inside. Women dressed in long gowns spun elegantly on the arms of tuxedoed men, their jewels glistening in the light of the chandeliers.

No doubt just one of those gowns cost three months' salary, he thought wryly. But he hadn't picked this profession for the money; he'd chosen it to put bad guys behind bars, and one of those bad guys was inside that villa.

The cell phone lying on the empty passenger seat began to buzz. Erik picked it up.

"Langston," he answered.

"Still chasing your tail in the middle of nowhere?"

Erik bit back a sharp retort, the jibe from his colleague and erstwhile partner grating on his nerves more than usual.

"What do you want, Kaminski?"

"Just checking up on you. Not everyone chooses to spend New Year's Eve stalking thieves with a track record of outrunning and outsmarting the FBI."

Judging by the slurring of his words and the sounds of revelry in the background, Erik thought it was safe to assume Kaminski was drunk.

"What I choose to do in my time off is none of your business," Erik retorted, though the fact that he was bothering to argue with a drunken asshole gave proof to the fact that he'd gone too long without any interaction with another person. Obviously, communing with nature wasn't his thing.

"Dude, I'm just saying, you're obsessed. Lay off the work and get a life. You won't make an arrest tonight, not alone. And how long has it been since you've been laid?"

"Fuck off." Erik hung up.

Before the call he'd been bored and cold. Now he was bored, cold, and pissed off.

It wasn't like he didn't get offers. Women tended to find him attractive, more so once they realized what he did for a living, but Erik chalked that up to too much television. Usually, he gave them a pass. It wasn't worth the hassle. Invariably he'd get hooked into the scenario of a woman relentlessly calling him, unable to take the hint when he didn't call them back. Then he'd feel guilty, once or twice allowing himself to be coerced into dinner with sex for dessert, and then he was in even deeper than before.

No thanks.

So he worked. And worked. This case in particular had been a thorn in his side for the better part of a year.

He'd been following the trail a thief who specialized in hacking the computers and bank accounts of some of the wealthiest people in the world. In an usual twist, those same people usually had some sort of link to organized crime. A vigilante masquerading as Robin Hood? Or just a talented thief with a taste for the absurd?

Erik had been tracking the hacker and their targets for months, always one step behind. Tonight, he'd hoped to turn that around. An anonymous tip had led him to this desolate spot in the Colorado mountains, where he'd been stuck watching the villa for the past two nights; that's how desperate he was to nail this case.

Muttering a curse, Erik climbed out of the SUV, pocketing his keys and holstering his gun. The snow crunched underneath his feet as he set off toward the villa. Crashing a New Year's Eve party wasn't usually his thing, but damned if he was going to be outsmarted again, and he was tired of waiting.

A few minutes later, he was knocking on the front door. A butler opened it, and with a flash of his badge and an admonition to alert no one to his presence, he was inside.

Jeans and a sweater may have passed muster at the office, but were decidedly lowbrow for this party, not that Erik cared. The guests had been dining, drinking, and dancing for hours. No one even gave him a second look.

She was here. His gut told him so, and he always listened to his gut.

Snagging an hors d'oeuvre off a passing waitress's tray, Erik popped it in his mouth, his practiced gaze scanning the crowd.

Clarissa O'Connell kept moving, though she'd spotted the cop immediately. Damn. How'd he find her?

It didn't matter. By the time he realized what was going on, she would be long gone.

She gave him one more look, since he certainly deserved it. Tall and broad-shouldered, his hair a deep mahogany, he stood out from the crowd, and not just because of his clothing. He carried himself with a confidence bordering on arrogance. In another lifetime, Clarissa might have tried her luck with him. But not tonight.

Hurrying back to the kitchen, Clarissa discarded the tray of food from which the cop had plucked his morsel. Loitering by the servants' staircase, she waited, patiently watching for the moment when no one was noticing her. When that time came, she soundlessly climbed the darkened steps to the upper floors, pulling on a pair of latex gloves as she did so.

If she did this right, she'd finally be free.

The information she'd been given was accurate, and several minutes later she was standing in front of a computer monitor, waiting for the program she'd uploaded from her flash drive to go to work.

"Solomon said you'd show up tonight."

Clarissa's hand went for the gun strapped to her thigh.

"Ah, ah, ah," cautioned the man now standing directly behind her. He'd blended with the shadows and not made a sound. Now the cold metal of his gun pressed against her bare neck. "I wouldn't do that if I were you. Hand it over."

4

Moving slowly and deliberately, Clarissa gave him her gun, turning so she faced him.

"I see why Solomon chose you," he said with a snort. "Not exactly a looker. I bet you blend in real well."

Clarissa ignored his insult, thinking furiously, her palms damp with sweat. "Solomon told you about me?"

"Yep. Looks like your boss thinks you've outlived your usefulness. I'm here to tie up loose ends."

"That's not what I was promised."

"Deals change, sweetheart."

Clarissa's smile was sweet as molasses as her fingers closed over the heavy silver letter opener lying on the desk at her back. "So they do."

Quick as a snake, she struck, shoving the arm holding the gun as she buried the letter opener to the hilt in his side.

He grunted in pain, snarling curses as they struggled. Her knee came up, nailing him in the crotch. The gun dropped to the floor as he dropped to his knees. An elbow to the back of the neck and he was out cold at her feet.

She retrieved her gun then reached over, typed a few commands into the computer, and waited impatiently for the files to be copied. When it was finished, she snatched the flash drive out of its slot. If Solomon wanted those files, he'd have to pay dearly for them, the lying bastard.

A few keystrokes later, information began to upload to her remote server, not that anyone would notice if they sat down in front of the computer. The program was both silent and invisible to all but the savviest of technicians, and even then nearly impossible to get rid of unless the drive was wiped clean.

Clarissa felt the usual thrill of satisfaction from seeing her work in action. Software was easy, logical; the rules it followed never wavered or changed. Unlike people. People lied to you, betrayed you, used you. The only way to stay alive was to never trust anyone, ever. That lesson had saved her life more than once.

And now it was past time to leave.

Clarissa hurried to the door, checking to make sure the hallway was clear. A shadow in the corridor made her whisk back inside, out of sight.

She never heard the gunshot, just a searing pain ripping through her. Reacting automatically, she spun, took quick aim, and pulled the trigger. Her would-be assassin fell back to the floor and didn't get up again.

The wound in her side was bleeding. If she hadn't moved at the last moment, she'd be dead. It wasn't that bad, though it hurt like hell. The blood mated with the black fabric of her uniform, darkening it, but thankfully not standing out. No one looked, really looked, at the waitstaff. She'd just slip out the back door with no one the wiser.

Pressing her hand tightly to her side, Clarissa eased into the hallway. The gunshot had gone unnoticed, it seemed, possibly not heard over the revelry of the midnight celebrations below. The New Year had arrived at a very opportune moment.

At least, it seemed that way until she rounded the corner and ran right into the cop.

Erik's hands shot out, grabbing the waitress's upper arms before she fell backward from their collision. A little thing, her arms seemed fragile enough for him to break with his bare hands. He eased his hold, not wanting to hurt her.

"Are you all right?" he asked.

She didn't answer, the surprise on her face somewhat comical. He repeated his question.

"No hablo Inglés," the girl stammered, her eyes wide.

Erik frowned, releasing her. He watched as she hurried down the hall, glancing back at him once before disappearing down a set of stairs. Dismissing her with a shake of his head, he turned back to the empty hallway. He could have sworn he'd heard a gunshot from up here. If he'd been downstairs, he would've missed it, with the party in full swing. But he'd been exploring the upper floors when the unmistakable sound had rung out.

Opening yet another door, Erik saw the faint blue glow of a computer monitor reflecting off the large picture window behind a desk. Casually flipping on the light, he froze when he saw the body on the floor.

Erik raced forward, crouching to turn the man onto his back. A gun with a silencer attached lay beside the body, the wound in his chest deadly accurate. His eyes stared straight ahead, sightless, while something protruded from his side. Grasping it, Erik pulled out a silver letter opener.

The waitress. Shit!

Jumping to his feet, Erik peered out the window to the grounds below. Sure enough, he saw her, hurrying away from the villa toward the bank of cars parked for the guests. Clutching awkwardly at her side, she disappeared among the steel maze.

Erik ran down the hall, racing down the stairs toward the front door, gun in hand.

A woman spotted him, saw the gun, and screamed, pointing, "He has a gun!"

Cries of alarm spread through the guests as Erik pushed his way through them. Dammit! This was taking too long. She was going to be long gone if he had to stop to explain who he was and what was happening.

The butler who'd let him in earlier now stood uncertainly in front of the doorway, blocking Erik's path.

Erik pointed his gun at him as he ran. "Open it!" he ordered.

The butler blanched, then scurried to do his bidding, flinging open the door just in time for Erik to launch himself through the opening and out into the frigid night.

Panting for air, Erik skidded to a halt, scanning the cars through the thickening snow falling from the sky.

There. A sedan was pulling out of the lot on the far side. Erik's smile was one of satisfaction. That car was a bad choice on a night like tonight in a place like this. He ran to his SUV.

Clarissa blinked hard, trying to clear her vision. The damn wound in her side hurt more than she'd bargained for, the loss of blood making her slightly dizzy. Damn Solomon and his double-crossing ways! This job should've been a piece of cake; had been, until the hired gun had showed up. She'd even slipped past the cop.

Lights in the rearview mirror caught Clarissa's eye. Someone was chasing her, and catching up fast. Alarmed, she stepped on the gas, the sedan's wheels spinning on the fresh snow as it picked up speed.

Clarissa had memorized the map of roads for the area, though some of them barely deserved the name, being little more than clearings just wide enough for one car to pass through. Forcing herself to concentrate, she put both hands on the frigid wheel, hoping the uniform she wore was tight enough to keep the bleeding down. Consulting her memory, she suddenly stepped hard on the brakes, spun the wheel, and hit the gas again. The car fishtailed at the abrupt turn before the wheels found purchase and she shot down the road.

Snow lay on the evergreens overhead, their laden branches hanging low and brushing the car as she flew past. The snowfall was heavy, the flakes coming down thick and fast. Glancing in her mirror, Clarissa saw the lights still behind her, the pursuer taking the sudden turn in stride and eating up the ground between them.

Clarissa cursed her decision to take the sedan rather than searching the lot for a more appropriate vehicle. At the time, expediency had seemed to be the wisest course, but she hadn't known she'd have someone chasing her. Someone who appeared quite relentless.

Consulting the map in her head yet again, Clarissa wavered in indecision. She thought she could make the turn ahead, but that road was filled with dangerous switchbacks. One more glance in the mirror and her lips thinned into a tight line. There really wasn't a choice, not if she wanted to lose the guy behind her.

A brief thought flashed through her mind—she hoped it wasn't the cop. He was doing his job and didn't deserve to be killed for it. She just really didn't have time to be arrested, even by a cop as mouth-wateringly gorgeous as that one.

Sending up a quick prayer to anyone who might be listening, Clarissa took a deep breath, then slammed on the brakes, spinning the wheel as fast as she dared before stomping on the gas again. The sudden, sharp movement caused a flash of pain in her side, but she gritted her teeth, tightly gripped the wheel, and ignored it.

The car fishtailed again, the wheels spinning, and the back of the sedan slammed into a tree. Clarissa jerked in her seat at the impact but didn't let up on the gas. Bouncing off the tree, the wheels caught and she was racing down the road. She let out the breath she'd been holding. That had been close.

Watching in the mirror, she saw the SUV skid and slow, then back up to make the turn.

Clarissa cursed under her breath, jerking her attention back to the road. It was rougher, the beams from the headlights dancing crazily as the car bounced and dipped over the uneven patches.

A sharp curve loomed ahead, and Clarissa's hands tightened until her knuckles were white. Fear lapped at her, but she fought it. There wasn't any time to be scared.

Bracing herself, she slowed the car. The empty space beyond the bend in the road made her blood turn to ice. If she didn't make it, it was a long way down. She turned the wheel.

The car slid past the edge of the road, and Clarissa choked back a cry. But luck or an angel was with her because just when she felt sure her next breath would be her last, the car shot forward again.

Her heart pounded in her chest, while her palms were damp and slick on the steering wheel. Watching in the mirror, Clarissa held her breath while the SUV easily made the turn.

Damn! How was she going to lose him?

Looking back at the road, Clarissa screamed, instinctively jerking the wheel and slamming on the brakes to avoid hitting the deer standing directly in her path.

The car swerved with a sickening lurch, spinning 180 degrees before sliding off the road and down a steep embankment. Slamming into trees, it broke branches before flipping once end over end.

Clarissa's heart was in her throat, the world upside down and righting itself around her. The sound of wrenching metal was loud in her ears as she was flung against the steering wheel, her head slamming against something so hard the pain caused instant nausea.

Her last terrified thought was that she was going to die.

Erik stomped on the brakes, bringing the SUV to a skidding halt. Vaulting from the seat, he watched as the sedan came to a shuddering stop at the bottom of the embankment. The metal was twisted and dented, a telling path of destruction left in its wake.

His feet slid in the snow as he made his way down to the car, gun in hand. The last thing he wanted was the girl getting the drop on him, though he'd be very surprised if the crash hadn't done permanent damage to her.

"FBI!" he shouted, the words immediately muffled by the falling snow. "Put your hands where I can see them!"

No response. Steam rolled from underneath the hood, the engine exuding a quiet hiss as escaping liquid touched the hot metal. The woods were quite still now, the idling of the SUV a distant purr as Erik cautiously approached the car. Snow squeaked and crunched under his boots as he walked. He never took his eyes from the windows and saw nothing move inside.

The twin glow of the SUV's headlights cut through the darkness, the falling snow grabbing the light and reflected it into the night. Erik was close enough now to see the glass had shattered in the driver's side window. Acutely aware that this woman had just shot a man less than fifteen minutes ago, Erik held his gun steady.

"FBI," he repeated loudly. Still nothing. Cautiously, he bent to peer into the car.

The woman was crumpled in the driver's seat, her head lolling forward on her neck, forehead nearly touching the pristine steering wheel.

The steering wheel. Completely intact, with no limp airbag hanging from its center.

Erik pressed two fingers to her neck, underneath her jaw, hoping she wasn't dead. It would be just his luck to have his hunt for her end with her dead from a car crash. A steady pulse beat under his fingers.

Making what he hoped wouldn't be his last decision, Erik swiftly holstered his gun before reaching for the door handle. Though he pulled, it refused to open. Muttering a few choice curses, he put his back into it, but still the mangled steel wouldn't budge. Well, that really left only one option.

He reached through the window, feeling his way through the dark to where the seat belt latched, holding the woman firmly in place. As he pressed the button, the seat belt relaxed, retracting as the woman slumped forward against the steering wheel and Erik's arm.

Hoping nothing vital had been broken, and not caring overly much if it had, Erik maneuvered until he had grasped her beneath her arms. He pulled her through the window. The fact that she wasn't wearing a coat helped to get her through the small space. Erik glanced up at the hill he'd just climbed down. Nice. Getting back up to the

SUV while carrying her was going to be a complete pain in the ass.

Hoisting her in his arms, he began the climb. Thankfully, she was a little thing and didn't weigh much. Still, Erik slipped and slid up the hill, losing his footing and going down to his knees a couple of times. The falling snowflakes coated his lashes, and he blinked them away, keeping his gaze on the ground in front of him.

He struggled on, the woman in his arms oblivious to the difficulties she was inflicting on him. His foot slipped again, and Erik cursed as his hand shot out to grab a tree to keep himself upright. Clarissa moaned, the sound quiet and pained, as he lost his grip on her legs.

Erik's lips pressed into a grim line as he carefully readjusted her in his arms. He was almost there; he just had to be more careful. No more falls.

As he neared the vehicle, he could see her a bit clearer, the headlights cutting through the shadows. Her hair obscured part of her face, but Erik thought he could see the dark trail of blood. Unconsciously, his steps quickened.

Finally, he reached the SUV. Sweat coated his skin underneath his thick coat and sweater, the frigid air he sucked in burning its way down his throat and lungs. He opened the back door, easing her onto the seat. Standing back, he took a moment to catch his breath, his back aching from the climb. Looking at her, he frowned. She was wearing that little black uniform, her legs encased in nylons, while her arms were bare against the cold.

By all rights, he should let her freeze her ass off. That's what Erik kept telling himself as he dug in the back of the

SUV, pulling out the emergency blanket he'd put there, just in case. He tossed it over her still form, giving it a rough tuck under her legs, protecting them from the cold leather seats.

He slammed the door shut, reminding himself that she could very well be playing him, just waiting for the chance when his back was turned to attack. Just because she was little didn't mean she was any less dangerous.

Another trip down the hill to the car and Erik retrieved the two bags he found inside, stowing them in the back of the SUV. His muscles burned from the exertion as he finally climbed into the driver's seat and shifted the car into drive. His hand stuck slightly to the gearshift. Curious, Erik glanced at his palm.

It was smeared with blood. Her blood.

Shit.

The nearest hospital was two hours away, probably more in this weather. Erik grabbed his cell, only to see that the storm had eroded what slight service he'd had: the display showed no bars. His only choice was to take his chances and try to get her to the hospital as quickly as he could.

Erik drove, retracing his path through the woods as best he could, though the snow and darkness made it slow and difficult. The switchbacks appeared as if from nowhere, their dangerous curves threatening to send the SUV plummeting to unseen depths. The road grew uneven, the tires dipping into gouges covered in snow. After hitting a particularly rough patch, Erik heard a soft whimper from the backseat. He glanced in the rearview mirror, but the girl hadn't moved. His hands tightened on the steering wheel.

After driving for another forty-five minutes, Erik was forced to admit that he was lost. The chase she'd led him on had turned him around, his sense of direction utterly screwed by the snowstorm, the map and cell phone lying on the seat next to him utterly useless.

Each minute that ticked by seemed to mock Erik. The sticky blood on his hand as he gripped the steering wheel reminding him that he had a responsibility to the girl, even if she was a criminal and cold-blooded killer.

Up ahead, the beam from the headlights glinted off something metallic. Squinting through the snow, Erik realized it was a mailbox. Wondering how in the hell anyone got mail out here—and his respect for postmen inching upward a notch—Erik aimed the SUV toward it, turning in to the tiny drive that led deeper into the thick woods.

A few minutes and several rough bounces later, a log cabin came into view. No cheery lights burned from the windows, but it was shelter.

He pulled to a stop in front of the cabin, noticing no other vehicles or tire tracks. The snow had piled up, and it came to Erik's shins when he cut the engine and climbed out of the SUV. Deciding to leave the girl in the car while he checked out the place, he grabbed a flashlight from the trunk and headed to the front door.

The slam of the car door penetrated the girl's consciousness, her eyes slitting open as the fog slowly lifted from her mind.

Where was she?

It was dark, and cold, though she had a blanket over her. She sat up, then gasped at the sharp stabs of pain the movement produced. Her side felt like it was on fire; her head ached as though she'd drunk a gallon of Guinness last night.

Lightly touching her forehead, she winced, and her fingers came away wet. What happened? Why was she in this condition? Her hair felt funny, and with a quick tug, she pulled off a wig, tossing it aside.

She seemed to be alone. Whoever had driven the car was no longer there. Had they left her behind?

Opening the car door was more difficult than it should have been, the pain in her side knifing through her until she was breathless. She kept at it until she stood shivering in the knee-deep snow. Her mind spun in confusion as the icy snow landed gently on her face and arms, the tiny pinpricks of cold unrelenting. Where was she? What should she do? Fear made her breath come faster as she clutched her side, struggling to see through the pitch-black woods. A cabin stood not far from the vehicle, a lone lamp burning in a near window.

A light suddenly danced across the snow. Someone was coming. The flashlight arced across her face, momentarily blinding her, before coming back in an abrupt jerk. She raised her hand to shield her eyes.

"Hey! Don't move!"

The shout broke the silence of the woods, startling her. The light was coming quicker now, the beam erratic as its owner struggled through the drifts.

Panic hit hard, and the cold rush of adrenaline flooded her veins, temporarily numbing the pain in her side and head. Turning, she ran.

Erik cursed as he saw her disappear into the darkness. She was an idiot if she thought she was going to escape him. In this weather, clad as she was and obviously hurt, she'd die.

That thought galvanized him, and he picked up speed, thinking of what he'd like to do to her for making him run through the damn snow after carrying her ass up that embankment.

He followed where he'd seen her disappear, his foul mood turning more disagreeable with each passing moment. Icy water dripped from his wet hair down under the collar of his sweater, his legs practically numb from the knees down as the stiff, cold denim of his jeans abraded his skin. The boots that had seemed impenetrable in the store proved even they couldn't withstand a Colorado snowstorm, and his feet squished inside their damp socks.

"I am not chasing you through the damn woods in the middle of the night!" he called out. No answer. He played his flashlight through the trees, grudgingly admiring how quickly she'd hidden herself, though it had been a stupid move. "Come out," he demanded. "You'll die out there otherwise." Not that he cared overly much at this particular moment. His toes were numb now.

Erik waited. Still no answer. He tried again. "I'll give you to the count of five to come out. I know you're hurt. You won't make it far, and there's nothing and no one for miles." Silence.

"One…two…"

Nothing. The flashlight illuminated no movement among the silent trees.

"Three…four…"

The thought occurred to him that maybe she was unconscious again, unable to come out because she was even now collapsed in the freezing snow. That image had him moving forward again.

"I'm here."

Erik spun around, wondering how the hell she'd gotten behind him, only to see something dark hurtling through the night. He dropped the flashlight, but was still too late to stop the heavy tree branch from landing hard in his gut, knocking the breath from his lungs.

The branch fell to the ground as Erik's temper ignited. The girl turned to run, and he launched himself at her, tackling her to the ground. He rolled as they fell so he wouldn't land on top of her, but didn't ease the tight hold he had on her arms.

She struggled in his grip, managing to get one arm free and scramble to her knees in the snow. Erik latched his arm around her waist, yanking her back down.

A strangled cry of pain made him freeze. The girl didn't move now, curled on her side with her knees drawn up, her eyes squeezed tightly shut. Her breath came hard and fast, the puffs of cold air visible in the night.

Erik's anger drained away, and he got to his feet, grabbing the flashlight and slipping it into his pocket. His eyes adjusted to the ambient glow from the snow as he bent, pulling her unresisting body into his arms. She shook like a leaf, her skin like ice and her clothes wet through.

Without a word, Erik carried her into the log cabin.

CHAPTER TWO

The inside of the cabin was cold, but not like it had been outside. Erik turned on a lamp and put the girl down on the couch in front of the fireplace. She didn't speak or open her eyes, her lips pressed tightly together, and Erik got the impression she was trying to not make a sound, though she had to be in pain.

He shut and locked the front door before shedding his wet coat. The absent owner had thoughtfully left a stack of wood in the corner, and Erik spent the next several minutes building a fire in the grate. Once that was done, he searched through the bathroom cupboards, turning up some rudimentary medical supplies, and grabbed a blanket from the nearby bedroom before returning to the huddled form on the couch. She hadn't moved.

Now he could see her properly and realized he'd been right about her injury. She had a nasty cut on her forehead and a livid red mark that was already darkening into a bruise. Dried blood crusted the wound and trailed down her starkly white face. Erik saw he'd been wrong about her hair; she must have been wearing a wig earlier, because the brunette locks were gone, replaced with deep, rich, red strands pulled back into a haphazard bun.

Erik reached down and pulled off her shoes. Her eyes flew open, the brilliant green of her gaze pinning him.

"What are you doing?" she asked. He could hear a touch of fear and panic in her voice.

"You're hurt and soaked. The wet clothes have to come off so you can get warm and I can see your injury," Erik answered.

It scared her, the matter-of-fact way in which the unknown man spoke about undressing her. Did she know him? She struggled to remember, but drew a blank.

"Who are you?" she asked, scooting away from him as he grabbed some scissors from the nearby table and started cutting the hem of the dress she wore.

"Special Agent Erik Langston," the man replied, ignoring her attempts to get away from him as he cut through the thick fabric.

"Special Agent?"

He looked up then, his eyes a clear, pale blue. "FBI."

Her eyes widened. FBI. That sounded ominous. What did he want with her? And he was still cutting. "Stop that," she ordered, pushing his hands away. The movement pulled at the wound in her side, and she sucked in a breath at the stab of pain. She was so cold. Part of her really wanted to get the icy dress off, but she didn't want to do it with this man watching.

The self-proclaimed FBI agent wasn't a little guy. The sweater he wore couldn't conceal his bulk. The thickness of his biceps was apparent even through the fabric. The muscles in his thighs pulled the denim of his jeans taut as he sat beside her on the couch, her nylon-encased legs pressed against the back cushions. She felt uncomfortably small next to him.

"Despite the fact that you hit me with a tree trunk," Agent Langston said wryly, "I'm trying to help you."

"It was a branch, not a tree trunk," she corrected him, warily watching as he handed her the blanket.

He gave her a look, then resumed cutting. She pulled the blanket to her chest, trying to get warm. Shivers were making her hands shake.

"You were chasing me," she accused. "What was I supposed to do?"

The cold metal of the scissors slid against the skin of her hip as he cut the formfitting uniform.

"If you weren't a criminal, I wouldn't be chasing you," he responded.

The girl stared at him in shock before finally finding her tongue. "Are you crazy? I'm not—"

A cry of pain left her lips as he parted the cut uniform, the fabric pulling at the bloody wound. The skin was torn, and blood still oozed sluggishly from the gouge in her side. She couldn't tear her eyes away, even as the image swam and blurred.

Erik's lips twisted in a grimace as the girl passed out. Some deadly villain she was, fainting at the sight of blood.

She had collapsed against the cushions, her eyes rolling upward, and Erik took the opportunity to get the wet fabric off her. His movements quick and efficient, she was soon divested of her wet uniform and mangled nylons. After a brief hesitation, he left intact the scraps of black satin and lace that preserved her modesty.

Erik examined the wound, which looked like a bullet had caused it. The girl was extremely lucky. It had just grazed her and taken a chunk of flesh from her side. He cleaned and tightly bandaged the wound, though without stitches it would leave a nasty scar on her soft, perfect skin.

Erik shut down the trail those thoughts led to, uncomfortably aware of her nakedness. Petite though she was, her body was perfectly formed to please a man. Slim ankles led to curved calves, indenting sweetly at her knees. Her thighs were smooth, flaring to hips that would fit nicely in his hands, before yielding to the deep dip of her waist. A soft, flat abdomen begged to be touched, and her breasts made his mouth water.

Abruptly jerking the blanket, he covered her, feeling like a sick voyeur, ogling her while she was unconscious.

Not to mention that she was wanted by the FBI, he reminded himself.

Getting a washcloth, Erik gently cleaned the blood from her face. She wasn't classically pretty so much as she had an interesting face. Her eyes had been clear, intelligence shining from their green depths. Her nose, small and tipped up at the end, was covered with a smattering of freckles. A strong, square jaw led to a pointed chin that seemed to advertise a stubborn nature.

Telling himself he was only making her more comfortable and not trying to ease his own curiosity, Erik reached over, removing the pins holding her hair until it framed her face in a fiery tangle.

Her picture hadn't done her justice.

After bandaging the cut on her forehead, Erik decided he'd had enough of wet clothes. He heaved a tired sigh as he got up. Taking his keys and gun with him, no sense leaving temptation within her reach, he took a shower in the master bath. The hot water went a long way to easing his mood.

Searching the closet, he was able to find a pair of jeans that fit him, but the shirts were too small. The closest he found was a T-shirt that was still tighter than he usually wore, the material stretched to its limits to cover his shoulders and upper arms. It would do while his clothes dried.

It appeared the owner lived alone, as there were no clothes for a woman anywhere to be had. Erik grabbed another T-shirt for her to wear and a pair of flannel pants that would likely swallow her. It didn't matter. At least she'd be covered.

The warmth from the fire had chased away the chill when he returned, though the girl still appeared to be asleep. He searched the kitchen, unearthing a few bottles of liquor. Choosing one filled with whiskey, Erik poured himself a healthy shot and tossed it back. The liquid burned a welcome trail of fire down his throat.

"Can I get some of that?"

Erik turned, surprised to see she had awakened and managed to sit up. Grabbing the bottle and a second glass, he took them into the living room and sank down onto the couch, careful to avoid her legs. Although he noticed she'd pulled the blanket to her chin to cover herself, he didn't say anything. He poured her a shot and handed her the glass.

She took it and drank it quickly down, then handed it back for a refill. He eyed her but poured more into the glass. Hopefully, the pain-numbing effects of whiskey hadn't been exaggerated, she thought, drinking the second helping down.

"You should take it easy," Agent Langston said. "You probably have a concussion."

She silently handed him her empty glass, raising an eyebrow until he poured more.

"What happened?" she asked, sipping more slowly at the liquid now. "How did I get here?"

"You don't remember?"

"Would I ask you if I did?" she retorted, trying to ignore the pain in her side. She wanted to bite back her words at the look he shot her. Schooling her features into what she hoped appeared contrite, she said, "I mean, no, I don't."

Agent Langston's expression told her she wasn't fooling him for an instant. He snorted and took another drink before answering.

"After you killed that guy—who was he, by the way?—I followed you, chasing your car until you ran off the road and crashed. I picked you up, put you in the back of my car, and ended up here."

"Killed a guy? What are you talking about? I didn't kill anyone!" The thought was absurd.

"Yes, you did," he said. "And judging by the fact that you're alive with just a bullet wound while he's dead, you had better aim than him."

"I don't know why you'd tell me these lies, but there's no way I would ever kill someone." The man was crazy!

He shrugged his shoulders as though bored with the conversation. "Save it for the judge. I already know you're guilty."

A knot of fear grew in her belly. This FBI agent thought he'd caught some dangerous criminal. "This is ridiculous," she spluttered. "I'm not a murderer! I'm—" The sentence cut off abruptly as realization struck. "Oh my God," she whispered.

Langston looked at her, his cynical gaze sharp. "Is it all coming back now?"

She ignored him. "I'm...I'm..." But the words wouldn't come. They seemed like they were right there, right on the tip of her tongue, but refused to come out.

"Guilty? Don't confess now, I don't have any witnesses."

"You don't understand," she gritted out, her hands moving to clutch her head. "I can't remember." She tried harder, her eyes squeezing shut. It had to be there. No one just forgot their own name.

"You hit your head," he reminded her. "A concussion plus bullet wound plus shock. You'll be fine in the morning."

"It's not that," she said, dropping her hands and meeting his gaze. "I can't remember. Anything. I don't even know my name." The horror of saying the words aloud made panic twist in her gut. This couldn't be happening to her. Her. She had no name to even refer to herself by.

A shout of laughter made her jump, and she jerked her head up to see Langston was finding great humor in her situation. She ground her teeth, her hands clenching into fists so she wouldn't hit him.

"You think this is funny?" she accused him, ice in her voice. What a jerk. Typical cop. Wait. Why had she thought that? Did she know a lot of cops? The fact that she didn't know the answer to that question scared her.

His laughter trailed away, and he wiped his eyes with the back of his hand. "It's a stroke of fucking genius," he replied finally. "I must say, I didn't see that one coming."

"I'm not lying," she insisted.

He nodded his head, clearly not believing a word of it. "Sure you're not."

"You asshole!" she yelled. "I'm telling you the truth! I don't know who I am!"

The fear in her voice must have gotten through to him, because his expression turned hard.

"You want to play this game?" he asked coldly. "Fine, I'll tell you who you are. You're Clarissa O'Connell, daughter of Flynn O'Connell, sister to Daniel O'Connell, and currently wanted by the FBI. You've been a criminal your whole life, following in the footsteps of dear dad and big brother. You're currently wanted for multiple counts of fraud, money laundering, and racketeering, all crimes you've racked up while working for a mob boss who goes by the name of Solomon. In the past few hours, you added murder to that list. Shall I continue, or are we done here?"

He slammed his empty glass down on the table and got to his feet. Giving her a contemptuous look, he said, "I suggest you get some sleep. We leave in the morning." He tossed a bundle of fabric at her and disappeared into the bedroom, leaving the door open behind him.

Clarissa stared after him, stunned at the avalanche of information he'd just poured on her. A criminal? She was wanted for a list of felonies, including murder?

The thought rattled around inside her head. Murder. According to the FBI agent, she'd killed someone.

Her hand went to her side, the pads of her fingers brushing the bandage. She'd been shot, that much was true. Maybe she'd killed in self-defense.

Clarissa released a pent-up breath of relief. Self-defense was different from outright murder. It was okay to defend yourself. She couldn't feel guilty for something she not only didn't remember, but had been an act of self-preservation.

And at least she had a name now.

"Clarissa O'Connell," she whispered to herself, letting the name roll around her tongue like the whiskey had. The name had the warm feel of familiarity to it but stirred no memories.

Clarissa touched the bump on her head, wincing at the tenderness. She'd seen movies where people hit their heads and lost their memories. It was usually temporary, wasn't it? She had to believe that. The possibility that it might be permanent was too horrifying to think about, so she wouldn't.

Suddenly, Clarissa had a burning desire to find a mirror. It was an odd feeling, not knowing what she looked like. Touching her hair, she saw that it was long enough to pull a lock of it around to see the color. Red. Hmm. Not too crazy about that.

Getting up from the couch proved unpleasant, the bullet wound was painfully tender and her head still ached. The blanket dropped, and cold air brushed her skin. Clarissa cast a quick glance into the darkened bedroom but couldn't see anything. Aware that the cop might be watching her, she pulled on the T-shirt and pants as quickly as she could. The pants were about six inches too long, and she had to roll the waistband several times to get them to stay up.

The cabin wasn't terribly large, the main space given over to a large expanse of windows along the back. The ceiling arched high overhead, and Clarissa could see the snow still falling outside. Now that she was inside and warm, she could appreciate the beauty of the scene, and paused for a moment to watch. The snow clung to the already laden branches of the fir trees, weighing them down even more.

The drifts looked as though they'd been sculpted by an artist, rather than the careless wind.

The warmth of the fire was at her back, and despite her current predicament, Clarissa smiled to herself. She liked the snow. Maybe she always had? Or maybe not. Regardless, it made her feel less like a stranger in her own skin.

Speaking of which…Clarissa resumed her search for a bathroom, and consequently, a mirror. Easing through one of the two closed doors, she found an office space, complete with a heavy oak desk. A computer monitor stood on top of the burnished wood's surface, and Clarissa stopped to stare at it. She felt drawn to it, almost an itch in her hands to sit down at the keyboard. How odd. Resisting the urge to satisfy her curiosity, and seeing as there was no attached bath, she retreated. Only a closet full of coats, boots, gloves and other assorted winter paraphernalia lay behind door number two.

Which left only one option.

A clock above the fireplace showed a half hour had passed since the cop had gone to bed. Surely he'd be asleep by now? He'd seemed exhausted, with lines of fatigue around his eyes. Not that Clarissa should care if he was tired. Sure, he'd saved her, but he'd been chasing her in the first place, accused her of lying, and was going to turn her in to the FBI.

She'd have to do something about that part.

Pausing inside the doorway, Clarissa let her eyes adjust to the darkness. The glow from the fireplace wasn't much, but enough so she could just see the outline of the bed. An inky rectangle to her left seemed to promise an open doorway to the bathroom.

Clarissa carefully skirted the bed, on which she could now make out a lumpy form that could only be Agent Langston. Her gaze caught on a slight metallic reflection on the table next to the bed.

Keys.

Okay, change of plan. Apparently, she was adaptable. Forget the mirror, she had keys. Keys that would get her inside the car outside and take her far away from this man who'd hunted her, seemed to know way too much about her misdeeds, and wanted to put her in jail.

Clarissa stood very still, barely breathing, just listening. She could hear Langston breathing too, slow and deep. Her steps on the thick carpet were silent as she reached for the keys, her fingers brushing the cold metal.

A hand clamped down like a vice on her wrist. Clarissa cried out in surprise, the metal keys pressing sharply into the palm of her hand as she reflexively clenched them.

"Going somewhere?"

The cop's icy voice sent a shiver of alarm up Clarissa's spine. She fought for nonchalance as she said, "The thought crossed my mind."

Keeping a tight grip on her arm, Agent Langston reached out and flipped on the bedside lamp. Clarissa blinked in the sudden glow, though it wasn't very bright.

Despite her attempts to resist him, Agent Langston turned her hand palm up and pried the keys from her grip.

"Not going to happen," he said, pushing the keys into the pocket of his jeans.

Clarissa swallowed hard. Agent Langston had taken off his shirt to go to bed, and the light from the lamp revealed a broad expanse of male skin. The muscles in his chest and arms were flexed as he held her captive.

It really was too bad he was a cop, Clarissa thought.

"You can't blame a girl for trying," she said sweetly, pulling at her arm until he released her. She rubbed her wrist, not that it hurt, but for something to do so she wouldn't stare at him. Her heart was racing so fast she was sure he could hear it, though she hoped he attributed it to her botched escape attempt rather than him.

How absurd, her reaction to him. You'd think she'd never had a boyfriend before.

Had she?

The thought sobered her. She had bigger problems than a sexy, half-naked FBI man.

"Looks like we're going to have to do this the hard way," Agent Langston said.

Clarissa watched with too much nonprofessional interest as he got up and grabbed something off the bureau. When he turned around, her eyebrows shot upward.

"Oh no," she said, backing away. "You are not going to use those."

Agent Langston opened the metal handcuffs with a quick flick of his wrist. "You don't leave me much choice."

"I swear I'll be good," Clarissa offered. "I won't try to escape."

"You're right. You won't."

He had her cornered now.

"Wait!" she said.

He paused.

"I have to...you know..." She jerked her head toward the bathroom.

"Fine," Langston said. "You've got five minutes. Don't make me come in after you."

Clarissa disappeared into the bathroom, flicking on the light before closing the door. It was a windowless room; no help there. Turning on the faucet to cover any noise she made, she began searching.

"Time's up," Langston called through the door a short time later.

Clarissa briefly contemplated putting up a fight, but he was a lot bigger than she was and she'd probably end up being the one hurt. She decided to bide her time. The more she cooperated, the more off guard he would become, the easier it would be to escape. She opened the door.

Langston was waiting, cuffs in hand. The cold metal locked around her wrist. She looked up at him, but he was looking down, concentrating on making sure the handcuff was secure. He was so close she could see the thickness of his eyelashes and catch the scent of his skin.

It wasn't a bad smell at all. In fact, she rather liked it.

"Come on," he said, tugging the cuffs so Clarissa had no choice but to follow him. When he approached the bed, Clarissa's brows climbed.

"You're handcuffing me to the bed?" she asked, glancing at him. "If I'd known this was standard operating procedure, I would've gotten arrested sooner." To her surprise, the quip caused a faint red to tint his ears. How adorable was that?

"I have to keep my eyes on you, and I need some sleep."

The urge to see the cop get even more embarrassed was too strong to resist. "You sure you don't want to keep more than your eyes on me?" Clarissa asked with a mischievous grin. So he was an FBI agent who believed her to be a criminal, thought she was lying to him about her memory, but turned red at her teasing innuendos. He was a bit of a contradiction. How interesting.

Erik clenched his jaw, trying to hold on to his temper. He was tired, pissed off at how this whole thing had gone down, and irritated that he was stuck in the middle of Nowhere, Colorado, riding out a snowstorm with a woman who looked more like a college girl wearing her boyfriend's clothes than a hardened criminal and murderer.

"Sit down," he ordered.

She looked down, then back up at him.

"Sit," he repeated.

"On the floor?" she asked, her tone bewildered.

"Yes, the floor."

O'Connell's forehead puckered. "No."

Erik's eyebrows shot up. "Excuse me? 'No,' did you say?"

"It's cold and hard on the floor," she pouted. "And I've been hurt. You shouldn't make me sleep on the floor."

"The carpet's thick; you'll be fine," Erik said, ignoring the niggle of guilt in the back of his mind.

For a moment, he didn't think she was going to do it, which left him wondering how exactly he would make her, but she finally gave in, sitting down with a dignity and grace that belied her overlarge clothes. After locking the other handcuff around the bedpost, he gave it a jerk to make sure it was secure. He was turning away when he saw a quick wince cross her face. Erik hesitated.

"You all right?" he asked before he could think better of it.

32

O'Connell gave a stiff smile of long-suffering that made Erik wonder how many times she'd had to practice that in front of a mirror.

"If it wouldn't put you out too much for a pillow and blanket?" she asked.

As Erik grabbed the requested items, he had a quick flash of what his mother would say if she saw he was making an injured woman sleep on the floor, handcuffed to the bed. She wouldn't care that said woman was wanted by the FBI. Erik grimaced at the thought of the lecture he'd get.

"Here," he said, depositing the pillow and blanket next to her on the floor. He watched as she awkwardly struggled to position the pillow with one hand before arranging the blanket. When her breath caught and she froze, her face draining of color, Erik's conscience reared its head.

Before he even realized what he was doing, he'd unlocked the handcuff and picked her up. After depositing her on the bed, he snagged the metal again, quickly locking it around the iron bars at the head of the bed. They were topped by a thick piece of wood, making an interesting headboard and a very convenient spot to cuff O'Connell.

She caught his eye and lifted a delicately arched brow. "Is this your side or mine?"

"Yours," he bit out between clenched teeth. His tone didn't seem to faze her, the tiny smile she wore making him want to curse his mother for ingraining chivalry into his very bones.

O'Connell shook the handcuffs, causing an irritating clanging noise, which Erik ignored as he rounded the bed. It wasn't a big bed, but she wasn't that big either, so it would be fine. He certainly wasn't going to sleep on the floor.

"Thank you, Agent Langston," she said as he lay back down, keeping a good distance between them.

"Whatever," Erik sighed, closing his eyes. God, he was tired.

It was blessedly quiet for a few moments before, "So where are we?"

Erik didn't bother opening his eyes. "A cabin. In the woods."

"I see that," she said tartly. "I meant what country? State?"

Erik cracked an eye, glancing at her. "Still going with the memory thing?"

She did not look amused. "Just tell me."

"Colorado," he replied, turning away again. "We were near Vail. Now I don't know where the hell we are."

O'Connell seemed to process this, and Erik thought he'd finally be able to sleep. She quickly disabused him of that notion.

"What's going to happen tomorrow?"

"We're going to get out of here," he replied. "I'll drop you off at the office in Denver."

"Where will you go?"

"DC."

Silence.

"You said I had family. Where are they?"

"They're both in prison."

That shut her up, but only for a moment.

"What did they do? How long have they been in prison?"

"Armed robbery. Your dad's been in for fifteen years. Your brother's served two years of a twenty-five-year sentence."

"What am I doing in Colorado?" she asked. "How did you know I was here?"

Erik's temper flared. He abruptly sat up and leaned over O'Connell. She flinched backward in surprise.

"Stop this bullshit!" he demanded. "You know why your family is all in prison and why you're here. It's what Solomon had you doing—breaking into his competition's homes to embezzle their money and expose their secrets. I've been tracking you for months and got a tip on who the next hit would be. Now, I don't give a shit if you want to keep playing the damsel in distress card, but I'm not buying it. What I do want is for you to shut up so I can get some sleep!"

His voice ended in a near-shout, which he immediately regretted. Keeping a tight grip on his temper was something Erik took pride in; the fact that this girl was able to undermine that was disconcerting.

O'Connell's green eyes were wide as she stared at him. For a moment, Erik didn't move, his breath coming hard after his tirade. He realized suddenly how close their bodies were, his arms braced on either side of her as she lay half reclined against the pillows. His memory conjured the image of her pulling on the ill-fitting borrowed clothes while he'd watched from the shadows, unable to look away.

The firelight had danced across her skin, illuminating shadows and valleys and making her skin appear like warm ivory. The red of her hair was an echo of the flames, her fingers carelessly pushed through what Erik knew were silky, soft strands. Her arms had stretched over her head as she put on the shirt, and the black lace of her bra had seemed inadequate to hold the plump flesh that spilled from its confines. Erik had nearly groaned aloud at the sight before her breasts had disappeared from view.

In a move he was sure she had done just to torture him, she'd turned her back and bent at the waist to pull on the pants he'd given her. A light sweat had broken out on his forehead, and Erik wouldn't have blinked if a gun had been held to his head.

Then the show had been over, though the effect on his body had been damn inconvenient, just as it was now as he struggled to dispel the images in his head.

O'Connell didn't speak, but neither did she seem frightened. She looked more interested than anything else, studying him curiously. Her tongue darted out to wet her lips, and Erik's gaze fell to her mouth.

The electricity between them was suddenly thick, prickling Erik's awareness and heightening his senses. The silence was a living thing, the only sound the pounding of his blood in his ears.

"It sounds like you could really use a vacation," O'Connell said thoughtfully. And the tension was broken.

Erik collapsed back onto his side of the bed, a huff of laughter escaping him. "You've got that right," he sighed. Especially if he was going to start being sexually attracted to the criminals he hunted. He gave a mental shake of his head. Fatigue and stress were getting to him, that was all. And obviously going too long between one-night stands. Kaminski had been right, which was painful to admit.

Thankfully, she was quiet then. The bed dipped slightly with her movements as she got comfortable. He heard another sharp intake of breath, but Erik resisted asking if she was all right. After a few minutes, she settled, and he closed his eyes.

When he opened them, hours later, the weak sunlight of dawn had dispelled the darkness. Erik rubbed his eyes, which felt like sand had been poured in them overnight. Glancing to his left, he froze.

She was gone.

EPISODE TWO

CHAPTER THREE

Erik stared in amazement at the empty handcuffs still fastened around the bed spindle. That was certainly unexpected. Who was she? Houdini?

The sound of a car engine outside jerked his attention to the window. His hand automatically went to his jeans' pocket where the keys should be, but no longer were. O'Connell must have taken them from him last night, and he'd slept through it.

Damn.

He launched himself out of bed, shoving his feet into his still-wet boots. Not bothering to take time to put on a shirt, he threw on a coat and grabbed his gun. Erik was a bit surprised she'd not taken the weapon too. Ten seconds after hearing the car start, he was outside.

She hadn't made it far, the deep snow prevented that, but the chains on the SUV's tires were doing their job, moving the car farther away from the cabin.

Erik took off after her, the snow hindering his efforts to move quickly, but before long, he'd caught up to the vehicle.

"Stop the car!" he yelled through the window.

O'Connell ignored him, which only served to infuriate him further. Did she think she was just going to drive out of here and leave him behind? His anger fueled his strength, and Erik ran to the front of the car, taking up a stance and aiming his gun squarely at the driver.

"Shit!" Clarissa muttered. She knew she should've taken the gun. Unwilling to test how serious he was about shooting her, and definitely not wanting to run him over, she brought the SUV to a standstill.

Langston looked furious as he stood with the gun trained on her. She really should have cuffed him to the bed, but that seemed cruel, especially since she'd planned on…borrowing…his car.

"Get out," he called to her, his words making puffs of cold in the frozen early-morning air.

Clarissa turned off the engine with a sigh and opened the door. Sliding out into the knee-deep snow, she was glad she'd found some boots and a coat in the closet inside. Even with the garments, the chill wind made her shiver. Looking at Langston, she noticed he wore only his coat and jeans. The skin of his chest was bare to the cold. He had to be freezing. Guiltily, she chewed her lip as he walked toward her, the gun steady in his grip.

"Keys," he demanded, holding out his hand.

Reluctantly, Clarissa handed them over.

"Just going to leave me here to rot, were you?" he accused.

"I was going to send help." Just as soon as she was well out of his reach.

"Sure you were," Erik replied. "Let's go." He motioned with the gun, and Clarissa turned, leading the way back inside the cabin.

It was irritating that she'd been so close to escaping and now she was right back where she'd started. Clarissa threw herself onto the sofa, staring glumly into the glowing embers of the fireplace. Getting the cuffs open hadn't been that hard—the tie pin she'd found in the bathroom had helped with that—but getting those keys without waking the cop had taken her a long time.

She watched in silence as Langston added more wood to the fire, stirring it back to life. He disappeared into the bedroom, then reemerged while angrily jerking a T-shirt down over his chest. Clarissa briefly mourned the loss.

Langston went to the kitchen and rummaged through the cupboards. A few minutes and much angry clanking of pans later, Clarissa smelled food cooking. Her stomach rumbled. When Langston sat down at the table with a bowl and started eating, she warily approached him.

"Food's on the stove," he said curtly between bites. "And I'd rather you not use the pan as a weapon."

Clarissa scowled at him. As if she'd take him on. He was twice her size, for crying out loud!

Langston ate but watched her closely as she filled her own bowl, as though she were going to hit him over the head with a frying pan. It looked like he'd heated up some canned stew. Not something she'd have picked, but beggars couldn't be choosers.

It seemed unnecessarily rude not to sit at the table, though Clarissa was careful to sit across and not next to him. Langston's gun lay on the polished wood surface, close to where his hand rested.

They ate in uncomfortable silence for a few minutes. Langston finished first and remained at the table, watching her.

"How'd you get out of the cuffs?" he asked finally.

Clarissa shrugged, not answering. She didn't want to tell him. She might need to do it again at some point.

"Any other hidden talents I should know about?"

"I wouldn't tell you, even if I knew," Clarissa answered truthfully. She hadn't realized she could pick a lock, it had just kind of happened.

Langston gave a derisive snort.

Clarissa didn't take the bait. She didn't want to argue with him. Actually, he was rather interesting. He'd seemed very tightly strung last night. She was curious about him.

"How long have you been working for the FBI?" she asked.

Langston studied her, and for a moment she thought he wouldn't answer.

"Ten years," he finally said.

"After college?" Clarissa prompted, doing some quick math in her head.

He nodded. "Right after I got my criminal justice degree."

Which would make him about thirty-two, Clarissa decided. She abruptly wondered how old she was but decided against asking. He'd just get all pissed off at her again, since he didn't believe her memory loss.

"Why'd you pick the FBI?"

Langston's smile was devoid of humor. "You could say my father figured greatly into my decision."

When he didn't continue, Clarissa prompted him. "Your dad? Was he FBI too?"

"Did I miss the part where we decided to exchange life stories?" he retorted.

"I was just curious—"

"All you need to know is that I've dedicated my life to finding criminals like you and bringing them to jus-

41

tice," he said, leaning forward in his chair to emphasize his point.

A chill that had nothing to do with the temperature in the cabin ran down Clarissa's spine. It was obvious Agent Langston took his job very seriously and would have no qualms about turning her in, whether she had any memory of her crimes or not.

Her appetite gone, Clarissa set down her fork.

"Well, if you've been chasing me for as long as you said, then I must either be really good, or you're really bad." Her jibe made Langton's eyes narrow in anger and gave Clarissa a momentary satisfaction.

"You'll have plenty of time to think about that where you're going," he replied evenly.

With that parting shot, he rose from the table, grabbed his gun, and disappeared back into the bedroom.

Absently, Clarissa stood and cleared the table, washing the dishes in the sink. This was a hell of a mess she'd gotten herself in. Despite what Langston said, she couldn't help thinking that he was wrong about her. She didn't feel like a criminal, though how would she know what that was supposed to feel like? And whatever happened to being innocent until proven guilty? It seemed Langston had already tried and convicted her.

The running water from the faucet was loud, so she didn't know the front door had opened until she felt the chilled air. Turning, she sucked in a breath.

Two men stood mere feet away, each holding a formidable weapon, both pointed at her. Neither looked like he had just dropped by for a friendly chat.

"Looks like you did not get far, Clarissa," the bigger of the two men said with a smirk. He had a thick accent. Russian? "Though you are more resourceful than Solomon thought, it seemed. He is not pleased with you."

Clarissa's mind scrambled furiously, searching her memory for a clue as to who these men were and coming up empty.

"What do you want?" she asked.

"It's what Solomon wants that you have to worry about," the smaller guy said. He smiled. He was missing a tooth.

"Fine. What does he want?"

"What you owe him, stole from him."

"I didn't steal anything," Clarissa protested, playing for time. She eyed their guns. Langston had no idea they were here. If he appeared suddenly, unarmed, they'd shoot first and ask questions later. She couldn't let that happen.

"I am sure he will be able to explain it fully to you himself. You are coming with us."

"Like hell she is."

Both men turned at the sound of Langston's voice. Dammit! If he'd only waited a few more minutes! Her hand grabbed the only weapon available to her and swung.

Erik saw O'Connell land a wicked hit with the metal pot he'd warned her about, causing one of the intruders to drop his gun. They grappled, O'Connell getting in another hit with the pan before he retaliated, and then they were on the floor, struggling.

The other man decided Erik posed more of threat, and a spray of bullets came his way. Erik dived to the floor in front of the sofa, tipping it backward and propping his gun on the edge to take quick aim. His gun spit bullets, and the intruder dropped to the ground, lifeless.

O'Connell and the guy were still fighting. He threw her off and went for the gun that had skittered across the floor. Dammit! The bastard was going to shoot her. Erik leaped to his feet, but before he could get off a shot, O'Connell had grabbed the gun off the man he'd killed and turned, firing just in time.

It had happened so fast, and now two men lay dead on the kitchen floor.

O'Connell sat motionless, her chest heaving, staring at the men with wide eyes. Even from this distance, her hands trembled. Erik hurried toward her, only to be stopped in his tracks when the barrel of her gun swung his way.

"Don't come any closer," she warned.

Erik eyed the gun, then her. "So that's how you're going to play this?" he asked evenly. Something close to disappointment churned in his gut.

"I don't want to go to jail." Her voice was steady, but her hands were not.

"Then you're going to have to shoot me."

Her mouth was bleeding. The guy must have gotten a hit or two in before she'd shot him. Erik took another step forward.

"Stop!" she demanded. "I'll do it. I swear I will!"

Erik slowly holstered his gun. "You'd shoot an unarmed cop?"

She didn't answer, just watched him warily.

She might very well do just that, but Erik was betting she wouldn't. O'Connell could have killed him this morning while he slept, but she hadn't. He took another step, and another, then held his breath as her hands tightened on the weapon.

"You're not going to shoot me," he said with more conviction than he felt. "You know you're not. If you'd wanted me dead, you would have let them kill me." He took a step.

A gunshot shattered the quiet. Erik flinched as shards of wood from the bullet tearing a hole in the floor hit his jeans. He froze.

"I think you underestimate how much I don't want to go to prison," O'Connell said evenly, and now her hands were steady. "Get on your knees. Keep your hands up."

Clarissa's palms grew sweaty as Langston slowly complied, his eyes like twin shards of ice. Getting to her feet, she watched him closely, not putting it past him to make a move for his gun. She regretted having to do this, but it might be her only chance of escape. The men had to have gotten here somehow. She could take their car and leave Langston his.

Please don't let him try anything, she prayed, knowing she didn't have it in her to shoot him. He was just a cop doing his job. He didn't deserve to die.

The gun felt comfortable in her hands. The act of shooting the thug who would've killed her was not that bothersome. Both were facts that scared her if she dwelled on them. So she didn't.

"You're bleeding, you know," Langston said casually, motioning his head in her direction. "All that fighting probably tore that wound open again."

Alarmed, Clarissa glanced down. The T-shirt she wore was stained a garish red over the gunshot wound, the blood having leaked through the bandage. The thin cotton stuck wetly to her skin.

"Oh God," she mumbled, the image blurring as her head swam.

A sound made her tear her eyes away from the sickening sight of blood leaking from her body. She looked up just in time to see Langston launch himself at her.

Clarissa cried out, the sound abruptly cut off as they crashed together to the floor, his body landing on top and forcing all the air from her lungs. She tried to bring the gun around, but his hands locked around her wrists, pinning them in place above her head. He squeezed, the pressure increasing until she couldn't hold on to the weapon any longer. With a whimper, she was forced to drop it from her grip.

"Christ, you're dangerous," Langston huffed.

"I wasn't going to shoot you," Clarissa said, struggling to breathe properly under his weight.

"You could've fooled me," he growled, regarding her with suspicion in his pale-blue eyes.

Clarissa was abruptly aware of the fact that his body was pressed fully against hers. Lean and hard, he was touching her everywhere. His thigh lay between her legs, the breaths he took pushed his rib cage into hers, and his grip on her wrists brought his face very near.

She wondered how much blood she'd lost that she was again contemplating his attractiveness, even when he was pissed off. The day's growth of whiskers shadowing his jaw gave him an untamed look.

The atmosphere grew tense as they stared at each other and breathed. Clarissa could feel the calloused roughness of his hands against her skin as the tight hold on her wrists loosened ever so slightly. When his gaze dropped to her mouth, alarm bells started going off in her head.

"Could you get off me now?" she blurted. "You weigh a ton."

Langston sat up as though he'd been electrocuted, and Clarissa took the opportunity to take a much-needed deep breath. The injury in her side gave a sharp pang and she winced.

"Who were they?" Langston asked, glad to hear the usual detachment had returned in his voice. He took the gun from the floor and tucked it in the back of his jeans.

"I don't know," she replied with a shrug, pushing herself to a sitting position. "They said I'd stolen something from Solomon, wanted to take me to him, but I don't know what they were talking about."

"Don't know or can't remember?" he retorted, standing to grab a kitchen towel and run it under cold water.

"Either. Both," she shot back. "I know you don't believe me, but the first thing I remember is waking up in the back-seat of your car."

Erik used the towel to carefully clean the blood from her abused lip and where it had trailed down her chin. She didn't speak or protest while he did this, instead just allowing him to help her.

Her eyes were clear and guileless. A twinge of unease pricked him. What if she was telling the truth? What if she really couldn't remember her past?

No. It was bullshit. All of it. She lied for a living. It shouldn't surprise him that she was good at it. Telling the truth would be more of a stretch for O'Connell than lying.

"You're right," he said. "I don't believe you. And I don't care. You just pulled a gun on me. Why the hell would I believe you? What's important to me now is getting out of here before more of Solomon's men show up."

Something akin to hurt flashed across her face and was gone. She nodded wordlessly.

"You'll probably want to put a new bandage on that," Erik continued. No way was he doing it again. She could just learn to stand the sight of blood without passing out. "I'm going to get your stuff out of the car." It had occurred to him, albeit belatedly, that her bags might have clothes that fit her.

"I have stuff?" she asked, perking up.

She looked so hopeful, it almost cracked his shitty mood. Instead, he snorted, going to collect the gun from dead guy number two before heading outside. A few minutes later, he was back.

"Here," he said, depositing her two duffels on the floor. He'd searched them and removed two guns and a knife. No sense handing her another weapon to use on him. "Don't bother looking for your guns. I took them."

O'Connell glanced up from where she was crouched next to the bags. "Whatever," she said before resuming her examination of the bags' contents. Erik watched for a moment. She pulled out clothes and other items, electronics and a laptop, looking at each as though she'd never encountered it before. Frowning, she turned a gadget over in her hand, seeming unsure of what it was.

"I'll check the garage for snow gear," Erik said, interrupting her perusal. "Just in case."

She didn't reply, so he left her sitting on the floor surrounded by her stuff.

As he'd hoped, the cabin's owner was well prepared for the climate. In short order, Erik found a high-altitude tent, two down sleeping bags, snowshoes, and other assorted items necessary for survival outdoors in a Colorado winter. While he didn't plan on having to use them, it was best to be prepared.

When he came back into the house, O'Connell was gone. For a moment, he panicked, then he heard the shower running in the bathroom.

Ten minutes later, she emerged, dripping wet and wearing only a towel.

"Where the hell are your clothes?" he snapped, watching as she crossed to her duffel and began rummaging. The towel pulled up the backs of her thighs as she bent, stretching tightly over her—

Erik jerked his gaze away, hurriedly turning his back to her.

"I didn't like what I picked," O'Connell said, matter-of-factly.

"So you're just going to prance around here half-naked?"

When she didn't reply, Erik chanced turning around, then wished he hadn't. She was facing him now, and his eyes were drawn to the little bit of towel tucked between her breasts. One tug and the whole thing would fall. He swallowed.

"Prancing? Really?" The dry sarcasm in her voice made his gaze jerk up to hers in time to see her roll her eyes.

"Just, hurry it up," he barked, shoving his hands into the pockets of his jeans. "We don't have all day."

"Geez, you're a grouch," she muttered.

Erik breathed a sigh of relief when she disappeared back into the bathroom. It was bad enough that he couldn't seem to get the image of her out of his mind. He didn't need to add wet skin and a barely there towel to the gallery.

Jerking on his coat, Erik loaded the back of his SUV with the supplies he'd found, along with nonperishable food from the kitchen. By the time he was done, O'Connell had reemerged from the bedroom, this time respectably clad in jeans and a black, oversize sweater. She looked vaguely irritated as she pulled on boots and a coat.

"What?" he finally asked.

She shrugged. "The mirror was disappointing. I have red hair and freckles."

Erik paused while holstering his gun, looking askance at her. Her deeply scarlet locks and ivory skin contrasted markedly with the dark sweater, making her appear striking. The freckles dotting her complexion softened the sharp bone structure of her face.

"We all have our crosses to bear," he mocked. If she was searching for compliments, she could damn well search someplace else.

She shot him an irritated look, her lips curling in a smirk. "And yours is being a complete jackass?"

Her insult did nothing for his mood. "You bring out the best in me," he shot back, then turned on his heel, leaving her to repack her things while he went outside. And no, he wasn't running away so he could have the last word, dammit.

Searching the SUV the men had arrived in yielded nothing of use, though Erik did grab the cell phone one of them had carried. It had no signal, but he was hopeful it would contain data that would help track down Solomon.

Erik loaded the dead bodies into their black SUV, the sweat from the exertion instantly freezing on his skin. The cold temperatures would serve to keep the bodies from decomposing before he could get someone from the field office out here to pick them up.

Back inside, he saw O'Connell picking up her duffels. She winced, her face going white, but didn't so much as let out a peep as she endured their weight.

"Give them here," Erik said roughly, taking one bag from her and shouldering the other one. God knew why in the hell he was being nice. She'd shoot him with his own gun if he took his eyes off her or let down his guard.

As they stepped outside, O'Connell paused, frowning at the sky.

"I don't know if leaving now is such a good idea," she said uncertainly. "It looks like it's going to snow again."

"It'll be fine," Erik said, dismissing her. "It always looks like that here." He tossed the bags in the back.

"You know this?" she asked, getting in the passenger seat and glancing his way.

"Trust me," he replied. The engine turned over immediately, the quiet purr reassuring him. The snow began to squeak under their tires as they pulled out.

A few hours later, his hands were white-knuckled as they gripped the steering wheel, the blizzard of flakes falling from the sky a white curtain that prevented him from seeing more than three feet in front of the car.

They should have been out of the mountains by now. Erik was sure he'd know in the daylight where they were going. But the storm obscured everything, and he had no idea if he was getting somewhere or just traveling around in circles.

"Please," O'Connell said, her voice tight with stress. "Can we please go back? Just until the weather clears. I swear I won't try anything." Her eyes were glued to the windshield.

Erik's lips pressed tightly together as he maneuvered the SUV at a crawl through the snow. Talk about forfeiting his man card. He was going to have to tell her that they were completely lost, that he didn't even know the way back to the cabin, not in this storm. Hello, cliché.

At least she hadn't said "I told you so."

Erik brought the car to a stop. "I don't think we can get back, not in this." No sense telling her just yet that they were lost.

"What are we going to do?"

"I brought some stuff that'll get us through until the storm blows over. We'll just hunker down in here and wait it out."

"Wait it out?" The screech in her voice made him flinch. "You have no idea where we are, do you?"

"It's a little hard to see right now." He gestured to the storm raging outside.

"I told you it looked like it was going to—" she began.

"Don't," he warned, holding up a finger.

Her emerald eyes flashed at him, but her mouth closed, thank God.

"Listen," he said, "I have sleeping bags in the back, food, water. We'll be fine. Once the storm passes, we'll get out of here."

"Am I supposed to 'trust you' about that?"

"Maybe you could lose the sarcasm next time, rather than the memory," he bit out. "It'd be more helpful."

"Go to hell," she snapped, crossing her arms over her chest and glaring at him.

"I'm already there," Erik muttered, turning off the car before climbing into the back. They had to conserve fuel, so he couldn't leave the car running. They'd just have to use the sleeping bags to stay warm.

It was getting dark, night came early this time of year, and the storm didn't help matters. Erik grabbed a glow stick from his stack of supplies and broke it, filling the car with a weak golden glow.

"You'll have to come back here," Erik told her. He'd laid the backseats down to have room for the sleeping bags.

"Why?" O'Connell asked, eyeing him suspiciously.

"Because we need to conserve body heat," he explained, striving for patience. "But if you want to wait until you're freezing, by all means, be my guest."

Ignoring her, he spread out the down-filled bags, climbing into one before rummaging some more in the supplies.

Clarissa watched Langston with apprehension. She hated this. The confines of the car combined with the darkness felt like a physical weight on her chest. Snow was quickly layering on the windshield, obscuring the view outside. As she tried to make out the shapes of trees through the glass, it seemed to press in, making the inside of the car smaller.

"I have to…go outside first," she stammered.

"Why?" He sounded suspicious. As if she'd try to make a run for it in the middle of nowhere, during a blizzard.

"Why do you think?" Clarissa snapped back.

Langston rummaged in the back until he produced a roll of toilet paper. "I'll go with you," he said.

"Absolutely not," Clarissa argued. God, how embarrassing.

"With the storm, it's easy to get lost," Langston replied, climbing back over the seat.

"I am not about to have you watch me while I...I..." Good lord, she couldn't even say it.

Langston seemed amused. "For a woman who walks around wearing only a towel, you seem bizarrely shy about normal bodily functions."

"That's different," Clarissa spluttered. "And I don't want to discuss it. Just wait here. I'll be back in a few."

Before he could say anything to further mortify her, Clarissa climbed out of the SUV.

"Don't go far," he called out as she shut the door.

The snow was a blurry mass of swirling white, making her squint against the onslaught. She took a few steps toward the other side of the narrow road. Trees were there. She could find a spot among them.

It took longer than she would have thought to make her way against the wind, snow, and drifts to reach the stand of trees. Luckily, once she did, the wind was somewhat abated by the thick evergreens.

Clarissa paused to catch her breath, glancing back at the car. If she could see it, then Langston could see her. This was going to be a pain in the ass enough without doing it for an audience.

Pushing her way farther into the forest, she kept walking until she could turn and not see the car. Good. Now, to find an adequate spot.

Clarissa vowed to never again take indoor plumbing for granted. By the time she'd finished, her ass felt like a block of ice and she was cussing a blue streak. Oh, to have a penis at times like these.

Still cranky, she'd just started to make her way back to the car when a noise made her stop. Frowning, she turned, searching the woods.

Nothing. It must have been her imagination.

Taking another few steps, she heard it again. This time, the noise was unmistakable.

It was a growl.

CHAPTER FOUR

A chill that had nothing to do with the temperature raced across her skin, and the hairs on the back of her neck stood up.

Slowly, Clarissa turned to face the direction the growling had come from. Eyes glowed in the semidarkness. A wolf stood about fifteen feet away, staring at her.

Clarissa's breath caught in her throat. This was bad. This was very, very bad.

Keeping her eyes on the wolf, she took a step backward. It didn't move. She took another step. This time, it did.

As it came into the clearing, Clarissa got a good look at it. The gray fur was matted in spots, and it looked too skinny. Too hungry.

And if there was one wolf, there were probably more.

Oh God.

She had no choice. She was going to have to make a run for it.

Before she could change her mind, Clarissa turned and took off. Funny how panic and fear could propel you through snow quicker than a full bladder.

The wolf howled behind her. An answering howl to Clarissa's right made the blood ice in her veins.

A branch lay on the ground ahead of her. It must have broken off from the weight of the snow. Clarissa snatched it up, glancing behind her to see the wolf coming at her.

She screamed as she swung, a piercing shriek rending the air. To her shock, the branch connected with a solid *thunk*. The wolf yelped and fell back.

Clarissa stood her ground, the rough tree branch clenched in her grip. She held it like a baseball bat.

The wolf eyed her more warily now, its tongue lolling outside its mouth. Its teeth looked sharp, and there were lots of them. It paced a few feet away, not intimidated enough to retreat farther.

Suddenly, it came at her again. Clarissa tightened her grip, ready to swing—

A gunshot broke the quiet, and the wolf stopped, falling to the ground. Red stained the pristine snow underneath its body. It didn't move.

Clarissa whipped around to see Langston standing a few yards away, gun still at the ready. She let out a relieved breath.

"Come on," he ordered. "There's probably more of them."

No need to tell her twice. Dropping the branch, she hurried toward him, surprised when he took her elbow in a firm grip.

"I told you to not go far," Langston bit out, his eyes swiveling, watching for danger.

"Can you wait until we're back in the car before you start yelling at me?" Clarissa retorted. She'd nearly been dinner for a hungry wolf, and not the two-legged kind.

They were nearly at the car when another howl broke the stillness of the night. Langston stepped up the pace, nearly dragging her through the snow.

He jerked open the car door and motioned her to get in, keeping watch around them as she climbed inside. Clarissa hurriedly scooted over to her seat, not breathing properly until Langston was in the car and had shut the door behind him.

More howls sounded outside, sending a shiver through Clarissa. The sounds were lonely, terrifying, and beautiful all at once.

Langston sighed, swiping a hand tiredly across his face. It suddenly occurred to Clarissa that she owed him a thank-you.

"Thanks," she said, glancing at him. "I think you saved my life."

"I know I did," he snapped. "If you'd done what I'd said, it wouldn't have been such a close call."

Now Clarissa's temper was rising. "It wasn't like I was trying to get into trouble. I didn't know there'd be wolves out there. And it scared me out of my wits, so I don't need you yelling at me about it!"

Langston looked at her, his jaw clenched tight and his lips pressed into a thin line.

"Besides," Clarissa added, her temper abating somewhat. "I did something I'm going to regret."

"What's that?"

"I dropped the toilet paper." Which really, really sucked.

Langston didn't say anything for a moment, then made a noise. Clarissa looked up at him, curious, and was stunned to see him actually grinning. He was laughing. At her.

"Yeah, it's just a ball of laughs for you," she grumbled irritably. She couldn't be mad at him, though. It was the first time he'd smiled, and it took her breath away. He had dimples. Hard-ass FBI Agent Langston had honest-to-God dimples. Clarissa thought he probably had no problems at all getting women, not with those eyes, that body, and his smile. She bet he just crooked his finger and they came running.

Slutty bitches.

Okay, stop right there. Jealousy of imaginary women over a man who was more interested in her rap sheet than her…feminine assets…was just ridiculous. Clarissa shook her head in chagrin even as Langston seemed to regain control, his laughter fading.

Shooting her one more look, he climbed into the back.

"You coming or not?" he asked.

Jerking her gaze away from the windows, she turned to the back. Langton seemed blithely unconcerned, ignoring her presence entirely as he chewed on something. By the smell, it must be beef jerky. He was sitting inside a sleeping bag, another laid out beside him.

The seats being down made the inside of the car larger, but Langston's size negated that. He wasn't a small guy, Clarissa guessed he was maybe six three, and he had to slouch so he wouldn't hit his head on the ceiling.

The cold had begun to seep into the car, and Clarissa shivered, eyeing the sleeping bag with longing. She wanted to climb into it, but something held her back, though she couldn't put her finger on it. The light from the still-lit glow stick reflected off the windows, making them appear opaque.

"Looking at it won't keep you warm," Langston quipped, interrupting her thoughts.

Steeling herself, Clarissa climbed over the seat, which was a hard thing to do. Of course, Langston had made it look easy.

Clarissa's foot caught on the gearshift, and she lost her balance, toppling headfirst into the back. With a muffled *Oof!* she landed sprawled across Langston.

"Ow," she muttered, wincing at the ache in her side.

Langston's arms were around her, and Clarissa realized he'd caught her to some extent, not that she'd given him much choice.

"Sorry about that." She struggled to get up and suddenly found her wrist in a viselike grip.

"Watch where you're pushing," Langston said roughly.

Clarissa's face grew hot, realizing that in her haste to get off him, she'd accidentally touched places she shouldn't.

At least, not without dinner first.

That last thought made her giggle as he righted her.

"What's so funny?" he asked suspiciously.

Clarissa shook her head. "Nothing." Like she was going to tell him she'd had a flash of an image of him like he'd looked this morning as he lay sleeping in bed. His chest had been bare, rising and falling slowly with each breath. Hair tousled as though from unseen hands. An arm crooked behind his head had caused his bicep to flex and made Clarissa's eyes linger.

Getting those keys out of his pocket hadn't exactly been a chore. Langston could be quite charming...when he was unconscious.

Pushing the thought aside, Clarissa went to climb inside the sleeping bag.

"Take your shoes off first," Langston reminded her. "And your coat."

"You have your shoes on," she argued. "And won't my coat keep me warmer?"

He shook his head. "Too many layers and the air can't circulate. And I have my shoes on in case someone or something unexpected happens by."

Clarissa frowned even as she obeyed. "What are you? A Boy Scout?"

Langston just looked at her while he took another bite of jerky.

"Really?" she asked. "You're kidding." Though somehow, she wasn't surprised. His whole demeanor practically screamed "I play by the rules and do what's right."

"Always be prepared," he replied. A hint of a smile flashed briefly on his face. "Want some?" he offered, holding a piece of jerky out to her.

"Um, yeah, sure." Clarissa took the jerky and chewed a bite, watching him out of the corner of her eye. He got a water bottle out of a box and handed it to her before taking one for himself.

"Why are you being so nice?" she blurted.

Langston looked at her strangely. "You'd rather I starve you?"

"No, I just...never mind," Clarissa stammered, looking away. She took a drink of water. He was right. What a bizarre thing to ask him.

Clarissa tried to see out the windows, but it was impossible. In the woods, far from civilization, with a storm raging around them, the darkness was impenetrable. All she could see was her own wavering reflection, which didn't seem like herself at all.

Absently, Clarissa brushed a hand through her hair, watching the stranger in the glass mirror her movements. It was unsettling, this feeling of being an unknown entity to herself. And alone. She felt so alone. The only person she knew was the man beside her, and he not only didn't believe her memory loss, he actively disliked the person she used to be.

It was enough to depress anybody.

As she stared at the window, the feeling of pressure, of the confines of the car shrinking, began to rise again. Her breath came faster as she searched the darkness, her gaze darting frantically for a glimmer of anything. God, it was cramped in here.

"Hey."

The light touch on her shoulder startled Clarissa so badly she nearly dropped her water.

"You okay?" Langston was watching her, the usual suspicion in his eyes replaced by concern.

"Yeah, yeah," Clarissa replied hurriedly, surprised that she was breathless. "I'm fine."

Langston looked dubious, but just took another drink of water, his eyes still on her.

Clarissa focused on him. If she just didn't try to look outside, she wouldn't think about it. She just needed to keep her mind off it. Luckily for her, she had a prime piece of distraction, albeit a slightly prickly one. She was willing to risk Langston's temper if it meant she didn't have to think about how damn small this car was.

"So you said you joined the FBI because of your dad," she said. "Was he an agent too?"

Langston breathed a sigh.

"We're going to be stuck here for hours, we may as well talk," Clarissa prompted testily. For God's sake, was she not even worth carrying on a conversation?

"He didn't work for the FBI, he was wanted by the FBI," Langston finally said, surprising her. "I didn't know he was a crook until I was fifteen, when he left me and my mom high and dry. Turned out he'd been embezzling for years, raising the stakes by defrauding customers at the securities firm where he worked when the embezzling wasn't enough." He paused, glancing her way. "Sound familiar?"

His voice was hard and flat.

Clarissa stared right back, refusing to be intimidated. He could be as judgy as he wanted, but she was sure that if she really had done those things he'd said she had, she must have had a really good reason. She just didn't know what it was yet.

"We never saw him again," he continued. "The people he'd stolen from sued his estate and my mother. Eventually, we lost everything. Whatever he did with the money, I don't know, but we never saw a penny of it."

He told the story impassively, though Clarissa could hear the bitterness underlying his words.

"That's really awful," she said sincerely. "I'm sorry."

Langston shrugged. "It is what it is. I learned from it, and now here I am catching criminals. One day, maybe I'll catch him."

It was quiet for a few minutes, both lost in their own thoughts. Clarissa kept her eyes slanted Langston's way, however. No way was she looking at the windows again. He must have gotten tired of sitting hunched over because he lay down with a sigh, an arm bent to cushion his head, and his knees up since the SUV couldn't accommodate his height.

"Might as well get some sleep," he observed. "It's going to be a long night."

Clarissa scooted down until she was cuddled inside the sleeping bag. It was warm enough, and though the floor of the SUV was hard, it was better than being outside. She turned on her side to face him, away from the windows. It was odd, yet comforting, being here with him, a near stranger. Though she supposed everyone was a stranger to her now.

The light from the glow stick wasn't bright, but enough for her to see Langston. He stared up at the ceiling of the SUV, seemingly unaware of her eyes on him. Despite his epically bad sense of direction, she felt safe, which was incredibly foolish of her. Langston was a man who saw things in black and white, was unforgiving of those who broke the law, and his entire sense of purpose was to bring to justice the people who'd committed those wrongs.

"Stop staring," he said, breaking the silence and startling Clarissa from her musings. He turned his head, and their eyes caught.

"Sorry," she said softly with a slight shrug. "Nowhere else to look." She hid a smile at his disgruntled expression.

Langston turned back to stare at the ceiling again. "So I told you my story," he said. "Now tell me yours. Why the life of crime? You're a smart girl. You didn't have to choose your way of life."

Clarissa didn't answer. After a moment, he turned to look at her. "Still sticking with the amnesia thing?" he asked, his voice colder now than it had been.

"Langston, I can't—" she began.

"Spare me," he cut her off. "I was an idiot to think maybe you'd stop lying to me." This time, he turned his back to her.

Clarissa wavered between disappointment and anger. Just like a man to think he was always right, and Langston seemed surer of himself than most.

Although she would have liked to turn her back to him, too, she didn't dare. The windows were watching her. Clarissa shivered as she glanced at the window above Langston's head. It loomed over her like a faceless wraith, staring in silence at the occupants inside the car.

With a chill, Clarissa tore her eyes away, instead focusing on the center of Langston's back. She slowly inched her way closer to him until his body obscured the window. He was very near now, so close she could feel a bit of his body heat through the layers. His hair was thick and looked soft to the touch. Her hands itched to touch the russet locks, to run her fingers through them.

She was quite sure he would not appreciate that.

Clarissa couldn't help but smile as she imagined what he'd say, Mr. Oh-So-Serious FBI Man. Then she began to wonder what he would say, and do, if he weren't quite so proper and determined to follow the rules. Would he turn over? Kiss her? Put his arms around her?

These thoughts led to delicious fantasies, ones that would no doubt shock and horrify Langston, but which lulled Clarissa into slumber, still wearing a grin.

It was still dark when she opened her eyes, only this time the dark was absolute.

Clarissa blinked, but everything looked the same whether her eyes were open or closed.

Where was she? Her sleep-fogged mind struggled to clear before she remembered—the storm. They were in the car waiting it out.

But the knowledge didn't bring calm. Her eyes swiveled frantically, and her pulse jumped, her heart thumping wildly in her chest. Air. She couldn't breathe. The darkness was a smothering blanket, pressing the air from her lungs. Clarissa gasped, the noise loud in the oppressive silence. She tried to suck in air but couldn't.

Blindly, her hand struck out, landing on cold glass. Panic clawed at her as she continued to gasp for air. She had to get out, had to breathe.

"What—"

Langston's voice didn't even penetrate as her frenzied grasp fell on the door handle. With a jerk, she pulled, nearly falling out the door as it swung open.

"O'Connell! What the hell are you doing?"

Erik watched, stunned, as O'Connell scrambled to get out of the car. She was trying to escape? Now? Was she insane?

"Are you out of your mind?" he bit out, grabbing her arm and hauling her back inside before she could get her feet out the door. Feeling around with his free hand, he found another glow stick and cracked it. The light threw her face into stark relief, and Erik froze when he saw her.

O'Connell was stark white, her eyes like bruises in her face. She clawed at her sweater, as though it were binding her, and terror leaked from her eyes.

"Air, please," she choked. "Can't...breathe."

She was having a full-blown panic attack, right here, right now.

Shit.

Throwing open the hatchback door, Erik hauled her bodily through it. Once her feet hit the ground, she tore her arms from his grip, stumbling away from him and sucking in greedy gulps of air before falling. She struggled to her knees.

Erik winced at the sight of her bare hands buried in the bitterly cold snow. He hurried to her, wrapped his hands around her waist, and set her on her feet. Shit! She had no shoes on either. If he didn't do something, she was going to be in danger of frostbite.

Without asking permission, though he wasn't sure she was in any condition to answer, he scooped her in his arms. Going back to the SUV, he set her gently inside, letting her face the open air.

O'Connell was still breathing too hard and too fast. Her eyes were squeezed tightly shut and were wet, though Erik couldn't tell if it was because she was crying or if it was from the snow.

Erik felt powerless to help her. "Why didn't you tell me you were claustrophobic?" he asked, the words coming out sharper than he had intended.

Her eyes shot open, pinning him with an emerald glare. "Because I didn't know," she said. "I can't remember!" O'Connell's frustrated shout echoed in the woods around them. When she angrily dashed the back of her hand across her eyes, Erik realized it wasn't from the snow.

Ignoring a stab of guilt, Erik's gaze shifted around uncomfortably before again coming to rest on O'Connell. She was still glaring at him, but thankfully, her breathing had regulated and her cheeks were no longer the stark white they'd been previously.

"We need to get back inside," Erik said gruffly. "We can't survive out here."

Her face fell, but she recovered quickly, her lips pressing into a thin line. "Just give me a minute, okay?" she asked, her tone grim.

Erik nodded, shoving his hands into the pockets of his jeans.

Minutes passed. It had stopped snowing for the moment, leaving the woods hushed and quiet. The occasional tree branch creaking under the weight of the snow was the only sound.

The storm had left a few inches of snow covering the windows of the SUV. Erik figured that probably wouldn't help her claustrophobia. Digging under the front seat of the car, he produced a scraper and cleared the snow from the windshield and the four windows.

Dusting the snow off his clothes, he stored the scraper again and rounded the car.

"Any better?" he asked. He didn't want to rush her, but damn, he was freezing. And she had to be, too. Taking a good look at her, he saw the unmistakable sign of shivering.

"I think so," O'Connell said, her teeth rattling. She slowly backed farther into the car, leaving room for Erik to haul himself inside.

Her eyes were glued to the hatchback as he went to pull it closed, and he could almost see the panic start again in the widening of her eyes and the shallowness of her breath.

"Hey," he said. When she didn't respond, he repeated himself louder. "Hey!"

O'Connell jerked her gaze to his.

"Don't look at it," he said, pulling the door closed. "Just…look at me instead."

She nodded but didn't speak, her body wracked with shivers.

"Your clothes are wet," Erik said, taking stock of the fabric with a few swipes of his hands. "You need to change or you'll get hypothermia."

Leaning over the front seat, Erik started the car. They shouldn't use the fuel for this, but he had to get her warm. He'd leave it running for just a few minutes, just enough to take the chill out of the air. Digging in her duffel, he pulled out one of the few changes of clothing she had.

"Put this on," he said, handing the items to her.

O'Connell pulled the sweater over her head, and Erik averted his eyes, not that there were many other places to look. He couldn't really blame her for getting claustrophobic in here.

"Can you help me?" she asked, her voice shaky.

Erik turned, chagrined to see her still in just her jeans and bra, a feminine combination he'd always appreciated. Tearing his gaze from the black lace cupping her breasts, he saw the problem. Her hands were shaking too badly to undo her jeans, though she was fumbling in a fruitless attempt to release the button. O'Connell looked up at him, a pained expression on her face.

"I can't get it. Can you?"

Erik cleared his suddenly dry throat. "Ah, yeah, sure," he said. Undress her again? Yes, please.

Erik brushed her ice-cold hands aside as he leaned over her. She fell back to rest on her elbows, allowing him better access.

His fingers brushed the skin of her abdomen as he worked the button free. He tried not to take longer than he should, but he couldn't pretend that his pulse hadn't leaped, the blood heating in his veins as the button sprang free and he slowly lowered the zipper.

O'Connell didn't protest when he began to peel the wet denim off her. She lifted her hips slightly, allowing him to push the stiff fabric down her thighs. Erik tried not to think of what immediately sprang to mind when she lifted her body that way.

He worked assiduously, pulling the jeans off one leg, then the other, her sodden socks going as well. O'Connell's skin was cold and clammy. After a moment's hesitation, he began rubbing her legs, knowing his hands were warm.

"Need to get the blood circulating," he said in a voice much too rough for his liking. Yes, that was the reason he was touching her. Absolutely. It wasn't at all because he couldn't resist the temptation her body was to him.

Erik didn't dare look up at her, didn't want to see if she was looking at him with anger, or worse, amusement. She didn't speak, and she didn't pull away, so he continued.

Soft was too inadequate a word to describe her skin. Erik's hands massaged her calves, easing the tight muscles there. Shivering made the entire body tight as a bowstring, and while her shivers had subsided, the muscles were still in knots.

The backs of her knees were silken to the touch, and he lingered there, the delicate curve of her bones fitting into his palms while his thumbs stroked the area behind the joints. The pressure he exerted nudged her thighs, and they parted easily under his hands.

Erik's gaze lifted. O'Connell was watching him touch her. Her eyes were bright, her lips slightly parted as she breathed. He could see the pulse beating under her jaw. The smooth column of her throat moved as she swallowed. Her chest rose and fell, her breathing more rapid than it should have been, and Erik's gaze fell to her breasts. Their plump fullness seemed to strain against their confines. What he wouldn't give at this moment to see her bared to him.

Abruptly, Erik jerked his hands away from her skin. "It's warm enough. I better turn the engine off," he mumbled, climbing into the front seat. "You should probably get those dry clothes on," he said, fiddling with the keys once the engine was off.

"Yeah," he thought he heard her say, but her voice was too low to be sure.

O'Connell moved around, the sound of fabric and rustling in the back telling him she was doing as she'd been told. Erik squirmed in his seat, his jeans suddenly much too tight.

"I'm dressed now," O'Connell said.

Erik told himself he was glad of that as he climbed into the back again.

Bullshit, his body argued. He ignored it. Now was not the time to be thinking with his dick.

Clarissa nervously brushed her hair back from her face. She had no idea what had just happened. One minute she'd been shivering uncontrollably, trying not to let the panic of being closed in again consume her. The next, she was being undressed by Langston, the look on his face as though she were torturing him.

Then he'd touched her.

Clarissa hadn't been able to tear her gaze away from his face. His intense concentration as he'd massaged her legs mesmerized her. As did the feel of his hands on her, the rough calluses abrading her skin in a way that had made her heart pound and completely distracted her from the claustrophobia.

There was something between them, no matter what he did for a living or who she was. And Clarissa didn't think she was the only one who felt it, not by a long shot.

The tension was still high when Langston climbed back over the seats, and he seemed to deliberately avoid looking at her as he pulled his sleeping bag up around him.

"You should get inside your bag," he said gruffly, glancing at her before quickly looking away. He began rearranging her bag, since it had gotten tangled in her mad scramble to get out.

Clarissa obeyed, though the inside of her bag was icy cold. She'd had on her warmest clothes, so the long-sleeved shirt and cotton pants she'd put on weren't much help against the chill. And her feet were freezing.

As she hunkered down in the bag, she turned on her side to face Langston. He was flat on his back again, eyes on the ceiling.

Should she say something? Thank him for helping her? Tell him she hadn't minded his touch, had rather liked it in fact.

Instinctively, she knew he wouldn't welcome that, so she said nothing, and neither did he.

God, she was cold. Had she been this cold before? It seemed being temporarily warm from the heater only made it feel worse when it was shut off. A shiver wracked her. Clarissa huddled deeper in the bag.

Having already slept, she now found she couldn't turn off her brain enough to find slumber again. Worry ate at her. What was she going to do when Langston turned her over to the Feds? Would they put someone in prison who was suffering from amnesia? Or, like Langston, would they not believe her? Was there any way to escape before he turned her over? Any way to convince Langston to let her go? And if by some miracle he did release her, where would she go? The only thing she knew about herself was the name he'd told her, Clarissa O'Connell. She had no idea even where she lived.

Her stomach twisted at her thoughts until she felt nauseated. Despair beckoned. She had nothing and no one. Her only family was in prison and she was wanted by the cops. The future seemed bleak indeed.

The shivering began again in earnest. Clarissa clenched her teeth to keep them from rattling. If they got out of this, she swore that somehow she'd find a way to live someplace where it was always warm. A place with a beach, next to a warm ocean, where she could lie in the hot sand and feel the sun's rays against her skin…

"Come here."

Langston's voice interrupted Clarissa's fantasy, and her eyes popped open in time to see him reaching for her. He'd unzipped his bag and was now unzipping hers. With a quick tug, he pulled her close, leaned down, and zipped the two bags together.

"What are you doing?" she asked.

"I'm keeping you from freezing to death," he replied curtly. "You're shaking the whole car with your shivering."

"I'm fine," Clarissa protested, the brisk tone of his voice telling her he didn't want to do this, no matter what had gone on before.

Langston ignored her, settling back down and pulling her into him, moving an arm under her shoulders to cushion her head while the other wrapped around her waist.

Oooh, this was nice.

Langston was toasty warm, and Clarissa couldn't help but relax her body against his, absorbing the welcome heat. She wasn't quite sure what to do with her arms, though, as their current position squished against his chest wasn't all that comfortable. Squirming, she tentatively freed an arm, resting it on top of his. The bicep under her palm tensed, his fingers digging into her waist. But he didn't protest, so Clarissa left it there and he gradually relaxed.

This close, she could smell the spicy scent of his skin, feel the hard press of his muscles surrounding her. The sick feeling in the pit of her stomach began to fade, and with a start, Clarissa realized it was because of Langston. Despite his antipathy for her, he had kept her safe, killing the wolf who would've ripped her throat out. He'd helped her with the claustrophobia, and now he was doing what he could to keep her warm.

Despite what the logical part of her brain was screaming at her, Clarissa knew in her gut that she could trust Agent Langston. He wasn't going to let anything hurt her, of that she was certain.

As for the prison thing, well, maybe he'd come to see things her way, given enough time. She should be grateful for the storm. The more time she had, the more opportunity to convince him she was telling the truth and that he shouldn't turn her over to the FBI.

Langston was a good, decent man. He'd do the right thing once he realized she had no memory. He just had to.

Clarissa had to believe that. She had nothing and no one else.

The thought made her scoot even closer to Langston. She didn't feel so scared and alone with his arms around her. Clarissa released a pent-up sigh, nestling her head against his chest. His arms tightened around her, and she smiled.

Erik felt her sigh, her body pliant and soft against his. What the hell was he doing? His conscience was yelling at him, but he hadn't been able to resist holding her, not when she'd been wracked with uncontrollable shivering. He was just helping her get warm.

Yeah, right, that's all this is, his conscience mocked.

Choosing not to think about it, or anything else for that matter, Erik closed his eyes, concentrating on the feel of her in his arms. She was trusting, something he hadn't expected of Clarissa O'Connell, and it unnerved him. And that wasn't all.

He liked her. Yes, he was attracted to her, that was a given. But he also genuinely liked her. She had a smart mouth and a comeback for everything, which kept him on his toes. There wasn't a dumb bone in her body. Her very soft, very curvy body, which he only held back from exploring by sheer force of will. That, and the fact that he didn't want to abuse the trust she'd placed in him. He'd used her being cold to touch her inappropriately earlier. Erik wasn't about to use the same excuse to cop a feel now.

Against all logic, O'Connell brought out his protective instincts. Not that she would probably thank him if she knew. He was curious about her and wished she'd drop the amnesia thing and be honest with him. Why would she choose this life? How had it happened?

And if she could tell him these things while they were both naked and he lay between her soft thighs, that would be appreciated.

Langston's jaw clenched, the image making him choke back a groan. Why? Why did the one woman who intrigued him have to be a criminal? Where was the justice in that? It wasn't fair, but that wasn't a surprise either. Since when was life fair?

He should just knock it off and quit trying to play the romantic hero bent on saving the self-destructive damsel in distress. They'd get out of here and he'd head to the nearest field office. He'd turn her in and they'd take her away in handcuffs to meet her fate.

That thought kept Erik awake long into the night.

When he opened his eyes, weak light filtered in through the opaque windows, a layer of snow once again blocking the view outside. The storm had finally passed. Morning had come.

At some point during the night, he'd become even more entangled with Clarissa. She now lay half on top of him, straddling his thigh while her head lay cushioned on his chest. Her arm was carelessly slung across his stomach, her hair tickling his chin. Erik could feel the press of her breasts against his chest as she breathed. She made a slight sound, and he smiled a little. She snored. It was kind of cute, the little noise she made.

A sound outside alerted him, wiping the smile from his face, and Erik knew that was why he'd woken.

Someone was out there.

EPISODE THREE

CHAPTER FIVE

"*W*ait, *Danny! Wait for me!*"

The little girl with an unruly head of fiery hair ran down the street after the teenage boy. The teenager paused in his rambling, turning to wait as bidden. He bent down to take her hand as she drew near.

"Keep up, Rissa," he chastised her. A thick Irish brogue colored his words.

Clarissa beamed up at him, her gap-toothed grin one of adoration for her big brother.

"Where we goin'?" she asked.

"Into town, o' course," Danny replied, resuming his path down the cobbled street. Though evening was nearly upon them, the air chill and wet, people still bustled about, hurrying to get one last errand done, drink one last pint, before heading home.

Clarissa didn't care where they were going, just so it was away from home. Dad and Mary's constant fighting echoed through the house, up into her small room with the purple walls. She'd been sitting on her bed absently playing with her dolls and trying to ignore the yelling when she'd heard the floor creak outside her door.

Jumping down and hurrying to the door, she'd opened it to see Danny heading for the back stairs.

"Can I come too?" she'd asked, causing him to stop on the top stair and glance back at her. A crash resounded downstairs, and

Clarissa winced, knowing that dishes had started flying. She looked plaintively at her brother.

After a moment, he nodded. "Getchyer coat."

Clarissa hurried to pull on her boots and grabbed her coat, tugging it on as she walked behind Danny down the stairs and slipped out the back door.

They lived on the outskirts of the village, so it was a bit of a hike, but Clarissa didn't mind. It was peaceful and quiet out here, unlike at home. She'd paused to try and coax a stray cat close for a pat and fallen behind Danny. Now that they were in the village proper, she caught back up.

His hand was big compared to hers, as was he. Almost ten years older than she, Danny had taken care of Clarissa for as long as she could remember. She couldn't remember her mother, who had died when she was a baby. Her Dad had brought several women home to stay since then. Mary had been there longer than the others.

By now they'd reached the sweets shop. Clarissa didn't have to say anything; she just looked up at Danny, who grimaced.

"How can I say no to that look, Rissa?" he grumbled good-naturedly. He didn't resist Clarissa's tug on his hand to go inside. A few minutes later, they were back on the sidewalk, a lollipop stick protruding from between her lips.

They meandered a while longer, peering into windows and whiling away the time. They stepped inside another shop, browsing the aisles. Clarissa watched as Danny picked up a pack of fags, looked around, then slid them into the pocket of her coat.

"What are ya doin', Danny?" she asked. She'd never seen him smoke before.

"Hush, Rissa," he said firmly, taking her hand.

"But I don't want these," she protested again, pulling the pack out of her pocket.

"Leave them," Danny ordered, pushing the packet back inside.

"But—"

"I said, leave them!"

"What's goin' on here?"

Clarissa jerked around at the voice, having to tip her head back to see the shopkeeper looming over her. He was older, his wiry mustache gray, and was frowning as he looked at them.

"You best not be thinking of shoplifting, boyo," he warned Danny.

"I didn't take nothin'," Danny protested. "Search me if you don't believe me."

The shopkeeper eyed him suspiciously. "Better get goin' then, 'less you be buyin'," he said.

Danny just grabbed Clarissa's hand and pulled her outside with him.

Clarissa didn't say a word. She knew it wasn't right to steal and didn't understand why Danny had done what he did. The fags seemed to burn a hole in her pocket, but she didn't dare say anything.

Her short legs struggled to keep up with Danny's long strides, and he didn't speak to her until they'd gone the length of several blocks.

Finally, they stopped. The sidewalk was empty around them, night having settled in and with it, a thick fog.

"Good job, Rissa," Danny praised her, sinking down in a crouch. He took the packet from her pocket. "You did real good."

Danny tore open the cellophane and pulled out a fag. Putting it between his lips, he lit it and took a long drag. The heavy fog made his cap wet; the tufts of brown hair sticking out were also damp. He eyed Clarissa as he blew out a stream of smoke.

"We make a pretty good team, you and me," he said. "Would you like that?"

Clarissa hesitated. She didn't like the idea of stealing and wasn't sure what Danny was asking. Did he mean he wanted her to do that again? If she said yes, did that mean she'd get to be with him more?

Tentatively, Clarissa nodded.

Danny's lips split in a wide smile, and he took another drag. "Tha's good, Rissa," he said. "No one suspects the cute li'l ginger girl."

Clarissa frowned at him. "Danny, you said you wouldn't call me that anymore," she pouted. He knew how much she detested her red hair.

"Sorry," Danny said easily, standing back up. "I forget."

He pushed his hands into his pockets, and Clarissa did the same as they walked back to their house.

When they arrived, it was to see Mary throwing a suitcase into the backseat of her car. She was muttering to herself, her movements sharp and jerky. When she caught sight of them, she froze. Clarissa saw a bruise on Mary's cheek and a cut on her lip.

"Danny, Clarissa," she began, "I'm just…going to a friend's for the weekend."

Clarissa didn't say anything. She knew Mary was lying.

"Yeah," Danny said, his voice flat. "See ya, Mary."

Mary winced, then seemed to brace herself before coming toward them. She went to hug Danny, but he stepped back, thrusting his hand out instead. She stopped and awkwardly shook it before turning to Clarissa.

Crouching down, she reached out, and Clarissa couldn't stop the compulsion to step into her open arms. Mary was nice. She read stories to Clarissa, baked her cookies when it was cold outside, and braided her unruly hair into a soft plait that hung down her back. She'd been here for three Christmases. Clarissa hadn't dared to hope

Mary might stay forever, but it seemed her insides hadn't gotten that message. Her stomach clenched in knots as Mary held her.

"I wish I could take you with me," Mary whispered in her ear.

Clarissa wished that, too.

When Mary pulled back, her eyes were red and wet. "I love you, Clarissa, don't ever forget that," she said fiercely. An expression of anguish crossed her face before she abruptly stood. In a few moments, she'd started the car and was driving away.

It was then Clarissa noticed how wet her own cheeks were.

"C'mon, Rissa," Danny said gruffly, tugging on her hand. "Let's go in."

That night as Clarissa went to bed without a bedtime story, she stared at the ceiling. She had slipped Mary's pillow from Dad's bed—he wouldn't notice as drunk as he was—and now she hugged it to her chest. It still smelled of Mary's perfume.

She hated it, the hurt inside that tore her up. What was wrong with her? Why had Mary left her? She said she loved Clarissa, yet she'd driven away without her. Would Danny leave her too someday? Tears streamed unnoticed down her cheeks to dampen the pillow underneath her head.

In the quiet silence of her darkened bedroom, Clarissa vowed she'd never let that happen. She'd do whatever she needed to do, be whatever he needed her to be, so he would never want to leave her.

And she would never again trust anyone who said they loved her.

"Mary..."

She wasn't aware she'd uttered the name aloud until a hand clamped down over her mouth.

Clarissa's eyes flew open. Langston's face was inches from hers. She realized with a touch of embarrassment that she was lying on top of him. She tried to pull away, but his arm tightened around her waist, locking her in place.

"Be still," Langston hissed. "Someone's here."

Clarissa's eyes widened and her heart beat triple time. What if it was more of Solomon's men?

"Anybody in there?" The voice came from outside.

In one quick movement, Langston rolled, pinning Clarissa underneath him. His hand was still pressed tightly against her mouth, and Clarissa could taste the slight tang of his skin.

"Don't move. Don't make a sound," he ordered, finally releasing her. He reached for his gun.

"What about you—" she began, only to clamp her mouth shut at the look he shot her.

Without a word, Langston grabbed the sleeping bags and folded them over her, enveloping her in darkness and completely concealing her from view.

She heard the car door open, and Langston call out.

"Hey, yeah, I'm here."

Then the door shut and she could only make out muffled words as he spoke to whoever was outside.

Clarissa chafed with impatience and dread. What if they hurt Langston? Killed him?

She waited, sweating under the blankets and feeling as though she were slowly suffocating. Okay, she'd count to ten, and if he wasn't back, she'd find some kind of weapon and go after him. One...two...three...

"Oh, screw it," she huffed, unable to take another moment with the walls closing in around her. She threw off the sleeping bags just as the door jerked open. Clarissa instinctively jerked back, then let out a breath of relief when Langston appeared.

"You listen well," he said dryly.

"And this is a surprise?" Clarissa replied breezily, concealing her relief that he was unharmed. "So who's the guy?"

"Nobody we have to worry about, but he's offered to lead us out of here."

"That's great!" Clarissa forced a smile even as her heart sank. She'd hoped to have more time to convince Langston she was telling the truth, but now it seemed her time was running out fast.

Langston caught her gaze and paused, looking like he was going to say something. Clarissa waited, hoping, but he seemed to think better of it, turning away and rummaging for a scraper.

Clarissa put on her shoes and coat before emerging from the SUV. Langston had started the engine to warm it up while he pushed snow off the glass.

"I'll just be back in a few," Clarissa told him.

"Wait," he said, making her pause.

Oh lord, please don't say he's coming with me, she thought. Even after the wolves last night, she'd still rather take her chances on her own for this particular chore.

Langston dug around the back of the SUV before emerging.

"Always be prepared," he said, handing her another roll of toilet paper. His mouth tipped up slightly in a faint smile.

Clarissa laughed outright, her breath a puff of white in the frosty air. "Langston, you're my favorite Boy Scout ever," she said, grinning at him.

Erik was struck speechless for a moment, which was not a frequent occurrence. O'Connell's smile transformed the angular lines of her face, her eyes twinkling with mischief. Her laugh was warm, inviting him to share the joke. She was simultaneously someone he'd love to have a beer with and a woman he'd strip naked at the slightest invitation. The dichotomy was as perplexing as it was intoxicating.

Erik watched her disappear among the trees, waited impatiently for her to return, and didn't relax until she had. By then, the SUV was dug out and ready to go, thanks to some help from the off-duty forest ranger that had happened upon them.

Erik hadn't told the man that he was FBI, hadn't explained that he was transporting a prisoner. He didn't know why. When the man had asked what they were doing out here, Erik had told him they were on vacation and had gotten lost trying to get into town. The lie had sprung easily to his lips, which was a strange thing for someone who made a habit of always telling the truth.

A few minutes later, they were following the ranger's jeep through the Colorado backwoods.

Erik observed O'Connell out of the corner of his eye. She hadn't said much once she'd returned and now seemed lost in thought as she gazed out the window.

He wanted to talk to her, find out what she was thinking, but didn't know what to say. That was a bit disconcerting. Erik certainly didn't consider himself a smooth operator, but he usually didn't have problems knowing what to say to women either.

"There's some more jerky in the back, if you're hungry," he offered, when he could think of nothing else.

She looked at him, wrinkling her nose slightly in distaste. "I'm not that into jerky," she said. "Maybe you can buy me a proper breakfast once we reach civilization? We did just spend the night together, after all."

The mischief in her grin made Erik squirm uncomfortably in his seat, remembering too much about last night. He quickly returned his gaze to the road before clearing his throat.

"Yeah, sure, I can do that," he replied. She had to be starving. He certainly was. A hot breakfast of eggs and bacon with a side of pancakes and about a gallon of coffee sounded fantastic.

Erik's attention was drawn again to her as she picked up a manila folder resting on the dash.

"You can't look at that," he said, reaching for the file. "That's FBI property."

O'Connell maneuvered the folder out of his reach. "It has my name on it," she protested. "I should be able to read my own file, shouldn't I?"

"No, that's not how it works," he insisted. "Give it to me."

O'Connell raised an eyebrow. "Make me."

Shit.

Her lips twitched as he glared at her then reluctantly turned back to the road. The paper rustled as she turned the pages.

The file wasn't very thick, but Erik had memorized its contents. Among other things, it contained a brief history of the O'Connell family. Mother dead shortly after Clarissa's birth. The father hadn't remarried, but he'd had a string of live-in girlfriends. The older brother, Daniel, had been arrested for petty theft numerous times as a teenager, then graduated to grand larceny as he got older.

The father had been arrested, tried, and convicted of theft and manslaughter ten years ago. A security guard at the jewelry story he'd robbed had died while trying to intervene. Although Flynn O'Connell had said he hadn't meant to kill him, those things had a tendency to happen when you hit someone over the head with a brick. Flynn was currently serving a life sentence in Ireland's Mountjoy Prison.

Erik glanced back over, watching as O'Connell read. She was frowning, the skin puckering between her brows.

The file went on to describe what they knew of Daniel and Clarissa's ties to Solomon, though information on Clarissa herself was sketchy. When Flynn had gone to prison, Daniel and Clarissa had disappeared.

"You want to fill in the missing information?" Erik asked. "What were you and Daniel doing before he hooked up with Solomon?"

Clarissa glanced up from the file, not sure how to answer. It was like reading about someone else's life, not hers. When she'd gone into the woods this morning, she'd thought of her dream but hadn't been able to recall much of it. It was as though she could almost remember the elusive something just out of reach, but it disappeared like smoke when she got close. She'd been upset, that she'd known, had felt a deep sadness that dragged at her but hadn't known the reasons why she felt that way.

"I'm...not sure," she answered truthfully. To her surprise, Langston didn't react in anger, as she'd expected. He just looked at her, his expression unreadable before he turned back to the road.

"Who's Mary?" Langston asked.

The name provoked the same wave of sadness Clarissa had felt earlier. "I know I sound like a broken record, but I don't know," she said. "The name…it sounds familiar, but I don't know why." She shook her head in frustration, hating the feeling of helplessness, of not knowing things she should.

Langston didn't ask any more questions, so Clarissa continued reading the file.

There was no known address for her, which was disappointing. She'd been hoping they'd know where she lived, which was an idiotic thought. If the FBI knew where she lived, they would have arrested her before now.

The file held only one photo, a grainy profile shot taken at a distance. The woman had red hair tied back in a French braid and large black sunglasses. Clarissa stared at the photo.

"Are you sure this is me?" she asked, holding it up next to her face.

Langston glanced at the photo, then her. "I'm sure," he said, his voice flat.

"I don't know," Clarissa muttered. "Could be anybody, really."

"It's you," Langston insisted.

His vehemence sparked Clarissa's temper. "I think your evidence is a little thin to say that I'm this Clarissa O'Connell."

"Then why were you at that villa? Why did you kill that man? And why were you shot?" Langston's angry questions were rapid-fire.

"I don't know," Clarissa retorted. "Maybe I just got in the way or…something." She didn't really have any good answers for his questions, but dammit! She wasn't going to just let him win the argument because of that minor detail.

Langston snorted in derision. "I've spent the better part of a year digging up every piece of information on you, tracking down every lead, no matter how vague. Followed every trail, every whisper or rumor I heard. Grainy video footage in Monterey. A couple witnesses in Chicago. Trust me. I know who you are."

The fact that Erik had watched that video footage until he saw it in his sleep wasn't something she needed to know.

"The file isn't that thick," O'Connell observed.

"That's just part of it." Erik didn't want to say how he had three full file boxes in his apartment in DC.

"Where's the rest?" she asked, glancing in the back as though she might have missed something.

"Back in DC," Erik said evasively.

She frowned at him. "Aren't you FBI guys supposed to work in pairs? Don't you have a partner?"

Erik's lips pressed together at the thought of Kaminski. "I...had a partner," he reluctantly explained. "We had a differing of opinion."

"About what?" O'Connell asked, flipping again through the file.

"You."

Erik saw her turn and look at him again, but he deliberately kept his eyes on the road.

O'Connell was quiet for a few minutes, as though digesting this. Finally, she asked, "So what happens now?"

The quiet resignation in her voice made Erik's gut clench. His hands tightened on the wheel.

"Now," he replied, "I'm going to feed you."

O'Connell glanced out the window just as Erik pulled into the parking lot of a country diner. He gave a wave to the forest ranger, who drove on.

Putting the car in park and pocketing the keys, Erik turned to O'Connell.

"I'm starving. And I believe I owe you breakfast."

She smiled, and Erik decided he could really get used to that sight.

"I like chocolate-chip pancakes."

"With whipped cream or syrup?"

"Yes," she replied.

Erik bit back a grin.

"And bacon."

"A woman after my own heart," he quipped without thinking, then quickly moved on. "You're not going to run, are you? It's hard to eat if one hand is cuffed."

"Cross my heart," O'Connell promised.

∼

The diner was playing country classics on the radio and held only a handful of customers, most of whom were old men out for their morning coffee and ration of biscuits and gravy. The smell of bacon grease and coffee hung heavy in the air.

Clarissa took an appreciative whiff as she slid into the vinyl booth where the coffeepot-toting waitress had led them.

"What'll ya have to drink?" she asked, handing them each a menu.

"Coffee," Langston replied.

"Make that two, please," Clarissa added.

The waitress nodded, pausing at a nearby table to refill their mugs with the dark brew.

"Bad luck," Langston said, looking over the menu. "No chocolate-chip pancakes. You'll have to make do with plain."

"So long as there's plenty of butter and syrup, I'm good."

The waitress returned with their coffee and took their order. Langston ordered what seemed to be half the menu. Eggs, bacon, hash browns, biscuits with gravy, and a dish of fruit. Sheesh. Did he always eat like that? You couldn't tell by looking at him, that was for sure.

The crooning of Tammy Wynette imploring Clarissa to stand by her man filled the silence as she added cream and sugar to her coffee. She noticed Langston watching her.

"What?"

He tipped his head toward her mug. "If you've lost your memory, how do you know how you like your coffee?"

It was a good question, and it stumped Clarissa. "I just… knew," she replied with some surprise. "I didn't think about it." The thought excited her. It meant her memories were still there, just hidden behind a wall, but obviously some were leaking out. She'd had the dream, for one thing. And for another, "Just like I knew I liked chocolate-chip pancakes."

Langston looked skeptical as he sipped his coffee; black, she noticed. Of course.

"So is there a Mrs. Langston, Agent Langston?" she asked, changing the subject and causing him to choke on his coffee.

"Ah, no, there's not," he answered once he'd recovered sufficiently to speak.

"Why not?"

"That's a little personal, don't you think?"

Clarissa shrugged. "You and the waitress over there are the only people on the planet that I know. If I ask her a personal question, she may spit in my food. You're already going to turn me in to the Feds, so I have nothing to lose."

Langston took another drink of coffee before answering. "There's never been anyone I've been interested enough in to last more than a few months. For the most part, women are narcissistic, selfish creatures whose sole ambition is to land a man with either looks or money, preferably both."

"Ouch." Clarissa winced. "Did your high school crush break your heart or something?"

"What about you?" he asked, evading her question. "Boyfriend? Husband? Fiancé?"

"You tell me," she countered, raising an eyebrow.

"The data's inconclusive, though you've never been spotted with a partner, and no marriage certificate has been issued to you. You don't wear a ring." He glanced at her left hand. "And no mark from one that's been removed."

"Maybe I don't believe in marriage."

Their food came then, and it was quiet for the next several minutes as they ate.

"I can hear your arteries screaming in protest," Clarissa deadpanned, watching Langston shovel in a forkful of biscuit dripping with gravy.

"This coming from the woman who likes a little pancake with her butter?" he quipped. "Besides, that's what the fruit is for."

Clarissa skeptically eyed the little dish of cut-up fruit.

When the check came, Clarissa excused herself to use the restroom. Situated at the rear of the restaurant, she was relieved to see it had a window. Ten seconds later, she had removed the screen and lowered herself through the gap to drop to the ground outside.

"That was easy," she muttered to herself. Now to get as much space between her and Langston as possible. She was betting at least one of the pickups out front could be hotwired.

Clarissa felt a pang of disappointment to bail on Langston, not that he'd given her much choice in the matter. She liked him, and truth be told, it was terrifying to think she was running without so much as a dime to her name or any idea of where to go. But even the unknown was better than the inside of a prison cell.

Rounding the corner of the building, she scanned the area carefully. No one was around. Walking quickly, but not so quickly as to draw attention, Clarissa headed for the nearest pickup truck. God bless the old men who trusted their neighbors, she thought ruefully, climbing into the unlocked cab.

The passenger door jerked opened, startling a gasp from her.

"Going somewhere?" Langston asked.

His voice was hard with fury, his eyes cold.

"Langston, I—"

"Save it," he bit out.

A hard grip on her arm and sharp tug later, she was being dragged behind him to the SUV and pushed into the passenger seat.

Clarissa fumed, bitterly disappointed. She wasn't mad at Langston. He was just doing his job. She was mad at herself. She'd thought she'd gotten to a place of trust with him, eased him into complacency. Obviously she'd made her move too soon. Now she was back to square one with him.

Langston slid behind the wheel of the SUV, jabbed the key in the ignition, and stomped on the gas. Soon the diner was receding in the distance.

Anger rolled off Langston in waves, the atmosphere in the car stiff and silent.

The miles flew by as Clarissa stared unseeing out the window. Where was he taking her? Was her freedom now counted in hours? Minutes?

"Thanks for breakfast," she said when she couldn't take the silence anymore.

"Don't mention it."

Clarissa winced at the ice in his voice. She felt guilty now, and she hated that, so she lashed out.

"You're taking me to jail," she retorted. "For crimes I have no memory of committing. Did you think I was just going to trot along obediently?"

Of course she was right. Erik knew that. But that didn't ease the feeling of betrayal. He'd liked her. That had been his first mistake.

Trusting her had been his second.

He couldn't afford a third.

∽

Erik paced alongside the deserted highway, waiting for the cell phone to make the connection. Now that they were out of the woods, he had a decent signal.

He glanced over at the SUV. The keys were in his pocket, and he'd left O'Connell cuffed to the door. She wasn't going anywhere.

The ringing in his ear cut off as someone picked up the call.

"It's about time you called in. You're in a shitload of trouble."

"Why? What happened?" Erik asked.

"Only about two dozen witnesses who saw you fleeing the scene of a murder at some ritzy place in Colorado," Kaminski said. "You finally cracked or what?"

"I didn't kill the guy, she did."

"She who?"

"O'Connell."

"Was that before or after she got away again?" Kaminski's sarcasm set Erik's teeth on edge. He didn't know how he'd stood having the guy as his partner for as long as he had.

"No," he said flatly, keeping a tight hold on his temper. "I got her."

"You killed her?"

"No, I didn't kill her! I arrested her. Now will you put Clarke on the phone?"

Leonard Clarke was the SAC, Special Agent in Charge of the Solomon investigation. He'd been investigating Solomon and his empire for the past five years. No one knew more about the powerful crime lord than Clarke.

"Clarke here."

"Sir, it's Agent Langston. I wanted to report that I've apprehended Clarissa O'Connell."

"Excellent work! Has she said anything about Solomon?"

Erik hesitated. "Negative, sir." He went on to explain about the men who had come after them.

"All right, I'll send a couple of field agents out to clean up the scene. If she took something from Solomon, I want it, Langston, and I don't give a shit if she wants to cut a deal. Get it for me."

"Ah, sir, there's a slight problem." Erik wasn't even sure he should mention it, but knew he really had no choice, not if she was determined to keep it up.

"What's that?"

"She says she has no memory, sir," Erik blurted. Like a bandage, better to rip it off quickly.

A heavy pause. "What?" Clarke asked, incredulous. "Did I hear you right? She says she has no memory?"

Erik winced.

"What the fuck happened, Langston?" Clarke yelled into the phone.

"There was a wreck; she hit her head. Sir, I'm not one hundred percent positive that she's telling the truth. It's very...convenient."

"So does she or does she not have a memory?"

"I don't know, sir." The words felt like salt on his tongue. Erik hated that he was forced to admit he couldn't answer the question with any degree of certainty.

Clarke cursed while Erik waited in stoic silence for his orders. He glanced back at the car. O'Connell was watching him steadily from the window. His gaze caught hers and held. She looked...disappointed.

Erik jerked his gaze away, concentrating on the orders Clarke was giving him.

"...call in to the US Marshals office in Denver," he was saying. "They'll transport her to DC and we'll get it sorted out. She'll talk."

"Yes, sir."

"As for you, get on the first plane back here."

"Yes, sir."

Clarke's voice was replaced by Kaminski's. "We'll call the marshals and arrange the transport," Kaminski said, all business now.

"Thanks," Erik replied. "Will you look up a number for me, too? I need any information you can get on it." Erik read off the only number that had been dialed from the cell he'd picked off the dead thug. The phone was a disposable one with pre-purchased minutes.

"I'm on it."

Erik ended the call and slid the phone into the pocket of his jeans, his gaze unwillingly shifting back to O'Connell, who turned away.

He refused to feel guilty for doing his job. Erik would drop her with the marshals, who would get her to Washington, and they could figure it out from there. No doubt their interrogation would show O'Connell that it was foolish to continue the amnesia charade.

Unless she was telling the truth, his conscience prodded. Then she'd just be helpless, trapped in a web of federal laws and behind bars. Alone.

No, she'd have a lawyer, she'd be fine. The damn lawyers made his job harder each passing year. Hell, she'd probably get a sweet deal for testifying against Solomon.

So why did that thought not ease the anxiety churning in his gut?

96

~

Clarissa stared at the road ahead, deep in thought, as Langston drove. It was tempting to give in to despair. The future looked pretty bleak. She hadn't needed to hear Langston's conversation to know he was taking her in.

She had to get her mind off it. If she thought about it any more, she'd go crazy.

"Why did you and your partner split because of me?" Clarissa asked.

"What?"

"You said you had a disagreement with your partner over my case. Why?"

Langston's jaw tightened, but Clarissa didn't particularly care if he didn't want to talk about it.

"He and I held differing opinions on your importance to the case, your position within Solomon's organization," he answered.

"What did your partner think?"

"Kaminski was convinced you were a low-level tech, hired to do the occasional job for Solomon, nothing more."

Clarissa digested this for a moment. "And you? You didn't think that, I take it?"

Langston shook his head. "The pattern was too clear, the methods too precise. It was one person hacking into the accounts, all of which just happen to be Solomon's competitors'. He wouldn't give that kind of job to more than one person, and it had to be someone he trusted. If word got out he was behind the operation, they'd band together and go after him. As it is, he's doing the oldest play in the book." Langston turned and caught her eye. "Divide and conquer."

"And you think I'm the one who's doing this? I'm some sort of techno geek computer hacker?" The very idea was ludicrous. A hacker was some genius misfit with pale skin from too little sunlight and a problem with authority.

Well, maybe that last part...

Langston grimaced before turning back to the road. "You were identified as gifted when you were eight years old. By the age of twelve you were routinely hacking into commercial websites, which put you in and out of juvenile detention. By fourteen, you were writing your own software spiders that crawled the Internet, installing themselves on vulnerable systems. At sixteen, you hacked into MI6 but didn't cover your tracks well enough and got another slap on the wrist and stay in juvie. And when you turned eighteen," he paused, "you disappeared."

His cell phone rang, and he answered while Clarissa mulled over what he'd told her. Maybe that explained all that computer equipment in her bags.

"I can take her to their office—"

Langston's irritated tone made her focus on him again.

"Sir, I can't just—" His lips pressed into a thin line as he was cut off.

Clarissa could hear the voice on the other end but not enough to understand what it was saying.

"Yes, sir. Understood." Langston hung up and angrily tossed the phone onto the dash.

"Problem?" she asked dryly.

"The marshal's men don't have an agent to fly you to DC tonight. The soonest they have is tomorrow morning." He shot her a glare, as though it were her fault. "He doesn't want me leaving you with them overnight. I'm to keep you until then."

Clarissa breathed a quiet sigh, her eyes slipping closed. She'd gotten a reprieve. Now she just had to use it to her advantage.

CHAPTER SIX

Erik pulled in to the Walmart parking lot. It was about the only thing in the tiny town. They weren't far from Denver, but Erik didn't want to let O'Connell anywhere near civilization. If she got away from him in the city, he'd never find her again. He'd just make sure they got an early start in the morning.

"Why are we stopping?" she asked.

"Need some things," Erik replied curtly. "My luggage is back in a hotel, probably being thrown out even as we speak. Plus, I don't know about you, but I'd like a fresh pair of underwear."

O'Connell smiled sweetly at him. "I don't mind going without."

Christ. Like he needed that image in his head. Ignoring her comment, he leaned over and unlocked the handcuff from her wrist. She rubbed the reddened skin where the metal had chafed.

"I get to come too?" she asked. "I thought you'd just crack a window."

"I could tie you to the bumper instead," he shot back. "Would you prefer that?"

By her pout, he could assume the answer was a no.

"Come on."

Erik took her elbow as they walked into the department store. The traditional Walmart greeter was nearby taking down a display of New Year's decorations and offered them a belated "Welcome to Walmart!" as they passed by.

Grabbing a handbasket, Erik headed for the toiletries. He threw in a couple of toothbrushes and a box of tooth-paste.

"I don't like that kind," O'Connell protested.

Erik snorted. "Toothpaste is toothpaste."

"It is not," she insisted. "This kind is better." She snatched another box off the shelf and tossed it in his basket.

"Don't just grab stuff," he reprimanded her, sticking the box back on the shelf and tugging her away. "Like I care what kind of toothpaste you prefer."

Deodorant went in the basket, including a girly one that she'd snatched despite his orders not to do that. He grabbed a packet of razors and a comb. He noticed her slipping in a brush when his back was turned.

Erik headed for clothing next, trying to ignore O'Connell's presence as he grabbed a pack of underwear and hoped she'd keep her mouth shut. No such luck.

"Tighty-whiteys, Agent Langston?" O'Connell piped up. "I figured you more as a boxer type of guy. Kind of like these."

He shouldn't encourage her; he should just ignore her. That's what he kept telling himself as he turned to see her holding up a pair of SpongeBob SquarePants boxers.

"He's square, just like you!" She grinned.

Erik ground his teeth, jerked the boxers out of her hand, and tugged her out of the men's department, grabbing a couple of shirts on the way with barely more than a glance at the size.

"Should've gotten Oscar the Grouch instead," she muttered as he dragged her to the women's lingerie.

"Hurry up and pick something," he grumbled, watching as she began perusing a nearby rack of bras. "That one will do." He pointed to a plain white garment. It seemed serviceable enough.

"According to you, I'm soon going to be wearing US Department of Corrections–issued underwear." She grabbed a flesh-toned bra that seemed to be nothing but lace, and not much of it at that, and held it up to her chest for his approval. "The least you can do is buy me something pretty."

Erik swallowed and turned away. "Just make it quick."

"What's your hurry anyway?" O'Connell asked, looking through more lingerie. There was a ton of it in a rainbow of colors.

Erik gave a brief thanks that he was a guy and his choices were limited in scope and color, SpongeBob notwithstanding.

"I hate shopping," he replied, glancing at his watch. "It's a waste of time."

O'Connell eyed him as she shopped, moving on to another rack. He followed, not bothering to conceal his impatience.

"What do you do for fun, Langston?" she asked.

"Excuse me?"

"Fun. Entertainment. Rest and relaxation. You know, that thing you're supposed to do when you're not working."

She held up a see-through nightie, and Erik lost his train of thought. What had she asked? Oh, yeah. Fun. "I work."

O'Connell peeked at him over the top of the gossamer fabric, then replaced it on the rack. "I know you work. After work. What do you do?"

Her questions irritated him. It was none of her business what he did or didn't choose to do. And if he chose to work as much as he did, well, that was his prerogative.

Except her questions made him feel about a hundred years old.

"Chess," he blurted as she searched through piles of bikinis and thongs.

She looked at him as though he'd grown two heads. "Pardon?"

"For fun. I like to play chess."

"I see," she replied, turning her attention back to the scraps of underwear that were hardly worthy of the title. "And who do you play chess with?"

"Um," he hadn't been prepared for that question, "friends, I guess." He didn't particularly want to tell her he played in the park with Frank, the retired insurance sales-man whose kids had all moved away and who loved to tell Erik stories of his twenty years in the marines.

"I bet I know how to play chess," O'Connell remarked. "We should buy a set." She grabbed one more item off the rack, adding it to the armful she already had, and started walking.

"Where are you going?" Erik asked, though he had a suspicion.

She looked at him strangely. "The toy department, of course."

"We're not getting a chess set."

"You have any better idea for how to pass the time tonight?"

103

Erik had lots of ideas, all of which featured O'Connell modeling the lace and satin scraps in her arms.

"Fine," he growled, shoving the images to the back of his mind. "I have something else to get too."

O'Connell found a cheap chess set and added it to his basket. Erik swung by the sporting goods section next and grabbed a length of rope.

"What's that for?" O'Connell asked curiously.

"Handcuffs can't hold you, remember?"

"You're going to tie me up?" Her incredulous tone would have been comical if the situation weren't so serious.

Erik looked at her. "You give me no choice. You can't be trusted."

Her eyes narrowed. "Well, Agent Langston. Maybe you're not so square after all."

O'Connell's sarcastic bravado in the face of what awaited her inspired a reluctant admiration in Erik, a feeling that was both dangerous and decidedly unwise.

~

The town boasted one motel, which had seen better days. Clarissa dubiously eyed the room Langston had rented for them. The furniture looked old and worn, as did the cheesy print bedspreads on the two double beds, but it seemed clean. There were no questionable odors in the air or stains on the carpet.

With some irritation, Clarissa pulled at the ropes binding her wrists to the bed. Langston had gone into the bathroom to shower, tying her to the bed to ensure her continued presence. He'd ordered pizza and had oh-so-graciously untied her so she could eat.

This wasn't going as she'd planned.

Instead of getting him to talk to her, get to know her, and hopefully getting him to care what happened to her, Langston was just ignoring her. The few times she'd attempted conversation had been met with monosyllable replies or grunts. He wouldn't even look at her.

Whereas she couldn't stop looking at him, especially when he came walking out of the bathroom wearing only jeans. Clarissa watched him covertly as he grabbed a plain gray button-down shirt, tore the tags off, and pushed his arms into the sleeves. She let out a tiny sigh of disappointment when he did up several of the buttons on the front.

"Do I get to shower?" Clarissa asked.

Langston didn't answer, and his face betrayed nothing as he walked to her and untied the rope. She rubbed at her chafed wrists.

His deliberate apathy and distance irritated her. So he was going to pretend there was nothing between them? Act as if he hadn't wanted her last night? Jerk. Men were all alike.

When she was free, she bounced off the bed and into the bathroom. Before closing the door, she poked her head out.

"Want to watch, Langston? Make sure I don't escape again?"

As expected, her teasing made a red flush creep up his neck, but his expression remained stoically unaffected.

"There aren't any windows in there," he replied, grabbing the remote and lying down on the other bed. He bent an arm behind his head and seemed to dismiss her.

Clarissa's eyes narrowed in frustration. "I might slit my wrists, you know," she snapped.

The TV changed channels as he surfed. "You're not the type."

Dammit, he was right. In a fit of temper, she slammed the door.

After her shower, Clarissa held up one of the matching bra-and-panty sets she'd had Langston buy. If he wasn't going to connect with her emotionally, talk to her, she supposed she could try sex. She'd seen the way he looked at her. It was obvious he was attracted, and she certainly was.

But the idea of using sex to trick him into letting her go was a distasteful one. Even as desperate as she was, she wondered if she could do that. The survivor in her urged to do everything she could, to use every feminine wile in her arsenal. She decided she'd exhaust every other avenue first before resorting to sex.

Though it wouldn't hurt to stoke the embers a little.

With that thought in mind, she left her jeans off, choosing to wear just her shirt to bed. Her legs weren't bad. Maybe Langston would appreciate the view.

After brushing the tangles out of her wet hair, she emerged from the bathroom to find Langston watching some basketball game on the TV. Getting up, he went to tie her again, his eyes flicking briefly to her bare legs.

"I picked the lock, Langston," she blurted, eyeing the rope. She preferred handcuffs to rope. Rope hurt, dammit.

He paused, the rope looped around her wrist. "What?"

"I picked the lock on the handcuffs," she admitted. "But I don't have anything to pick it with now, I swear. You can search me. I'd just rather the cuffs than the rope." And at least with the cuffs, she'd have one hand free.

Langston hesitated, then tossed aside the rope, attaching the cuffs to her before returning to his previous position on the opposite bed. Clarissa didn't protest. Suddenly, she felt very tired. Langston's deliberate distance after last night made her feel more alone than before.

Her eyes stung, and she quickly turned away from Langston. If she couldn't stop herself from crying, she damn well didn't want him to see.

Maybe she just needed a good night's sleep, that was all. That was why she was feeling so hopeless. She was just tired. Things would look better in the morning. She'd come up with a different plan, one that would definitely work.

Clarissa thought all these things as tears slid down her face into the pillow underneath her head. She wasn't crying. She wasn't. She was just...having an emotional release. Perfectly normal; healthy, even. It wasn't good to keep things bottled up.

The bed dipped behind her and Clarissa stiffened.

"Um, are you all right?"

Langston's voice was gruff, as though he didn't want to be having to ask.

Clarissa quickly swiped at her face, refusing to turn around. "I'm fine," she said thickly.

He hesitated. "Are you sure?"

"I'm about to be sent to prison for who knows how long and can't even defend myself because I have no idea what I have or haven't done," she retorted. "You have me handcuffed to a bed, which under other circumstances would be a good thing, but not so much at the moment. How the hell do you think I am?"

"You know," Langston replied carefully, "if you tell the truth, they'll probably cut you a deal. Turn witness against Solomon. That's your best bet."

"What a fabulous idea," Clarissa muttered with a sniff. "Too bad I have no idea who Solomon is or what I know that could put him behind bars."

The phone rang in the room. Langston answered on the second ring.

"Hello...um, yeah, sure. I'll be right there." He hung up. "There's a problem with the credit card I used. I'll be back in a few minutes."

Before Clarissa could protest him leaving her cuffed to the bed, he was gone.

She heaved a sigh and stared at the ceiling. The sound of the basketball game playing on the television scratched at her already shot nerves. Glancing over, Clarissa saw Langston had left the remote beyond her reach, dooming her to having to listen to the damn game, the bastard.

To her surprise, the lock clicked on the door only minutes after Langston had left. Guess he'd realized without his coat, it was pretty darn cold outside.

The door eased open and a man slipped inside, but it wasn't Langston.

"It's about time the Fed left," he said casually.

Dressed all in black, the man wasn't that tall, maybe just under six feet. He had a wiry build and a pleasant face, which was ruined altogether by the menace oozing from him.

"Who are you?" Clarissa asked, sitting up.

The man stopped his progress toward her, a brief flash of confusion crossing his face. "Is that any way to greet me,

Clarissa? Especially when you've led me on a merry chase around this godforsaken wilderness."

"What do you want?" She couldn't imagine it was anything good, not with her luck.

"I know we've worked together in the past," the man said, "but you and I both know that loyalties in this business are fluid." He smiled as he loomed over her. "So please don't take this personally."

~

Erik headed for the motel lobby, wishing he had a bottle of bourbon nearby. He needed something to ease the tension. His body was like a guitar string pulled too tight; any moment he might snap.

His conscience wouldn't leave him alone. He was becoming more and more convinced she was telling the truth about losing her memory. There was little reason for her to lie at this point. They'd go easier on her if she testified than if she tried to sell them some cockamamie story about having amnesia. Surely she knew that. She was far from stupid.

It was ridiculous for him to worry about her. He knew better than anyone what she was capable of. It wasn't as though she was innocent.

Erik pushed open the door to the lobby. No one stood behind the desk. He hit the bell that sat on the counter and waited. Still nothing.

That sense of something not being right stirred in his gut.

"Hello? Anyone here?" he called out, meandering behind the desk and nearly tripping over the body on the floor.

Crouching down, Erik saw the skater-dude desk clerk had been knocked out. Not dead. That was good. A robbery?

A shadow on the floor alerted him a split second before the bat came swinging his way. Leaping to the side, Erik went for his gun but had no time to pull it before the attacker swung again. Erik ducked; the bat smashed a hole in the drywall. Scrambling to his feet, he backed away.

The guy was big, his head shaved, and a tattoo curved from his neck and disappeared under the tight black T-shirt he wore.

"Now stand still, little Fed," the man said with a smirk, a thick Irish accent coloring his words. "Just wanna rough you up a bit."

"I'd rather you not," Erik replied, eyeing the bat.

"I have me orders."

The guy swung, and Erik ducked again, then tackled his midsection. They grappled, and Erik swung his fist, connecting a hit to his jaw. Grabbing the bat, Erik yanked it out of his grip, shoving it forward again to nail the guy in the nuts. The man went down to his knees, groaning in pain. Erik landed another hit to his jaw, and the attacker fell over, unconscious.

Erik gasped for breath, his knuckles aching as he scrambled to make sense of what was going on. This guy had been sent to rough him up, not kill him. Why?

Clarissa.

Erik tossed the bat and pulled out his gun, flicking off the safety. Going to the door, he peeked outside, aware there might be an ambush waiting for him on the other side of the door. If he was unconscious or dead, he couldn't help Clarissa, and he had no doubt she was their target.

Seeing no one, Erik stepped outside, his gaze scanning the near-empty parking lot.

It was dark now. The fluorescent lights overhanging the walk to the motel's rooms glowed, though one or two had the telltale flicker of a bulb nearing the end of its life. Only a few cars passed on the nearby two-lane highway. The buzzing from the motel's neon sign could easily be heard.

Erik quickly eased by the rooms, his gaze steady on the room he'd rented for himself and Clarissa, number sixteen. His blood pounded in his veins. He was an easy target out here under the lights, but there was nothing he could do about it.

A television played in number seven, the canned laughter of the audience loud in the night as Erik passed by, a sense of foreboding creeping over him. He'd left Clarissa cuffed to the bed, alone, with nothing to defend herself with and no one to guard her.

Suddenly the door to number sixteen opened and a man stepped out.

"Freeze! FBI!" Langston yelled, aiming his weapon.

The man turned and smiled. A chill went through Erik. The face was familiar.

A car pulled up to the curb and the man got in. Erik fired a warning shot, then had to duck behind a nearby car as they fired back. When he popped back up, the car was speeding away and out of range.

Jumping to his feet, Erik ran to the motel door and pushed it open, terrified at the thought of what he was going to find.

The bed where she'd been lying was empty, the handcuffs nowhere in sight. The bedside lamp had been knocked to the floor, its light now casting strange shadows around the room. But there was no sign of Clarissa. Had they taken her?

"Clarissa!" he called, hurrying into the room. He glanced in the closet and shoved open the bathroom door…and felt his breath leave his lungs in a rush.

She was in the tub, facedown in the water, her arms cuffed behind her back. Her red hair floated in the water like a crimson halo. She was very still.

"Jesus Christ," Erik blurted, reaching into the ice-cold water and pulling her out. He gently laid her flat on the bathroom floor on top of the torn shower curtain. Water was everywhere. It looked like she'd put up a fight, what little she could with her hands cuffed.

She wasn't breathing.

Bending over her, Erik began CPR. He prayed to whatever god would listen as he worked. Erik had done this. He had left her alone when he should have known better, had known there were people looking to kill her.

"C'mon," he muttered. "You're tougher than this."

Her lips were frigid against his as he breathed air into her lungs in a sick parody of a kiss. Suddenly she began to cough, water pouring from her mouth and nose. Erik turned her on her side, digging for the key to the handcuffs and yanking them off her. He tossed them aside as she continued to cough and retch. Then she began to shiver in earnest.

The wet clothes had to go. As quickly as he could, Erik stripped off her sodden shirt, grabbed a handful of towels, and wrapped them around her. She'd curled into a ball now on the wet floor, and she was breathing, thank God. He pulled the wet, shivering mass onto his lap, cradling her in his arms as he leaned back against the wall.

"Shh, it's all right. You're safe now," he said, as soothingly as possible. Erik combed his fingers through her hair, her head tucked against his chest.

"He said it was a message," she rasped.

"What kind of message?"

"Solomon wants what I took, and if I say anything to the cops, he'll kill me."

She lifted her head, and Erik saw a livid red mark around her neck where she'd been choked into unconsciousness. Her lip was split and swollen, her cheek bruised. They'd hit her, and she hadn't even had her hands free to defend herself.

Erik's fists clenched with rage, and he struggled to keep it under control. All he wanted to do was to go after the bastard and kill him with his bare hands.

"Why did you let them do this to you?" he asked, as evenly as he could. "Why didn't you just give it to him?"

When Clarissa looked at him, the despair and hopelessness in her eyes was like a punch in the gut. God, how could he have been such an idiot? If she was faking the amnesia, no way in hell would she have let that guy do this to her. She would've given up what she'd taken. Clarissa was a survivor. You didn't get to where she was without a strong instinct for survival.

"I believe you," he said. Her eyes were limpid pools, sucking him in. Erik's hand brushed her cheek, the chilled skin soft to the touch. "I'm sorry I didn't before, and I'm damn sorry I left you alone."

Relief filled her gaze, and she ducked her head, resting against him again.

"It's about time," she mumbled.

Erik smiled humorlessly. That sounded more like her, and she was right. It was about damn time he believed her amnesia. Now, what was he going to do about it?

∾

They didn't stay in that motel. As soon as Clarissa had stopped shaking, he gave her a shirt of his to wear with her jeans. Once she was dressed, they hit the road. Although he went back to the lobby for the thug he'd knocked out, Erik wasn't surprised to find him gone.

It was late when they finally arrived on the outskirts of Denver. Erik found another hotel, one that was quite a bit nicer than the previous one, and checked them in. After settling Clarissa into bed, where she promptly fell into an exhausted sleep, he stepped outside and called Clarke, who answered on the third ring. Erik quickly explained what had happened.

"Did you get a good look at the guy?" Clarke asked.

"Yes, sir. I know I've seen him before. I just need to look through the Interpol database."

"You can do that tomorrow once you're back. Make that your first priority."

"Sir," Erik said hesitantly, "I don't know if handing her over to the marshals for transport is the best idea. She has amnesia, has nearly been killed twice, and is obviously a high-value witness."

"They're trained to handle just that, Agent," Clarke replied. "She won't escape. And I'm sure she'll have a miraculous recovery once she talks to her lawyer. They'll be waiting for you at Centennial Airport at oh nine hundred. Don't be late."

"Sir," Erik tried again, "O'Connell is a flight risk. She knows no one except myself—"

"You have your orders," Clarke interrupted. "I expect to see you tomorrow afternoon in my office."

"Yes, sir." Clarke hung up before Erik even got the words out. Now what?

Erik didn't see that he had any choice. He was going to have to turn her over to the marshals.

Erik returned to the hotel room, being careful not to wake Clarissa. Sitting on the edge of the other bed, he braced his elbows on his knees. He watched her sleep while he thought, trying to come up with a solution.

She looked different now than when he'd first laid eyes on her. Erik knew she hadn't changed; his perception of her had. Before, he'd only seen a criminal, wanted by the FBI for her ties to a ruthless mobster.

Now, he saw a woman who was scared and alone, the only thing standing between her and death being whatever she had taken from Solomon. Obviously, she'd known he was going to kill her and had taken measures to give herself leverage to exchange for her life. The only twist now being…she couldn't remember it.

~

Clarissa woke to the smell of cinnamon and coffee. Cracking open her eyes, she saw a steaming Styrofoam cup inches from her nose on the bedside table. Next to it was a paper plate topped with a huge cinnamon roll dripping icing.

"Thought you might be hungry," Langston said, sitting down on the bed across from her and taking a sip from his own cup.

"I am, thanks," Clarissa said, then wished she hadn't. Her voice sounded two packs a day and her throat felt like sandpaper.

She sat up and reached for the coffee, surprised to see he'd remembered how she took it. The hot liquid felt good on her throat.

"What time is it?" she asked, taking a bite of the cinnamon roll. It was gooey and practically melted in her mouth. Her stomach growled appreciatively.

"A little after seven," Langston replied. "We need to leave soon. We're meeting the marshal at nine to fly you to DC. He texted me earlier with the hangar number."

Clarissa suddenly lost her appetite. Langston was going to hand her over to the Feds. If she was in their custody, she had no hope of doing anything that might bring her memory back.

"If I'm in custody, I can't get what he wants," she said. "If I can't get what he wants, he's going to kill me."

Langston's face was grim. "You'll be safe, Clarissa. They'll put you in protective custody."

"For how long?" she asked. "Once they realize I don't know anything, which they'll chalk up to obstruction or label me an accessory, they'll charge me." Her gaze was unflinching as she looked at Langston. "You know he'll get me."

Langston cursed harshly, standing and walking away. He tossed his cup in the trash, his back still to her, his hands resting on his hips.

"Help me, Langston," Clarissa said. "If I can just have some time, I'm sure my memory will come back. I swear, once it does, I'll testify against Solomon." When he didn't respond, she added, "Please. I have no one else—"

"I can't, Clarissa!" he said, his voice loud in the room. Langston turned back to her and met her gaze. "I just can't. Don't ask me to. If I were to help you, I'd lose everything I've worked for."

Clarissa swallowed and was the first to look away. She couldn't blame him; not really. It was against everything he believed in to help a criminal like her. She had asked for the impossible. Like it or not, scared or not, she was on her own.

She gave a jerky nod. "Fine. Just give me a few minutes, and we can leave."

An hour later, they were pulling into Centennial Airport. The drive there had been nearly silent, both of them lost in their thoughts. Erik navigated to the specified hangar and parked.

Clarissa got out, and he took her elbow. They were met by a man with a US Marshals badge who stood about Erik's height, wore a cowboy hat, and sported a moustache. He shook hands with Erik.

"Randy Stiver," he introduced himself. He glanced at Clarissa. "This the prisoner, I'm guessing?"

"Clarissa O'Connell," Erik clarified. "She's to be delivered to the Hoover Building in DC. They'll remand her into custody from there."

"There's been a slight change in plan," Stiver said. "The private jet we had booked had some mechanical difficulties, so we're going commercial."

"That's not a problem," Erik said, more relieved than he wanted to examine. "I'm flying to DC. I'll just take her with me."

"No can do, Agent," Stiver said, pulling a pair of handcuffs out of his back pocket. "You know the law. She'll be waiting for you in Washington." Stiver turned Clarissa around, handcuffing her wrists behind her back.

Clarissa's gaze stayed locked on Erik's while she was cuffed, until he was forced to look away. The accusation in her eyes made guilt roil inside his belly.

"Do you have her personal effects?" Stiver asked.

"Um, yeah, just a second," Erik replied, hastily turning away as Stiver put Clarissa in the front seat of a nearby sedan. Erik had taken several steps toward the SUV to get the two black duffels containing Clarissa's things when a thought occurred to him.

"Wait," he said, swiveling to stare at Stiver, who stood waiting. "I never said she had anything with her."

"It was just a routine question, son," Stiver replied easily.

Something was off. Erik's gut was telling him something very different than his head was saying. He studied the marshal for a moment, trying to figure out what was bothering him. Then he saw it.

US Marshals carried Glocks, not Sigs.

Erik reached for his gun an instant too late. Stiver had drawn and fired. Erik dived for the SUV as Stiver threw himself into the sedan and took off, Clarissa locked inside with him.

EPISODE FOUR

CHAPTER SEVEN

Clarissa was thrown against the door as the marshal gunned the car out of the lot. Her shoulder hit hard, and she winced. She twisted in her seat, relieved to see Langston getting up off the ground through the rear window. When she'd heard the gunshot, her heart had lodged in her throat.

"Who are you? What do you want?" she demanded of the man who called himself Stiver. If he was a federal marshal, she'd eat dirt.

He shot her a look before glancing in the rearview mirror. "I'm to bring you in, just not to the Feds."

"Did Solomon send you?"

"Solomon ain't the only one after you, sweetheart."

The words sent a chill up Clarissa's spine. Whoever she'd been before, it obviously hadn't been a cashier at the Gap. My, what a dangerous life she'd led.

The scenery sped by as Stiver took her farther from the airport. Clarissa eyed the door. Stiver hadn't buckled her in, so she could try to make a leap for it, but at this speed and with her arms pinned behind her, chances were she would not come out of it unscathed.

When trees began to thicken outside the windows, the calm Clarissa had forced began to waver. Nothing good ever came from an abductor taking someone into the woods.

Stiver cursed, his eyes on the rearview mirror. He twisted in his seat to look, then turned back only to speed up even more.

"What?" Clarissa asked, turning to look as well.

"That Fed is following us."

Stiver was right. She could see Langston. Hope leapt as Clarissa saw his SUV barreling down the road after them. He was coming for her.

Clarissa lost sight of Langston as Stiver rounded a bend and she was again thrown against the door. Stiver spun the car around, skidding to a stop on the side of the deserted road. He pulled his gun from its holster.

"Time to end the Fed."

Panic raced through Clarissa. Reaching behind her, she yanked on the handle, and the door popped open.

"Don't even try it," Stiver growled, leaping across the seat and jerking her back inside before Clarissa could get out. He grabbed the seat belt and started to buckle her in.

Clarissa seized her chance. She didn't think; she just moved. If she did nothing, Erik might be killed.

That wasn't an option.

She slammed her forehead down, cracking Stiver on the bridge of his nose. He yelped in pain as blood spurted. Before he could recover, Clarissa twisted, swiveling in her seat and wrapping a leg around Stiver.

His gun came up, and Clarissa kicked it out of his hand with her other foot. Stiver's balance was precarious as he lunged for the gun, but Clarissa brought her knee up hard, hitting him on the chin and clamping his mouth shut. Stiver yelled again as blood trickled from his mouth.

Now both Clarissa's legs were around Stiver's neck. Crossing her ankles, she squeezed her thighs as hard as she could. Stiver clawed at her, the cramped confines of the front seat of the car working more to Clarissa's advantage than his. His face turned a mottled purple, his eyes bulging in his head.

The muscles in Clarissa's thighs screamed in protest, but she held on. Stiver grappled with something, she couldn't tell what, until he pulled the switchblade.

Panic gave her another burst of strength, and Clarissa twisted, throwing her whole body into it and slamming Stiver into the dash. His head snapped backward with a sickening crack. His body jerked once, twice, then collapsed on top of her.

Clarissa fought to breathe, the weight of the dead body pressing against her chest. Her arms were pulled up behind her back, her shoulders wrenched into a painful position.

Suddenly, the door behind her flew open. Clarissa stared up into the barrel of a gun.

Erik was breathing hard from his race to the car and took in the scene with a glance. He quickly holstered his weapon before reaching down to shove Stiver off O'Connell. The body fell to the side, and Erik was able to pull her out of the car. Her face was bloodless, and she struggled for air, pulling in short, quick breaths.

"Slow down," he admonished. "You're going to hyperventilate." A lock of her hair had fallen across her face, and Erik tucked it behind her ear before he even realized what he was doing. Once he did, he jerked his hand back, but if she noticed the touch or his hasty withdrawal, she didn't say anything.

O'Connell closed her eyes, obviously making an effort to calm down. Her wrists were still cuffed behind her back, which bothered Erik. He couldn't forget the sight of her facedown in the water last night with those damn cuffs on. Reaching into the car, he dug the keys off Stiver and unlocked the offending bracelets. Tossing them to the side in disgust, he wasn't sure whether to be impressed or horrified that O'Connell had managed to kill a man without the use of her hands or a weapon.

"Are you hurt?" he asked, anxiously watching as she rubbed her wrists.

She shook her head. "Other than the fact that I just killed someone, I'm hunky dory."

"Did he say anything?" Erik asked.

"Just that Solomon wasn't the only party interested in acquiring me."

Sirens sounded in the distance. Erik made a decision, one that he should have made hours ago. He knew with a fateful certainty that there would be no coming back from the consequences. So be it.

Giving her a moment to collect herself, Erik searched the marshal's car, taking two rifles from the backseat and another pistol. When he popped the trunk, he stopped dead.

"Well, I guess we know what happened to the real Stiver," he said.

O'Connell peered over his shoulder, and they both stared at the dead body shoved into the trunk of the car.

Reaching into the trunk, Erik felt the man's pockets until he pulled out a wallet. Flipping it open, he confirmed, "Yeah. This is Randy Stiver."

"So who's the guy I—" She cut off her own sentence, asking instead, "Who's the guy up front?"

"No idea." The sirens were getting closer. "Let's go," he said, closing the trunk and taking the weapons to his SUV.

"Wait, what do you mean?"

Erik paused, glancing back to see that O'Connell hadn't moved but was eyeing him suspiciously.

"The cops are coming," he said. The sirens grew louder by the moment. "Do you really want to be here when they arrive?"

"But I thought you didn't want to jeopardize your career—"

"I changed my mind," Erik interrupted. "Now let's get out of here before the cops haul both of us to jail."

"We can call it quits right here," O'Connell argued. "Dump the bodies, and I'll take this car and go my way, and you go yours."

"And what will you do then?" he asked. The thought of her on her own, with no one to help her, made him sick to his stomach.

She shrugged. "I'll figure it out." The bleakness and exhaustion in her eyes belied the casual words.

"You don't have to do it alone," Erik said. "I can help you. How far do you think you'll get on your own? You know no one and have nothing, not even a memory." More gently, he said, "Surely I'm a better option than going it alone." He held his breath. He wouldn't stop O'Connell if she decided to leave, but it would be a near thing. And not just because she was wanted by the FBI, but because he was afraid her life expectancy was growing shorter by the moment.

Erik's gaze locked with hers. Her green eyes seemed unusually bright. *Oh God, please don't let her be crying.* The thought made him panic slightly, though how she was holding it together after the past twenty-four hours, he had no idea. Any other woman of his acquaintance would have dissolved into hysterics long ago.

O'Connell cleared her throat, took a deep breath, and headed toward him. Erik let out his breath, relieved more than he wanted to admit that she hadn't left. He'd just gotten her back, amazingly enough unharmed, and he'd be damned if he was going to let her be hurt or killed because he was too much of a dumbass to figure out what was going on, which was obviously a hell of a lot more than what he'd been told.

He held the car door for her as she climbed in, refraining from touching her only with difficulty, and he wasted no time in getting them the hell out of there.

The miles flew by as Erik tried to get his head together. He was committed to a course of action now, aiding and abetting a fugitive. A fugitive that too many people wanted for reasons unknown, even by O'Connell herself.

Who had that guy been, and how had he known where they were going to be? The only explanation was that someone had known who was being transported. Someone had talked, laying a trap for him and O'Connell.

Grabbing his cell phone, Erik dialed SAC Clarke directly. When the man answered, Erik didn't waste time with preliminaries.

"Sir, this is Agent Langston—"

"Tell me you're on a plane, Agent," Clarke interrupted.

"Negative, sir. I regret to inform you that...well, sir, I believe we have a mole in the office."

"Just...wait, what?"

Erik heard a door shut and assumed Clarke was trying to get some privacy, which was a good thing considering what Erik had to tell him.

"We were ambushed, sir," he explained. "The marshal was a fraud. He killed the real marshal and impersonated him."

"Did he get the girl? Is she hurt?"

"No, sir. I was able to prevent that from happening. He's dead."

There was silence for a moment before Clarke spoke again. "All right, good job, Langston, but just because you think there's a mole here doesn't make it true. The mole could be in their office."

"Yes, sir."

"Looks like we're going to have to do this on the down-low. Let me get a map."

Langston waited, listening to papers shuffle on the other end of the line.

"Okay, there's a bit of nothing town in southern Colorado right near the New Mexico border, called Branson. They have a heliport there. I'll personally arrange a transport for O'Connell."

"Will I be coming, too, sir?"

"No. Get back to Denver once you drop off O'Connell and dig into the marshal business. I don't want to think one of my agents would betray his own like that."

That didn't sit well with Erik. He was responsible for O'Connell's safety, which had been precarious at best. While he didn't want to suspect his former partner, Kaminski was the one who'd contacted the US Marshals' office and the only one who knew where they were meeting. It was a bit too convenient to be mere coincidence, but he didn't say that to Clarke. Accusing a fellow agent without any evidence was a serious charge.

"Yes, sir."

Clarissa watched as Langston ended the call. "So what now?" she asked.

Langston pulled into a dilapidated gas station before answering, his thoughts busy contemplating his options. "My orders are to drive to a town close to the New Mexico border, meet up with a helicopter, and put you on it."

With that he got out of the car, slamming the door shut behind him.

Clarissa sat, utterly dumbfounded. He'd lied to her. Even after what had happened with the marshal, he was still going to turn her in. She'd been so sure he was going to help her, so relieved that she wasn't alone.

Though she had no memory, Clarissa felt that being alone was not a rare occurrence for her. You could only depend on yourself. No one could be trusted, not really. Wasn't everyone out for themselves, anyway?

Well, it was high time she got on with the business of looking out for herself. God knew no one else gave a damn. She was an idiot not to have gotten in that marshal's car and put the FBI agent far behind her.

Clarissa glanced around the gas station. It was empty of customers save for Langston. The windows into the building were dirty, and she couldn't see through them. She'd just have to hope the person inside was bored and not paying attention.

Reaching in the back, Clarissa grabbed one of the rifles Langston had tossed in. Keeping an eye on Langston—his back was turned to the window as he filled the tank—she checked to make sure the rifle was loaded. It was.

Clarissa opened the door and slipped outside, shifting her grip on the rifle before rounding the car. Langston looked up, saw the weapon leveled at him, and froze.

"This again?" he asked, his voice cold. He turned away, putting the fuel nozzle back in the pump before screwing the gas cap back on.

Clarissa swallowed, licking her dry lips. "Give me your keys," she demanded.

Langston crossed his arms, leaning casually against the side of the SUV.

"No."

Clarissa gritted her teeth in frustration. "Give them to me, Langston, or I swear I'll put a hole in you!"

Langston's eyes flicked down to the rifle in her hand, then back up. His blue eyes were calm and his voice steady as he said, "You're not running away from me."

"You said you'd help me," Clarissa fumed, hating the way her eyes stung with tears. She blinked them back. "You lied."

Langston's body was a coiled predator feigning ease as he pushed himself upright and moved toward her. "I didn't lie. I am going to help you."

"By turning me in?" Clarissa's voice was shrill, and her hands shook. She tightened her grip on the gun, taking a step backward as Langston slowly advanced.

"You're a strong woman," he said, eyeing her carefully, "but you're inches away from losing it."

Clarissa couldn't stop the tears now, which only made her more furious, and she dared not loosen her grip on the rifle to wipe them away. "You would be too," she spluttered angrily, "if you had no memory of who you were or what you'd done that had all kinds of horrible people wanting to capture or kill you! I've killed two people in as many days, done things, know things, that terrify me, and the one person I do know is hell-bent on turning me in to the cops so I can get sent to jail! So yeah, I think I'm entitled to be a little upset!"

Langston was blurry in her vision as he stepped closer until his chest was pressed against the rifle's muzzle. His hand lifted, and Clarissa knew with a sinking sensation that it was over. She couldn't shoot him, which was bad enough, but even worse, he knew it too.

To her shock, though, he didn't try to take the gun. Instead his hand brushed her cheek, wiping away the tracks of her tears. Confused, she looked up at him. His brows were drawn; his lips pressed tightly together as his eyes, so startlingly blue this close, studied her.

"I wasn't going to leave you alone, Clarissa," he said. "I planned on going with you, keeping you safe, helping you. I didn't lie to you."

Langston's hand was rough against her cheek even as his touch was featherlight. His thumb brushed her cheekbone as his palm cupped her jaw.

"I'm trusting you with my life," he said quietly, reminding Clarissa of the loaded weapon pointed at his heart. "Trust me in return."

Clarissa couldn't take her eyes from his. He seemed so sincere. Could she trust him? Did she have a choice? Would he betray her?

Even with all these things running through her mind, there was a deeper reason she didn't want to leave, one she'd refused to think about back at the marshal's car. The truth was she didn't want to leave him. Clarissa was an utter fool to feel that way; she knew Langston didn't feel anything for her, but she couldn't make herself give him up. She'd have to at some point, she wasn't stupid, but not just yet. Right now, he was all she had.

Lowering the rifle, she flicked the safety back on before looking back up at Langston. He hadn't moved away. If anything, he was closer now, though his hand had dropped back to his side.

The fact that he'd seen her cry embarrassed Clarissa. She wasn't weak and didn't want him to think that of her. "I'm not some weepy female who can't take care of herself," she muttered, dropping her chin so she wouldn't have to look him in the eye.

"I got that," Langston replied.

"I'm just tired. And...really don't want to go to prison."

"I got that too." Langston reached out and took the rifle from her hand. She didn't resist relinquishing the weapon, and neither did she resist when he cautiously wrapped an arm around her.

Unsure but obeying the gentle pressure on her back, Clarissa stepped into Langston's embrace. She tentatively slid her arms around his waist and rested her head against his chest. She was rewarded when his hold tightened, and he settled his chin on top of her head.

O'Connell's body was stiff against his, reminding Erik of a wild animal, hesitant and poised to run. He doubted she was the type of person who allowed others to see any weakness or vulnerability, with or without her memory intact. Her survival in the world she inhabited depended on it.

A few moments passed, and he simply held her, saying nothing. Ever so slowly, she relaxed into him. Erik tried not to think about how well the curves of her body fit against him. This was about comfort, not sex. He'd bet his next paycheck that O'Connell could really use a friendly hug right about now.

Considering what she'd been through—losing her memory, being captured, attacked, and nearly abducted—she'd held up remarkably well. It amazed Erik. Even though she had nothing and no one, she was determined to hold on to her freedom. He'd always known Clarissa O'Connell was an incredibly intelligent woman, albeit of a criminal bent, he just hadn't understood until now how truly extraordinary she was.

"What happened in the car?" he asked. "Did he attack you?" Erik had noticed the car had been pointing the wrong direction when he'd pulled O'Connell out. Had the fake marshal hoped to get her to talk by hurting or threatening her?

Pulling back slightly, O'Connell looked up at him. "He'd stopped the car so he could ambush and kill you." She gave a slight shrug. "So I killed him instead."

Erik looked at her, utterly taken aback. "You realize you could have waited until he'd killed me and then easily gotten away from him," he said.

"I just figured if anyone was going to kill you, it should be me."

The mischievous glint in her eye made his lips twitch. Damn. Hearing a woman casually discuss killing him really shouldn't be a turn-on. Something about that was very wrong, but he couldn't bring himself to care.

His gaze was drawn inexorably to her mouth. The hug that had begun as platonic was rapidly turning into something else. Erik was loath to let her go, even as he knew he should; his conscience screamed at him inside his head that O'Connell was a fugitive and thief. Her trust in him was precarious at best.

O'Connell seemed to sense the rising tension. Her tongue darted out nervously to wet her lips, and Erik's gut clenched in response. She moved to step away, but Erik's hold unconsciously tightened, preventing her escape. Her gaze darted up to his, questioning. The saline in her tears had turned her eyes a brilliant emerald.

The shrill ring of Erik's cell phone shattered the moment. O'Connell jumped, startled. Erik reluctantly released her before digging the phone out of his pocket.

"Langston," he barked, watching as O'Connell disappeared around the car and climbed back into the front seat.

"Hey, it's Kaminski."

Erik's attention was jerked away from where it never should have been in the first place.

"I'm glad you answered," Kaminski said, lowering his voice. "I wanted to warn you."

"Warn me about what?"

"About Clarke. It's weird. He's saying some strange shit..."

"Like what?"

"About you, man."

Erik paused in stowing the rifle back inside the car. "What do you mean?"

Kaminski's voice lowered even further. "He's saying you've gone off the reservation. That you're involved with this chick, Clarissa O'Connell. He says you killed two guys in some cabin in Colorado and killed the marshal I sent to pick her up. What the fuck, Langston? I mean, I know we're not buddies, but I just can't see you doing this shit no matter how hot the babe."

Erik listened, confused. What was this? Did Kaminski suspect that Erik might be on to him since the abduction had gone bad, hence the attempt to divert suspicion away from himself? But was Kaminski that clever? Erik's immediate thought was no, he wasn't, but perhaps his judgment was clouded by his own dislike of the man. He decided to play along and see where it led.

"I killed some men, but since they were trying to kill me and abduct my prisoner, I deemed it necessary," he replied evenly.

"That's not the story Clarke's spinning," Kaminski said. "Just...don't trust him. I have a bad feeling."

"He's sending a helicopter for O'Connell. I'm to have her on it this evening."

"Listen, let me look into it, see if it's legit. I'll call you back."

"Sure. Sounds good." Erik ended the call and stood for a moment, thinking. This was an odd turn of events. Clarke had been on this case and after Solomon for years. It made much more sense that Kaminski was trying to cover his own ass than Clarke being compromised did.

For now, Erik would head to Branson and wait to hear back from Kaminski. If he was "looking into it," then there might be yet another ambush. Only this time, Erik would be ready.

~

Clarissa covertly watched Langston as he drove. He'd pushed the sleeves of his shirt up to his elbows, and she studied his forearms and hands. He must work out; the muscles in his arms were too well-defined for someone who didn't. His hands were large. Strong. Capable. Much like the man himself.

It had been a surprising relief to lean on him, to give in to the overwhelming need to trust him. The hell of feeling so alone and without a single friend had abated when she was in his arms.

Clarissa felt her face heat, and she quickly turned to look out the window. The hug had been unexpected, a comfort that warmed the ice in her veins and eased the feeling of being hunted. She hated being afraid. She'd rather fight than just be scared. At least then she was proactively defending herself. Not knowing who or what might come after her next made the fear nearly paralyzing.

Then suddenly the embrace had turned into something entirely different.

The heat in his eyes, the hardness of his body as it pressed against hers, all of it had combined to steal her breath. She'd wondered if perhaps she'd been imagining it and had thought to take a step back before she embarrassed herself, but he'd stopped her. His hold had tightened and his gaze had fallen to her mouth. Had he been about to kiss her?

Then the damn phone had rung before she could find out.

It was probably for the best anyway. He was an FBI agent. She was a wanted fugitive. To think they could be together was like saying maybe a shark could go vegetarian. It just wasn't going to happen.

Clarissa glanced at Langston again. His hair had burnished red tones in the bright sunlight streaming through the window. The mirrored shades he wore suited him and gave him a mysterious air even as the gun holstered to his side added a dangerous edge. One arm rested on the console between them, slipping into Clarissa's space. His other elbow was braced against the door as he drove one-handed.

Yum. A night with him would surely be something to remember. And considering her shortage of memories...

No. Not going to happen except in her fantasies. Langston may be attracted to her, but his convictions of right and wrong would prevent him acting on it, she was sure. Which was too bad, she thought, her eyes lingering on his denim-encased thighs.

"So you're coming with me tonight?" she asked, partly to reassure herself, partly to get her mind off the track it had been happily breezing down.

"Yes." He glanced at her. "I promise."

The way he said the words was different from most people, as though he really meant them. Clarissa mused that she'd probably finally met a man who kept his word. So they really did exist, though few and far between.

"It would be really helpful if you could regain your memory," Langston said.

Clarissa raised a sardonic brow. "Ya think?"

The corner of his mouth turned up for a brief moment, and Clarissa felt a shot of pleasure that she'd amused him. Lord, if she wasn't careful, she was going to have it in a bad way for him.

"Maybe if you just relaxed, it would help," he suggested. "Things have been pretty...tense since the accident."

"The other night I dreamt something, a memory," she said. "But nothing last night." Not knowing anything about herself, even her own address, was getting old quick.

"Last night you nearly died," he said grimly.

Clarissa didn't want to think about last night. If she did, she could still feel the icy water closing over her head.

"Who was on the phone?" she asked.

"Remember that partner I told you about?"

"The one you disagreed with about me?"

"That's the one. I think he's been compromised. He arranged the marshal pickup. He could have very easily told someone about it and set up the ambush. Except he says the SAC, Clarke, is telling everyone I'm aiding you and murdered those men trying to get you away, that I've gone off on my own."

That sounded pretty close to the truth, in Clarissa's opinion.

Langston must have read her thoughts on her face because he said, "And no, that's not what I'm doing. Something's not right. I don't trust the FBI right now to keep you safe. Someone has an agenda, and it's not justice. I'm just not sure what it is or who's behind it." He glanced her way. "Until I do, you're staying with me."

Although the possessive words were meant in an entirely platonic fashion, Clarissa couldn't help the curl of pleasure they produced in her belly.

"Get some rest," Langston ordered. "You're going to need it, I'm sure."

Clarissa did as he said, leaning back against the seat. The sun was warm on her skin, and she sighed. She hadn't relaxed in what felt like a hundred years. The fact that she could do so only because she knew Langston would keep her safe was something she didn't want to dwell on. Doing so would only drag her in deeper with him. They'd part ways soon, she was sure of it. She needed to keep that in mind.

It was nice to have the help, and the company, but she knew you really could only count on yourself.

CHAPTER EIGHT

"They're comin' for me, darling."

Clarissa stared as her father hurried around his bedroom, throwing clothes into an already stuffed duffel bag.

"What do you mean? What happened?" The job her father and brother had pulled the night before had gone south; she knew that. Both of them hadn't said much since they'd gotten back in the wee hours of the morning.

Her father turned and looked at her, and for once his eyes weren't bleary from too much whiskey. "A man died, lovey."

Clarissa's jaw gaped. "What? What do you mean?" Never before had someone died on one of their jobs.

"A security guard," he answered, resuming his rushed packing. "It happened so fast, lovey. Awful thing, it was. An accident, at that. Wasn't supposed to happen."

"What about Danny? Are they comin' for him too?" A shot of fear went through Clarissa. Would the coppers take both her dad and brother? They'd go to prison and she'd be left utterly alone. Or worse, they'd send her back to juvie. No way was she doing that. It had been miserable enough without her computer, but having to put up with the other teens there had been near maddening. All of them in for petty theft, substance abuse, or other forms of teenage delinquency. None of them had known her crime, and she hadn't enlightened them. Frankly, there had been no one there worth telling. Immature idiot children, the lot of them.

"No' if I can help it," he said.

Just then Danny poked his head in the door. "Dad, they're here!" His face was white with panic, which scared Clarissa. She'd never seen Danny afraid of anything. At twenty-five, he was her invincible older brother, always outsmarting the coppers and bringing home his stolen treasures to show off to Clarissa.

Flynn O'Connell froze in his packing just as a knock sounded downstairs.

"We know you're in there, O'Connell! This is the police! Come out peacefully with your hands up."

Clarissa's heart was in her throat as she watched her dad. Flynn was looking at Danny, and something unspoken passed between the two of them.

"Take care of your sister, me boy," Flynn said roughly. "Do right by her. Prison's no place for a girl."

Realization hit and Clarissa panicked. "No, Dad!" She ran to him, and he caught her up in his arms. Flynn O'Connell was many things, a drunkard, liar, and thief, but he loved his daughter.

"I know I haven't been the best dad for ya, lovey," her dad said, his rough hand smoothing her hair. "But try to remember me well."

Clarissa was crying, holding tight around his waist as he pressed a kiss to the top of her head. He was right; he hadn't been a great dad, not having any idea what to do with a girl. His quick temper had put an end to the relationships he'd had over the years, though he'd never raised a hand to Clarissa.

But he and Danny were all she had.

The cops yelled again downstairs, banging on the door even more fiercely.

"Take her, Danny," Flynn said.

Clarissa felt Danny prying her arms from her dad.

"No!" she cried. "Dad, wait! Don't go!" Tears poured down her face, but Danny held her fast as Flynn gave them one last look before disappearing through the bedroom door.

Clarissa drew in a breath to yell again, but Danny clamped his hand over her mouth. She tore fruitlessly at his fingers. She had to get to her dad, couldn't let him just give himself up, leave them forever. She fought Danny, but he was too strong.

"Shhh, Rissa, hush. They'll hear you."

She could hear the men talking downstairs, heard her father go outside and car doors slam. Soon she heard the crunch of gravel as they drove away. Clarissa slumped against Danny, exhausted and sobbing.

"C'mon, Rissa," he said. "They're gone. We've got to get out of here before they come back." He let her go, and Clarissa sank to the floor, wrapping her arms around her legs and resting her head on her knees. "Rissa? Are you listening to me? We have to go."

"Go where," she asked tonelessly. She didn't know where they would go or how they'd pay to get there. Despite the thieving, they had little money.

"I don't know, but we have to get away from here. We'll find a job, get some dough, maybe go to America." He knelt down next to her. "You'd like that, wouldn't ya?"

Clarissa didn't answer. Her world was falling apart. Again. She thought she'd guarded herself well over the years, never letting any more of Dad's girlfriends get too close, not after Mary. And she'd been right to do that. Eventually, they all left. And now, even Dad was gone. The hole in her chest she'd thought was healed now gaped, and she realized it had never healed, merely patched over.

"We's all we got now, Rissa," Danny said quietly. "Best look after each other. Unless ya don't want to come with me?"

Clarissa looked up at Danny, panicked. His expression was compassionate, though his gaze was shrewd.

"O' course I'm comin'," Clarissa said. "You're not leavin' me."

"Ya know I'm a thief," he cautioned her. "If ya come, you'll have to earn your keep."

"Ya been usin' me to steal since I was small," she said with a snort. "Not so much be changin', I'm thinkin'."

"Then let's get out o' here," he said, standing up. Holding a hand outstretched to her, he helped her up. "Only pack what ya can carry in one bag."

Clarissa nodded, swiping her hands across her eyes.

Satisfied that she understood, Danny turned to leave. "Twenty minutes tops," he tossed back as he headed down the hall.

Clarissa gazed around the room, in somewhat of a dazed shock. In the space of ten minutes, her world had been turned upside down. Dad was gone. And there was no time to grieve, no time to even accept what had happened. She had to pack and leave the only home she'd ever known, probably forever, and all she could take was what could fit in one bag.

Hurrying to her father's room, she pulled out his bottom dresser drawer, digging and unearthing the contents until she found what she wanted. A gold pocket watch dangled from a chain. It was a gift from her mother before she died. She had to take this. A little of both her father and mother she could carry with her.

Clarissa slipped the watch into her pocket and hurried to pack. Even with Flynn's admonition to take care of her, she wouldn't put it past Danny to leave her behind. Careless and reckless to a fault, she was sure the last thing he wanted was to be responsible for a sixteen-year-old girl. It was a good thing she was useful to him. She grabbed her laptop. It went in a backpack all its own.

She felt the tears come again but forced them back. No time to cry. Time to go. Time to run...

Erik was loath to wake her, but it had been hours since she'd eaten and it might be hours yet if they didn't grab something now.

"O'Connell, wake up," he said, giving her a gentle shake.

She mumbled in her sleep, frowning. Erik leaned closer, trying to make out what she was saying.

"Don't leave me," she muttered. "I'll be good." She frowned even more fiercely, her lower lip puckering out like a child's, and tears leaked from the corners of her eyes.

All of it sent a chill through Erik. She was dreaming again, and not of unicorns and rainbows. The idea of O'Connell begging anyone for anything was unsettling, but at some point she'd begged someone not to go. Who? Her father? Brother? Friend? Lover?

The last thought sent a flash of jealousy through Erik, which was utterly ridiculous. What, was he going to pretend she'd never had a lover? And he shouldn't care anyway; it wasn't as though he had any claim to her.

"Wake up," he repeated, shoving those thoughts away. He shook her a bit more roughly this time.

O'Connell's eyes shot open, and she jerked upright, breathing hard. Her eyes were wide and fearful, her expression confused.

"Do you remember what you were dreaming?" Erik asked.

She turned his way, her eyes clearing as she focused on him.

"Yeah, a bit," she said.

141

Erik noticed her accent was much more pronounced when she spoke, the Irish lilt softening the consonants.

"They were arresting my…dad, I guess. And my brother was there. We were packing…"

Her voice faded and her gaze grew distant.

"So do you remember?" he asked.

O'Connell slowly shook her head. "The dream, it's familiar, but I can't remember it in context, ya know? It's like watching a movie without knowing the beginning or how it ends."

Erik was disappointed but still encouraged. "At least you're dreaming. I think your memory will come back any day now."

O'Connell nodded, still appearing deep in thought.

"Let's get some food," Erik suggested.

It wasn't until he was paying the check for their dinner that his cell phone rang. It was Kaminski.

"I checked on the copter thing," Kaminski said. "It's bogus."

"What do you mean it's bogus?"

"I mean there's nothing in the official channels about a helicopter transport request for you. Clarke hasn't said a word about it."

That was strange, but again, was Kaminski lying or telling the truth?

"I don't know what's going down," Kaminski continued, "but I wouldn't get on that chopper if I were you."

"You think I should disobey a direct order?" Langston asked, skeptical. "And I'm supposed to believe that you're trying to help me and not sabotage my career? Since when did you give a shit?"

"We may not like each other, but that doesn't mean I'm going to look the other way with something weird like this," Kaminski said stiffly. "You can take my advice or not, whatever. I just know if it was me out in the field and you saw something off, I'd hope you'd tell me, one agent to another."

Langston grudgingly considered this. Kaminski's argument was valid, but that didn't mean he could be trusted.

"I'll think about it," he said, offering no commitment either way. "Thanks for the intel." He ended the call.

If Kaminski was the traitor, then the path to safety was getting on that flight and escaping whatever, or whomever, he had lying in wait for them. If he was telling the truth, then it was a trap and getting on the chopper was a bad idea. Either way, Erik's choice might get both him and O'Connell killed.

No pressure.

"Who was that?"

Erik looked up to see that O'Connell had returned from the bathroom, a somewhat gratifying occurrence considering what had happened the last time he'd let her use a public restroom.

"Kaminski," he said. "We have a decision to make."

Once they were back in the SUV, Erik explained what Kaminski had said as well as his doubts about whether he could be trusted.

"So if we show up, we'll at least know who the traitor is, right?" O'Connell asked. "Kaminski or Clarke?"

"We should," he agreed.

"Then let's do it," she said.

Erik glanced at her, trying to determine if her bravado was real or fake. He couldn't tell. If she was scared, she concealed it well, which didn't surprise him. She was a good liar, had to be, in her line of work.

∼

The town was indeed a mere blip on the map, a blink-and-you-miss-it bump in the road. Langston had googled the location via satellite imagery, finding a place for them to park a ways from the heliport. After concealing the car, they approached on foot.

Night had fallen some hours ago and brought the chill of winter with it. Clarissa shivered in the cold, and she caught Langston glancing at her.

"I'm fine," she whispered, anticipating his question, though "fine" was relative at this point. The next few minutes could go very, very badly.

There wasn't really any grass, just dirt and scraggly weeds braving the dry terrain. Clarissa and Langston passed a couple of houses that had their lights on, and she could see people moving around inside, but mostly Langston kept to the shadows.

The howl of a coyote made the hair stand up on Clarissa's arms, the lonely sound foreboding and ominous. Her ears seemed to twitch with every new sound, she was so keyed up. Uneven ground caused her to stumble, tripping into Langston, who steadied her. Without a word, he took her hand as he resumed his pace.

When they neared the heliport, Langston led her into the deep shadows next to a darkened house.

"Stay here," he whispered. "I have a plan."

The sound of his words was nearly drowned out by the roar of a helicopter approaching. They both watched as it flew overhead and settled on the ground about a hundred yards away. Its engine cut off and the rotors began to slow.

Clarissa grabbed Langston's arm as he made to leave.

"Wait! Let me come with you," she said, but Langston was already shaking his head.

"If it's no good, I'll give you a signal. Hightail it back to the car and get the hell out of here." He handed her his keys.

"Aren't you afraid I'll just take these and leave?" she asked. The cold metal pressed against her palm as she clutched the keys.

His face was barely discernible in the darkness. "I'm trusting you."

Clarissa shook her head sadly. "You're a fool, Langston." Why would he trust her? She certainly wouldn't have had their positions been reversed.

"For having some faith in you?" he asked. His lips twitched in an almost smile.

"You could be walking into a trap," Clarissa warned, ignoring his question. She realized her hand still gripped a fistful of his sleeve, so she let go. "What if they kill you?"

"Then no one on the planet will know where you are," he replied.

His gaze was steady, and though Clarissa knew he meant that as reassurance, it was hardly comforting.

On sudden impulse, she leaned forward and pressed her mouth to his in a quick, firm kiss. When she pulled back, he looked as stunned as if she'd stripped naked and danced the hula.

"I'm Irish," she explained with a shrug. "A kiss for luck."

Langston jerked her into him, making her gasp in surprise. "Then I'll take a real one," he rasped.

Before she could think, he bent his head and was kissing her, only this wasn't anything like the chaste kiss she'd given him. His mouth slanted across hers, demanding her response. Soft and warm, his tongue brushed against the tender skin. With a sigh, Clarissa parted her lips and he quickly took advantage, deepening their kiss.

His hand cupped the back of her head and his fingers tangled in her hair, while his other arm around her waist locked her against him. Clarissa twined her arms around his neck and felt the cold wall of the house at her back as he pressed her into it.

Her pulse raced as their kiss became even more heated, each second that passed marking time they didn't have. Langston's tongue stroked hers in a dance that set fire to her blood. The shadow of whiskers on his face softly abraded her skin. His hair was silky, and she couldn't resist from pushing her fingers into the thick strands, which he must have liked, judging by the masculine groan that met her ears.

When he finally lifted his head, both of them were breathing hard.

"Probably shouldn't have done that," Langston muttered, his thumb stroking her jaw.

Her skin tingled from his touch, as though electricity were flowing from him into her. "Do you hear me complaining?" she asked.

He almost smiled. "I've got to go," he said. "I'll be back, and if I'm not, you know what to do."

Langston released her, pulling his gun and checking the ammunition cartridge before sliding it home again. He motioned for her to get down, and Clarissa obeyed, crouching behind some shrubbery.

Langston melted into the shadows. Clarissa stayed down, watching as he emerged into the glow cast from the lights overhanging the tiny heliport. He crossed the dirt road, and Clarissa saw two men get out of the helicopter, the breeze from the gently turning rotors ruffling their clothes and hair.

The men seemed affable enough as they greeted Langston. Clarissa watched them talk, her nerves on edge. The keys to Langston's SUV felt as though they were burning a hole in her pocket. What if everything was fine and Langston told her to come out? Yes, he'd be with her on the helicopter, but what then? He couldn't stay with her once she was arrested and in federal custody. He wouldn't be able to help her or protect her. And her options for helping herself would be severely limited.

Clarissa eased to her feet, still watching the men talk. It seemed as though everything was legit. Any moment now, Langston would turn and motion to her, then it would be over.

She hated to betray his trust, but like she'd said, he was a fool to trust her.

Clarissa kept to the shadows as she crept away. Guilt ate at her, but she ignored it. Escaping now was the smart thing to do, the logical thing.

A loud *pop!* sounded behind her, making her instinctively drop to the ground as it sounded again. How she knew that was a gun, she had no idea. She just did. Glancing back over her shoulder from where she lay in the dirt, she saw the two men from the helicopter had collapsed and weren't moving. Langston stood, his hands in the air and looking at someone.

A man was approaching him, gun in hand. Clarissa's heart was in her throat as she watched, stunned at the turn of events. She scrambled to her feet, wishing she had a gun. Two men came up on Langston from behind, taking his gun from him.

Clarissa choked back a scream as one of them clubbed Langston over the head and he dropped like a rock. Together, they each grabbed an arm and dragged him into a nearby clapboard building, little more than a shack. The last man holding the gun glanced around once, twice, before stepping over the dead bodies and following his accomplices. The door closed behind him.

Clarissa sucked in a breath. It was the same man that had nearly killed her in the motel.

She stood, her heart racing and adrenaline pumping as she thought furiously. What could she do? Her fingers brushed the keys in her pocket. Wait—Langston had taken those rifles from the marshal. She had access to weapons, thank God.

Looking up at the shack, her eyes narrowed, and she calmed. She had an objective now, and she had to move fast. Anger replaced her panic as she swept through the logistics in her mind, discarding plans and approaches in favor of others in an almost clinical way before settling on a course of action.

Clarissa didn't know who that bastard was or how he'd found them again, but Langston was her FBI agent, by God, and she wanted him back.

~

Cold water splashed on Erik's face, jerking him awake. He grimaced, the pain in the back of his head lancing through his skull.

"Welcome back, Agent Langston."

Erik pried his eyes open as memory flooded back. The other agents, shot. The man from the motel and the two thugs that had knocked him unconscious.

God, he hoped Clarissa had gotten away. She was smart and had a strong instinct for self-preservation. No doubt she was miles away by now after seeing how things had gone down, which was a good thing, no matter how his gut was in knots about what his immediate future entailed.

"What do you want?" Erik asked, forcing his body upright from where it was slumped in the wooden chair to which he was tied.

"Where's the girl?" the man asked. His eyes were shards of black, his expression bored.

"I don't know what you're talking about," Erik said.

The man gave a nod, and that was when Erik saw one of the henchmen standing slightly behind him, the other a bit farther away, watching. Without warning, the closest guard struck out, nailing Erik in the jaw with his fist and making Erik's head snap backward. Another blow, and his lip split, the metallic tang of blood hitting his tongue. A punch in the gut made him want to double over, but he couldn't, tied as he was to the chair.

Erik bit back a groan as pain ricocheted inside his head. That was gonna leave a mark. Turning to the side, he spat a mouthful of blood. Gritting his teeth, he blinked hard, squeezing his eyes shut before focusing on the head guy. As he did, it finally clicked who he was.

"I know you," he said, his breathing ragged. "Xavier Mendes. Interpol has had you flagged for years. Ties to the Russian Mafia." He paused. "You know, murdering federal agents isn't going to go over real well."

Mendes smiled, though it did nothing to soften his face. "What an excellent memory you have, Agent. Though I'm not surprised. Agent Erik Langston. First in your class at the academy and rising through the ranks faster than your peers, despite your rather unfortunate parentage. You were the first to see Clarissa's importance to Solomon, and I have no doubt that you know exactly where she is right now. So let's make this easier on everyone, shall we? Tell me where you've hidden her."

"She must have something pretty good for him to put you on her trail," Erik mused, ignoring the question. "If you want her so bad, why didn't you just take her last night?"

Mendes's smile faded, his expression turning glacial as he said, "If things had gone according to plan, she would be dead. Now things have changed, and I want her alive."

"Why?"

Mendes smirked. "You hardly need to know, Agent. And with or without you, I will find her. And she will very much regret making me chase after her." He gave another nod to the guard, and Erik braced himself.

An explosion sounded from outside, making all of them turn toward the door.

Mendes gestured to one of the guards. "Go see what's going on."

The guard hurried to obey, disappearing through the door.

Mendes's gaze narrowed as he watched Erik. "I certainly hope Clarissa didn't take it into her head to attempt a rescue operation. She should be thanking me for taking care of you."

Erik didn't like the context of how exactly Mendes would be "taking care" of him. As for a rescue, well, he wasn't naive, and Clarissa wasn't an idiot. He tugged on the ropes binding his hands, but they held fast, biting into his skin as he tried to work a hand free.

Mendes pulled out his gun as he walked to a window, careful to stay to the side and out of the direct line of sight. He motioned to the guard. "Watch him closely."

The guard took up a position right next to Erik.

"I don't like this," Mendes said. "And I don't like being sitting ducks in here." Peering out the widow, Mendes slowly smiled. "I'll be damned," he said. "She blew up the helicopter." He turned to Erik and said with some admiration in his voice, "Clarissa is quite clever, you know. And I am guessing by my associate's failure to return that she has reduced our numbers by one."

Shit. Instead of being miles away, Clarissa was outside, trying to be a badass and rescue him. As if the fact he needed rescuing wasn't humiliating enough, his female prisoner was the one attempting it.

Erik worked harder at the ropes tying each wrist to the chair. He'd be damned if he'd sit here tied up and helpless.

Suddenly, the lights went out, plunging them into darkness.

Erik took his chance, swinging the chair around and ramming it into the guard. Though he was still tied to it, it made an excellent weapon.

The guard stumbled backward, slamming into the wall. Erik blindly swung again, getting him in the knee-caps. The guard cried out in pain and went down. Erik lost his balance and fell hard. Luck was with him, as the chair cracked apart on impacting the floor, and Erik jerked his hands free.

He grappled with the guard in the dark, hitting him as the guy pulled his gun. Erik made a grab for his wrist just as the door flew open.

The figure of a man was starkly outlined in the doorway, the orange glow of the fire behind him casting him in utter darkness. As everyone watched, he fell into the room. The guard fighting Erik stopped for a moment, confused.

The figure suddenly raised its arm and fired. The guy next to Erik dropped. Before he'd even hit the floor, the shooter switched aim.

Mendes shot the man, his head exploding into a gooey mass of blood and brain matter. To Erik's amazement, the man's arm didn't drop, instead firing another bullet and hitting Mendes in the arm.

Mendes dropped the gun as another bullet hit him in the opposite shoulder, flattening him against the wall.

The headless body on the floor flopped onto its back, and O'Connell leaped to her feet, her gun still trained on Mendes.

Erik's breath rushed out of him as he gazed at her. She'd ditched the sweater she'd had on, instead wearing a black tank with her jeans, and had tied her hair back at the nape of her neck. Golden light from the doorway bathed her face, revealing an impenetrable expression and eyes that glittered as she gazed at Mendes.

She was breathtaking in the same way as a gazelle staring into the eyes of a lioness stalking him. Beautiful and deadly, the danger she posed no less fascinating for its menace.

Stepping forward, she used her foot to send Mendes's gun sliding across the shack's wooden floor. Her gun remained steady, pointing at him.

"You nearly killed me last night," she said, her voice cold. "If it wasn't for the agent here, I'd be dead."

Mendes smiled tightly at her, his hand clutching at the wound in his shoulder. "Clarissa. You always did know how to make an entrance."

"Do I?" she asked. "That's good to know. I bet I'm also the type of person who's not really into turning the other cheek."

"Wait!" Erik interjected, afraid she was going to kill Mendes. "Don't kill him."

O'Connell froze but didn't look at him. "Why the hell not? He was going to kill you."

"Kill him in cold blood? That's what you want to do?"

"At the moment, yes." Her tone was dry as dust.

"I don't want to see that, Clarissa."

Her name on Langston's lips startled Clarissa. He'd never called her by her first name before. His voice was a sad plea, though leaving the assassin alive was decidedly unwise. A mantra pounding inside her head told her so.

Eliminate the threat. Leave no trail.

It felt as though her head were going to explode, the words nearly a compulsion. She squeezed her eyes shut, trying to block it. After a moment, she refocused on the man who'd hurt her, and Langston faded from her mind. She aimed the gun...

Langston tackled her, knocking her to the floor. They hit with a muffled thud, and he quickly pried the gun out of her hand.

"He presents no threat, Clarissa," Langston said as he lay on top of her, his breathing harsh. "You can't just kill him. I won't let you."

"God, Langston, you're so naive!" Clarissa spat, shoving him off her and getting to her feet. "He'd kill us in an instant if he could."

"That doesn't mean we should do the same."

They stood glaring at each other until a laugh from Mendes broke their staring contest.

"I must say, this is quite entertaining," he said, still chuckling. "An FBI agent trying to give Clarissa a conscience? Good luck."

His words sent a chill through Clarissa. Was she really like that? A criminal with no conscience? Was she just like the man who'd tried to kill her?

"What in the hell is going on here?"

They both turned to see two men with rifles, locals by the looks of it, had entered the shack. Langston held his hands up, pointing the gun at the ceiling.

"I'm Agent Erik Langston with the FBI," he said. "This man killed those two men outside and held me hostage. If you let me, I can show you my ID."

They kept their rifles trained on him until he produced his badge, then they relaxed.

"I need this man guarded until the FBI comes to collect him," Langston said. "Can you do that?"

The men agreed. Langston promised to have the FBI there in a few hours before taking Clarissa by the elbow and dragging her out the door.

"Where are we going?" she asked as they passed the smoking wreckage of the helicopter. "We're not waiting for the FBI?"

"No," Langston said, his strides eating up the ground. "The FBI wants to arrest me."

Clarissa nearly stumbled. "What? Why?"

"Those guys were seconds away from disarming me and taking my badge. I'm now wanted for murder as well as aiding a fugitive."

"That's insane!" Clarissa spluttered. "You didn't murder anyone! Well, at least not anyone who wasn't already trying to kill you."

"I know."

Langston's expression was hard, preempting any further questions from Clarissa. She didn't know what else to say anyway. Langston was being pursued by his own people for what he'd done to help her. Why he wasn't putting her in cuffs and dragging her to the nearest FBI office to clear his name was beyond her.

They were at the car now, and he held his hand out for the keys. Clarissa gave them to him, wincing as she noticed the blood and bruises on his face. She'd gotten there in time to save his life, but not spare him pain. Clarissa glanced away uncomfortably as she climbed into the car. It was her fault they'd taken him, hurt him. Protecting her had nearly gotten him killed, not to mention put him well on the path to destroying his career.

"What the hell were you thinking anyway?" he bit out, once he got in the car. "I told you to leave, not play Sarah Connor and rush in with guns blazing." He hit the gas, and gravel spewed behind them as they shot down the road.

"You'd rather I left you there?" Clarissa retorted.

"I'd rather you'd have done what I said!"

"Well, screw you! I wasn't going to run away and let you die."

Langston stomped on the brakes; the SUV fishtailed as it came to a shuddering halt. He threw it into park before turning to her.

"I can't trust you if you don't do what I say," he said.

"Getting rescued by a girl got your knickers in a twist?" Clarissa sneered. "Don't worry. I won't tell."

"Dammit, Clarissa! Don't you see—"

Clarissa knew only two ways to shut up an angry man, and she was fresh out of bullets. Which only left one option.

"Shut up, Langston," she cut in. Fisting a handful of his shirt in her grip, she jerked him toward her, planting her lips on his. He went still, and her lips curved in a smile. Then he was kissing her like before, cradling her face in his hands, and she could taste the blood he'd shed for her.

After a long moment, he pulled back just enough to look in her eyes. She grinned at him. "You're much too pretty to let die," she said.

"Is this the part where I'm supposed to thank you?" Langston said, but it was without rancor. The roughness in his voice as his eyes devoured her made her stomach do flips.

"I thought you just did?"

He snorted before putting the car back in gear and heading down the road, this time at a more reasonable pace.

"So where to now?" she asked.

"Well, we need a safe place to stash you until I can figure out what to do next, someplace no one will look, not even the FBI."

"And you know a place like that?"

He nodded. "I think so."

"And that would be…"

Langston glanced at her, grimacing as he said, "My mother's."

EPISODE FIVE

CHAPTER NINE

The motel this time was little better than the one before, but on the road in the middle of west Texas, there was little to choose from. Erik paid with cash, knowing his credit cards could and would be tracked.

Erik had called the incident in to the closest field office, avoiding a conversation with SAC Clarke, and told them to take Mendes into custody. He'd briefly contemplated his next move; should he call Clarke or Kaminski? Then decided it would have to wait until morning.

He was tired, and his body ached from the abuse it had taken at the hands of Mendes and his honchos, then having to drive a few more hours in the middle of the night to put some distance between them and the dead men. He should probably go take a shower, but he couldn't make his body move from where he sat on the edge of the bed.

"Let's see what the damage is."

Erik looked up to see O'Connell holding a washcloth while she squeezed between his spread knees. She frowned as she began gently cleaning the dried blood from his face, the warm cloth sliding over the cuts and bruises. He reached up and grasped her wrist, halting her ministrations.

"That's not necessary," he said stiffly. "I can do it."

She seemed taken aback, looking at him strangely. Her wrist felt too fragile, like he could snap it with a quick twist of his hand, and Erik had to remind himself that just hours ago this woman had killed two men without batting an eye.

Killed them on his behalf, his conscience reminded him.

"You're exhausted," she said, tugging herself free. The cloth swiped again at his skin.

O'Connell's nearness disconcerted him. The memory of the heated kiss they'd shared reminded him of the consequences for not keeping a tighter control on his impulses. He shouldn't have kissed her, shouldn't have crossed that line. He was an FBI agent. She was his prisoner. Circumstances required them to cooperate, but those circumstances could and would change.

Erik grabbed her wrist again, his hold tighter this time. "I said I can do it," he repeated.

Their gazes caught. Her eyes searched his, then her delicate jaw locked tight.

"Fine," she said curtly, dropping the cloth and jerking her wrist out of his grasp. "Just trying to help, Langston. No need to be an ass." She dropped down on the opposite bed and picked up the remote, flipping on the television.

Erik watched her for a moment, but she studiously ignored him, randomly switching channels. He could tell she was irritated, though it wouldn't have taken Sherlock Holmes to figure that one out.

"O'Connell—"

"Save it," she cut him off. "Prim and proper FBI man is regretting that kiss now, right? Well, don't worry. Your virtue is safe with me. Wouldn't want you to get your hands dirty with a filthy thief now, would we? Even if I did save your life."

Her sarcasm grated on Erik. "I can't let my emotions cloud my judgment."

"Oh, your emotions are what's clouding your judgment?" she snapped. "I thought the culprit was a bit further south." She tossed the remote and bounced off the bed, swiping some clothes from the duffel nearby before disappearing into the bathroom. The door shut with a resounding *bang* behind her.

Erik sighed and rubbed a hand across his forehead, wincing as his fingers brushed against a scrape. God, what a mess. As if it wasn't bad enough having mobsters after O'Connell and the FBI hunting him, now he had to deal with a pissed off woman. A woman he absolutely had to keep his hands off of, no matter what.

That resolve was put to the test when she emerged from the bathroom wearing nothing but one of his shirts. Enough buttons were undone to leave the valley between her breasts tantalizingly bare. Her wet hair left random drops sliding down under the cotton, causing the fabric to cling damply to her skin.

"Your own clothes are unavailable?" Erik snapped.

"You didn't buy me anymore and I'm not sleeping in the ones I have." She plopped down again on the bed. The shirt slid up her bare thighs.

Erik quickly looked away, grinding his teeth in frustration. The sight of her wearing his shirt stirred something possessive in him, just as the memory of her fighting to free him stirred something primal. Both feelings were best dealt with under the spray of a cold shower.

When he emerged twenty minutes later, the room was empty.

"Shit!" he exploded, dropping the towel he was using to dry his hair and running for the door. He couldn't believe he'd been stupid enough to trust her alone for even a second. She was going to get herself killed, taking off alone.

The door swung open just as he reached it, and Erik skidded to a halt.

"What's your problem?" O'Connell asked, eyeing him as she slipped past him to the bed. Thankfully, she'd put on a pair of yoga pants. She popped the top on a can of soda in her hand. When Erik continued to stare at her, she said, "I was thirsty, okay? What, did you think I'd run off?"

"Where'd you get the soda?" he asked, ignoring her question. No need for her to know he'd panicked at her disappearance.

She rolled her eyes. "Vending machine, obviously."

"How'd you get the money?" Erik was quite sure his wallet had been with him.

"Well, there was a guy there and I told him I'd give him a blow job for a buck."

Erik glared at her and waited.

"Oh, relax," she huffed. "It was an old machine, okay? I pressed a few buttons and got a free soda."

"You pressed a few buttons?"

She shrugged. "I just kinda…knew to try a couple things, and one of them worked. Not a big deal."

"So you hacked into a vending machine and stole a soda." Why was he not surprised?

"It's just a soda, Langston."

"It's stealing," he said. "And it's wrong."

"You're just mad because you thought I left," she shot back. And the thought had crossed her mind. But Langston had put his life and career on the line for her. While her survival instincts may have dictated she scurry out the door and not look back, her conscience wouldn't let her. So she'd ignored the keys sitting on the table and just gone in search of something to drink instead.

"Why don't you make yourself useful and open your laptop," he countered. "Maybe you can figure out why you're so popular."

Clarissa flushed at this. She'd been so consumed with thoughts of Langston and his rejection of her attempt to help him that she hadn't remembered the laptop they'd been carting around. But she wasn't about to admit that to him. Bad enough that he'd practically shoved her away earlier. As if she was throwing herself at him, for God's sake. Please.

She brushed past Langston and went to dig out her laptop, trying to ignore his half-naked state. Jeans did not qualify as fully dressed. Didn't the man ever put on a damn shirt after showering?

Clarissa felt his eyes on her as she set the laptop on the tiny table in the corner and booted it up. She felt more than heard him approach to look over her shoulder.

The confines of the tiny motel room seemed even smaller with Langston so close, and she had to nearly bite her tongue to keep from telling him to take a step back. No way was she going to let on how much his nearness affected her.

The laptop put a quick dash to her hopes for information when a log-on screen appeared.

"Well, so much for that," she snorted in disgust. "I can't remember my birthday, much less a password." She turned away, intent on putting some space between her and Langston, when he snagged her around the waist.

"Wait," he said. "Passwords are automatic. They're practically muscle memory. I'd have to type my password in order to spell it. I bet if you tried, your fingers would remember without your brain having to."

It was a good thought, Clarissa grudgingly admitted. She wished she'd thought of it instead of him. Nothing worse than a self-righteous do-gooder know-it-all with abs that looked like they'd been Photoshopped.

Clarissa glanced down pointedly at where his hand still rested on her waist. The warmth of his touch seeped through the thin cotton of the shirt she wore as though to brand her skin. At her look, he yanked his hand back as though he hadn't even realized what he'd been doing.

Their eyes met, but his gave nothing away.

Stepping back in front of him, Clarissa bent over the laptop, resting her fingers lightly on the keys. "Now what?"

"Um, I don't know," Langston said. "Close your eyes maybe. See what comes to you."

Clarissa did as he suggested, heaving a sigh. "I feel ridiculous," she said after a moment. "Like I'm playing with a Ouija board or something. Oh, spirits," she mocked, "will the quarterback ask me to the prom?"

There was a snort of muffled laughter behind her. Clarissa's spirits lifted somewhat. She'd made him laugh.

"Try reaching for each key," he suggested. "Maybe your fingers just need a little prompting."

Clarissa really didn't think this was going to work; her fingers felt nothing, but she was aware of a strong desire not to disappoint Langston. That was odd and made the grin fade from her face. She should not care one way or the other what he thought of her. If she started caring, then she'd be under his control, her actions subject to his approval.

That wouldn't do.

While she was thinking all this, her fingers were unconsciously moving, until—

"You did it!" Langston crowed.

Clarissa's eyes popped open. He was right. She'd somehow managed to type in the right password. She immediately hit a few more keys until a window popped up.

"What are you doing?"

"I'm changing the password, of course," she said. "Just because I got it once doesn't mean I could do it again."

Clarissa pulled out the cheap wooden chair and sat down, looking curiously through the laptop's menu of options and clicking on one for e-mail. But she was disappointed at what it contained.

"Paranoid much?" Langston said dryly, looking over her shoulder at the empty folders.

"Obviously with good reason," Clarissa replied. "You've met my fan club." She checked her Sent and Deleted folders. All were empty. "Without an Internet connection, the e-mail is useless."

"We're lucky this place had indoor plumbing," Langston said. "Wi-Fi's a bit much to ask for."

Clarissa closed the e-mail client and started browsing through the files, looking for ones most recently modified, but the names meant nothing to her, nor did the lines and lines of color-coded gibberish when she opened them.

"None of this rings a bell?" Langston asked. "You can't read computer code anymore?"

Clarissa slowly shook her head. "No." Well, that was disappointing. Though there had to be something on here that would tell her more about herself. But no matter what files she opened or where she looked, there was nothing personal. Not a music file or photograph, nothing. After several minutes, she sat back in the chair with a sigh, closing the laptop.

"We can try again when we get somewhere with Internet," Langston said, backing away as Clarissa got up and went back to lie down on the bed. Though she'd forgotten about the laptop, she was still disappointed at not finding anything that would help.

Langston watched her for a moment before moving to his own bed. Reaching over, he shut off the light, plunging them into darkness. A meager glow filtered in between the heavy drapes, and Clarissa's eyes quickly adjusted.

"So now what?" she asked.

It was a moment before Langston responded. "Now we get some rest. Tomorrow we'll drive to San Antonio. Don't worry. We'll figure something out."

Clarissa stared at the spot where Langston lay, his body cloaked in shadows. It was kind of sweet, him trying to reassure her, even after his earlier rejection. It surprised her how much she wanted to go to him, though she knew she wouldn't be welcome. She'd become way too dependent on his solid presence for her peace of mind.

~

The shrill sound of the alarm clock woke Erik from a dead sleep. He slammed his hand down on the offending noisemaker, silencing it.

Shit. He flopped onto his back. A few more hours' sleep would come in handy, but the drive to San Antonio would take all day, so he'd only allotted them a short time to be off the road.

A feminine sigh close by startled him. What the hell? It seemed O'Connell had joined him in his bed at some point during the night.

She was still asleep, curled up next to him under the covers. He could feel the warm press of her body against his. She'd removed the yoga pants, and Erik didn't resist the urge to slide his hand up the soft skin of her thigh, settling his palm over the curve of her hip.

Why was she here? Did she have a nightmare in the middle of the night or something?

These thoughts were running through his head even as he nudged her closer. The voice in the back of his head that had castigated him so harshly yesterday for kissing O'Connell was nowhere to be found.

She'd come to his bed. Who would blame him for taking her up on the invitation?

It was a matter of a moment to unbutton the shirt she wore.

Erik found himself holding his breath as he slipped his hand between the folds. He felt like a kid on Christmas morning. His hand brushed her warm skin and her eyes fluttered open.

Erik froze. But O'Connell just smiled sleepily at him, her green eyes soft in the early morning light. She curled an arm around his neck, tugging his head down. His lips brushed hers—

Erik jerked awake, his hand groping for the shrieking alarm clock. When it was again blessedly quiet, he collapsed back on the bed, his chest heaving. Remembering, his gaze flew to the other bed, where O'Connell was mumbling in her sleep.

A dream. It was just a dream.

Damn.

Christ, he was losing it.

"Let's go, O'Connell," he said roughly, hauling himself out of bed.

She mumbled something in reply and burrowed deeper under the covers.

"C'mon," he said, giving her shoulder a shake.

"All right, all right, I'm up," she groused, throwing off the covers.

Her hair was tousled from sleep, and she pushed a hand through it as she headed to the bathroom. Erik's gaze followed her, his dream still too fresh in his mind for his liking, or comfort.

Thirty minutes later, they were on the road after stopping at a gas station to fill up and grab some coffee and food. The sun hadn't been up for long but was already bright enough for Erik to don his sunglasses.

"How long until we get there?" O'Connell asked, sipping from her steaming Styrofoam cup.

"Nine hours, give or take."

"And taking me to your mother's is a good idea because…"

"Because first, we need cash. She'll loan me some money. Second, we need time to figure out our next move. Third, no one will look for us there. It has no ties to you."

"And your mother's not going to mind you bringing home a fugitive?"

Erik hesitated. He hadn't thought of that. "Let's not... discuss that with her," he said.

"Then who am I and why are we visiting your mother?"

O'Connell's matter-of-fact questions irritated Erik. "Listen," he said, "I don't want to upset my mother. She's been through enough as it is. We'll just say you're a...friend...and leave it at that." Right. Because his mom wasn't going to be insanely curious about him bringing a girl home. Shit. He really hadn't thought this through.

"All right, sheesh, chill," O'Connell said. "We're friends. Fine."

Blessed quiet for a few minutes before, "How did we meet?"

"What?"

"If we're friends, we had to have met somewhere. She may ask. So how did we meet?"

"I don't know. It doesn't matter. Just make something up." Lying to his mom didn't sit well with Erik, but he had no choice.

"So we met at a strip club. I was one of the dancers. You wanted to save me."

"For God's sake, no!" Erik spluttered. "Don't tell my mother something like that!"

Clarissa laughed. It was way too easy to get under Langston's skin. Maybe the nine hours locked in a car with him wouldn't be so boring after all.

"We'll say we met...at church," he said.

Clarissa snorted. "When was the last time you went to church, Langston?"

"My mother thinks I go every week," he answered, evading the question.

Clarissa rolled her eyes. "I bet. Okay, so we met...at church. Do I sing in the choir?"

Langston's grip tightened on the steering wheel and he didn't answer. Clarissa grinned.

"Okay, so if we're friends, why aren't we involved?"

"What?"

"Well, we met at church so I must be a good girl, the kind of girl your mother would approve of, so she's going to want to know why we're not dating." Clarissa gasped. "I know! It's because you're secretly gay, right? And I'm your quirky-but-straight BFF and you've confided in me that you're having all these conflicting feelings—"

"I'm not gay! What the hell? Don't tell my mother I'm gay!"

Clarissa slumped in her seat, overtaken by a fit of giggles at Langston's obvious horror.

However, the sudden ring of Langston's cell phone made her amusement vanish.

Langston looked at the display, then glanced at Clarissa before answering.

"Langston."

Clarissa chewed a ragged nail as she listened. Whoever was on the other end of the line was very likely the person who either tried to have them killed or was out to arrest Langston.

"I'm sorry, sir. I can't say...no, sir...she's unharmed... it was an ambush...Xavier Mendes...I believe he's working with Solomon, sir...I'm sorry, sir, but I can't do that."

Langston winced, holding the phone slightly from his ear, and Clarissa heard the tinny sound of someone yelling on the other end. She tried to make out the words but couldn't. After a moment, Langston cut them off and his voice was like ice.

"Sir, with all due respect, someone ambushed me and would have killed me last night. Whether or not you choose to believe it, the FBI has a mole in their office, specifically as it relates to this case. Until such a time as you discover and apprehend that person, I'll keep the witness safe. I'll be in touch."

Langston ended the call, turned the phone off, and tossed it onto the dash.

Clarissa eyed him. The sunglasses hid his eyes, but the set of his jaw and the tightness of his body betrayed his anger. She didn't particularly want to antagonize him further, but thought it would be prudent to know what was going on, especially as it greatly concerned her immediate future.

"So I guess you won't be getting that pay raise," she joked halfheartedly, hoping to break the tension.

Erik glanced at O'Connell. She looked vaguely nervous.

"Clarke wasn't particularly on board with my change of plan," he said, which was putting it mildly. The man seemed more concerned that O'Connell was not yet on her way to DC than the fact that one of his agents had been ambushed...twice.

His explanation didn't seem to satisfy her; the nail she chewed grew even more ragged than before.

"What's the matter?" he asked.

She shook her head. "I...just...why are you doing this?"

Erik was startled. "Doing what?"

"This." She gestured between them with her hand. "You're going to ruin your career by helping me. Or get killed."

"Possibly."

"So why, then? I can't figure out why you're not just dumping me on the side of the road, or hauling me in so you can clear your name. I'm nobody to you except a thief." The confusion on her face would have been cute if her questions weren't so serious.

Why *was* he helping her?

"Because," he said finally. "It's the right thing to do."

"The right thing to do?" She sounded incredulous. "Erik Langston, FBI agent and former Boy Scout, thinks aiding and abetting a wanted thief is the right thing to do?"

"Until you recover your memory, you're useless to the FBI," he said, trying to justify his logic. "Once you can remember what you took from Solomon, you'll be able to help us nail him." All of which was true. She didn't have to know about the compulsion he now felt to protect her, and he certainly didn't need to acknowledge it.

"So you'll help me so long as there's a possibility I'll turn out to be useful," O'Connell said, and now Erik detected a slight bitterness in her voice, but he wasn't going to lie to her.

"Yes."

"And what if I don't recover my memory and my usefulness ceases to be an option?"

Erik didn't know how to answer that, so he didn't.

"Thought so," she said grimly, and fell silent.

It was silent for a long time.

~

It was after dark when they pulled into a little subdivision on the outskirts of San Antonio. Clarissa was roused from her drowsy lethargy by the slowing of the SUV's speed, and she sat up in her seat, rubbing her eyes.

"Are we there?" she asked, her voice husky with sleep.

"Nearly."

Langston had driven all day, despite Clarissa's offers to take a shift. How he'd kept going, she had no idea. Even now, he didn't seem tired. The man was a machine, she thought ruefully.

A few moments later and they were parking in the driveway of a brick two-story home on the corner of the cul-de-sac. A large tree obscured the front of the house, but it looked like a nice place to Clarissa. A place she could see Langston growing up in.

She got out of the car while Langston grabbed the duffel bags and rifles; his pistol remained in his holster. Clarissa wondered if his mother would be surprised to see her son on her doorstep toting numerous weapons and a strange girl.

Following him to the front door, she waited while he rang the doorbell. After a moment, the porch light flipped on and the door was flung open.

"Erik!" a woman exclaimed, throwing her arms around him.

"Hey, Mom," he said, awkwardly trying to hug her back. "Surprise."

"It is a surprise! I thought you weren't coming home for the holidays? That you had to work? What happened to your face?" She retreated while she talked, and Clarissa followed Langston inside the house.

"Goes with the job sometimes, Mom," Langston said.

The woman gave a disgusted *harrumph*, then her eyes widened when she saw Clarissa. "Erik! You've brought a girlfriend home. How wonderful!"

Clarissa could get a good look at her now, and she immediately liked her. Langston's mom was about her height and appeared younger than Clarissa would have thought, maybe early fifties. Slim with dark-silver hair pulled back in a clip at the nape of her neck, her eyes were warm and friendly. Her face was wreathed in a welcoming smile as she surveyed Clarissa.

"And what's your name, dear?" she asked.

"Mom, this is Clarissa," Langston said, unloading the bags in the foyer. "Clarissa, this is my mom, Vivian."

Clarissa held out her hand, but Vivian waved away her hand and pulled her into a hug instead.

"I'm so pleased to meet you, Clarissa," Vivian said.

Clarissa was stiff with surprise and had no chance to respond before Vivian released her.

"Um, yeah, same here," Clarissa managed with a wan smile.

"Mom, Clarissa's just a friend of mine," Langston interjected, eyeing where Vivian had her arm around Clarissa's waist.

"Don't try to pull that one over on me," Vivian said with a laugh. "I've been waiting years for you to bring home a young lady. Now come in. I'm guessing you two are probably hungry."

With that, Clarissa was ushered into the kitchen and sat at a table in a breakfast nook while Vivian began pulling dishes out of the refrigerator.

Vivian kept up a steady monologue as she worked, talking to Langston as he came and sat next to Clarissa at the table. "And you know the Wilsons, just down the street? Their oldest boy, Jason, remember him? Well he just got married not two weeks ago. Isn't that nice? I went to the wedding. Beautiful ceremony, and such a sweet girl. Now Mrs. Carmichael from church—she used to babysit you when you were little—she's been diagnosed with lung cancer, isn't that awful? And never smoked a day in her life. Where's the fairness in that, I ask you? Oh, and rumor is that Betty and Lewis Foster are getting a divorce. Supposedly he's been having an affair with some paralegal in his office. Personally, I hope she takes him for everything he's got, the cheating ass…" And on it went.

Occasionally, Langston would say something, but for the most part, his mother talked, filling him in on the latest gossip and news while she heated up food. Finally, she set two steaming plates in front of them. The smell of ham filled the air and Clarissa's stomach growled appreciatively. She dug in as Vivian took a seat opposite them.

"So tell me," Vivian said. "Where did you two meet? How long have you been together? Will you be staying long?"

The rapid-fire questions made Clarissa glad her mouth was filled with food. Langston would have to step up.

"We're not together, Mom," he said. "Clarissa just needed a ride to DC and I was in the neighborhood…working. Thought I'd swing by here while we're on our way, stay a couple of days."

"Oh." Vivian looked crestfallen as she looked from Langston to Clarissa, the one word containing a world of disappointment. Clarissa actually felt kind of bad. Then Vivian's eyes took on a slightly crafty look. "That sure is an awfully long way to drive someone who's just a friend, Erik," she said.

Langston shifted uncomfortably. "Yeah, well, Clarissa is…afraid of flying. And I'm just a nice guy, what can I say?" He smiled tightly.

Vivian just smiled back before turning her attention to Clarissa. "And what do you do for a living?" she asked. "Are you an FBI agent, too?"

Langston choked on his food and Clarissa shot him a dirty look.

"I'm in acquisitions," she directed toward him, slapping his back with perhaps slightly more force than necessary. "Freelance. Right, Erik?" Her smile was like saccharine.

Her use of his first name didn't go unnoticed it seemed, as his face darkened under her gaze.

"Well that sounds…interesting," Vivian said, her brow furrowing.

"So what have you been doing, Mom?" Langston quickly changed the subject and Clarissa smothered a grin.

"Well, Lee Anne and I are planning to go on that cruise, you know."

"That's right. When do you leave?"

"The end of the week."

"Where is it going again?"

Vivian talked about her upcoming cruise to the Bahamas while Langston and Clarissa ate. She'd never been on a cruise before and was really looking forward to going, especially with Lee Anne, who was such fun and had been on several cruises before…

A full stomach and the long day had Clarissa covering yawns before too long, and her eyes were heavy.

"Goodness, I've been prattling on and it's obvious you're both exhausted. Driving will do that to you. Let's get you settled."

To her surprise, Langston took Clarissa's hand as they followed Vivian up the stairs to the second floor. Was it an unconscious gesture? Or was he just being considerate in front of his mother? Either way, the warm feeling it gave Clarissa in the pit of her stomach disturbed her. Her hand was swallowed by his; the warm calluses on his palm gently abraded her skin, making her much too aware of him.

"Here you go," Vivian said, stopping in front of a room.

Langston seemed to hesitate. "Clarissa can sleep in the guest room, Mom."

"Oh no she can't, sweetheart," Vivian said. "I've been using it for my craft projects. It's a complete mess and unsuitable for company. You'll have to stay in your room, I'm afraid." She smiled.

Langston stiffened. "I can sleep downstairs on the couch then. Clarissa can have my room."

"You'll do no such thing! I have plans in the morning, a couple friends who pop by for coffee and a chat, and don't want you sacked out there in my living room." Vivian opened a nearby closet and pulled out a stack of blankets, which she loaded into Langston's arms. "You'll just have to sleep on the floor."

Clarissa caught a twinkle of mischief in Vivian's eye as she turned away, and wondered if Langston's mom might be trying her hand at playing matchmaker.

"Good night, you two. Sleep well!" In seconds she had disappeared through another door at the end of the hall.

"Cheer up, Langston," Clarissa said conspiratorially as she pushed open the bedroom door. "At least I didn't tell her you were gay."

CHAPTER TEN

E rik took a deep breath. Patience. Control. He followed O'Connell inside his bedroom, flipping on the light switch before dropping the stack of linens on the floor.

O'Connell stood in the middle of the room, surveying her surroundings. Erik felt a flash of unease. His mom had pretty much left the room untouched since he'd left for college, and it still contained much of the memorabilia from his youth.

Baseball and swimming trophies were displayed prominently on the bookshelves in the corner, along with photos his mother refused to put away.

"Nice acid-washed jeans, Langston." O'Connell grinned as she held up a photo before replacing it on the shelf. "Looks like you were quite the competitor."

Erik shrugged. "Kept me out of trouble."

She glanced at him. "Somehow I doubt you were a wild child."

Erik was slightly insulted, which was ridiculous. And yet, "I had my moments."

Her eyebrows lifted. "Oh really? Do tell." She dropped down onto the double bed, scooting backward until she rested against the headboard. "Love the poster, by the way." She nodded toward the door.

Shit. He'd forgotten about his old Captain America poster on the back of the door. How she was able to make him feel like an awkward fifteen-year-old with a girl in his bedroom for the first time was beyond him, but that's exactly how he felt.

"So you were going to tell me about all the hell you raised when you were a teenager?" Her teasing smirk was both infuriating and a turn-on. Dammit.

"I got a speeding ticket once," he blurted, wracking his brain. Despite his bravado, he actually had been rather well known for his straitlaced ways.

"Ooooh," she breathed, her eyes wide in mock astonishment. "What a rebel. What else?"

The sight of her in his bed, albeit his younger self's, was the stuff boyhood fantasies were made of, and he couldn't look away. He would have given a limb to have had a girl like her all to himself when he was a teenager. Gorgeous, sexy, with an edge to her that whispered of danger and excitement. She was everything he shouldn't want, and that just made her irresistible.

"We'd better get some sleep," he said sharply, haphazardly spreading a blanket on the floor. "You can use this bathroom. I'll use the one in the hall." Erik was out the door before she could reply.

It wasn't until he was toweling dry from another cold shower that he realized he had been in such a hurry to finally put some space between himself and O'Connell, he'd forgotten to grab some fresh clothes.

He wrapped a towel around his waist and hoped O'Connell was asleep by now as he entered the bedroom. As luck would have it, he could hear the water running in the bath attached to his room. She must still be in the shower.

Moving quickly, he dropped the towel and rummaged through a nearby drawer. He always kept a few things here so he didn't have to cart a suitcase when he came to visit.

"Wow."

Erik spun around to see O'Connell staring open-mouthed at him, the bathroom door ajar behind her. It looked like she'd helped herself again to his wardrobe, this time wearing an old Guns N' Roses T-shirt, and that was all. Her penchant for going without pants was starting to wear thin.

"I thought you were in the shower," he accused. His immediate instinct was to cover himself, but he squelched it. It seemed...unmanly somehow.

O'Connell didn't answer, just stood there staring. Her gaze drifted across his chest before slowly dropping lower. Her mouth formed a little *O*.

"My eyes are up here, O'Connell." Erik's voice was harsh, but her unabashed admiration made him stand just a tiny bit straighter, not to mention the effect it was having on other parts of his anatomy. "O'Connell!" he barked when she didn't reply.

"Hmmm?" She seemed wholly unconcerned with his irritation, and if he wasn't mistaken, she'd inched closer.

Erik's imagination kicked into overdrive of what he could do next, none of which he thought O'Connell would mind at all based on how she was devouring him with her eyes.

But it would be wrong and put him in an untenable position, given her status as his prisoner and a wanted fugitive.

Erik started toward O'Connell. Her gaze flew to his. He didn't stop until he stood directly in front of her.

She stared at him, her green eyes wide and unblinking. Her breath came faster, and Erik could see the rapid beat of her pulse through the delicate skin under her jaw. Her tongue darted out to wet her lips, and Erik's gaze fell to her mouth.

"Clarissa," he said, dropping his voice to a low growl.

"Yes?" she murmured.

"Turn around."

"Turn…what?"

Erik took hold of her upper arms and turned her to face away from him.

"I'd like a little privacy, if you don't mind," he said. Yanking open a nearby drawer, he grabbed a pair of flannel pants and pulled them on.

"You know, Langston, you're a real tease."

Erik hid a smile at the irritation in her tone. She'd crossed her arms over her chest and looked every inch the petulant child thwarted from getting her way as she stood with her back to him.

"You can turn around now," he said.

"Oh, go to hell," she muttered, ignoring him entirely as she spun around, flounced to the bed, and got under the covers. She was still muttering to herself as she arranged the covers over her with quick, angry jerks, but Erik couldn't hear what she was saying. He caught the word *ass* but thought she was probably using it as an adjective and not a noun.

Erik took the other pillow from the bed and arranged a place on the floor, turning off the light before settling down. The blankets did little to ease the discomfort of lying on the hard floor. Erik bent his arm behind his head and stared at the ceiling, uncomfortably aware of O'Connell only feet away in his bed.

"You don't have to sleep on the floor, Langston," she said. "You didn't make me sleep on the floor, so allow me to extend you the same courtesy."

Erik squeezed his eyes shut. Shit. Talk about waving a red flag in front of a bull.

"It's all right. I'm good," he said stiffly. Erik may have been able to sleep beside O'Connell in a bed four days ago and keep his hands to himself, but he didn't trust that he could maintain that same control now.

"Jesus, Langston! You'd rather sleep on the damn floor than be in the same bed with me?"

Erik winced. If he didn't know better, he'd swear she sounded hurt underneath the irritation.

"Go to sleep, O'Connell."

Something soft smacked him in the face.

"What the—" he spluttered, grabbing the offending pillow she'd thrown at him.

"Be glad I didn't have something heavier nearby," she retorted.

He was, actually.

"Now give it back to me," she said.

"Forget it," Erik said, tucking the second pillow underneath his head. That was slightly better. "You shouldn't have thrown it. You should really learn to watch that temper of yours. Could get you into all sorts of trouble."

"Langston! Give me back my pillow!"

"No."

She started cussing a blue streak at him. Langston smirked, waiting. When she stopped, he said, "Try to watch the mouth in front of my mother, will ya?"

He heard her flop back onto the bed, and he was quite sure that if she'd had something else close at hand, it would have been launched at his head.

≈

Something woke Erik. His eyes popped open and his senses were on immediate alert. He stayed still, listening. It was still dark, not yet morning.

A whimper, mumbled words from the bed.

Crying.

Erik was on his feet and by O'Connell in seconds. The streetlight outside sent dim rays slanting across her face, and he could see she was again in the throes of a nightmare. Her cheeks were wet with tears, her eyes tightly closed. She was curled into a tight ball, as though protecting herself.

He was loath to wake her, despite it being a nightmare. The more she dreamed, the better chance she had of getting back her memory.

"No…stop…don't touch me…"

The words were mumbled but coherent and sent a jolt of alarm through Erik. "Don't touch me." What the fuck was she dreaming about? Screw that shit about not waking her.

"Clarissa, wake up." He sat next to her, untangling the blankets that had gotten wrapped around her. "Clarissa," he said again, taking hold of her arm. That got a reaction.

She sat bolt upright, yanking her arm away, then started fighting like a hellcat.

"Clarissa! Stop!"

She was silent, still in the grip of the nightmare, and Erik tried not to hurt her as he grabbed her arms, pinning them to her sides. He hauled her writhing onto his lap, her back against his chest. It took both his arms wrapped around her to hold her still.

"It's me, Clarissa," he hissed in her ear. "It's Erik. I'm not going to hurt you."

The words finally seemed to penetrate, and she went still in his arms. Her chest heaved as she struggled to catch her breath. Her entire body was trembling.

Erik loosened his grip on her, but didn't release her. Her hair gently tickled his face and chin as he held her. After a moment, he said softly, "You want to talk about it?"

He didn't think she was going to answer, but finally she spoke.

"I was…in an apartment. I dinna know where. I think my brother lived there with me. He was gone…out on a job. Told me to stay put, he could handle it alone. I was worried. Danny always overestimated himself."

Erik stayed quiet, listening. Her voice had regained the lilting Irish brogue, but was strained, as though the words were being pulled from her throat.

"A man was there…a friend of Danny's. His name was Sam. I…I must have had a crush on him, I think. I was nervous, excited that he'd come by when Danny wasn't home. He told me I was a pretty li'l thing."

An awful feeling of foreboding swept over Erik. *Please, God, don't let this be going where I think it is.*

"He…kissed me. My first kiss. And he touched me. It was nice. Thrilling, even. I was stupid."

Erik's eyes squeezed shut as her voice turned cold. He forced them back open. "What happened, Clarissa?"

"He wanted me to take my clothes off. I dinna want to. I was scared. He grabbed me, tore my shirt. Hit me. I yelled at him, told him Danny would kill him. He said…he said…"

"What did he say?"

"He said he knew where Danny was, what he was doing. That he'd call the cops on him if I dinna let him…" Her voice trailed away.

Rage coursed through Erik like he had never felt before. It took everything he had to control it. O'Connell didn't need his anger right now.

"So I did."

O'Connell's voice was toneless, her admission matter-of-fact, yet her body still shook in his arms. Erik wondered if she'd ever told anyone what she'd just told him.

"What happened then?" he asked, hoping Danny had killed the man slowly.

"You woke me."

Shit. So he'd let her go through all of that again in her nightmares and she still didn't have her memory.

Erik shifted her around sideways and tucked her head against his chest. She curled into him without protest, her trembling subsiding somewhat. She felt small and fragile in his arms, nothing at all like the same woman who had ruthlessly done what was necessary to free him last night. Erik had never known a woman with such strength and courage, who could still allow herself to be vulnerable with him.

Erik's conscience was silent for once. At the moment, he couldn't give a shit about keeping an "emotional distance" or that she was his prisoner. O'Connell was alone and hurting, yet had trusted him enough to tell him the horror of what had happened to her. And now, even after how Erik had treated her, she was allowing him to comfort her.

He was one lucky bastard.

And after all this was over, he was going to track down Sam and rip him limb from limb. Starting with his dick.

Erik shifted, pulling the covers back and settling her on the bed. Reaching down, he grabbed a pillow from the floor and tucked it behind her head.

"Erik?"

"Yeah?"

"Don't leave yet." Her voice was a whisper in the dark, and Erik knew it must have cost her something to make that request. The lingering effects of the nightmare were no doubt worse than she was letting on.

"Wasn't planning on it," he said. He grabbed the other pillow and arranged himself next to her before pulling the covers up over them. He didn't ask permission and she didn't protest when he snagged her around the waist and tucked her spoon-style against him.

His arm settled in the curve of her waist, and Erik felt her body relax as she released a deep sigh. Her hand found his and she threaded their fingers together.

Erik's chest suddenly felt too tight and the air too thick in his lungs. Whatever he had been repeating inside his head all day about keeping his distance from O'Connell, he couldn't lie to himself any longer. He wanted to keep her, protect her, make love to her. He wondered how far he'd go to do all three, and just how much it would cost him.

Clarissa woke feeling more rested than she had in days. It took a moment to remember where she was, but the feel of Langston's body pressed against her back, his arm curved around her waist to settle between her breasts, quickly brought back memories of last night.

A chill went through her as she recalled the too-real nightmare. She didn't know what had happened to Sam, but if she got her memory back and she hadn't already killed him, she would. She shivered, the fear and helplessness she'd felt in the dream still too present in her mind.

"You all right?" Langston's voice was a husky baritone in her ear. His arm tightened protectively around her.

Clarissa smiled, amazed at how attuned to her he was, even while asleep. Hadn't he just told her yesterday that he needed to keep a distance? And yet he'd thrown that all aside when she'd needed him last night.

"I am now," she said, squirming until she faced him.

His hair was tousled from sleep, his jaw shadowed with whiskers. Clarissa abruptly decided Langston had the definition of "bedroom eyes." He looked at her as though he had nothing but sex on his mind.

Butterflies fluttered in her stomach, but she did nothing. After all he'd said yesterday, she wasn't about to put herself in the position of being rejected again.

"Thanks," she said, trying to break the sudden tension between them. "For last night. I really—"

But his mouth was on hers, and she couldn't finish her sentence, even if she'd remembered what she was going to say.

Clarissa eagerly opened her lips, her blood heating in her veins as Langston deepened their kiss, his tongue sliding against hers. She had a brief thought that she wished she'd taken a moment to brush her teeth, then dismissed it. Who the hell cared when he was kissing her as though he couldn't get enough?

His body lay half on top of her, his leg insinuated between her thighs. The thin pants he wore did nothing to hide his arousal, and Clarissa couldn't hold back a moan.

Langston dragged the T-shirt she wore up and over her head, tossing it aside. His hands pressed against her spine, encouraging her to arch her back. She did so eagerly, her eyes slamming shut as his mouth settled over her breast.

Clarissa gasped, her fingers digging into Langston's shoulders, the muscles hard underneath her hands. Her blood thundered in her ears as his whiskers abraded her tender skin, his lips and tongue a searing heat against her flesh. Desire burned in her veins. God, she wanted him.

Hooking her leg around his waist, she dragged at his pants, working them down. He helped, lifting his hips, and she triumphantly pushed the fabric down his legs. He was bare now, and she mewled in pleasure at the feel of the incredible ass she'd glimpsed last night. She couldn't remember if she'd ever seen a better one, but somehow she doubted it.

"Oh, Erik," she breathed.

Langston's mouth left her breasts, burning a trail up her neck to kiss his name from her lips.

"Say my name again," he whispered, pressing his mouth to her cheek, her jaw, her brow.

"Erik. ErikErikErik." His name was a mantra she was only too happy to repeat, just so long as he didn't stop what he was doing.

He shifted, settling himself fully between her thighs. His sizeable erection pushed against her flesh, sending Clarissa's arousal to a fever pitch. The feel of his naked body against hers was more intoxicating than she would have believed. The only barrier between them now was the scrap of silk she wore, and even as she thought that, his hand was pulling at the fragile fabric.

There was a sharp rap on the door. "Erik, breakfast is ready if you and Clarissa want to come down."

Langston was up and off her so fast it would have been funny if it didn't make her want to scream in frustration. But she was treated to the view of a fully aroused Erik Langston—before he hurriedly pulled his pants back on.

"Um, yeah, we'll be right down," Langston called out. Somehow, his voice was steady.

Clarissa heard footsteps moving down the hall. For trying to be a matchmaker, Vivian had shitty timing.

"Shit, Clarissa, I'm sorry." Langston shoved a hand through his hair.

Clarissa frowned. "Why are you apologizing exactly?" Tossing away the covers, she turned on her side to face him. She bent her elbow and rested her head on her hand. The pose accentuated the dip of her waist and displayed her breasts to full advantage.

Erik swallowed. Hard. He could not believe he'd nearly made love to O'Connell while in the same house as his mother. And after what she'd told him last night, too. What if she thought he was taking advantage of her? She'd been open and vulnerable to him last night; was this how he repaid her? By groping her the first chance he got?

"I didn't mean to take advantage of you," he said, trying to keep his eyes above her neck.

"Take advantage of me? Was I saying no?"

"Clarissa, you've lost your memory, we're running for our lives, you're having harrowing nightmares about the life you led—it's natural to feel lost and alone."

She sat up abruptly. "What are you saying? That you felt sorry for me? That's all that was?"

Erik couldn't take it anymore and started searching the floor for the shirt he'd taken off her. He couldn't think straight with a raging hard-on and O'Connell nearly naked.

"No," he said, finally finding the shirt and snatching it up. "It's just...wrong of me to take advantage."

She'd stood now, and Erik handed her the shirt.

"You know, Langston," she began, "it always amazes me how men never stop to think that maybe they're the ones being used for sex. And that's all it is. Just sex. It doesn't mean a damn thing."

Erik winced inwardly at the ice in her voice but didn't look away from her gaze. After a pregnant pause, she turned away and disappeared into the bathroom, the door slamming closed behind her.

If anything, Erik was now even more grateful for his mother's timely interruption. What O'Connell had told him last night, what she'd unknowingly revealed just now, was how little her feelings were involved with sex. Erik wondered if O'Connell had ever had a real lover, someone who wanted to give and not take, someone she could trust to open up to and bare her soul.

Her first experience with sex had been to be raped, he harshly reminded himself. A sacrifice to save her brother, who was no more worthy of that kind of act than anyone else.

Regardless of the heat between them, Erik didn't want to be in the same category as any other man who'd been with O'Connell. How to go about that…well, it would just have to wait until this was all over. His first priority was to keep her safe, the second to find a way to trigger her memory.

With that thought in mind, he dressed and went downstairs. A short while later, Clarissa came down to find him and Vivian sitting at the kitchen table.

"Good morning!" Vivian said cheerily. "You must be starving. Sit down and eat."

Clarissa gave Vivian a wan smile as she sat down, making sure to put a seat between herself and Langston. She avoided his gaze. "Thank you."

Vivian chatted with Langston while Clarissa ate. She watched him drink his coffee while he talked with his mom. He'd put on a pair of jeans and a navy button-down shirt. It was obvious that he and Vivian got along really well, and Clarissa remembered how he'd told her what they'd gone through when his dad had left them.

"So Clarissa," Vivian said. "I noticed you have a slight accent. Where are you from?"

"Ireland originally," Clarissa answered, remembering what she'd read from Langston's file on her.

"And your family?"

Clarissa really didn't want to tell her that her dad and brother were in prison. She liked Vivian and doubted she'd want her son associating with someone whose family reunions had to be held under maximum security. "My mother died when I was young," she said, evading the question slightly. "I don't really remember her." That was certainly true.

"I'm so sorry to hear that," Vivian said sympathetically.

Clarissa thought she would have said more, asked another question, but Langston cut in.

"We have some work to do, Mom, so we'll just be in the living room."

"Oh. Okay, well don't let me keep you then."

Vivian started clearing the dishes, despite Clarissa's protests that she'd help. Anything, really, to delay having to be alone with Langston.

"Don't be silly," Vivian said, taking the plate from Clarissa. "You're a guest."

Clarissa reluctantly followed Langston to the living room, sorry for the loss of Vivian as a buffer. Langston had already set up her laptop on the coffee table in front of the couch.

"Internet's not a problem here," he explained. "Let's see if you have any e-mail."

Clarissa didn't say anything as she sat down. So it was all business now? Fine with her. It's not like she wanted to discuss what had happened.

She didn't know what to make of Langston. It was obvious he was attracted to her, wanted her, but refused to give in to the impulse to have sex with her. She could only assume his sense of duty, him saying it would be wrong, precluded sex. At least, with her. Maybe if she really had been the good girl he'd met at church...

But there was no point in following that line of thought. It was what it was. Langston was a white hat, an FBI agent who fought on the side of the law. Clarissa was a black hat, a criminal and thief who'd apparently done enough bad things to have dangerous people expending considerable resources to find her. The two of them together was a recipe for disaster.

The silence between them was fraught with tension. Clarissa was hyperaware of Langston sitting next to her, watching as she entered her password and pulled up her e-mail.

It didn't take long before two messages came in. Both were from the same e-mail address, dated two days ago, and very short.

Transfer complete.

The second was just as cryptic.

31°33'34.01"N 91°24'40.78"W

"Those are coordinates," Langston said.

"To where?" Clarissa asked, but Langston was already typing the coordinates into his phone.

"Natchez, Mississippi," he said.

Clarissa noticed a flashing icon in the lower right-hand corner of the screen. She clicked on it, realizing it was a message from someone named Killall.

"Instant messaging," Langston said, scooting closer. Clarissa could smell the spicy scent of his aftershave.

Bout time u came online. Where u been?

Clarissa stared at the prompt, her fingers poised over the keys.

"Type something back," Langston urged.

She shot him a look. "I will. Give me a second."

Looking back at the screen, she typed.

Ran into problems.

"Your handle is Calamity?" Langston said with a snort. Clarissa ignored him.

The response came back quickly.

Everything's uploaded and now offline. When r u coming for pickup?

Clarissa glanced at Langston, who was sitting much too close so he could see the screen. "You think this is the one who e-mailed the coordinates?"

Langston hesitated. "Maybe. Ask him if the coordinates are still good."

Clarissa typed, *Any change in coords?*

No. Time?

"We can get there by tonight if we leave soon," Langston said, looking at his watch.

Tonight. 9 pm. Clarissa typed.

Got it, came the response, then, *Wtf, Calamity?! No IP mask?!! R u insane?!!! The feds are always watching!*

His icon went dark.

"What's he talking about? Where'd he go?" Clarissa asked in surprise.

"Shit!" Langston exclaimed, slamming down the lid on the laptop. "He's right. I didn't even think about it."

"Think about what?" Clarissa was utterly confused, but Langston's reaction was making her extremely nervous, as were Killall's last words.

"If he traced our IP address, then so can the FBI. We have to go," Langston said. "The sooner, the better. Pack up the laptop."

He disappeared into the kitchen. Clarissa could hear him talking to Vivian as she put the laptop back in the duffel. When he returned, Vivian was following him.

"Erik, I'm not just going to pack up and leave for my cruise two days early, especially if you're not going to tell me why."

"Mom, it's better if I don't tell you. Just trust me."

Vivian crossed her arms over her chest, her face taking on the same stubborn expression Clarissa had seen Langston sport more than once.

Langston sighed and pushed a hand roughly through his hair. "Fine. Mom, Clarissa's not a friend. She's a prisoner. Wanted by the FBI."

Ouch. Well, he'd certainly not sugarcoated that. Clarissa felt embarrassed, which was irritating. She stiffened her spine as she met Vivian's gaze. She was who she was, and that was that.

But it had been nice to have Vivian think highly of her, even if it had been temporary.

"But…there have been problems. It's not cut-and-dried. I'm trying to help her," Langston continued. "I just need more time to sort things out."

"What sort of problems?" Vivian asked.

Langston hesitated. "Clarissa has amnesia."

Vivian's eyebrows climbed. "I take it this means you weren't just in the neighborhood and this wasn't just a friendly visit? You're actually on the run with her?"

Langston winced. "Kinda."

"For goodness' sake! Why didn't you just tell me last night?"

"I didn't want to worry you."

Vivian rolled her eyes. "I swear, Erik, you treat me like I'm some fragile flower, which is sweet but can get downright irritating. So are you going to go to jail for this?"

Langston hesitated. "Dangerous people are after Clarissa, including people inside the FBI. If they find her, they'll kill her. So, whether or not I end up in jail isn't really figuring into the equation right now."

Vivian cast a shrewd glance at Clarissa, who squirmed uncomfortably.

"I didn't ask him to help me," she said. "I've tried to get him to let me go numerous times. But he won't."

"So will you leave?" Langston asked Vivian, ignoring Clarissa. "We need to leave too, but I need to know you're out of harm's way."

Vivian nodded. "An extra day or two in Florida certainly won't hurt me. I'm nearly packed anyway."

Langston's shoulders slumped in relief. "Good. I'm going to get some things we need, then we'll get out of here. You too, Mom." With that he headed up the stairs, taking them two at a time.

Clarissa was left with Vivian, who gazed silently at her.

"Is it true?" she asked Clarissa, her voice hard. "Do you have amnesia? Or are you tricking my son?"

Clarissa didn't flinch from Vivian's gaze. "I swear to you, it's not a trick. The first thing I remember is…him."

Vivian's features softened slightly. "Erik never was one to ignore someone who needed his help. But this isn't just about the job. I know my son, and he wouldn't put his career or his life in jeopardy for just anyone."

"I'm really sorry," Clarissa said, and she was. Even if Langston made it out alive, his career was destroyed, all on account of her.

"I just hope you don't break his heart."

That bombshell was still hanging in the air when Langston reentered the kitchen. Clarissa was saved from having to come up with a reply, not that she had any idea of what to say. Vivian seemed to be under the impression that Langston had feelings for her. Clarissa could have disabused her of that notion pretty quick. He didn't even like her enough to sleep with her.

"Mom, please," he said. "Time is short."

"All right, all right, I'm going." Vivian went upstairs and returned within moments, carrying a suitcase. Langston put it in the trunk of her car while she gathered a few more of her things. "Be safe," she said, giving Langston a tight hug.

"I will."

Vivian approached Clarissa and hugged her as well. Clarissa awkwardly hugged her back.

"Remember what I said," she whispered to Clarissa.

While they watched Vivian drive away, Langston asked, "What did she say to you?"

"It doesn't matter," Clarissa replied stiffly, turning to head back inside. Langston followed her.

"Should I pack some food or something?" Clarissa asked.

"Shh." Langston waved her silent. "Look."

He pointed behind her, and Clarissa turned to see a little television nestled into a corner on the counter. The news was on, and Clarissa recognized the little shack they'd been in last night in Colorado. Langston grabbed a remote and turned up the volume.

"…four men dead, including two FBI agents and two locals," the voice-over was saying. The screen flashed and pictures showed two smiling men.

"Those are the men I left to watch Mendes," Langston said.

"Looks like that didn't work out so well."

"This man is wanted for questioning regarding the murders," the anchor continued, and the photo changed. "Special Agent Erik Langston of the FBI."

EPISODE SIX

CHAPTER ELEVEN

The silence was thick with tension as Langston drove. Clarissa thought maybe she should say something, but wasn't sure what it should be. Langston hadn't said much at all since they'd seen the news anchor declaring him a man wanted for murder. Considering how hard he'd worked at his job, the idea that he was now on the wrong side of the law had to be killing him.

And it was her fault.

Clarissa didn't like the nagging guilt that thought produced, and she squirmed uncomfortably in her seat. It wasn't her problem that Langston was determined to stick with her. She'd told him several times now to just let her go, that she'd figure things out on her own. It wasn't her fault he had an overactive sense of responsibility toward her. With any other man, she'd say it was just a ploy to sleep with her, but Langston's continued rebuffs negated that as a possible motive.

Best to just go ahead and address the elephant in the car, she decided. "So," she said with fake cheeriness, "how does it feel to be a wanted man?"

Langston glanced her way. His expression was unsmiling and his eyes were unreadable behind the mirrored sunglasses.

"Just trying to lighten things up a little," she muttered.

His only response was to turn his attention back to the road.

"Listen, I'm really sorry about all this," Clarissa said. "But I'm sure you'll be able to clear your name once you explain what happened."

Langston sighed. "It's not your fault. Mendes must have escaped, killed those men guarding him, and removed the bodies of his buddies. Though how he escaped, I don't know. Unless he had help."

"Help from who?"

"Kaminski," Langston answered. "I'm almost positive he's the mole."

Clarissa frowned, thinking. "So you and Kaminski don't get along, right?"

"Right."

"Well, who was your partner before? Did you get along with him? Maybe he could help you." Clarissa thought that an excellent idea.

"He can't," Langston said curtly.

"Why not?"

"He's dead."

Well, that was unexpected. Langston's voice was flat, but Clarissa knew him well enough by now to realize he was deliberately being that way, hiding his emotions.

"I'm sorry," she said, reaching out to lay her hand on his arm. He glanced her way. "How did it happen?"

"It was a robbery," Langston finally answered. "A luxury jewelry store in New York. Two men walked in, pulled guns, demanded the gems. They were in and out in under two minutes. Unluckily for them, my partner and I happened to be nearby when the call came in. We saw them escaping in their getaway car and went after them. They crashed into another car, immobilizing one of the robbers. The other took off on foot.

"I stayed with the one who was injured, waited until the cops got there, which wasn't very long," Langston continued. "Then I went after my partner. I got there just in time to see him gunned down."

Clarissa didn't know what to say. Langston stared at the highway, the muscles in his arm stiff under her hand. Without a word, she slid her hand down to his, threading their fingers together. Langston didn't acknowledge the gesture, though his grip tightened on hers.

"Did the guy get away?" she asked.

Langston shook his head. "I was able to take him down."

There was silence for a minute. Then he said, "Peter was married. Had a kid. A little boy. I'm his godfather."

Somehow Clarissa wasn't surprised that the boy's parents had chosen Langston to be their child's godfather. When it came to role models, she doubted there was a finer one than him.

"The last thing he said was to watch over his son," Langston said. "So I try and do what I can, which isn't much since they moved away. She was from Ohio, so she moved back there not too long after he died."

"How long was he your partner?"

"Four years. He died in my arms."

The story was horrifying and heartbreaking and Clarissa thought she could understand more now of Langston's deep antipathy for criminals. It was personal. No crime was without a victim, even if some of them were unintended. She thought of the security guard that had been killed in her dream, the one her father had gone to prison for, and wondered if he'd had a family. No doubt there had been people who'd depended on him, loved him.

And what about herself? What all had she done that she didn't even know about, but had affected other people? Innocent people.

Dread formed a hard knot in Clarissa's stomach. Suddenly, she wasn't sure if she wanted her memory back or not.

～

Erik stopped at a tiny gas station in the middle of Nowhere, Louisiana to fill up. He handed O'Connell some money.

"What's this for?" she asked.

"I need a hat," he said. "They'll have some inside. A baseball cap will do."

She went inside and Erik gassed up the SUV. Erik would have gone in himself, but there might be cameras. He'd chosen this gas station because it looked like it probably hadn't seen a technology upgrade in about fifteen years, but it paid to be careful.

O'Connell had just returned when he climbed back into the driver's seat.

"Here you go," she said, handing him a cap.

Erik took it, then did a double take. On the front, above the bill, were giant letters:

Got Wood?

He looked at O'Connell, who snorted in amusement.

"Couldn't resist," she said with a grin. "It was on clearance." She reached behind her back and tugged out another cap she'd been hiding, then handed it to him. "Relax. I got you a Saints cap."

Her teasing lightened Erik's mood. That seemed to happen a lot. O'Connell wasn't put off by his temper or morose silence. After reliving what had happened to Peter, he'd felt pretty damn bleak. But she'd made him smile with the ridiculous hat.

"I'm starving," she said. "Is food on the agenda any time soon?"

Erik found another diner that had seen better days on the outskirts of Baton Rouge. O'Connell's eyebrows climbed, but she didn't say anything as they slid into a booth with faded, torn vinyl held together by duct tape. When this was over, Erik decided he'd take her somewhere nice, someplace where you didn't order by a number on the menu.

The waitress came by for their orders and Erik took a sip of the steaming black liquid that was their version of coffee. Strong and bitter, it was a far cry from the gourmet blends he usually drank.

"So tell me, Langston," O'Connell said, adding a splash of milk to her mug. "There's no Mrs. Langston, but do you have a girlfriend? Ex-girlfriend? Friend with benefits?"

Erik choked on his coffee. "Friend with benefits?" he echoed.

O'Connell shrugged as she took a delicate sip of her coffee. "Your mom seemed to think you were unattached, but that doesn't mean you don't have an...arrangement with a friend."

"No, I don't have a friend with benefits," Erik said. "And no, there's no girlfriend. My last ex was three years ago."

"Why'd you break up?"

Erik's eyes narrowed. "What is this? Dr. Phil?"

"Just making conversation, Langston. Don't get your knickers in a twist."

Erik surveyed her. "Fine," he said. "We broke up because she didn't like how much time I spent working rather than being with her, and I didn't like her enough to bother changing. We were together four months before we broke it off."

"So how much time *do* you spend working?"

"A lot."

O'Connell looked thoughtful, and Erik braced himself for whatever overly personal question she'd come up with next.

"So what do you do for sex? Just one-night stands? Or do you play a lot of five-on-one?" Her green eyes twinkled at the joke.

"Christ," Erik huffed. He could feel his ears heating. It had been years since a woman had made him blush. "Is nothing off-limits for you?"

"Just wondering," she said nonchalantly. "You're good-looking, great body, have a steady job. You're not into relationships, but I'm guessing you don't have a hard time getting company for just an evening."

"I'm not a man-whore, if that's what you're insinuating," Erik said stiffly, though he couldn't help the warm satisfaction he felt at hearing her describe him. "So you think I'm good-looking and have a great body?" he asked, his lips twitching into a half smile.

O'Connell looked him right in the eye. "Give me an hour and a can of whipped cream and I'll erase all doubts."

Holy shit. Erik hastily took another gulp of coffee, his mind building that image much too quickly. O'Connell's mischievous grin made him want to drag her to the back of the SUV and finish what he'd started this morning.

He was saved from having to reply by the waitress delivering their food to the table, and he concentrated on eating. Anything to get his imagination to stop replaying the memory of O'Connell's body underneath him, willing and ready. At the moment, Erik was having a hard time remembering exactly why he'd stopped.

"Tell me, Langston," O'Connell said after a while. "Do you know…I mean…you have my file and all…"

Erik wondered what she was trying to ask. She was pushing her food around on her plate and didn't look up as she spoke.

"Do I know what?" he prompted.

"Those guys, back at the cabin, and the fake marshal. I killed them." She finally lifted her gaze to his. "It seemed awfully easy. Too easy. And I was wondering if you knew…if I'd killed anyone else."

Erik's fork stopped halfway to his mouth. He was surprised at her question. He took a moment to think before answering.

"To my knowledge, you've never been involved in a crime where someone innocent was killed, no."

"Then why was it so easy for me to kill those people?" O'Connell asked, her voice tight.

"Hey, don't overthink it," Erik admonished, reaching out to lay his hand on top of hers. "I'd guess you've had self-defense training, quite advanced training from what I've seen. If you're trained well, then it's supposed to be automatic, instinctual. It doesn't mean you're a killer."

After the harrowing memories she'd dreamed about last night, Erik thought O'Connell had most likely decided that no one would ever rape her again and had taken steps to ensure it. Given what he knew of her personality, he doubted she'd let something like that happen twice, not if she could help it.

"Then what did Mendes mean when he said I had no conscience?"

Erik's lips thinned. "Mendes is a paid assassin. I wouldn't take anything he had to say to heart."

O'Connell nodded, but Erik could tell she wasn't eased by his comment. "What's this about? Why do you care?" he asked. Why was she so concerned about her past?

O'Connell's gaze was steady. "Maybe I don't want to be a bad guy anymore," she said baldly.

Erik's breath caught, and he couldn't help the hope that burned inside him at her words. "Why is that?" he asked, striving to be casual. He was just curious, that was all. It wasn't that he was daring to hope her change of heart might have something to do with him.

"The job doesn't seem to have a real long life expectancy, for one," she said, ticking the items off on her fingers.

"True."

"Not to mention there's no health insurance. Or 401(k)"

Erik's lips twitched. "Also true."

"And I know not everyone is fond of those who make their living illegally." Her eyes met his and Erik couldn't hold back a tiny smile.

"That's not exactly true," he said. Her brows lifted in question. "You can...be fond...of the person, just not what they choose to do."

"What if I don't ever get my memory back, Langston?" she asked.

Erik's gut tightened at the note of fear in her voice. "Don't worry," he assured her. "Even if you don't, you're not alone."

The look of trust in her eyes made guilt hit him hard as he tried, and failed, to convince himself that he wanted her memory to return too.

$\approx$

It was just before nine p.m. when they rolled into Natchez. The coordinates Killall had given them were next to the river. Langston parked the SUV a couple of blocks away in a shadowy lot. Clarissa stood by the vehicle, taking in the quiet streets as she waited for Langston.

"I'll be with you, just out of sight," he said, emerging from where he'd been rummaging in the backseat. He shoved a newly loaded clip into his gun and racked the slide. "If he sees you with someone, it might scare him off."

"I got it," Clarissa said, rolling her eyes.

"Did you just roll your eyes at me?" Langston sounded affronted.

"Of course not," Clarissa lied. "I admire the way you state the obvious."

She'd hoped to make him smile, but his expression remained serious.

"Here, take this." He tucked the gun in the back of his jeans and shrugged out of his jacket, then held it for her to put on.

The gesture, chivalrous and protective, was unexpected. Clarissa pushed her arms into the sleeves. Langston lifted her hair from under the collar and Clarissa shivered when his fingers brushed the skin on the back of her neck. The jacket smelled of him, which was surprisingly comforting.

"Be careful," Langston said, pulling the lapels of the jacket closed.

Clarissa looked up at him. Their eyes caught, and for a moment she thought he might kiss her again. His eyes dropped to her mouth, but she flashed him a quick smile and stepped away.

"See you soon," she said, then turned and began heading toward the river. An empty park, dimly lit by lonely streetlamps, was her destination.

She felt nervous, exposed. The name *Killall* didn't exactly provoke thoughts of bunnies and rainbows. Clarissa reminded herself that Langston was nearby. He wouldn't let anything happen to her. Though she disliked the idea of her safety being in someone else's hands, she trusted him.

Burying her hands deeper in the pockets of Langston's jacket, she headed for the trees that lined the park. She could hear the sound of the river below the banks. It was peaceful, and if she hadn't been so keyed up, she might have enjoyed the walk.

There was a bench nearby, and Clarissa walked toward it. The cold of the metal soaked through her jeans when she sat down, and she huddled deeper inside Langston's jacket. She felt as though she were being watched, and didn't know if it was because of Langston or if Killall had arrived.

"Don't turn around."

The words came from behind Clarissa just as she felt something hard press against her back. A gun. She froze.

"I have it," the man said. "But tell your boss I want double what he paid me before I hand it over."

Nice. Another criminal out to screw her over. She really needed to find better friends.

"You expect me to pay you without knowing if you have the goods?" she asked without turning. "How do I even know you're really who you say you are?"

That seemed to stump him for a moment. "Who else would I be?" he said. "And I said I have it, so you just have to trust me that I have it. Call your boss."

"You're holding me at gunpoint," Clarissa said frostily. "Trusting you isn't gonna fly." Where was Langston?

"One move and it'll be your last."

It was Langston. Clarissa breathed a quiet sigh of relief.

"Hey, man, don't shoot!"

"Give me the gun," Langston said.

"It's not a real gun, I was faking," the guy blustered.

Clarissa stood up at that and turned around. Her assailant wasn't quite what she'd pictured.

Killall was short and stocky, about her height, and young, maybe only nineteen or twenty. He had a mop of unkempt curly brown hair, wore glasses, and sported a Batman T-shirt under a well-worn jacket.

"What do you mean you were faking?" she asked, irritated to have been even momentarily afraid of this clown.

"It's just a banana. Here, take it." He shoved his hand into his pocket.

"Freeze!" Langston barked.

Killall obeyed, his eyes glued to Langston's gun. He gulped.

"Now take your hand out, nice and slow," Langston ordered.

Sure enough, the idiot had an honest-to-God banana in his pocket.

Clarissa grabbed the front of his T-shirt and got in his face. "Did you really just threaten me with a goddamn banana?" she hissed furiously.

"Hey, I'm sorry!" he spluttered.

"You're gonna be sorry—"

"Take it easy," Langston said, sliding an arm around her waist and tugging. Clarissa was forced to release the guy, and she glared at him as Langston pulled her back.

"Are you Calamity?" Killall asked Langston, shifting nervously from one foot to another as he warily eyed Clarissa.

"*I'm* Calamity, asshole," Clarissa retorted.

Killall looked taken aback. "But…but you're a—"

"Say it and you'll be one too," Clarissa threatened. Langston's arm tightened around her and she heard what sounded suspiciously like a laugh before he stifled it.

"I'm so glad this amuses you," she sneered, jerking out of his grasp. She turned back to Killall. "Give it to me."

Clarissa held her hand out expectantly. When Killall didn't immediately respond, her eyes narrowed. "Now," she demanded, snapping her fingers.

"Okay, okay" he groused, digging in his jacket pocket before handing over a tiny flash drive.

"What's on it?" Clarissa asked.

"I don't know, man," he whined. "I just downloaded the data like I was told. That's all."

"Bullshit," she snapped. "What's on it?"

"I'd answer her," Langston said. "She's still pretty pissed off about the banana."

When Killall still hesitated, Clarissa took a step toward him. She was looking forward to inducing some pain in the little twerp.

"Wait, I'll tell you," he said quickly. Clarissa paused. "It's transactions, okay? Thousands of them. But I don't know where they were coming from or where they were going to."

"Well guess what?" Langston said. "You're going to help us figure it out."

"What? No way, dude. That wasn't the deal."

Langston flashed his FBI badge. "It is now."

"Aw, man!" Killall whined again. "I *knew* I shouldn't have taken this job. Listen, I didn't do anything illegal—"

"I'm not arresting you," Langston said. "But that'll change if you don't help us."

Killall looked defeated. "Fine. But we'll have to go back to my place."

"Let's go." Langston led the way to the SUV.

Twenty minutes later, they were driving through a ramshackle trailer park.

"Twister bait," Erik mused. Tornadoes always seemed to go for trailer parks. They were like magnets.

"It's the last one on the left." Killall pointed.

Erik parked the SUV, then he followed O'Connell and Killall inside.

If the outside looked unimpressive, the inside wasn't any better. A sofa that had seen better days took up the living room space, facing an unexpectedly expensive-looking flat-screen television on the wall. Gaming equipment littered the battered coffee table along with dirty dishes and a pizza box.

Killall and O'Connell headed to the back and Erik took a quick detour around to the kitchen area before following. If they weren't alone, he'd rather know sooner as opposed to later.

When he reached the back room, Killall and O'Connell were sitting in front of a computer. There were three monitors, but one seemed to be displaying a game of some sort.

The room was dimly lit with just one lamp. More dirty dishes and computer equipment littered the space. The wall was covered with posters of comic-book characters, none of which Erik recognized. The one poster he did recognize was a vintage Star Wars movie print.

"So you're Calamity," Killall said as he plugged in the flash drive. He shot O'Connell a sideways look. "You know, you're kind of a legend around here. I mean…not *here* here, but you know, with the guys I know on the Net."

The reverence in his voice made Erik's eyebrows climb. If he didn't know better, he'd think the boy seemed almost smitten, even after O'Connell had threatened him.

"Really," O'Connell said, sounding wholly uninterested. "If I'm such a legend, then why did you try to scam me for more money?"

Killall flushed, looking abashed. "It's just business. Nothing personal," he muttered.

O'Connell raised an eyebrow, staring him down until he turned back to the computer.

Files opened up and Killall began typing. "It'll take a few minutes to start tracking them down," he said.

"That's fine," Erik said.

"So, Killall. What's your real name?" O'Connell asked.

Killall turned puppy eyes to her. "It's Andy," he said. "My name is Andy."

"Why Killall then?"

Andy frowned. "Uh…it's kinda obvious, right?"

O'Connell stared blankly at him. "Because you're a real badass?"

"Yeah, I mean, no." He shook his head. "You know… Unix. Killall."

She caught on at the same time Erik did. This was something she should know as a hacker.

"Oh yeah, right," she said quickly, waving her hand. "Killall. Clever." She held something up, a black rectangle about five inches long. "So if you had a stun gun, why did you use a banana?"

Erik frowned. Andy had a stun gun? If he'd used it on O'Connell, Erik would have kicked his ass.

"Uh, yeah." Andy's pasty skin flushed. "It's…um…broken."

"You stunned yourself, didn't you," O'Connell said.

Erik knew she was right as Andy turned an even brighter red. He couldn't hide a grin.

"Listen, you want something to eat? Or drink?" Andy jumped to his feet. "I've got some leftover pizza in the fridge—"

"That's okay. We're good," Erik said. The idea of eating anything out of this kid's refrigerator was enough to put him off food for a week.

"Oh. Okay." Andy seemed somewhat crestfallen as he resumed his seat. Erik thought he probably should find

Andy's infatuation with O'Connell amusing instead of irritating. Did the kid have to sit so close to her? He was practically crowding her.

"Hey, it's coming through now," Andy said excitedly, distracting Erik. "Let's take a look."

The kid typed some more, pushing his glasses up his nose as he examined the screen.

"Um, wow," he said, sitting back in his chair.

"What?" said both Erik and O'Connell.

Andy glanced at O'Connell, newfound respect shining in his eyes. "These are banking transactions."

"They are?" Erik asked, coming closer to peer at the screen, which was a useless exercise. Nothing on there made a bit of sense to him. "For what? And to whom?"

Andy squinted as he studied the screen. "Here," he said, pointing to a section of lines that looked very similar. "From what I can see, they're all transferring a small amount of money from one account, but the money's going into lots of different accounts, and there are thousands of transactions."

"How much money total?" O'Connell asked.

"Um, I don't know. Gimme a minute."

More keystrokes. Erik waited, his nerves on edge.

"It looks like…wow…like about a hundred million." Andy slumped back in his chair. "Whoa. Dude. That's a lot of money."

O'Connell looked up at Erik. Her face had gone white.

"I mean, you did an awesome job scattering it," Andy said, squinting again at the screen. "It's in hundreds of accounts. It would take a team of hackers months to follow those trails, if they could even tie them together, which is doubtful," he scoffed.

"Oh my God," O'Connell breathed. "Why would I do that?"

Erik had no answer for her. But now they knew why Solomon was after her. He wasn't going to let one hundred million just disappear without a fight. And someone would probably die in the end.

"Can you send it back?" O'Connell asked Andy.

He shook his head. "No way. Not without the original program that sent all these transactions." He squinted at the screen. "And maybe not even then."

"Why? What is it?" Erik asked, his voice grim. Surely it couldn't get any worse?

"The way you did this," Andy said, glancing at O'Connell. "I think...I think you hacked into SWIFT." Now his voice bordered on awe.

"I did what?" O'Connell asked.

"What's swift? What are you talking about?" Erik chimed in. Maybe he was wrong. Maybe it could get worse.

"SWIFT," Andy explained. "It's an acronym. It stands for the Society for Worldwide Interbank Financial Telecommunication."

Erik's heart sank. It had just gotten worse.

"It's a secure, supposedly hack-proof network that banks use to send transactions to each other. I've never heard of someone who even got close to hacking it, though lots have tried." Andy jerked his head toward the screen. "Just look. There's no mistaking the header on those packets. It can only be SWIFT.

"Oh, man! That's so sweet!" He chortled. "High-five, Calamity!" He held his hand up expectantly.

O'Connell ignored him, her panicked eyes on Erik's. Andy awkwardly lowered his hand.

"Langston—"

"I'm on it," he interrupted, hurrying from the room. He was back in minutes, carrying her laptop.

"Here," he said, handing it to her. She booted it and logged in.

"Can you look at that and see if it's the program?" O'Connell asked, turning the laptop so it faced Andy.

Andy rolled his chair away from O'Connell, his eyes narrow with suspicion. "You're not Calamity, are you? Who are you?"

"Of course I am," O'Connell said in disgust. "I'm just… having some issues remembering things."

Andy didn't seem fazed. He just crossed his arms over his chest.

O'Connell sighed. "Listen, I really need your help." She seemed to brace herself before forcing out, "Please, Andy. You're the only one who can help me."

Erik rolled his eyes. She was really laying it on thick. Her eyes were wide pools of green in her pale face as she gazed at the kid. He didn't stand a chance.

Andy's expression softened at her plea. He cleared his throat and studied the screen with its lines of code for a few minutes. Erik watched him, hoping he'd have good news. He should have known better.

Finally, Andy shook his head. "I'm sorry, but this isn't it."

O'Connell's hand shook slightly as she closed the laptop lid. After a moment, Andy spoke.

"You know," he said hesitantly, "this really wasn't part of the deal. I mean, it's awesome that you hacked into SWIFT, but dude, it could bring some serious shit down, you know?" He glanced uneasily at Erik. "So, like, maybe you guys have what you want and can leave now?"

"Sure, Andy. We'll leave," Erik said, pulling his gaze from O'Connell's. "Just as soon as you tell us what you know about where Calamity lives." If the program wasn't on her laptop, maybe she'd done it from home.

Andy's eyes nearly popped out of his head. "What are you talkin' about, man? I don't know anything like that. Why would you want to know something like that?"

"Do I look stupid to you?" O'Connell snapped, her ploy at helpless female evaporating. "You expect us to believe you'd take a job like this without knowing anything about me?"

"Just tell us what you know and we'll get out of here," Erik coaxed, playing good cop to O'Connell's bad.

Andy's panicked gaze swiveled from O'Connell to Erik and back before he finally answered. "Okay, listen, all I know is that Calamity was given my name by someone in New Orleans. There's this chick there, and if you let her know what you can do, she'll hook you up. That's how I got this job. If you find her, she'll know more about Calamity."

"Who is she?" Erik asked.

Andy shrugged. "Beats me. All I know is her handle— Raven."

"How do we find her?"

Andy turned away and started searching through a stack of papers before finally pulling out a single sheet. He handed it to O'Connell.

"There's this club, in the French Quarter somewhere. I've heard she hangs out there." He lowered his voice. "And dude, it's a lesbian club. Word is that Raven is…you know."

O'Connell was already on her feet.

"Hey." Andy jumped up. O'Connell glanced back. "Sorry about the banana," he said with a sheepish shrug.

"Be careful who you do that to," she replied. "Someone else might just shoot first and ask questions later."

"It's too late to get there tonight," Erik said once they were in the car. He headed back along the dirt road out of the trailer park. "We won't be able to get inside that club until tomorrow." Shit. Another night in a motel with O'Connell.

He could really use a drink.

O'Connell didn't say anything.

"O'Connell? Did you hear me? We'll need to find somewhere for tonight, get some sleep—"

"Stop the car," she interrupted.

"What?"

"I said stop the car! Stop the car! Stop the car!"

Her frantic demand had Erik swerving to the side of the gravel road. He hadn't even come to a full stop before O'Connell was out of the car and running.

"What the—"

Throwing the SUV into park, Erik jumped out and tore after her.

It was pitch-dark, and the ground was uneven beneath his feet. He stumbled but caught himself. Muttering a few choice words, he resumed his pursuit.

"O'Connell!" he yelled. "Come back!" What the hell was she doing?

Erik's eyes adjusted to the darkness and meager light cast by the moon. He stopped, searching and listening. How had she disappeared so fast? He was abruptly reminded of that first night with her and how quickly she'd disappeared into the snowy trees. Even hurt, she'd moved like a wraith in the night.

Up ahead, he thought he caught a glimpse of a shadow. O'Connell. Erik ran toward her as she disappeared over a hill.

When he reached the same spot, he looked down and saw the unmistakable inky black of the Mississippi River about eighty yards away. O'Connell stood at its shore.

"What the hell is going on?" he asked when he reached her.

"Go away, Langston," she said, her voice flat. Her arms were crossed over her abdomen as though she were holding herself together.

"Not going to happen," he replied. "So you might as well tell me. What prompted this unexpected field trip?"

She rounded on him. "Did you hear what he said? Were you listening?"

"Of course I—"

"I stole a hundred million dollars, Langston. *A hundred million.* From someone who's not just going to look the other way. And not only that, but I hacked into…that thing he said…to do it." Her gaze met his and the hopelessness in her eyes was like a physical pain to Erik. "I'm not going to make it out of this alive," she said quietly. "You and I both know that."

Everything inside Erik rebelled, even though he'd thought the same thing. "That's bullshit," he spat. "You did this for a reason and it wasn't to sign your own death warrant. We just need more information."

"*We* don't need anything," O'Connell snapped. "You're out of this, Langston. Starting now." She turned away.

Erik grabbed her arm, yanking her back to him. "You think I'm just going to let you walk away? We're in this together. I promised you I'd help you and that's what I'm going to do. No one is going to kill you, not if I can help it."

O'Connell smiled a sad little smile. "You're a good man, Langston," she said. "Much too good for someone like me. And much too good to die for me."

Erik opened his mouth to argue, but then she was kissing him, her body pressed against his, her arms looped around his neck. The warm heat of her mouth was an intoxicant.

O'Connell kissed him with a desperation Erik matched, desire for her igniting inside him like a match to tinder. He wrapped his arms around her waist, holding her as close as he could, cursing the clothes that prevented the warm touch of skin against skin. He lost track of time and place, his every sense overwhelmed by her.

Suddenly, she stepped back, out of his arms. Her eyes shone wetly in the moonlight.

"I'm sorry," she whispered.

O'Connell thrust her hand out and Erik barely had time to register that she was holding something before pain knifed through him and his knees buckled. He hit the ground, then knew nothing at all.

CHAPTER TWELVE

Clarissa tried not to think about how she'd left Langston lying in a heap on the banks of the river, his body motionless after the electric charge from the "broken" stun gun she'd swiped from Andy. At the most, he would have been out twenty minutes or so. He'd be fine.

It had only taken her three attempts to find a car that had keys in it once she'd backtracked to the trailer park. She'd driven during the night, pulling off occasionally on a side road to sleep for a half hour or so when she'd gotten too tired. Now she was pulling into New Orleans just as the morning rush hour was hitting.

Guilt ate at her, but she ignored it. She'd done the right thing. Langston was the kind of man who would have stuck by her, defended her, protected her, no matter what. But that path would undoubtedly get him killed.

No need for him to share her fate.

Clarissa had no idea why she'd taken that money or what she'd planned to do with it, but she wasn't stupid. Solomon would never stop hunting her. And once he found her and realized she couldn't give the money back…well, Clarissa just hoped he'd kill her quickly, though she had her doubts.

Langston had done enough for her. It had been time to cut him loose.

Clarissa pulled up to a coffee shop. It was busy with several people going in and coming out.

"Here goes nothing," she muttered, getting out of the car. She needed money, and there were few options for obtaining it. She'd refused to take any off Langston. That somehow seemed more wrong than stealing from a complete stranger.

Though she'd kept his jacket. She hadn't been able to make herself leave it behind.

The shop smelled of roasted coffee beans and pastry, making Clarissa's stomach growl. She pretended to check out some merchandise on the shelves while observing the queue of people waiting to be served.

One man caught her attention. A businessman, judging by his suit and tie, he was wearing a Bluetooth earpiece and was busy texting on his phone. When the barista asked what he wanted, he didn't even look up as he barked his order at her.

Clarissa looked him up and down, judging his height and where he most likely kept his wallet. When he grabbed his coffee, she made her move, stepping into his path as he headed for the door. They collided, coffee splashing from the little hole in the lid of his cup.

"Dammit!" the man exploded.

"Oh crap!" Clarissa said, feigning surprise as she stumbled back, one hand disappearing under Langston's jacket. "I'm so sorry!"

The man's hands were full with his phone and coffee as he glared at her. "Just watch what the hell you're doing, will you?" With that, he pushed by her and went out the door.

Clarissa waited a moment, then followed, glad to see he'd gone the opposite direction from where she'd parked. A few minutes later, she was several blocks away, examining the expensive brand-name wallet.

She was in luck. The wallet held four hundred dollar bills and some twenties along with several credit cards. First order of business: food.

The Café du Monde was hopping with tourists, though the traditional revelry area of Bourbon Street was quiet this morning. Clarissa ordered and ate the sugary pastry as she walked a few blocks. A second-hand vintage clothing store was her next stop. A couple of questions to the woman working there as she was checking out and she knew where Queens of the Night, the name Andy had scrawled on the piece of paper, was located.

Stowing her purchases in the backseat of the car, she drove by the club. Situated right on the corner of St. Louis, it had a pink facade with the club's name in shining gold letters.

Clarissa cruised the streets until she found a beat-up motel that looked like she wouldn't have to show ID to get a room. Sure enough, a hundred dollars got her a key and no questions.

After showering, she lay on the bed, the rough fabric of the cheap linens abrasive against her skin. As tired as she was, she couldn't fall immediately to sleep. She stared at the ceiling, thinking of Langston.

Was he angry with her?

Well, that was an easy question. Clarissa was sure he was furious. She hoped he would see that she'd had no choice, and that she'd left to protect him. She hoped he'd understand.

Had he gone back to Washington? Gone back to clear his name? The stun gun would have left marks. That would prove she'd overpowered him and escaped, that he hadn't let her go. They'd believe him.

There was an empty ache in the pit of her stomach when she thought of Langston.

God, she missed him. Missed his calm strength and absolute conviction that he was doing what was right, even with the danger they'd faced. She missed making him laugh in spite of himself, missed teasing him until his ears turned red. Missed watching him get dressed, the hard planes of his chest rippling as he moved. And the way he'd kissed her, as though she alone could give him what he needed, wanted.

A shiver ran through her, and Clarissa pushed thoughts of Langston from her mind. The truth was she was on her own and on the run—with no memory. It terrified her.

As did the thought of exactly how long it would take until Solomon caught up to her. The clock was ticking and she knew her time was running out.

∿

Erik's headache was matched only by his anger, which poorly concealed his frantic worry.

She was gone. O'Connell had nailed him with the stun gun he hadn't even seen her take from Andy, and taken off, leaving him on the cold ground by the river. She'd even distracted him first with the oldest trick in the book.

On some level that wasn't either angry or worried, he had to admire her resourcefulness and courage. Somehow she'd gotten far enough away that he hadn't been able to find her when he'd regained consciousness.

Erik had stumbled his way back to the SUV, fully expecting to find it gone. Hope had flared briefly that she'd changed her mind, that she'd be inside, but it had been quickly dashed. He'd gone back to Andy's, thinking maybe she'd gone there, but no luck.

But he knew her destination.

Andy had told him the name of the club, and now Erik stood outside it, the glowing letters of the sign like a beacon in the night. The music was loud with a thumping bass he could feel. Crowds filled the street, laughing and talking as they flowed around him, drinks in their hands.

O'Connell would come here tonight. And he'd be waiting.

The bouncer let him pass without a word, and Erik stepped into the darkened club.

Strands of multicolored lights were hung on the walls and draped from the ceiling. The club was filled with people, though Erik noticed he was certainly in the minority. Women were the primary clientele, for obvious reasons. The getups some of them wore had Erik's eyebrows climbing. His jeans, black button-down shirt, and sport coat seemed decidedly out of place.

Making his way to the bar, he ordered a beer from the bartender, who seemed to be a man in drag. Maybe. Erik wasn't sure and didn't think it would be in his best interest to ask.

Taking a swig of the beer, Erik scanned the room. O'Connell shouldn't be too difficult to spot, not with her red hair. From where he was, he could see most of the bar. No one with red hair stood out.

As Erik waited, he thought about what O'Connell had said before she'd kissed and subsequently stunned him.

You're a good man. Much too good to die for me.

Had she thought she was protecting him? That running away from him would make him just give up? Let them find her? Kill her?

The thought just served to piss Erik off. Did she not believe him when he said he'd protect her? Or did she just not trust him to keep her safe?

An hour and two beers later, Erik saw her. His breath left his lungs in a rush.

She'd just walked in. Tousled waves of red hair brushed her shoulders, and her eyes were smoky with shadow, mysterious and alluring. But the hair and makeup weren't what held Erik's attention. It was the dress.

Skintight, the dress she wore was long sleeved and came up to demurely circle O'Connell's neck. But the modest lines were pointless since it was made entirely of black lace.

The hemline stopped at the tops of her legs, giving a tantalizing view of inner thigh as she walked. Strategically placed lace was the only thing that seemed to preserve her modesty. Black stilettos held on her feet with a thick leather strap around each slim ankle made her legs look like she'd walked right out of one of Erik's fantasies. Not that he had fantasies about her.

Right.

O'Connell didn't see him as she went by, and Erik slid off his stool, his eyes never leaving her as he followed. Her hips swayed as she walked, the lace whispering across her skin. Erik struggled to keep his eyes above her waist, but the battle was futile. She wore a flesh-toned g-string under the dress, and Erik wanted to groan at the leap his imagination was already making.

Seeing she was safe brought his anger to the surface again. He'd been worried sick, terrified he'd find her already dead in New Orleans. And instead here she was, looking for Raven in a dress he'd get on his knees and beg to be allowed to peel off her.

She paused uncertainly about halfway into the bar, near a small alcove. Erik saw his opportunity and moved in behind her.

"What's a girl like you doing in a place like this?" he said directly by her ear. The music was loud, but by the stiffening of her body, he could tell she'd heard him.

Clarissa spun around, a scathing put-down on her lips, and froze in shock.

Langston.

Her heart leaped to see him, and tears sprang to her eyes. He'd followed her. She knew she should be upset that he had, but she couldn't lie to herself. But she had to lie to him, so she schooled her features into a mask, blinked back the tears, and hoped he hadn't been able to tell how relieved she was to see him.

Clearing her throat, she said, "That's the best line you've got? No wonder you don't have a girlfriend."

"Well, I briefly considered asking where you're hiding your stun gun in that dress."

Clarissa's eyes narrowed. "What are you doing here, Langston?" she asked. "Didn't you get the message? I don't want you here." She made to push past him.

Langston snagged her around the waist, yanking her back and into the empty alcove. He leaned in close, imprisoning her with his body.

"I don't recall asking your permission," he hissed in her ear.

Clarissa's pulse raced. He was so close she could feel the heat of him through the nearly nonexistent material of her dress. She struggled to keep her wits about her.

"Did you think you could pull your disappearing act and I'd just meekly give up and go home?" he said. "You were very...very...wrong."

Langston's breath was warm in her ear, a phantom caress. His hands lay possessively on her hips, his grip not tight enough to hurt, but enough to let her know she wasn't going anywhere. Despite her wearing shoes that were killing her feet, he still loomed over her.

Clarissa couldn't think straight. The music was pounding in her head like the blood did in her veins. The flashing disco light over the dance floor in the corner briefly illuminated Langston before throwing him back into shadows. His wide shoulders blocked her view of anything but him.

The touch of his tongue to the skin just under her ear made her gasp. He sucked lightly, sending a bolt of heat through Clarissa. Her nails dug into his shoulders. When had she moved to grip his shoulders?

Then rational thought was lost again when his hands moved from her hips to the hem of her dress and under, cupping her rear and pulling her even closer. Clarissa could feel his arousal against her abdomen.

A part of her was stunned at Langston's audacity. Clarissa never would have taken him for the making out in public type, yet here he was, leaving a hickey on her neck while his hand determinedly traced the elastic line of the tiny scrap of lingerie she wore. The fact that they were surrounded by people in a public place and she was hidden only by Langston sent a thrill of excitement through her. Maybe she was an exhibitionist?

Or maybe it was because it was Langston.

Clarissa briefly thought she should push him away, put a stop to this, but she couldn't. Willpower must not be one of her virtues, not that she probably had that many to start with.

The corner of the alcove pressed against her back as she clung to Langston. His denim-clad knee urged her thighs apart as the fragile fabric of her dress bunched around her waist. She struggled to remain standing, the persistent movement of his fingers making her knees nearly buckle.

"Kiss me." His rough command had barely reached her ears before his lips were on hers, his tongue sliding into the warm cavern of her mouth.

Clarissa's legs weren't really holding her up now, just the wall against her back and Langston's arm around her. She heard nothing, felt nothing but him kissing her and his intoxicating touch between her legs. Her breath came in pants as he kissed her jaw, her neck, her shoulder.

"Erik," she moaned. "Oh God...please don't stop..." She really would kill him this time if he stopped now.

Her words must have encouraged him. He groaned, his fingers moving more purposefully now.

Clarissa's body was like liquid fire, her hand tangled in Langston's hair, holding him close as he licked and sucked the tender skin under her jaw. Just before she fell apart, he kissed her again, smothering her cries as she splintered into a thousand pieces.

She clung to him, struggling to catch her breath, when she felt his breath again by her ear.

"You're beautiful, Clarissa."

His words were reverent, and the way he said her name made an ache bloom inside Clarissa's chest. Langston's hands were gentle as he rearranged her clothes so she was once again presentable.

Their gazes caught and held. Words she shouldn't say lingered on the tip of Clarissa's tongue, so she grabbed a fistful of Langston's shirt and pulled him in for a kiss. She tried to put a lot into that kiss, including a promise she didn't know if she'd be able to keep.

Erik's head swam, nearly giddy with the knowledge of how much she'd let him in. Not to mention what she'd just allowed him to do to her. He felt like a stranger had inhabited his skin, a stranger with no willpower or self-control when it came to O'Connell. He couldn't have stopped himself from touching her if the club had caught on fire. Speaking of which...

He reluctantly pulled away from her kiss. "Let's go find Raven," he said, his voice rough. That was really the last thing he wanted. What he would have liked to have said was, "Let's get in the car and drive until no one knows or cares who we are."

O'Connell nodded. "Yeah, okay."

Taking her hand, he led her to an iron circular staircase that went upstairs, guarded by another bouncer. He'd been watching earlier and that seemed to be a section for VIPs only. Erik bet that Raven was probably up there, if she was here at all.

The bouncer moved to block his path and Erik reached for his badge, but before he could flash it, the guy saw O'Connell. He gave a quick jerk of his head and moved aside for them to pass.

"You think he recognized me?" O'Connell hissed.

Erik nodded, then let her precede him up the stairs. He followed closely behind, preventing the dress she wore from giving too much of a view to anyone who might be watching. The possessiveness he'd felt earlier toward her had magnified tenfold after their interlude in the alcove. Erik didn't like the way too many people, men and women, looked at O'Connell as she passed by.

The upstairs wasn't as crowded as below, the music not as intense. Erik and O'Connell paused, taking in the room and its inhabitants.

"Over there," Erik said, nodding in the direction of the corner. O'Connell turned to look.

A strikingly beautiful woman seemed to be holding court. She sat on an antique pink sofa and sipped from a martini glass. Her hair was jet black and hung nearly to her waist. She was dressed in a long black gossamer dress that was transparent, revealing a black corset underneath.

O'Connell gripped his hand tighter as she led them over. Erik's palm itched to have his gun in his hand, but he had to settle for its reassuring presence in the small of his back. He wanted to get in front of O'Connell, to shield her in case things turned ugly, but it made more sense for her to go first. Raven would recognize her, not him.

Sure enough, when they were closer, Raven's gaze fell on O'Connell.

"Darling! There you are! Where have you been?" Raven rose quickly to her feet. Her heels made her slightly taller than Erik. Hurrying forward, she grasped O'Connell's hands, tugging her from Erik's grip, and planted a kiss right on her mouth.

Erik froze, jaw agape. Raven stepped back, tugging O'Connell with her to the couch. With quick fluttering motions of her hands, she shooed away the other people nearby.

"Away with you," she said. "A dear friend has finally returned." She settled artfully back onto the couch, and O'Connell sat beside her.

If O'Connell was surprised or shocked by Raven's manner of welcome, she didn't show it. The woman had nerves of steel, Erik decided, breaking himself out of his immobility and following her to the couch.

"And who is this?" Raven asked, glancing at him as he settled into an antique Queen Anne chair. "Did you pick up a boy toy, Clarissa?" She winked. "He's fantastic."

O'Connell seemed to enjoy Erik's dismay. "He is," she agreed. "I hope you don't mind my bringing him with me."

Raven waved her hand. "Of course not. Having a man around is so handy sometimes. For eye candy, if nothing else."

Erik wasn't sure he enjoyed being talked about as though (a) he wasn't there, and (b) like he was a stick of furniture. He frowned darkly at O'Connell, who merely smiled at him.

"What's your name, sweetie?" Raven asked him.

"Erik."

"Ooooh, nice voice," she purred, glancing back at O'Connell, then she seemed to dismiss Erik entirely.

"So where have you been? I've been worried sick, you know. Did that geek boy I hooked you up with screw up the job? He came highly recommended, but you never know."

"No, he was fine." O'Connell hesitated, then said, "Raven, I need your help. I've run into some trouble—"

"No, don't," Erik interrupted. They knew next to nothing about Raven. O'Connell shouldn't tell her anything.

"How are we supposed to get anywhere without telling her?" O'Connell retorted.

Raven watched them argue. Then she pointed her finger imperiously at Erik. "You," she said. "Stop talking. Order Clarissa around again and I'll have you thrown out, no matter how lovely you look."

Erik pressed his lips together, eyeing the more serious-looking bouncers that hovered nearby, just out of earshot. They watched carefully for any sign from Raven.

"Clarissa, you know I'll help you, if I can," Raven said. "Just tell me what's going on. Something went wrong with that last job, didn't it." It wasn't a question.

O'Connell hesitated. "Sort of," she hedged. "To make a long story short, I need you to tell me everything you know…about me. I…can't remember."

Raven looked confused. "Can't remember what?"

"Anything."

Raven sat back on the couch, looking stunned.

"There was an accident," O'Connell continued. "Erik was there and helped me. But I hit my head, and now I can't remember."

"You have amnesia?"

O'Connell nodded.

"Oh, darling," Raven cooed, taking O'Connell's hands again in hers. "Of course I will help you. What do you want to know?"

"Where do I live?"

"Outside the city, in a house I've tried to get you to sell for years," Raven said. "But it's over a hundred years old and you love it, though God knows how you stand to be out there in the wilderness." She gave a delicate shudder.

"Who do I work for?" O'Connell asked.

Raven raised a perfectly arched brow. "Lately you've been working for that bastard, Solomon, not that you wanted to."

"What do you mean?"

Erik waited, holding his breath.

Raven looked sad as she spoke, as though she didn't want to have to tell O'Connell the answer. "He's blackmailing you. Has been for, what, nearly a year now?"

The relief Erik felt was nearly overwhelming. O'Connell had been forced to get involved with Solomon. Then relief was swiftly followed by rage. The bastard had put O'Connell in grave danger, from others, and now from him.

"Blackmailing me with what?" O'Connell asked. She looked relieved too.

"That no-good brother of yours, that's what," Raven said with a disgusted snort. "When he went to jail, Solomon said he could pull strings, get him out somehow, if you did some work for him." She shook her head. "But you've done job after job and he's done nothing to get Danny out. He's been stringing you along for weeks."

"Can you give me directions to my house?" O'Connell asked.

"Sure, sweetie." Raven snapped her fingers and a nearby lackey hurried to do her bidding. When he returned, she jotted something down and handed it to O'Connell. "You know, you don't have to go all the way out there. You're always welcome to stay with me." She glanced at Erik. "I bet the three of us would have a really good time."

"Ah...thanks for the offer, but we're good," O'Connell said hurriedly. Was she blushing?

Raven laughed, a throaty sound designed to be enticing. "I see amnesia hasn't changed your sensibilities," she teased O'Connell. "I've been trying to entice her into my bed for years," she said conspiratorially to Erik.

O'Connell jumped to her feet, and this time Erik was positive she was blushing, her cheeks a flaming red. "Thanks so much for your help, Raven," she said. "Does anyone else know where I live?"

"I don't think so. It took years before you told me." Raven dropped all humor now as she stood and hugged O'Connell. "Be safe," she said earnestly. "Solomon isn't to be trifled with. Finish this and get out."

O'Connell smiled tightly. "I'm trying." She glanced at Erik and headed for the stairs.

Raven stopped Erik with a hand on his arm.

"Keep her safe," she said, and now Erik could see the stark worry she'd kept hidden from O'Connell. "Solomon will kill her if she crosses him."

"I will," Erik promised.

He caught up with O'Connell at the bottom of the stairs. Erik didn't put it past her to leave him behind again, but she was waiting for him. He paused, their eyes meeting for a fleeting moment, then took her hand and led her out of the club and down the street to his car.

The quiet inside the SUV was a welcome respite from the noise outside, the streets even more crowded as the hour grew later.

"You all right?" Langston asked.

"Yeah. Maybe. I'm not sure," Clarissa said, pushing a hand through her hair. "It's just...a lot to take in."

"Which part?"

Clarissa gave a humorless laugh at the wry note in his voice. "Well, being kissed by another woman definitely took me off guard." She glanced at him.

"Yeah, wasn't a huge fan of that," he said.

Clarissa frowned slightly. Was that jealousy she heard? Impossible.

"Then the news that apparently I'm being blackmailed to try and free my brother. Which obviously hasn't worked out so well."

"But you found out the truth," Langston said. "You weren't involved with Solomon of your own free will. He coerced you, using the one thing guaranteed to get you to cooperate. Your brother."

"So why did I take a hundred million dollars from him?" Clarissa asked. "That certainly wasn't going to help free Danny."

"Unless you decided to turn the tables. He's blackmailing you but refusing to deliver, so you blackmailed him. He gives you what you want, you give the money back."

Clarissa stared at Langston, sure he was right. "The only problem is that I can't give the money back. I don't know how. And no one else can either, since I'm the only one who's hacked SWIFT."

Hopelessness assailed Clarissa. She leaned her head back against the seat with a sigh. She saw no way out of this. No way to escape.

"Hey." Langston's voice was soft. She turned her head toward him. He reached out to gently cup her cheek. "Don't give up," he said. "I'm not, so you damn well better not."

Clarissa gave a slight shrug. "I don't know what else to do."

"Well, for starters, we'll go to your house. Andy said the program wasn't on your laptop, so it has to be there. And maybe being there will help jog your memory."

Clarissa brightened. Maybe he was right. Maybe seeing the house she supposedly loved would bring back her memories. God, she was glad to have Langston back. She managed a small smile, turning her head farther to nestle into his hand.

Langston gave one last caress to her cheek. His gaze dropped to her chest and lower before looking quickly away. He cleared his throat.

"You're cold," he said, turning on the car. "Let's get going."

"Wait," she said. "I need you to drive me by my car first. I have some stuff I need to get."

All her things were in there, including Langston's jacket. He stowed her stuff in the back of the SUV, not saying anything about her taking his coat.

"So where is this place?" he asked.

Clarissa dug out the paper with the directions on it. "Take Interstate Ten east to the Slidell exit."

Forty minutes later, Langston was driving on a tiny dirt road barely wide enough for the SUV. There were no streetlights, just empty darkness around them.

"Are you sure this is right?" he asked.

Clarissa double-checked the directions. "Pretty sure. Turn left up there." She peered through the windshield as Langston turned into a drive being quickly overtaken by vegetation. "Wait—is that it?" She pointed.

A large shadow of a house loomed ahead of them, the windows darkened. Clarissa struggled to remember something about it but came up blank.

"Dammit!" She slammed a hand on the dash.

"What?" Langston asked, pulling to a stop. "What's the matter?"

"I don't remember anything." It was so frustrating. She'd been so hoping…

"Take it easy," Langston said. "We just got here. I can't even tell what it looks like. Give yourself a break."

"You're right." Clarissa sighed. "I'm just tired, I guess."

"Well, look on the bright side," Langston said. "You get to sleep in your own bed tonight."

Clarissa smiled. That man could see the silver lining in anything.

"Alone?" she asked, raising an eyebrow.

The look in Langston's eyes changed, becoming more predatory. His mouth tipped up slightly at the corner. "Only if you want to be," he said. The husky promise in his voice sent a jolt of heat through Clarissa.

Well now *that* was more like it.

Clarissa's heels sank into the damp earth as they walked to the front door. Four steps led up to a wide porch with a hammock strung up on one side. Langston handed her a set of keys.

"Where did you—"

"They were in your bag," he said. "Remember?"

Vaguely. It seemed like forever ago since she'd gone through her things in the Colorado cabin.

The third key she tried worked, and she stepped cautiously over the threshold, listening. All was quiet. The only thing she could hear was the hum of the refrigerator. But still...she held up her hand to halt Langston.

"Something's not right," she whispered. She didn't know how she could tell, she could just feel it. Had someone been here in her absence? Her eyes strained to see into the dark room.

She moved blindly toward the wall. There had to be a light switch somewhere.

Her searching hand touched fabric stretched across warm skin. She jerked back with a sharp cry.

Someone was in there with them.

EPISODE SEVEN

CHAPTER THIRTEEN

A hand closed like a vise around Clarissa's wrist, and she reacted instinctively, twisting her arm free as she lunged in close, her hands feeling for the vulnerable parts of the body. A hit to the intruder's throat and he began choking. Clarissa moved fast, groping in the dark, and jabbed at his eye.

The man let out a strangled yell just as Clarissa grasped his shoulders and threw all her strength into kneeing him in the nuts. He collapsed at her feet, moaning.

Someone seized her from behind. Clarissa whipped her head back, cracking him in the face. He grunted and his hold on her loosened. She spun around, ready to give his family jewels the same honor she'd bestowed on the other asshole, when the lights suddenly came on.

"Move and he dies."

Clarissa froze at the tableau in front of her. Two men held Langston, one sporting a busted and bleeding nose, while Mendes held a gun to Langston's head. Langston's mouth was bleeding.

"I have no use for him, so the choice is yours," Mendes said with a careless shrug.

Well…fuck.

Clarissa held up her hands, and the guy that she'd cracked in the head grabbed her, pinning her arms behind her back.

The guy Clarissa had nailed in the nuts regained his feet.

"Fucking bitch," he spat at her.

"I'm surprised I could even find your balls, they're so tiny," Clarissa said sweetly.

"Don't," Mendes warned when the guy started for her with murder in his eyes. "I need her."

The thug stopped, but it looked like a near thing.

"Xavier," Clarissa said. "I'd lie and say it's nice to see you again, but I'm trying to turn over a new leaf. New Year's resolution and all." She glanced at Langston and hissed, "Told you we should have killed him."

"You're picking *now* to say 'I told you so'?" His tone was incredulous.

"I just want the record to show that I was right," she retorted.

Langston rolled his eyes. "Fine. So I'm just supposed to let you kill someone whenever you want?"

"I'm just saying."

"Enough!" Mendes interjected, his irritation at their bickering obvious. "The money, Clarissa. Where is it?"

Clarissa gave a derisive snort. "What? You think it's here? Right, like I'd just walk around with it in my purse. Or do you think I hid it in my mattress?"

"Give it to me, or your boyfriend will pay the price." Mendes was implacable.

Clarissa started to sweat. "I swear, I don't have it." She couldn't give Mendes the accounts, not until she could figure out how to get the money back to Solomon. If he knew exactly how useless she was to him, he'd kill her immediately.

"Hurt him."

"No!" Clarissa cried, but it was too late. One of the thugs holding Langston jerked his arm up and back.

Langston yelled, his face contorting at the pain, and his knees faltered. They'd dislocated his shoulder, but somehow he was still on his feet. His breathing was harsh, and sweat broke out on his face, now drained of color. He gritted his teeth and pressed his lips tightly together to keep from making another sound.

Fury consumed Clarissa. "I'm going to kill you for that," she hissed at Mendes.

"You're in no position to be making threats." His smile was malicious. "Now where is it? Or should we have another demonstration?"

Before Clarissa could answer, Mendes had nodded toward the thugs.

"No—stop!" Clarissa struggled against her captor but was helpless to do anything but watch as the two men unleashed a brutal assault on Langston. "Please! I'll tell you—just stop hurting him!"

Mendes gave a sharp whistle, and the two men paused. Langston was slumped on the floor now, and he coughed as he tried to push himself upright. Blood flowed freely from a nasty gash on his forehead. He grunted harshly when he slipped and crashed down onto the floor again, landing on his abused arm.

Langston's form swam in Clarissa's vision. *Oh God. Please.* He couldn't die. Not now. Not after all this.

"I...I have it," she stammered. "What you want. The accounts."

"Now that wasn't hard, was it?" Mendes sneered.

"But you have to let him go."

His smirk disappeared. "Like I told you before, you're not in a position to bargain."

"Having the accounts will get you nowhere," Clarissa said. "I'm the only one that can get the money back." She lowered her voice to a hiss. "And if you hurt him again, I swear to God I'll rot in hell before Solomon sees a dime of that money."

"Clarissa, no. Don't—"

Langston's protest was cut off by a vicious kick in his side. He grunted again, and Clarissa flinched at the sound.

"Xavier—" Clarissa warned, her gaze locked on Mendes.

"Enough," Mendes ordered, his eyes studying her. "Take him into the swamp and dump him. Leave him alive." He raised an eyebrow at Clarissa. "That's the most I'll do."

It was better than the alternative. This would give him a chance at surviving, which was more than she could say for herself. Clarissa was under no illusions as to what would become of her when Mendes was through. She swallowed hard and gave a jerky nod. "Agreed."

In moments, they had Langston on his feet. Clarissa cringed when they grabbed his arm. His face went white, and he gritted his teeth to keep from making a noise. It was nearly a physical pain to watch.

"Clarissa, dammit, no!" Erik struggled, the pain shooting through his arm pure torture. His logical side was lost in a haze of rage and fear. He couldn't leave her. Mendes was going to kill her; he knew it. "Clarissa!"

They were dragging him toward the door. O'Connell wouldn't look at him, her gaze fixed on Mendes. She looked so small and frail surrounded by the hulking men, but her face was an unreadable mask. If she was afraid of the near-certain death that loomed, she didn't show it, calmly bargaining for his life with the only leverage she had.

Herself.

That was the last glimpse he had of her before they shoved him out the back door. An SUV was parked not far from the house. Erik knew they weren't just going to let him go, no matter what Mendes has promised O'Connell, though it had been real sweet of her to try.

Sweat poured from Erik's body despite the cold, the agony in his shoulder reminding him of how much he detested hand-to-hand combat. It always hurt like a sonofabitch. His arm hung useless at his side.

Well, that was certainly inconvenient, but he had to work with what he had. Now that it was two on one and not pitch-black like it had been when they'd first jumped him, it was time to take control of the situation.

Erik stumbled, going down on one knee just as they were near the car. His right hand slipped under the hem of his jeans as the guy nearest him went to grab his arm to pull him to his feet.

Erik leaped up, and the blade in his hand flashed. A moment later, the thug was clutching his neck, blood seeping through his fingers from the deep gash. His eyes were wide in shock. Erik had already turned to the other threat before the first guy even hit the ground.

His remaining captor went for his gun but was too late, the knife buried to the hilt between his ribs. He collapsed as well.

Erik's gaze flashed back to the house, but there was no movement inside to indicate that anyone suspected what had just happened. Keeping an eye out, he searched and took the two guns off the men at his feet, retrieved his knife, then silently disappeared into the trees beyond the small clearing surrounding O'Connell's home.

Time to fix his shoulder.

He found a solid tree with a thick trunk that looked like it could withstand a hit. Knowing he couldn't make any noise, Erik grabbed a dry stick about as thick as his finger and bit down on it. Taking two deep breaths, he braced himself, then rammed his shoulder into the tree as hard as he could.

The pain was agonizing and his knees weakened, sending him flat on his ass on the ground. Black edged his vision.

No. There wasn't time to pass out.

He spit out the stick and stuck his head between his knees, taking slow, deep breaths. The pain was passing, though the shoulder was sore and tender. He wouldn't be getting his full use out of it for a few days.

At times like these, a desk job sounded like heaven on earth.

Shouts from the house had Erik jumping to his feet and melting into the dark shadows of the trees. Moving silently, he found a position where he could see one of the other guys examining the bodies on the ground.

He was too far away to shoot with the pistol Erik had, so he moved closer. But before he could get in range, the guy had disappeared back inside. Shit. Now they knew he wasn't dead.

A strangled cry came from inside the house.

O'Connell.

Panic leaped in his veins, but Erik forced himself to calm. He'd be no use to her if he panicked.

Picking his path carefully, Erik approached the side of the house, sticking as much to the shadows as possible. Dawn was near, the sky lightening ever so slightly.

O'Connell's house was of the Old South style, a wraparound porch on the first floor, with a wraparound terrace gracing the second. Erik climbed up on the porch balustrade and grasped the floor of the terrace about his head. His shoulder muscles screamed in protest, but he gritted his teeth and pulled himself up until he stood, panting, on the second floor.

Using his knife, he jimmied the lock on the window, raised it soundlessly, and slipped into the house, landing in a crouch inside the darkened room.

Erik listened, straining to hear where the four people in the house were. He knew Mendes was probably with O'Connell, but what about the other two?

Knife in hand, Erik crept to the open doorway and peered around the edge.

There. At the end of the hallway near the stairs. The two men stood together, the one O'Connell had nailed in the nuts talking.

"You watch up here," he ordered. "I'll take downstairs. I want first crack at that bitch when Mendes is through with her."

"He ain't gonna wanna mess around," the other guy said. "He's gonna want her dead so we can get outta here."

"There'll be enough time to do what I gotta do."

With that chill warning, he headed down the stairs. Erik listened carefully to his footfalls. There. A squeak on the seventh step down. Quiet the rest of the way.

The second guy gave a shrug and checked his ammunition clip before turning away to walk down the hall. Erik supposed he was going to check the rooms.

Silently, Erik crept after him. The guy paused, and Erik had a split second to jump inside an open doorway. He held his breath. Had he seen him? Erik's grip on his knife tightened.

But there was nothing. He slowly exhaled.

Peering around the doorframe, he saw the guy go into the last room at the end of the hall. Hurrying as fast as he dared, Erik followed, ducked into the room next to it, and waited.

After a moment, the knob turned and Erik breathed, tensing. The guy stepped inside and past where Erik was hiding behind the door. Erik pounced, grabbing him by the hair and slicing his knife across the man's throat. Blood spurted everywhere. He dropped to the ground.

Adrenaline was spiking hard, burning away the pain in Erik's shoulder and from the beating. He didn't like having to kill these men, but he didn't see that he had a choice. Not if he wanted himself and O'Connell to get out of here alive. And she was right on one count—they'd kill him in an instant if they could.

Shouting from downstairs brought Erik's head up. He crept to the stairs.

"You need me, Xavier!" O'Connell was shouting.

"I have everything I need," he replied calmly. "You've been more trouble than you're worth, Clarissa. And you and I both know it's best to tie up loose ends. Finnegan, take care of her and call me when you're through."

"Xavier! You bastard!"

O'Connell's furious shout was drowned by the slam of the front door. Not a moment later, O'Connell cried out in pain, and the sound of furniture breaking reached Erik's ears. Sheathing his knife, he grabbed the gun from the small of his back and racked the slide.

More sounds of struggling downstairs; the man cursed viciously, then glass shattered.

Everything inside Erik was screaming for him to run, hurry, stop the bastard from hurting O'Connell. But he had to stay calm and think. If he got himself killed, O'Connell was dead.

But that was a lot easier said than done when he heard her scream.

"Fuck it," he growled.

Clarissa moaned, clutching her stomach. She'd gotten a good hit in with the heavy bookend she'd grabbed off a shelf, but he'd retaliated, punching her in the stomach and throwing her. She'd screamed, the sound abruptly cut off when she landed on a glass-and-wood coffee table. The glass had shattered on impact. Now she lay facedown on the rug that covered the wood floor.

Hands closed around her ankles, jerking her backward. Clarissa struggled, her fingers scrabbling against the carpet. The rug burned against her skin, the tops of her thighs, her stomach, as the fabric of her dress bunched. She knew what was coming, and bile rose in her throat. Her fingers found a shard of glass just as she was flipped onto her back.

Clarissa surged upward, wielding the glass like a dagger. In a flash it was embedded in Finnegan's chest, but it was too fragile and broke before going in very far.

He yelled and backhanded her. Pain exploded in Clarissa's head at the impact, and she collapsed again to the floor.

A shot rang out.

Finnegan grunted in pain, then somehow stumbled to his feet. Clarissa managed to raise her head, then stared in shock.

Langston.

He stood at the bottom of the staircase, a smoking gun in his steady grip. His shirt was torn and stained with blood, which was also oozing from the gash on his forehead. His hair was matted with sweat. Bloodstains marred the hand that held the gun.

"We figured you'd run off," Finnegan said, holding up his hands in surrender. "Decided to play the hero instead?"

"O'Connell, you all right?" Langston asked her. His eyes stayed locked on Finnegan.

Clarissa got painfully to her feet. Blood dripped lazily from her hand; the glass she'd used had cut her as well. The metallic taste of blood was also in her mouth, and she could already feel her cheek swelling. Her hands shook as she smoothed her dress back down.

"I'm fine," she rasped, her voice hoarse from screaming.

Langston's eyes flicked to her and widened. He looked her up and down carefully, and when his gaze returned to Finnegan, his face was a cold, hard mask.

"You gonna arrest me?"

"Not this time."

The gunshot startled Clarissa, and she jumped then watched, jaw agape, as the man crumpled. Langston looked completely unfazed as he hurried toward her, tucking the gun behind his back.

"You shot him," she said, stunned.

"Yes, I know."

"But…you don't just kill people. You arrest them." His behavior was incomprehensible.

"I just served up justice and saved the taxpayers a lot of money." Langston gently slid an arm around her waist and guided her into the kitchen. He started the water in the sink and held her bleeding hand under the flow.

"But…why?"

Langston finally looked her in the eyes. "Because he deserved it," he said. His hand cradled her cheek, his thumb gently brushing the bruise forming there.

It suddenly hit Clarissa that he was here, alive, when she'd never expected to see him again. He'd saved himself…and her.

"Where else did he hurt you?" he asked, studying the cut on her lip from her teeth.

Clarissa shook her head and pushed his hand away.

"What—"

Clarissa reached for him, yanking him down for a searing kiss. Her arms wrapped around his neck, her fingers threading through his hair and holding him as close as possible.

Langston needed no urging, his tongue surging inside to tangle with hers. A hand cupped the nape of her neck while his other arm pressed tightly against her waist.

Passion, desperation, urgency. She could feel all of it in his kiss. And the only thoughts going through Clarissa's mind: Langston was alive and she was living on borrowed time.

When Langston pulled away, they were both breathing hard.

"We need to get out of here," he said. "What happened with Mendes? What did you give him?"

"There's a computer in the other room," Clarissa said, struggling to focus. He still held her, his thumb absently stroking the back of her neck. "My files were on it along with the account list. He copied them to a flash drive and left."

"Will he be able to get the money?"

She shook her head. "No. I put an encryption password on it as it was downloading. He doesn't know it yet, but those files will be inaccessible without it."

"So you remember now?"

Langston's tone made her pause. "Not really. Maybe it was the pressure of what was going on, I don't know, but when he made me copy the files, I was just trying to think of some way to stop him, and it came to me. Kind of like how I knew how to pick the handcuffs."

Something close to relief flashed across Langston's face.

"Let's grab the computer and get out of here." He stepped away and took her hand.

Clarissa held tight to Langston, closely following him as they went to retrieve her second laptop from the den. She should probably take a moment, get a grip, but she couldn't make herself step away or let go of him. She'd been moments from dying, and the fact that they were both alive was astonishing. By all rights, they should be dead.

She followed him upstairs to the bedrooms as he searched for a room that looked to be hers. Clarissa saw the dead man on the floor in one, a pool of blood underneath the unmoving corpse.

"That's gonna leave a stain," she murmured absently, unable to tear her gaze away.

"What?" Langston asked, pulling her past the room.

She shook her head. It wasn't worth repeating, and she didn't even know why she'd said it. Everything seemed to be in slow motion, though Langston was moving quickly.

Her bedroom was foreign to her, the furnishings simple. It held a double bed with a plain white comforter, an old-fashioned rocking chair by the window, and a dresser. A couple of photos in frames were on top of the dresser. Herself with a man, his arm around her shoulders. She recognized him from her file that Langston had. That must be Danny, her brother. The other photo was of Danny as well, only this time she must have been the one taking the picture, because he was by himself.

Langston grabbed some clothes from a closet and a pair of shoes. Taking her hand again, he led her back downstairs and helped her into his SUV. Moments later, they were speeding down the gravel road, the sun just now appearing over the horizon. Langston grabbed his sunglasses and put them on.

He cast a few glances at Clarissa as he drove. She stared straight ahead.

"You're still shaking," he said.

Surprised, Clarissa glanced down. He still held her hand, and he was right. She could feel the fine tremors now. Weird that she hadn't noticed. She looked at Langston, her brows raised.

"Sorry? I'll stop?" Sarcasm edged her words. She didn't know what he expected her to do, exactly. It wasn't like she could control it.

Langston didn't reply. His lips just thinned and his grip tightened on her hand.

Clarissa looked back out the window. "I guess Raven betrayed me," she mused. Not that it should have surprised her. Not that it did. "Do I know no one who won't stab me in the back?"

"I won't."

Langston's fervent declaration made Clarissa's eyes sting. She refused to look at him, didn't want him to see, and continued to stare out the window while tears rolled down her cheeks.

~

Erik's concern for O'Connell only grew as he drove. She was silent as she stared out the passenger window, and the tight grip she had on his hand didn't let up.

She'd stopped trembling, thank God, but if he had to guess, Erik would say she was in shock. The trauma of this whole experience was bound to have an effect at some point, and her mind was already damaged from the amnesia.

But he couldn't do anything about that. All he could do was take care of her, keep her alive, and make sure she knew she wasn't alone.

"Where are we?" O'Connell asked when he pulled into the driveway of a three-story antebellum home on the outskirts of New Orleans.

"A friend of my mom's owns this place," he said. "We need a place to clean up, get some rest, and figure out our next move." Erik got out of the car and grabbed his jacket from the back. He opened O'Connell's door, then swung the jacket over her shoulders. It concealed the worst of the damage to her dress.

Her eyes were bloodshot and red-rimmed from crying. Erik's gut twisted.

"Let's go," he said.

He led her up the wide stairs to the porch, then knocked on the door. A few moments later, a woman answered. She looked surprised to see him.

"Erik?" She took a good look at him. "Oh my goodness! What in the world happened to you?"

"Hi, Mrs. Cooper," he said. "It's a long story, but we really need a place to stay where people won't ask questions. Do you have any rooms available?"

"Of course, of course. Come in." She hurriedly stepped aside, her brow creased with worry as they crossed the foyer. "It's the off-season and Mardi Gras isn't for a few weeks yet, so there are plenty of rooms."

The interior of the home was lavish and reeked of southern elegance. A staircase straight out of *Gone with the Wind* led to the upper floors, which was where she led them.

"The top floor is empty and will give you the most privacy," she said, taking them up another flight and showing them to a room at the end of the hall. After opening the door, she handed a key to Erik. "Let me know if you need anything."

"Do you have a medical kit?"

She did and agreed to get it right away. Erik saw the questions in her eyes and the way she kept glancing at O'Connell, but he didn't elaborate. While he felt bad for not giving Mrs. Cooper a fuller explanation, all his attention was focused on O'Connell.

The room they were in was spacious, its decor understated elegance done in creams and ivories. A large tester bed took up a full corner, while a sitting area occupied the opposite corner, which also held a fireplace.

He settled O'Connell on a loveseat in front of the fireplace, crouching down in front of her. "I need to get some things from the car," he said. "I'll be right back."

Panic flared in her eyes, and she clutched at his arm. "I'll go with you."

"No. It's okay," he assured her, gently removing her hand. "I'll be right back. I promise."

She still seemed unsure, but she didn't try to stop him again.

Erik hurried, grabbing their clothes and her laptop from the car. He was back in minutes after retrieving the med kit from Mrs. Cooper, who'd met him on his way up.

O'Connell jerked around when he opened the door, her hands curved into claws as though she were expecting to fight, but she relaxed when she saw it was him.

He deposited their things on a nearby chair and kicked off his shoes. Kneeling in front of her, he removed the killer stilettos from her feet. The leather had left marks around her ankles, and he gently massaged the angry red welts.

"C'mon," he said, rising and pulling O'Connell to her feet.

He led her into the bathroom and started the shower running, adjusting the temperature until it was nice and hot. After checking that there were plenty of towels, he unwrapped the soap for her.

O'Connell stood, silently watching him. Erik was sure she was still in shock. If he got her clean and warm, she'd be okay. She had to be.

Erik frowned as he examined her dress. No zipper or buttons. Okay. Guess it just went over her head then.

He remembered how much he'd wanted to strip this dress off her last night. Somehow, this hadn't been the scenario he'd imagined.

Once she was naked, he tried to keep his eyes above her neck as he helped her into the shower. The warm spray hit her skin, and she seemed to stir from her stupor, turning her face up to the water. In seconds, her hair was streaming with water and her body seemed to relax. Erik breathed a sigh of relief and turned to go, but she stopped him with a single word.

"Stay."

CHAPTER FOURTEEN

Erik swallowed. His mouth was suddenly dry as dust. He couldn't stop his gaze from dropping. The water sluiced like a lover's hands over her skin, her shoulders, her breasts, before rippling down her abdomen and disappearing between her thighs. With effort, he lifted his eyes to hers.

"If I stay, I'll make love to you," he said baldly. His voice was a rasp of sound. "I won't be able to stop this time. And you don't need that. You need to recover and rest."

"All I need is you," she said simply.

Indecision kept him immobile. O'Connell stepped close to him, close enough for him feel the heat from the water on her skin. He couldn't look away from her eyes, so green and full of trust as she looked at him. It made him want to kiss her until she knew without a doubt what he felt for her. No matter what.

"You're wearing too many clothes," she said softly. She began slipping the buttons from his shirt, one by one.

Erik could no longer keep from touching her. While she worked assiduously on removing his shirt, he reached out to rest his hands on her waist. She felt so fragile, her bones small compared to his. He hated the thought of all she'd had to endure on her own, hated the fact that she'd been blackmailed into nearly forfeiting her own life for her unworthy and ungrateful brother.

O'Connell tugged his shirt free of his jeans and rose on her toes to push it off his shoulders. He had to briefly remove his hands from her to get the shirt off, and he did so with irritation, yanking it off and dropping it to the floor.

She started on his belt, but Erik barely noticed. His mouth was at her shoulder, tasting the warm, sweet skin there. She sighed softly, encouraging him.

Impatient now, with the blood thundering in his veins, Erik quickly shed his remaining clothes before stepping into the shower with her.

Steam shrouded them, the air currents swirling the misty vapor and making it appear as though Erik had fallen into an otherworldly dream. Though he doubted he could ever have dreamed someone as amazing as O'Connell.

Her cheek was black-and-blue from where Finnegan had struck her. Erik bent down to her, lightly cupping her jaw as he brushed his lips gently across the abused skin, as though he could heal the damage by the sheer force of his will.

A washcloth hung on the nearby rack, and Erik picked it up, wetting it before carefully wiping the dried blood from her face and hand. Taking the soap, he lathered his hands and set the bar aside. He began at her fingers, gently using his hands to wash her. When he was empty of soap, he lathered again, learning every inch of her skin, every curve, dip, and hollow.

Erik touched her as though she were made of the finest porcelain, as priceless and beautiful as she was delicate and rare. Her heartbeat raced under his palm, her little panting breaths and sighs a melody to his ears. The full globes of her breasts were slippery under his soap-covered hands, their feminine weight filling his palms. His thumbs brushed the rosy tips, eliciting a moan from O'Connell.

He bent his head, reverently touching his tongue to a nipple. O'Connell gasped, and he licked the warm, wet peak before taking it fully into his mouth. His hands gently massaged her rear while he suckled her breasts, her moans and whimpers urging him on.

Dropping to his knees, the spray of the water hit his back as he again lathered his hands. She was a slick, wet heat between her legs, so aroused that she cried out at the mere brush of his fingers. Erik's aching cock twitched at the sound.

He urged her legs wide, needing to see her, taste her. She complied, her fingers digging into his shoulders as his tongue parted the flesh bared to him.

Erik worshipped her with his mouth, prolonging her pleasure even as she panted and begged him, bringing her to the edge again and again. He intimately tortured her until her entire body trembled beneath his hands and his name fell in a constant litany from her lips. Only then did he allow her release, sliding a finger inside her heat and sucking her tender flesh until she screamed and her nails dug into his skin.

Clarissa's legs felt unable to hold her weight, the wall at her back and Langston's hand on her hip the only things keeping her upright. Opening her eyes, she looked down. He was still on his knees, pressing open-mouthed kisses to her abdomen. She could feel his finger still inside her, languidly moving in and out.

Loosening her grip on his shoulders, she threaded her fingers through his wet hair. He turned to look up at her. Their gaze caught and held. The blue of his eyes held her mesmerized. Her breath caught on a gasp as he pushed another finger inside her. The blazing passion in his eyes branded her even as his touch marked her.

"Make love to me," she said.

Langston didn't waste any time. Standing, he scooped her in his arms and carried her to the bed. Their bodies were wet, but Clarissa was beyond caring. She wanted Langston, needed to feel him on her, inside her.

He kissed her as he settled between her legs, and she could feel the hard length of him against her thigh.

"Hurry," she breathed against his lips.

His hands grasped her hips as he slowly pushed inside her. Too slow. Clarissa made a noise of frustration, lifting her hips to take more of him. Langston groaned, lifting his head to look at her.

"I don't want to hurt you," he rasped.

"Either you think I'm really fragile or you have a very high opinion of yourself," she shot back, raising an eyebrow.

His lips twitched. Then he was kissing her again, claiming her mouth as he claimed her body. And if he didn't have a high opinion of himself, Clarissa certainly did. His cock was as spectacular as the rest of him and worth the wait. She wrapped her legs around his waist, her fingers threading through his hair as his tongue mimicked the movement of their bodies.

Clarissa's heart was racing, or was that his? Their chests pressed together until she couldn't tell his heartbeat from her own. Langston tore his mouth from hers, his breath a hard pant against her skin.

"Oh God oh God oh God." Clarissa squeezed her eyes shut. It was perfect. He was perfect. The magic he'd done to her body in the shower was building again. "Harder. Faster," she begged.

Langston complied, his hips pistoning into hers, his arms imprisoning her. Clarissa's body was on fire, whimpers and moans escaping her. "Erik, oh God," she cried out, her orgasm crashing through her.

His mouth swallowed her cries as he continued to thrust, his cock thicker and harder than before. His body jerked into hers, pushing her over the edge again. Clarissa's nails dug into Langston's back, his hoarse shout muffled by their kiss.

Clarissa struggled to catch her breath. Langston must have realized his weight was pressing on her and made to move, but she tightened her legs, holding him in place.

"I'm too heavy," he said, bracing himself on his elbows.

"I like it," Clarissa said. A sheen of sweat covered his skin, and she lightly ran her fingers down his back.

He pressed a kiss to her forehead, then the corner of her eye, her cheek, her lips. Looking in her eyes, he brushed her hair back from her face. His gaze was intense, reminding Clarissa of how he'd touched her in the shower, as though this was more to him than just sex.

This was just sex, right?

"Langston," she began.

"Erik," he corrected softly, brushing his lips along her jaw.

"Erik," she said. "That was amazing—"

"I thought I had too high an opinion of myself," he interrupted, gently biting then sucking her earlobe.

"That was the best sex I've ever had," Clarissa said bluntly.

"Considering as how you can't remember the other sex you've had, I'm not sure that says all that much, but I'll take it in the manner in which it was intended."

Langston's teasing made her smile, but his arms were still locked tight around her, his body covering hers, as though he wanted to still maintain the connection with her, even after the act itself was over.

Her stomach twisted. This couldn't happen. He was behaving as though this meant something, as though this changed things.

"Erik," she said carefully. "I know we just went through an intense time, this morning, but let's not...make this more than what it is."

He froze, lifting his head to look at her. "What?" His incredulity might have been tinged with anger.

Clarissa licked suddenly dry lips. "I'm just saying, I don't want you thinking that this means something more."

"I'm still inside you and you're already giving me the 'let's just be friends' speech?"

Okay, no mistaking the anger that time.

"I didn't say that, exactly, I just—"

"You're trying to pretend this is just physical," he interrupted.

Clarissa heaved a frustrated breath. "It's been a tense few days, Langston. We've been together constantly, in life-and-death situations. It's only natural we'd end up in bed together."

He abruptly pulled back, sitting up on the bed and turning away from her. Clarissa sat up too, grabbing a pillow to shield her nakedness. Suddenly, she didn't want to be vulnerable in front of him.

Langston shoved a hand through his hair and blew out a frustrated sigh. He glanced at her. "So you're going to try and tell me that you bargained for my life because you...what? Were grateful for my help? I don't buy it, Clarissa."

Clarissa squirmed uncomfortably under his steady gaze.

"I don't buy that you don't feel more for me than that. Look at me," he said when her gaze fell. "Look me in the eye and tell me that."

When Clarissa didn't respond, he moved closer, tipping her chin up so she was forced to look at him. His blue eyes seemed to see into her, through her. "Tell me."

"Stop it!" she snapped, jerking away. "Be logical about this, Langston. What do you think is going to happen, can possibly happen, between us? In case you've forgotten, I'm a thief with a hundred-million-dollar bounty on my head. Do you think there's any kind of future for people like me?"

"There can be."

Pain twisted inside Clarissa. Hope. He was offering her hope. Hope was a dangerous thing. Dangerous and ephemeral. Better to believe in fairy tales than hope.

"Then you're even more foolish than I thought," she said quietly.

Langston looked as if she'd hit him, then seemed to recover, his expression turning to cold, hard granite.

"Who are you trying to protect?" he hissed. "Me? Or yourself?"

Then he was gone, disappearing inside the bathroom with a slam of the door.

Clarissa huddled on the bed, her knees to her chest. She'd hurt him. She hadn't meant to, didn't want to. But it was better for him to not be under any illusions now as to how this was going to end.

Tears stung her eyes, and she hurriedly blinked them back. Langston was right, she did care about him. Too much. It terrified her, though she couldn't put her finger on why exactly, just a panicked, twisted feeling on the inside.

Feelings couldn't be trusted, not his or her own. Feelings changed, were fickle, undependable. The only thing that could be trusted was what you had to offer in exchange for loyalty. Right now, Langston needed her to prove his innocence. Once he didn't need her anymore, the tie between them would dissolve, no matter what she felt for him.

No matter how in love she was.

The realization struck her with the force of a sucker punch. She was falling in love with Langston. She would have laughed at the absurdity if she could have drawn a breath.

Langston walked out of the bathroom, a towel wrapped around his lean hips. He ignored her, going to the pile of clothes he'd brought in from the car. Dropping the towel, he pulled on a pair of jeans and a black T-shirt.

Clarissa couldn't take her eyes off him as he dressed. He was beautiful, the muscles in his back and thighs flexing and rippling as he moved. He'd run his fingers through his hair to comb it, the thick, dark strands still damp. His jaw was shadowed again with a day's growth of whiskers.

God, she wished she could keep him.

"I'll be back," he said, heading for the door.

"Wait! Where are you going?" She practically fell off the bed in her haste to stop him. Was he lying? Would he really be back? Or had he finally decided to ditch her? Clarissa didn't stop to examine why the thought of him leaving sent her into such a panic. She didn't want to.

"To find some food," he replied, his voice clipped. His gaze dragged down her body.

Clarissa flushed, wishing she'd kept the pillow as armor. She nervously crossed her arms over her breasts; her nakedness made her too acutely aware of what they'd just done.

His eyes darkened at the gesture and his jaw clenched tight. He stepped into her personal space, forcing her to lift her chin to look at him.

"You can try to shield yourself from me and pretend there's nothing between us but a survival instinct, but I know all about you, Clarissa O'Connell, and a week ago, I would have arrested you without a second thought. But it's too late now. I've seen the good and the bad, your weaknesses and strengths, and I want you in spite of and because of them." He paused, adding more gently, "We've both changed, and there is no changing back."

Then he was gone.

Clarissa rubbed her face, trying to hold it together in the face of what he'd just said. "I have got to get a grip," she muttered to herself. She had grown too dependent on Langston, the words he'd said to her making her chest ache. The thought of him leaving sent her into a tailspin.

She stood in front of the bathroom mirror, inspecting the damage done by Finnegan. She tried not to dwell on how Langston had saved her from him, risking his own life to do so, and how he'd taken care of her when she was too much in shock to do so herself. These feelings she had for him, they did nothing but make her weak. And though he may not agree, any feelings he had for her made him weak too. She knew it even if he refused to acknowledge it.

Maybe he's telling the truth, a little voice whispered inside her head. Maybe it was real, what he'd said.

But it didn't matter if he believed it or not. When feelings dictated actions, there was always a risk. The only thing that could be depended on was someone looking out for their own self-interest. That was a universal truth that applied to everyone, even a man as good and honorable as Langston.

~

Erik placed the tray of food Mrs. Cooper had prepared for him down on the coffee table near the fireplace. The room had a chill in the air, and he could hear the water running in the bathroom. O'Connell would be cold. He flicked the switch on the wall, and the fireplace sprang to life, the flames dancing across the fake logs.

He sank into a chair, resting his elbows on his knees as he stared into the fire. He'd had time to cool off now, and he thought again of what she'd said to him.

The sweat hadn't even dried on their bodies before she was putting an emotional distance between them, demanding he acknowledge that it had meant nothing. At first, he'd been hurt, angry, confused. It had taken stepping back and looking at the situation from the outside in for him to see.

Erik knew a lot about Clarissa O'Connell. He'd been tracking her, studying her, for over a year. Given the dreams she'd shared with him and the time he'd spent with her, he knew even more now.

A woman like her didn't survive the world she inhabited without developing a healthy distrust of everyone and everything. Erik imagined she'd learned that lesson the hard way, and had ingrained the belief that the only person she could count on was herself. Well, she was wrong about that. She wasn't alone, not anymore, and he'd prove that to her... somehow.

And pray her memory didn't return.

The bathroom door opened, and O'Connell stepped out. She was wrapped in a robe, her hair a damp mass of tangles. She eyed him, judging his mood, he supposed.

"Come eat," he said. "You've got to be starving."

She obeyed, coming to sit on the rug in front of the fire. The tray he'd brought held grapes, strawberries, crackers and assorted cheeses, and a bottle of Perrier with two glasses. Erik watched as she perused the selection before making her choices.

Sitting cross-legged, O'Connell munched on her plateful of goodies, absentmindedly running her fingers through the tangles in her hair as she watched the fire.

"Are you angry?"

She spoke so quietly, still staring into the flames, Erik wouldn't have even heard had he not been watching her so intently.

He shook his head. "No."

"Then why aren't you eating?"

"Too busy thinking."

She raised an eyebrow, casting him a sideways glance. "About what we do next?"

"About you."

O'Connell swallowed, then took a drink of water. Erik wondered if she was going to say anything to his straightforward reply.

"It's not worth going hungry over," she finally said. Her pragmatism almost made Erik smile. Ever practical, she wasn't a typical woman, at least not in his experience.

Grabbing a cluster of grapes, she scooted between his spread legs.

"Gotta eat, Langston," she said, leaning to rest against his chest as she held a grape to his lips.

Erik watched her as she fed him, the firelight making her hair appear the shade of the sunset. Regardless of what she'd said earlier, it seemed she didn't want any more space between them than he did, returning with more food when the cluster of grapes was gone.

"So what now?" she asked.

"Now I want you to tell me what I've done to make you not trust me."

O'Connell's body went stiff. After a moment, she tried to draw back, but Erik had a hold of her robe and she didn't get far.

"I'm telling you the truth," he said. "This isn't just sex for me, and I wouldn't be here with you now if I didn't care about you."

"This is pointless," O'Connell said. "It doesn't matter what you feel or what I feel. In the end, I'll be—" She stopped.

"You'll be what?" Erik prompted. She didn't speak. "Dead? Is that what you meant?" He could tell by the resignation in her eyes that he was right, and it made him angry.

"I'm not going to let that happen," he vowed. "I promise you. I won't betray you, and I won't leave you."

"You have to," she insisted. "I won't let you throw your life away trying to save me."

"It's not your decision to make."

O'Connell's eyes searched his.

"Do you believe me?" he asked.

Hesitantly, she nodded, her brow furrowed as though she were in pain.

Erik pulled the tie at her waist, loosening her robe. A brush of his fingers and it fell in a cascade to the floor, baring her to his hungry gaze.

"You're beautiful," he rasped. "And I don't want to be without you. Tell me you feel the same, Clarissa. Tell me I'm not imagining what's between us."

Clarissa felt not only physically naked, but emotionally as well. She was stripped bare to Langston, her innermost fears and hopes laid out for him to see. Hope that, impossibly, this would end and she'd survive...to be with him.

He leaned forward, his lips caressing the line of her jaw. "Tell me," he whispered.

His touch was like a drug, and her eyes slipped closed. She tilted her head to the side, allowing him access to her neck. His hands drifted down her back to her waist.

"I do," she whispered. The words were difficult to get out, like she was making a promise she knew she couldn't keep.

Clarissa felt more than heard his growl of satisfaction, then he pushed her backward, his arm at her back as he gently laid her on the floor. He stripped off his clothes, and Clarissa was captivated by each inch of skin he bared.

Recriminations echoed in the back of her mind, but she ignored them. She wasn't going to throw away a few hours of happiness just because it wouldn't end well. She had no memory of anything else happy—only nightmares. She was entitled to a small bit of happy, dammit. Wasn't she?

Then all thoughts were driven from her mind as she gave herself up to the moment, and to Langston.

~

"...and that was my first fistfight."

Clarissa smiled. "Somehow it doesn't surprise me that you'd risk getting beat up by trying to help the little guy."

Langston shook his head. "I just hated bullies. Still do."

They were lying in the bed underneath the sheets and comforter. The sun was nearing the horizon, and still they lay, propped on their elbows facing each other, talking. Clarissa had a burning desire to know as much about Langston as she could, so she'd gotten him talking, asking questions about his childhood, his career, past girlfriends, his hobbies. The picture she'd drawn in her head from his answers made her heart ache a little.

She'd never actually believed men like him existed.

Between talking and making love, the hours had passed as though they were stolen out of time. And Clarissa knew they were. The clock ticking inside her head told her so.

"I want to go see Raven again tonight," she said.

"Why?"

"I want to know why she betrayed me." That and Raven should know how to reach Solomon, but she didn't say that to Langston.

Langston shook his head. "It's too dangerous."

"We'll be careful." He still didn't look convinced. "Please," she said. "I have to know."

He finally gave in. "All right, but we don't stay long enough for her to warn Solomon. We get out when I say."

"Agreed."

~

Bourbon Street was already busy despite the fact that the night was still young. Erik tucked his gun into the back of his jeans and pulled his shirt down to cover it. O'Connell stood on the sidewalk, waiting for him.

Her jeans were skintight, as was the short-sleeved T-shirt she wore. He took a moment to appreciate the view. Erik didn't want to be taking her into danger again. If it were up to him, he'd have locked her in their room, and he would have gone to confront Raven alone.

As if O'Connell would have let that be an option.

She glanced at him and he gave a curt nod. He followed her into Queens of the Night. The crowd was thicker than last night. Erik trailed O'Connell as she walked up to the bouncer guarding the stairs that led to the top floor.

She asked him a question that Erik couldn't hear, and he shook his head. They exchanged a few more words and he shook his head again. Then O'Connell did something Erik couldn't see, and the guy froze, his face turning white, then a mottled red.

Frowning, Erik looked closer, then grinned. O'Connell had the guy's balls in a viselike grip. Erik couldn't help admiring her guts, not to mention he found it a complete turn-on when she was a badass.

The guy gritted something out at her, his face a grimace of pain, then she let go, turned around, and headed back outside.

"What was that all about?" Erik asked once they were free of the noisy club.

"She's not here."

"Then where is she?"

"It took a little persuasion, but he gave me her home address," she said. "Let's try there."

Getting back in the SUV, they drove to the address. A few blocks up from Bourbon, the house they pulled up to was a two-story redbrick home, the wrought-iron terrace on the second floor giving it French Quarter flair. A large magnolia tree in front lent privacy to the residence, though it was situated right on the street.

Erik parked and they went up the stairs to knock on the door. Before long, the door opened, revealing a man dressed in black slacks and a black T-shirt. Asian in descent, Erik guessed him to be late twenties.

"May I help you?" he asked politely.

"We're looking for Raven," Erik said, flashing his badge. "Is she here?"

The man hesitated, then nodded. "Come in. I'll see if she's available."

He led them into a parlor, the decor quite feminine and akin to the upstairs of Queens of the Night with the antique furniture done in pink pastels and creams.

O'Connell went to a sideboard in the corner where a decanter filled with amber liquid sat. She grabbed a glass and poured herself a drink, downing half of it in one swallow.

"You all right?" Erik asked, concerned.

She gave a curt nod and drank the rest.

"Clarissa! Oh my God!"

Raven rushed into the room, the pink gossamer dressing gown she wore billowing behind her as she ran to O'Connell and threw her arms around her.

"I was so afraid they'd kill you!" she said, her voice choked with tears.

In seconds, O'Connell had Raven on her knees, her arm twisted behind her back, and a knife to her throat. *Where the hell had she gotten a knife?* Erik certainly hadn't given her one.

"You betrayed me," O'Connell said.

"I didn't want to," Raven replied. She was very still, the knife millimeters from her skin. Mascara stained her cheeks, and her eyes were red from crying. "I had no choice."

"Why? You had to have known they'd kill me."

"I swear to you, he told me he wasn't going to kill you, that he just needed you to give him something."

O'Connell's grip tightened on Raven's hair, jerking her head back farther. Erik stiffened.

"You're not stupid," O'Connell hissed. "Solomon can't be trusted."

"It wasn't him!" Raven's eyes were wet now with more tears. "It wasn't Solomon. It was the FBI. I swear."

"The FBI?" Erik asked. "What are you talking about?"

"This man came by two days ago. Wanted to know where you lived. Said I was supposed to call him if you came by."

"And you gave me up, just like that?" Erik winced at the bitterness in her voice. "I thought you were my friend!"

The look in O'Connell's eyes was one he had seen before, and it alarmed Erik. He didn't want her to kill Raven, no matter how she'd been betrayed.

"Mom!"

Erik turned, just in time to catch the teenage boy who'd run into the room, straight for O'Connell. The boy struggled, but Erik held him fast.

"What the hell, Clarissa?" the boy yelled. "What are you doing?"

O'Connell stared wide-eyed at the boy.

"Hush!" Raven commanded. "Jake, stop!"

The boy went still, his chest heaving from his exertions.

"Jake's why, Clarissa," Raven admitted. "I know you don't remember him, but you were teaching him. He loves computers, found you online. It's how we met. The FBI, they threatened to take him away. Said it would be easy to pin something on him, that he'd hacked into something and stolen credit cards, something like that.

"I had no choice," Raven continued, and now tears streaked her face. "Don't you think I knew this was exactly what would happen? If you survived, I knew you'd come looking for me, would kill me. But it was me or my son. I love you, Clarissa, but I'd do anything for my son."

O'Connell hesitated, her eyes lifting to meet Erik's, then dropping to stare at Jake.

"Please don't kill my mom," Jake begged. He was crying now too.

Shit. What a clusterfuck this was turning into.

"She's not going to kill your mom," Erik assured the boy, though he couldn't say for sure whether he believed that. His hands were full holding Jake. Erik didn't think he'd be fast enough to stop O'Connell if she decided to use the knife.

"Don't do it in front of him," Raven said to O'Connell, her voice barely above a whisper. "That's all I ask."

O'Connell gritted out a curse, then abruptly released Raven and sheathed her knife. "I'm not going to kill you," she said.

Raven's eyes slid shut as her body slumped with relief. Erik released Jake, who ran to his mother and threw his arms around her.

Langston sidled up to Clarissa. "So where'd you get the knife?" he asked.

"Try to take it from me and you'll regret it," she said evenly.

Their eyes caught. He didn't look pleased, but neither did he make a move to disarm her.

Raven stood, her arms around Jake, and faced Clarissa. She looked nothing like the self-assured diva of last night.

"I'm so sorry," she said sincerely.

Clarissa wanted to believe her, but she'd been burned too much, so she just nodded.

"Tell me more about this FBI guy," Langston said. "What was his name? Was it Kaminski?"

Raven shook her head. "He said his name was Clarke."

"Clarke?" Clarissa turned to Langston. "Isn't that your boss? I thought you said Kaminski was the mole."

Langston looked momentarily stunned, then his jaw tightened. His eyes were cold when he glanced at her. "I thought he was. Clarke's been after Solomon for years, poured blood, sweat, and tears into this case. I never would have thought he'd sell out." He turned his attention back to Raven.

"Did he say anything else?"

"Just that he wanted Clarissa. It seemed like he had someone he was working with, because when I told him where she lived, he made a call."

Realization struck. "He was the one working with Mendes," Clarissa said. "Not Solomon."

The Asian butler who'd answered the door suddenly appeared, holding a phone.

"Excuse me," he said. "But there's a phone call."

"Later, please, Tom," Raven said.

Tom held the phone out. "It's actually for Miss O'Connell."

Clarissa's every sense went on alert, and she instinctively moved to place herself out of the line of sight through the windows.

"Get down," Langston ordered Jake and Raven, who quickly complied. He hurried to the side of a window, peering slightly around the edge to look outside.

Clarissa accepted the phone from Tom, then took a deep breath.

"Hello?"

"Miss O'Connell, finally. You're a difficult woman to track down."

"Who is this?"

"I believe Raven has told you all about me. My name is Clarke. You know, you would have done me a great favor if you'd just killed her."

Clarissa glanced at Langston and made a motion with her hand, pointing to her eyes, then the room. He nodded that he understood. Someone was indeed watching them.

"Yeah, well, sorry to disappoint you," she said.

"Mendes brought me the accounts," Clarke continued. "While he was very useful at some things, he wasn't always the brightest bulb in the room."

"Was?"

"He's dead now. My temper got a little out of hand when I realized you'd encrypted the files right under his nose."

"Yeah, I can be a real pain in the ass."

Langston shot her a look, and Clarissa shrugged. Maybe antagonizing him would bring him out of the shadows.

"If my agent had done what he was told, I'd have you by now, and we'd be spared all this unpleasantness."

"I'm sure it would've been a real walk in the park for me," Clarissa shot back.

"Tell Agent Langston that I'm looking forward to seeing him again."

The threat sent a chill down Clarissa's spine, and her gaze went to Langston.

"Give me the password," Clarke demanded.

"Yeah, see, here's the thing," Clarissa said. "If I give you the password, you'll empty those accounts, leaving me with no bargaining chip for Solomon. I need that money, so I'm going to have to say no, sorry, you don't get the password."

"I had a feeling you might say that, so *here's the thing*," he mocked her. "Someone like you has very few weaknesses; you're too smart for that. So while there aren't many, I've managed to find one."

A sense of foreboding came over Clarissa. "Oh, really?" she asked, pretending nonchalance. "And what's that?"

"Your brother, of course."

Clarissa's eyes slipped closed. Dammit. How had he gotten Danny? All this work she'd supposedly done for Solomon, and now a crooked Fed had her brother.

"So here's what's going to happen," Clarke continued. "You're going to meet me tomorrow at the Oak Alley plantation along the river road. Alone. You'll transfer the money to me, and in return, I'll hand over your brother."

"This could all be a bluff," Clarissa argued. "How do I know you really have him? Solomon was supposed to get him."

Clarke laughed. "So clever. All right, you want proof, hold on."

Clarissa held her breath. Would he put Danny on the phone? How would she even know if it was really him? She couldn't remember anything. Her hand clenched in a fist at her side, her unseeing gaze on Langston as she waited. Finally, a voice came on the line.

"Rissa?"

The nickname went through her like an electric shock and her knees gave out. She slid to the floor, her head swimming.

And she remembered.

EPISODE EIGHT

CHAPTER FIFTEEN

*S*he'd told him not to do it.

The heist was too dangerous, too unpredictable, and the stakes too high. But as usual, Danny ignored her. The payoff had proven irresistible, though Clarissa had been leery of Danny getting involved with such a well-known and infamous crime boss as Solomon.

She'd followed him that day, just in case Danny got himself into a jam he couldn't talk or fight his way out of. Little did he know that she'd helped him from the shadows on more than a few occasions. His arrogance knew no bounds, and she was afraid he'd overestimated himself with this job.

She'd been right.

Chased by cops, Danny had nearly gotten away. Then he'd pulled a gun.

Clarissa had watched in horror as Danny fell to the ground, the cop's bullet striking him in the chest. She'd been too far away to help, not that she could have done anything anyway. She wasn't going to sign her death warrant by getting into a gun battle with the cops.

Danny had survived the gunshot wound, only to be sent to prison.

Clarissa had felt cast adrift and had moved away to New Orleans. Her every move had been orchestrated and dictated by her brother since she was a young girl. It felt strange not to have that anymore, not to have anyone anymore.

For the first time in her life, she took a legitimate job. Writing software from home for a tech company based in California. It had felt good to not be looking over her shoulder constantly. To not be under the constant strain of wondering which of their so-called partners would turn on them, rat them out, blow the job.

Then the phone call had come. Solomon had a proposition for her, an offer she couldn't refuse. Not if she wanted to ever see her brother again. That's when Clarissa knew. She'd only been living in a fantasy world. It didn't matter what she wanted or what she did, she'd never be able to escape her past or the people who wanted to use her.

A year. An entire year of her life she'd given, trying to fulfill Solomon's demands while he kept his promise of freeing Danny dangling on a string. Each job was harder than the last and more dangerous. She'd lost count of all the close calls she'd had, barely escaping death or capture.

The assassin sent by Solomon to kill her after that last job in Colorado was proof that he'd never planned on living up to his side of the bargain. Luckily, Clarissa had already decided to take back control of her life, even knowing it would likely seal her fate.

She'd die, that hadn't changed, but it would be on her terms.

~

Erik glanced at O'Connell as he drove. She hadn't said much since they'd left Raven's house. Even now, she sat in silence, staring out the window.

Not that he could blame her.

The scene with Raven was still fresh in his mind, her absolute certainty that O'Connell would kill her bothering him more than he wanted to admit. Yes, O'Connell was dangerous, but not unreasonable. Not the O'Connell that he knew, anyway.

But what about the O'Connell he didn't know? Would she have killed Raven?

Erik refused to believe that. O'Connell believed Raven had betrayed her, sent killers to trap and murder her. He could understand why she'd reacted the way she had. Betrayal was the flip side of loyalty. Those who felt great loyalty would also feel the deepest of betrayals. And if there was one thing that defined O'Connell, it was loyalty. She'd been loyal to a fault with her brother. What she'd done, had endured, because of him was astonishing. And sad.

"So when are you supposed to meet Clarke?" he asked.

"Sunrise tomorrow at a plantation outside the city. Alone."

Erik frowned at her curt reply, glancing her way again, but she refused to meet his eyes.

"Well, obviously you're not going alone," he said. That got a reaction.

"Obviously?"

"I'm not going to let you walk in there by yourself so he can kill you." That fact seemed pretty damn obvious to Erik.

"It's not like we can call the cops or the FBI for backup," O'Connell argued. "We have no proof that Clarke is behind this, and if they see you, they'll arrest you."

"You're not going alone."

"He wants to exchange the money for Danny," O'Connell said. "And I know he has him. I spoke to him."

"How are you planning on getting the money to him when you can't remember how to do it?" Erik asked in exasperation.

O'Connell shrugged and turned away again. "I'll figure something out."

"Winging it with someone like Clarke is going to get you killed," Erik said. "He's got nothing to lose at this point. If he doesn't get that money, he'll kill you *and* your brother. And even if, somehow, you get the money to him, he's still likely to kill you both."

"I have to take that chance."

O'Connell's determination to throw her life away for Danny made Erik want to yell and pound the steering wheel in frustration.

"Someone's following us."

"What?" Erik glanced in the rearview mirror.

"That black sedan's been three cars back ever since we left Raven's."

Erik frowned, looking again in the mirror. There was a turn up ahead and he made it, watching to see if the sedan followed. It did.

"We need to lose them," O'Connell said.

"No shit." Nothing like stating the obvious.

"Don't get snippy," she retorted. "Give me your gun."

"No way," Erik said. "You're not just going to start shooting at people until we know who they are and what they want."

"Because *that's* worked out so well before."

Her sarcasm grated on him, and it wasn't because she was right, dammit.

"When you're with me, you've got to play by my rules," he said.

O'Connell snorted and rolled her eyes. Erik ignored her.

Erik stomped on the gas, and the car shot forward. He maneuvered carefully between cars, enduring more than his fair share of honks and middle fingers flipped his way.

"They're getting closer," O'Connell said. She was twisted around in her seat now, watching behind them.

"Here, you drive," Erik said.

"What? Why?"

"In case we do have to start shooting; I have a badge and you don't," he explained.

"Fine. But for the record, I'm a better shot than you are."

"For your information, I was the youngest kid awarded the rifle shooting merit badge in my troop," Erik said, holding the wheel as she climbed across him.

"Is that supposed to impress me?"

"Just enough to get you back into my bed." She took over the gas pedal and Erik slid out from underneath her.

"It takes more than fancy shooting," she said loftily, making a sharp turn.

Erik was thrown against the door. "Would you warn me before you do that?"

"It's a car chase! What do you expect?" She laid into the horn, cutting off any retort Erik might have made.

"Can you let them get close enough so I can see who they are?"

"Sure," she said. "Just don't get shot."

Without warning, O'Connell stomped on the brakes and did an illegal U-turn. Horns honked around them and tires squealed. Erik was flung against the door again, then back as she gunned it.

"Out your side," she said.

Erik looked out his window and saw they were now speeding toward the sedan in a game of chicken. At the last second, O'Connell swerved and they skimmed the side of the car, missing it by inches. Erik got a good look at the man driving.

"It's Kaminski," he said.

"Who?"

"My partner."

"I thought you two broke up?" O'Connell swerved down a side street, made three more turns in rapid succession, and lost him.

"We didn't 'break up,'" Erik said. "We just don't work well together."

"So why is he here?"

"No idea."

"You thought he might be the mole, but it turns out Clarke is," O'Connell reminded him.

"I know, but he's here." Erik glanced at her. "They might be working together."

"Or maybe he's your partner and you've been missing for days and he's trying to find you," she said.

"What an uncharacteristically charitable thought from you, O'Connell," Erik said.

She shrugged. "Guess your bleeding heart is rubbing off on me."

They spent the rest of the car ride in silence until she parked in the lot at the bed-and-breakfast, and Erik took O'Connell's elbow as they went upstairs to their room. Mrs. Cooper had thoughtfully left a tray of cold sandwiches for them. Despite their appearance upon arrival, it seemed she thought this was a romantic getaway. Erik noted the bottle of wine and two glasses also on the table.

He sat on the loveseat, bracing his elbows on his knees and steepling his hands under his chin. He observed O'Connell. She seemed strung out with nervous energy, pacing the room, picking up knickknacks here and there before putting them back down again. Erik wasn't sure she even realized she was doing it.

"Do you think Kaminski knows what Clarke is planning?" she asked.

"I don't know."

"If he's Clarke's backup, he's definitely planning to kill me," she said.

"Which is why you need me there."

"We've been through this—" she began.

"He won't know I'm there unless he makes a move on you," Erik interrupted. "I just want to protect you."

For a moment, he thought she didn't hear him. Then she spoke.

"Danny is a convicted criminal, Langston," she said, finally ceasing her pacing as she stared into the flames dancing in the fireplace. "You're an FBI agent. Even if things do go according to plan, are you just going to let him walk away?"

The question gave him pause. O'Connell was nobody's fool. She knew him well enough by now to know he'd want to follow the law and put Danny right back where he'd come from. But he also knew that if he did that, she'd never stay with him. She'd understand that he had to do what he had to do, but she'd leave.

He took a deep breath. "I would," he said. "For you."

O'Connell's gaze snapped to his.

"If the only way I won't lose you is by letting your brother go free, then that's what I'll do," he said.

A breath of silence passed as he waited to hear what she'd say.

"You'd let him go?" she asked, disbelief edging her words. "Just like that? When you know what he's done?"

Erik got up and went to her. "I promise you," he said.

She searched his eyes, her brow furrowing. "You're lying."

"I'm not, I swear to you." He cupped her jaw in his palm, his thumb brushing gently over her cheek. Her skin was satin soft. "Look in my eyes. I'll let him go. Trust me."

"You don't want to be with me, Langston," O'Connell said softly. "Even if Clarke keeps his word, I still have a target on my back. Solomon will never stop looking for that money, only now I won't have it to give back to him. You've got to know that."

Her eyes were blue pools of sadness and resignation. It made Erik ache inside to see her hopelessness.

"I don't care. We'll find a way. I'll protect you." Even if it was the last thing he did, he silently vowed.

God help her, Clarissa believed him.

She shouldn't. She knew enough, remembered enough, to know that everyone lied. Even her, as she stood there in front of Langston. He was putting everything on the line, baring his soul to her, and she couldn't even bring herself to tell him that she remembered. She remembered everything.

And what would he say if he knew? Would he tell her the truth? The truth he'd been hiding all along?

The weight of the world felt as though it rested on her shoulders, and Clarissa thought with some chagrin, no wonder she'd lost her memory. Her life was empty, tragic, pointless. Who would want to remember it, if given the opportunity? Hell, *she* didn't even want to remember, though she no longer had any choice.

No choice but to remember all the bad decisions, the left turns when she should have turned right, the times she'd said yes when she should've said no. Maybe if she'd said no, she might be worthy of this man standing in front of her, looking at her as though she meant more to him than his next breath.

"I'm not worth it," she managed to whisper. Tears clogged her throat, but she swallowed them down. Clarissa O'Connell did not cry. Ever. A fact she'd forgotten along with everything else. Tears showed weakness, and she wasn't weak.

"That's bullshit," Langston said fiercely.

"You—" Her voice broke and she swallowed again. "You don't know what I've done."

"I know everything you've done," he said, "and none of it matters. Not to me. Not anymore."

Well. The only correct response to that was for Clarissa to wrap her arms around his neck and pull him down for a kiss.

The same desperation Clarissa had felt at her house when she'd kissed Langston filled her again, only this time, she knew why that clock inside her head was ticking. It had nothing to do with Solomon and everything to do with her. Because once Langston found out what she planned to do, he wouldn't feel this way about her anymore.

He cared about a woman who didn't exist, a woman with no memory of her misdeeds or knowledge of exactly how far she'd go.

One more time. One last time. To be with him, to know how it felt to be cherished, protected, cared for above all others.

And one last chance to show him in return.

Clarissa unbuttoned his shirt without breaking their kiss. Their mouths melded together as though they couldn't get close enough. She memorized his taste, the texture of his lips against hers, the feel of his arms holding her.

His chest was warm and hard to the touch. Her palms skated over his abdomen, the muscles there contracting at the light brush of her fingers. Langston's belt was a minor hindrance, quickly done away with, then she was unbuttoning his jeans and lowering the zipper.

He groaned against her lips when she freed him from the denim, heavy and hard in her light grip. Pulling back, she dropped to her knees in front of him. Before he could say or do anything, she had touched her tongue to his cock, a slow lick that made Langston hiss between his teeth.

Clarissa looked up at him. The firelight danced off the skin of his chest, bared from his open shirt, and his eyes smoldered with molten heat.

"Watch me," she said, though the order seemed unnecessary. It didn't look like he was even blinking.

Clarissa slowly took him in her mouth, her hand wrapped around the base of his cock. She relaxed her throat, taking in as much of him as possible. The sweet tang of his skin, the slightly musky scent of his body, the sight of him watching her do this to him, all of it filled her senses. The flesh between her thighs grew warm and aching.

Langston had gone commando today, and Clarissa could only give thanks to the gods above as she cupped his perfect ass in her palms. She'd willingly pray at the altar of his body all night long.

His breath was coming in pants, his hips thrusting into her mouth as she encouraged him, moaning around his cock. And still, he watched her, their eyes locked together.

Clarissa's arousal was at a fever pitch, her body humming with desire. She quickly undid her jeans, slipping a hand inside.

"No," Langston gasped, pulling away. In seconds, he was down on the floor with her, tugging off her jeans. "You'll come with me inside you."

He wasn't going to get an argument from her. Her shirt was ripped over her head and flung aside. Langston pulled her astride his lap, thrusting inside her.

Clarissa gasped while Langston moaned. Their tongues tangled in a heated kiss before Clarissa pulled away, panting for breath.

She placed her hands on his chest and pushed until he lay flat on the floor. Reaching behind her back, she undid her bra and let it slide down her arms. She rose and fell on him, his thick length filling her. His hips took up her rhythm, stroking between her legs until she cried out, convulsing around him.

Langston's hands bit into her hips as she lay on top of him, thrusting hard into her already swollen flesh.

"Come again for me, Clarissa," he ground out.

Her body was too sensitive and she wanted to get away, but he wouldn't let her, the pressure unrelenting until, unbelievably, she felt her body tighten again.

"Erik! Oh God!" she sobbed, splintering apart.

Langston gave a muffled shout, jerking hard into her, his orgasm prolonging hers, perfectly in sync, until she couldn't tell his body from her own.

O'Connell lay against his chest, her body boneless and slight. Erik had released her hips and now his hands moved up and down her back, lightly stroking her skin. She seemed impossibly small for all she was capable of.

She was unlike any woman he'd ever known. Feisty, incredibly smart, fearless, loyal, independent. Yes, she was also a thief and wanted woman, but that didn't matter anymore. They'd find a way out of this mess, and when it was all over, nothing would stop them from being together.

O'Connell lifted her head to look at him and smiled a slow, sexy smile. The surge of possessiveness that filled Erik took him by surprise. He felt almost caveman in the way it was nearly a physical need to hold her close.

He cupped her cheek, his fingers threading through her hair. She closed her eyes, tipping her head into his palm. The sight made his chest constrict.

"Clarissa," he said, his voice rough. She opened her eyes. "I love you." The words seemed to fall out of their own accord, but Erik realized it was true. Somehow, he'd fallen in love with the one woman he never would have suspected.

O'Connell's smile faded and her face paled under his hand. Her eyes were wide but her voice steady as she said, "Don't get sappy on me, Langston."

Before, those words would have angered him. Now he knew fear prompted them.

"It's true," he said. "And I know you're afraid, but that's okay."

"Don't be ridiculous," she snapped, pulling away. In moments, she was off him entirely. "I'm not afraid of any-thing."

Erik was on his feet now, and he grabbed her arm, pre-venting her from escaping him. "That's not quite true, is it? You're afraid of letting someone in, of letting me in." Some-thing was different with her. Something was off. It nagged at him, but he pushed the thought aside.

Her eyes shot daggers at him. "I don't take kindly to being held against my will, Langston," she said. "Let me go."

"I love you, Clarissa," he said. "And I'm not going any-where."

She moved then, so fast Erik didn't even have time to react. One second, he had her by the arm, the next he was flat on the floor, eating carpet.

Ow.

Erik couldn't decide what was worse, the damage she'd just inflicted on his body or his ego.

"I warned you," she said coolly.

Erik turned over onto his back. He had a brief satisfac-tion at seeing O'Connell's eyes flick down his naked body. She swallowed, then hurriedly glanced back to his face.

"See something you like?" he asked, bending an elbow behind his head.

Her lips twitched slightly. She arched a brow and put a hand on her hip. "Not turned off by a girl that just laid you out flat, Langston?"

Oooh, he loved it when she got all badass. He felt his body stir. "Not in the slightest," he replied honestly.

Her gaze flicked downward again and she licked her lips. That got a reaction, and he bit back a groan. But damn, the floor was hard and uncomfortable.

Erik got to his feet, aware of her watching him, and tried not to preen at the frank admiration in her eyes. Preening was not manly.

He stalked her, their eyes locked, until she had to retreat. O'Connell stopped when she hit the bed, and Erik drew close until he just touched her. Her breath caught in her chest and her pupils dilated.

"I'd appreciate it," he said softly, "if you refrained from kicking my ass for a few hours."

"My, what stamina," O'Connell teased, her eyes now glinting with desire instead of fear.

"You have no idea."

~

Clarissa took a moment to gaze at Langston. He was sacked out in the bed, the sheet pulled barely to his waist. And well he should be exhausted. The last few hours had been amazing.

Their last few hours.

With an inward sigh, Clarissa tied her shoelaces, hesitating before she grabbed Langston's jacket and slid her arms into the sleeves. She dropped his keys and his cell phone into the pocket then looked around to make sure she had everything.

"What are you doing?"

Langston's question made her spin around even as her heart fell. Damn. She'd been hoping to get out while he was still sleeping.

"O'Connell, what's going on?" He went to sit up, but was brought up short by the handcuff around his wrist, binding him to the heavy, wooden bedpost. "What the hell is this?"

"It's time for me to go," she said, careful to keep her voice matter-of-fact. "Sunrise is in a few hours."

"Why the fuck am I handcuffed?" he fumed.

"Isn't it obvious? You can't come with me, Langston."

"What are you talking about? We agreed—"

"No," she cut him off. "I didn't agree. It's time to finish what I started. And you can't come."

He looked at her, studying her, then his lips pressed into a thin line. "How long?" he bit out. "How long have you had your memory back?"

Clarissa met his angry gaze unflinchingly. "Since the phone call with Danny."

Langston looked stunned, but he recovered quickly. "So you know how to recover the money? You remember how?"

She nodded.

"That's great," he seemed to force out. "Uncuff me. I'll come with you, have your back."

Clarissa just looked at him. "There's no good reason for me to do that," she said, "and so many reasons not to."

Langston froze, his eyes darting to hers. "What do you mean?"

"Your promise," she said. "Your promise to let Danny go."

He didn't say anything.

Clarissa's lips felt almost frozen as she forced out the words. "Did you think I wouldn't remember? Is that why you didn't tell me?"

A silence that was too oppressive filled the air between them.

"I don't know—"

"Don't lie to me!" she exploded. "You know *exactly* what I'm talking about. Did you think I wouldn't remember the circumstances of Danny's arrest? That I wouldn't put two and two together?"

He still just stared at her.

"Did you think I wouldn't find out that my brother is the one who killed your partner?"

Langston said nothing.

Clarissa gave a slight shrug, despair like a living thing inside her. "Maybe you meant it, what you said about letting him go. I don't know. But either way, I can't take that chance. The chance that you were lying…or that you were telling the truth."

He frowned in confusion. "What—"

"If you let the guy go who killed your partner, you won't be able to live with yourself, Langston," she said. "Eventually, you'd regret it. You'd resent me for being the reason you let his murderer go. I'm not going to let that happen." She paused. "Or you'll resent the fact that you never followed through with your original plan. You know, the one where you avenge your partner's murder by putting the killer's sister behind bars. Or was it in the grave?"

That finally got a reaction.

"I was never going to kill you."

His tacit admission that she was right sent a shaft of pain through Clarissa. Even after knowing what she now knew, she'd hoped, somehow, that she was wrong. Her eyes closed involuntarily.

"Listen, please," he said. "Yes, I was obsessed with you because of what Danny did. I was going to put you behind bars no matter how long it took. But things changed. And at first it didn't matter what you knew or didn't know about me, and then it became too late to say anything. I wanted you to trust me."

Clarissa grudgingly admitted that she could see that. When would have been a good time for him to say, "Oh, by the way, your brother killed my friend and partner, so I've been hunting you down to punish him." She would have felt betrayed and lied to no matter what. And if he'd told her that from the beginning, she never would have trusted him.

"Look at me."

Clarissa opened her eyes. Langston was staring at her, his imprisoned hand clenched in a fist.

"I got to know you, who you really are, and I realized you're not who I thought you were."

"You don't know me," Clarissa snapped. "You know a girl who doesn't exist, who lost her memory, who had no idea what she was."

Langston was calm as he asked, "And what is that?"

"Someone without a future."

O'Connell picked up Erik's gun, expertly ejecting the magazine to check that it was fully loaded before slamming it back in place. She tucked it into the small of her back under his coat.

"Why are you taking my gun?" Erik asked, a sense of foreboding coming over him.

"The only way out of this is to kill Clarke and give Solomon back the money, once I have Danny."

Alarm shot through Erik. "You can't do that," he said. "Crooked or not, he's a federal agent. If you get caught, they'll bury you. And if Kaminski is there, he'll shoot you no matter whose side he's on."

She shrugged, not even looking his way as she gathered up her clothes into a small stack.

"Just…tell me why," Erik said. "Tell me why you'd want your brother out of prison. He killed someone. My partner. He had a wife, a kid, a family."

O'Connell's movements faltered. She was listening.

"He deserves to be in jail," Erik continued. "Why would you help him escape that?"

She finally looked at him. Her face was stark white. "Because he's my brother," she said so quietly he had to strain to hear her. "I owe it to him."

"You owe him *nothing*," Erik gritted out, unable to suppress the hatred he felt for Danny. "He's used you for years, and he's still using you from inside a prison cell. He's in prison because of *his* mistakes, not yours. You don't owe him anything, much less your life. Don't you see that?"

"He's all I have, Langston." Fear underlined her words.

"That's not true. I swear to you that's not true," Erik said. "You have me. Uncuff me and I'll prove it. I'll have your back. I won't betray you. I can help you out of this without anyone getting hurt."

"No one can do that," she said, going to pick up her sack. "You'd just get killed, and even though you lied to me, I don't want that."

When she faced him again, her face was unreadable. "I'll call the FBI. Tell them I left you here, that I'm responsible for those men being killed. That should clear you." She headed for the door.

His time was up.

"No! O'Connell, don't you dare walk out that door," he warned. He pulled at the handcuff, the metal biting into his wrist as she ignored him. "Trust me—I can help you— O'Connell!" His desperation finally seemed to make her pause halfway out the door. "Please," he begged. "Please don't do this. He'll kill you."

"Not if I kill him first. Have a nice life, Langston."

Then she was gone.

CHAPTER SIXTEEN

Blood seeped from the cuts in Erik's wrist, sluggishly trailing down his arm as he pulled with all his strength, trying to snap the bedpost. But no matter how hard he tried, it remained firm; only a telltale creak indicated he'd even bent the wood.

The tester bed had a wooden roof, for lack of a better term, that sat atop the four posts. Erik had tried standing on the mattress and lifting it off, but it was fastened tight and nothing he did would budge it.

O'Connell had left him strung up pretty damn good.

She'd remembered. She'd known the entire time they'd made love that he'd lied to her.

Dammit, he couldn't think about that right now. He had to concentrate, get out of here, save her.

The phone was across the room, so he couldn't call anyone. No one else was on this floor, so there was no one to hear him yell for help. By the time Mrs. Cooper came in the morning, it would be all over for O'Connell.

Sunrise was only four hours away.

Erik stared at the cuff, thinking. O'Connell had picked her way out of these. They'd even taught him at the academy how to do it so he'd be aware of how a prisoner might escape. But what could he use as a pick?

The only thing close by was the lamp on the bedside table. Seeing it sparked a memory of an old *Mythbusters* episode he'd watched. Erik grabbed the lamp and pulled off the shade. Thank God. Mrs. Cooper hadn't gotten around to changing her old-style incandescent bulbs for the fluorescent kind.

Carefully cracking the glass bulb on the table, Erik removed the wire supporting the fragile filament. It was a strong enough gauge for what he needed.

It took him an embarrassingly long time to pick the lock, especially considering how quickly O'Connell could do it, and it was nearly an hour before Erik was finally free.

He dressed and called a cab, hurrying downstairs to wait for it. All O'Connell had said about where she was meeting Clarke was that it was a plantation. There were a dozen or more plantations outside New Orleans, and Erik had no idea which one was the right one. But he knew someone who might.

~

Clarissa sat in the SUV, the glow from her laptop's screen illuminating the car. She'd turned on Langston's phone and tethered her laptop to its Internet connection. It was slow, but it worked.

Her fingers flew over the keys as she typed, commands scrolling on the screen as she wrote the code to transfer the money she'd "borrowed" into one account.

She could still smell him on her skin.

Her keystrokes faltered.

No. She couldn't think about him. Special Agent Erik Langston was a part of the past now. Thinking about him would only make her hesitate, second-guess herself, and that could get her killed.

Clarissa stared out the window as she waited for the transactions to go through. Regrets consumed her. Regrets for the path she'd taken, the choices she'd made. Granted, she hadn't had much choice when Danny had first brought her to America, but she'd stayed with him, continued to help him in one get-rich-quick job after another. He would've ended up in jail long ago if she hadn't been there, though that was a fact Danny never seemed to appreciate.

Just like now. Langston was right. Danny should be in jail. Clarissa had always told him that if he killed an innocent bystander on a job, she'd leave. She wouldn't go through what had happened to their dad.

But if she let him go back to jail, what would she do then?

Then you'd finally be free.

The thought sprang into her mind, and she immediately felt guilty for even thinking that, however briefly. Danny was her brother. He'd taken care of her since she was small. She owed him her loyalty.

But not her life.

Dammit! This was all Langston's fault! If he hadn't said all those things, she wouldn't be thinking them now.

But look at all she'd sacrificed!

The past year had been hell.

∽

"If you're going to do this, then you must be trained." Solomon lectured her as she stood in front of the polished oak desk behind which he sat, fingers steepled on his chest, observing her. "Your self-defense training isn't enough. You'll be on your own, many times surrounded by people, men, wanting to kill you."

Gee, that sounded fantastic, she thought ruefully, though she was careful to keep her face blank.

"I have someone, an expert in these sorts of things, he'll train you in hand-to-hand combat, weapons, the tools you'll need to succeed in your task."

She'd had no choice in the matter, not really. Not that training from an expert was a bad thing. Clarissa was always willing to find more ways to help her stay alive and one step ahead. What she hadn't counted on was the pain.

Her body hit the mat for the umpteenth time and she groaned, sweat making her tank stick to her body.

"You think too much," Jaleel said. "You need to react instinctually. Your pauses give your enemy opportunity."

He wasn't even breathing hard, Clarissa thought sourly as she peeled herself off the floor.

Jaleel used to be Mossad, or so she'd gathered from what little he'd told her of himself when he wasn't kicking her ass.

It took weeks of training, but eventually she held her own against Jaleel as he taught her the finer points of hand-to-hand combat, the many varied ways to kill someone up close and personal, and how to shoot over a dozen different guns, timing her loading and firing them until he was satisfied that it was second nature to her.

Clarissa had been grateful for his unrelenting training on her first job, when she'd been cornered by two armed guards. They'd tried to take her prisoner. They'd failed.

The transactions had finished and now the cursor flashed expectantly at her, dragging Clarissa from her memories. There was nothing to wait for anymore, no reason to not head to the meeting place. She closed the laptop and set it aside, slumping down in the seat and staring sightlessly out the window at the empty street.

She wondered if Langston had found a way out of his cuffs yet. He was a resourceful kind of guy. Clarissa doubted he'd stayed bound for long.

God, she missed him already.

Her body was sore in the best possible way after the things he'd done to her. She shivered, remembering. But it was the things he'd said that made her stomach twist inside.

Had Langston been telling the truth? Did he really love her? He'd lied by omission to her, not telling her the truth about how his partner had died. Other than that, he'd never lied, not once.

Maybe, just maybe, he really did love her. And if he did, how did she feel about him?

That wasn't a hard question to answer, though she shied away from putting a name to it. She'd never felt this way about anyone before, and now that her memory was back, that statement held weight.

Okay, change of plan. She wouldn't kill Clarke. She'd give him the money in exchange for Danny, but then she'd tell Danny it was over. Her debt to him was paid.

Once she was rid of both Clarke and Danny, she'd find Langston, turn state's witness, and help him put Solomon behind bars. Then maybe they could be together. If he wasn't still totally pissed off at her leaving him handcuffed to a bed.

Well, there were ways to make up for that.

A sudden movement outside her window startled her. A man stood outside. He had a gun pointed at her head.

"FBI. Get out of the car."

Shit.

∼

Tom answered the door again despite the lateness of the hour, his expression wary as he surveyed Erik standing on the front step.

"I'm not here to hurt her," Erik clarified. "I just need to speak to her."

Tom still looked skeptical, but he allowed Erik in the door. "Wait here," he said, leaving Erik in the foyer.

It took a good fifteen minutes before Raven appeared, and Erik paced while he waited, the minutes crawling by with agonizing slowness. Where was O'Connell? Was she somewhere still in the city, close to him?

"What do you want?" Raven asked, tying her satin ivory dressing gown closed. Her tone was not exactly friendly.

"I need your help," Erik said.

"Why would you think I'd help you? I was nearly killed because you brought Clarissa here."

"I didn't know she was going to do that," Erik said. "But you said yourself, it wasn't unexpected. You knew she would come. Just like you knew she wouldn't kill you."

Raven didn't reply, but Erik knew he was right.

"You know she isn't a cold-blooded killer," he continued. "Even if your son hadn't been there, you knew she wouldn't kill you. So don't pull this martyr crap with me. I need your help. *She* needs your help."

"Fine," Raven capitulated. "But you realize you led another FBI agent to me."

"What do you mean?"

"He came by shortly after you left earlier. Said his name was Kaminski and that you were his partner. Wanted to know if I knew where you were."

"What did you tell him?"

She shrugged. "I told him the truth, that I had no idea where you two were staying. But he seemed to think that you were being held against your will by Clarissa."

Well, that was a little demoralizing, Kaminski thinking a girl could keep him hostage for days on end. *She probably could*, a little voice reminded him. Whatever.

"Did he say anything else?"

Raven shook her head. "No. He made a phone call to someone as he left, something about tracking, but I didn't hear all that was said."

"He must be trying to track my cell phone," Erik said. He'd turned it off days ago, but O'Connell had taken it. Surely she'd know not to turn it on? But then why would she have taken it?

"Where's Clarissa?" Raven asked, interrupting his thoughts.

"That's what I need your help to find out." Erik explained the deal she'd made with Clarke and what she planned to do. "If I don't find her, Clarke is going to kill her. He's too deep into this to leave any loose ends."

"How am I supposed to help you find her?"

"You know how to reach Solomon, don't you?" With Raven's ties to the underworld, it was a gamble Erik hoped paid off.

"I can't reach him directly," she said, "but I know where his headquarters are in the city."

"Good enough."

"You can't just go walking in there," Raven protested. "An FBI agent? They'll kill you on sight."

"I have to take that chance," Erik said. "I don't have any other choice."

"Why?" Raven asked, her eyes narrowing. "Why would you do that? Are you so set on arresting Clarissa that you'd risk your own life?"

"I don't want to arrest her," Erik said. He took a breath. Raven was unlikely to help him if she didn't know the truth. "I love her."

His declaration seemed to momentarily stun Raven as she stared, open-mouthed, at him.

"Please," he said. "I can't lose her. Help me."

Raven's mouth shut with a snap. "Follow me," she said.

He followed her into the same room they'd been in before. She went to a table in the corner and wrote something down on a slip of paper, which she handed to him.

"You'll find them there. Ask for Liam. Tell him Raven sent you." She opened a nearby drawer and handed Erik a gun. "You may need this," she said.

Erik gratefully took the address and gun from her. "Thank you. And…I need one more thing."

Raven raised a brow in question.

"Can I borrow your car?"

~

Clarissa was thrown none too gently against the car and frisked. Kaminski found Langston's gun and took it from her before cuffing her wrists behind her back. She was spun around again to face a furious FBI agent.

"This is my partner's gun," he gritted out. "And you were using his phone, which, coincidentally, is how I found you. Now where the hell is he?" He moved in close to her face. "Did you kill him?" he hissed. "Just like you did those other agents?"

"Kaminski," Clarissa said as realization struck. "You're Kaminski."

"That's right. And I'm pretty fucking pissed that my partner has been missing for days. You'd better tell me right now what you did to him, or you may have an unfortunate accident while resisting arrest."

Clarissa swallowed. The rage in his eyes and menace in his voice were real. Although Langston had indicated that he and Kaminski weren't particularly close, it seemed that didn't really matter when it came to life-and-death situations.

"I know your brother killed Langston's old partner," Kaminski continued, "and that Langston put him in jail for it. So what did you do? Kill him for revenge?" He suddenly grabbed her by the throat and squeezed. "You fucking bitch," Kaminski snarled. "If he's dead, I promise you, you won't live another day."

Clarissa struggled to force words out, the pressure on her throat making it hard to breathe. "I didn't...kill him," she managed. The grip on her throat loosened slightly. "He's fine. I swear. I didn't kill him."

"You'd better be telling me the truth," Kaminski said. "Or you're going to regret it."

He released his hold on her and Clarissa doubled over, coughing and sucking in air. Kaminski yanked her upright. "Let's go."

~

The address Raven had given him was for a high-end club on the outskirts of the French Quarter. The interior was very dim, obscuring the faces of those who sat in the leather booths lining the walls. A small stage in the corner held a jazz trio, the smooth sound they made filling the room.

Erik felt the stares of people watching him as he went to the bar. The bartender wore a black shirt and slacks with a gray vest and black bow tie.

"What can I get you?" he asked.

"I'm looking for Liam," Erik replied.

"What do you want Liam for?"

The question came from behind, and Erik turned to see two big guys flanking him. They stood close enough to block his exit should he try to leave.

"That's really between me and Liam," Erik said.

"Liam doesn't take well to people just dropping by," one of them said.

"Raven sent me."

The one who'd spoken to Erik narrowed his eyes. "Did she, now? Well, let's go see if Liam wants to see you." He turned away and the other guy gave Erik a shove to follow.

They walked through the club into the back until they stopped in front of a closed door. After knocking, the head guy opened the door and they walked inside. The room was a spacious office, the kind you'd find in any high-rise downtown.

Before Erik could get a good look, he was spun around and searched. They found his wallet and Raven's gun, which they took and gave to someone behind him.

"FBI Special Agent Erik Langston."

Erik turned. "That's me."

"To what do we owe the honor of your presence?" The slightly mocking words were said by the man seated behind the desk. His gaze was shrewd as he observed Erik. Lean and long-limbed, he was dressed impeccably in a tailored suit.

"I have some important information for your boss."

Liam's smile was as cold as his eyes. "I am the boss, Mr. Langston. And you're either incredibly brave or incredibly stupid to come here."

Erik didn't wait for an invitation and sat in one of the chairs in front of the desk. "I'm on a tight schedule," he said, "so let's cut the bullshit."

Liam wasn't smiling now, reminding Erik of the very dangerous gamble he was taking. Worst-case scenario, Liam wouldn't have any knowledge of Solomon's dealings with O'Connell. If that was the case, well, it wasn't going to end well.

"I know your boss has a very important project going on," Erik continued. "And I know he hired Clarissa O'Connell to do it. But she double-crossed him, took a lot of his money. And in two hours, she'll give it to someone else." He paused. "I can help you. She trusts me."

Liam's eyes narrowed. "You seem to know an awful lot, but yet are ignorant of a very important fact," he said.

"And what's that?"

"Clarissa's been captured by the FBI."

Erik couldn't hide his surprise.

Liam stood and rounded the desk to Erik. "Apparently your partner tracked her down. I do believe he thinks she murdered you."

"He won't hurt her," Erik said, hoping it was true. Agents took it very personally when one of their own was involved. Kaminski wasn't the best rule follower, which had been another reason he and Erik hadn't clicked.

Liam laughed. "The question, Mr. Langston, isn't whether he'll hurt her, but whether she'll hurt him."

~

Clarissa fished the keys out of Kaminski's pocket, finding the one for the cuffs and quickly unlocking them. He groaned when she grabbed his arm, cuffing it to the steering wheel.

The deflated airbags hung limply from the dash, and Clarissa was glad they'd deployed as they were supposed to. She wanted to escape, not kill him. It looked like he'd have only some scrapes and bruises as mementos of his encounter with her.

It wasn't her fault. She'd tried to convince him she wasn't working for Solomon anymore, but he'd refused to believe her. She'd had no choice but to escape. Sitting in jail wasn't an option.

She went to grab Langston's gun and phone back from Kaminski, when she found her wrist caught by Kaminski.

"Wait," he said, forcing his eyes open. "Just…tell me where he is."

"Langston?"

He nodded.

"I told you, I left him alive," she said, jerking her arm free along with the gun and cell. "Though I don't think he'll take too well to you working with Clarke."

"I'm not…working for Clarke," he gritted out, his face creasing in pain as he sat up in the seat.

"Then how did you find us?" she asked.

"I followed Clarke to New Orleans, tracing his phone just like we traced Langston's."

Just then, said phone in Clarissa's hand rang.

"So you're not working for Clarke?" she asked Kaminski again.

He shook his head.

"Prove it." She hit the button to take the call and put it on speaker.

"Kaminski," he said, watching Clarissa.

"Kaminski, it's Langston."

"Shit," Kaminski breathed, rubbing his free hand over his face. "Man, where the fuck are you?"

"Is O'Connell with you?"

"Yeah."

"Don't hurt her, okay? She didn't do anything to me."

"Yeah, don't hurt me," Clarissa mocked Kaminski in an undertone. He shot her a glare.

"You're lucky she didn't kill me with that stunt she just pulled."

"What are you doing, Langston?" Clarissa asked. "Still cuffed to the bed?"

Kaminski's eyebrows shot up, but she ignored him.

"I'm resourceful," Langston said. "Learned from the best."

Clarissa couldn't help the thrill of pride and admiration she felt. He'd gotten loose. She'd known he would. "I thought I told you to sit this one out," she said.

"I do what I'm told about as well as you do."

"Where are you?"

A pause. "I'm with some…friends of Solomon."

Clarissa's heart stuttered, then she went from zero to furious bitch in 2.3 seconds. "Are you fucking kidding me, Langston?" she yelled. "What the hell did you do?"

"Ow," he said. "Quit yelling, please."

Clarissa fumed, wishing she could crawl through the phone just so she could make sure he was safe…and then kick his ass.

"I thought it best if Solomon knew Clarke was planning to double-cross him."

"He'll thank you for that information by killing you," Clarissa retorted.

"Gotta go with the chick on this one, man," Kaminski said.

"Did you just call me a *chick*, you prick?"

"Settle down, sweetheart," he sneered. "Don't get so emotional."

"I'm going to kill him," Clarissa warned Langston. "He's a total dick and you can do better."

"Knock it off, you two," Langston said. "You can kill each other later. For now, I've struck a deal. Kaminski, you go with Clarissa and take down Clarke before she has to transfer any money."

"What about you?" Clarissa asked, looking at the phone as though she could see him through it.

"I'm…collateral. To ensure you give the money back to Solomon."

"Dammit, Langston! Why couldn't you have just stayed put like I said?" All of this was going to hell, and while she couldn't give a shit if Kaminski got caught in the crossfire, Solomon holding Langston hostage was a headache she didn't need.

"I told you that I wasn't going to let you do this alone. Nobody's going to die tonight."

She sincerely hoped he was right.

"Now where are you meeting Clarke?"

"Oak Alley," Clarissa reluctantly answered. "Outside Vacherie."

"Okay. I've gotta go," Langston said. "Good luck, and Kaminski?"

"Yeah?"

Langston's voice was low and earnest now. "Take care of her. Please."

Kaminski shot her a look, understanding dawning in his eyes. "Will do." He ended the call. "Looks like it's you and me," he said, then jangled the cuff still attached to the steering wheel. "Better unlock me."

Clarissa moved to do just that. "I'm already regretting this," she groused.

"Cheer up," Kaminski said, rubbing his wrist. "I'm a better shot than Langston."

"Like I give a shit," Clarissa shot back. "I'm a good enough shot for both of us. Besides," she leaned toward him, "he's way hotter than you."

That shut him up.

∽

Erik handed the phone back to Liam. "I told you. She'll do whatever I tell her to. She trusts me."

"And you're sure you can get her to transfer the money back to Solomon's account?"

"If she thinks I'm in danger, she'll do it."

Liam smiled. "You *are* in danger, Mr. Langston. Don't kid yourself about that."

Erik didn't smile back. "Don't kid yourself into thinking that you'll ever get that money back without me or her. Threaten all you want, but I know your boss wants that money. If he hadn't reneged on the deal he made to free Danny and sent someone to kill her, he wouldn't be in this mess right now." Erik pointedly looked up at the camera hanging from the ceiling in the corner of the office. "Isn't that right, Solomon?"

The phone on the desk rang, and Liam picked it up. He listened for a moment, his face paling slightly.

"Understood. Right away," he said before hanging up the phone. "It looks like you may not be as smart as you think you are, Mr. Langston. Solomon would like to see you." He leaned close to Erik. "Perhaps you don't know this, but few have ever seen Solomon who then lived to tell the tale," he hissed.

"Then I'll make sure to shoot you on my way out," Erik hissed back.

"Take him," Liam barked.

Erik smiled, his gaze locked on Liam's as the two guards grabbed him and hustled him out of the room.

~

"So," Kaminski began. "You want to tell me what the hell's been going on?"

They'd gone back to Langston's SUV and now were heading out of town toward Vacherie. Kaminski had insisted on driving. Just like Langston, Clarissa thought. Maybe they had more in common than they thought.

"I don't have to tell you squat," she shot back. "Only that Langston hasn't done anything wrong. He's lucky to be alive after your guys nearly killed him."

313

"Not our guys," Kaminski said. "Clarke."

"So how did you realize it was him?" Clarissa asked. "Langston wasn't sure if you were in on it too."

Kaminski's jaw tightened. "Nice. Some partner he is."

Clarissa shrugged. "Better to be alive and wrong than dead and right. He had no choice but to be suspicious."

"Well, maybe if he'd given our partnership a chance, he'd know I'd never do that."

Hmm. That was interesting. "So what happened between you and Langston?"

Kaminski glanced warily at her. "What did he say happened?"

Clarissa shrugged, feeling more than a little like she was mediating two middle schoolers fighting than two grown men. "He said you two disagreed over my importance to the case. That you had a falling out about it."

Kaminski snorted. "That was just the straw, sweetheart—"

Clarissa flicked open a switchblade and quick as a flash, held it between his legs. "Call me sweetheart again and you'll be singing soprano," she threatened.

"Jesus Christ!" he exclaimed. "All right, all right! Just, can you put the knife away? Please? How the hell did you get my knife?"

Certain he'd gotten her message, Clarissa flipped the knife closed and pocketed it. "You should be more aware of your surroundings. Now, you were saying?"

"Uh, yeah. The thing with you. He was fixated on you, to the exclusion of nearly everything else. His apartment is filled with boxes and boxes of research on you, anything he could dig up. He'd watch video footage of you nonstop." Kaminski shook his head. "That's not healthy, man."

Clarissa stared at him, her hands like ice. Langston hadn't said anything to her about this. Yes, he'd told her he'd been hunting her for nearly a year, but she hadn't realized the extent of his obsession to find her.

"Was he…do you think he wanted to kill me?"

Kaminski glanced at her, then back at the road. When he spoke, he didn't answer her question. "You know, Langston and me, I thought we'd get along fine. But nothing I did was good enough. And I got that he'd just lost his partner, that shit's rough, but he just never let up."

"Well, maybe you weren't good enough," Clarissa said stiffly.

"I'm a good agent," Kaminski said evenly. "Sometimes a little too spontaneous, too go-with-my-gut, but that's why Langston and I should've been a good team."

"Because he's such a by-the-book hard-ass?"

Kaminski grimaced. "You caught on to that, did you?"

"It's kind of hard to miss," Clarissa admitted. "Which was why it was so difficult to believe when he—" She stopped.

"When he what?"

Clarissa sighed. "When he wanted to help me, said he'd protect me from Solomon." Her chest hurt, and she absently rubbed her breastbone.

"Lady, no offense, but why in the hell would Langston help a criminal like you? He hates you. When I got in his face about removing himself from the case, giving it a rest, he damn near broke my jaw. Told me to mind my own fucking business and that we were through as partners." He paused. "I'd find it easier to believe that he set you up to pull in the big fish—Clarke and Solomon. You're just collateral damage at this point."

Clarissa jerked her gaze to his. "You're wrong," she said. "He wouldn't lie to me." And yet, he'd already lied to her once about Danny.

"He's a federal agent," Kaminski said. "Why *wouldn't* he lie to you?"

~

They blindfolded Erik before they took him from the room, which didn't surprise him. Solomon was one of the most elusive figures in organized crime. If they didn't kill Erik, they certainly wouldn't want him to be able to find him again.

He was driven somewhere, but not that far away. It was a lot quieter when he got out of the car, the smell cleaner than the congested Bourbon Street area.

Erik was led inside a building, carpet thick under his feet. It was even quieter there. He'd guess it was a house, not a hotel. Not even in New Orleans could you get away with leading a person blindfolded through the lobby of a hotel.

"Sit," one of the guards said, pushing him roughly backward into a chair. It was padded, the fabric thickly textured, with a straight back. Erik's wrists were tied to the arms of the chair.

"Thank you, that'll be all for now."

The voice was different from the guards', and Erik said nothing, listening intently as the guards' footsteps left the room. A door shut quietly behind them.

"Special Agent Erik Langston, I believe?"

Erik swallowed. A part of him couldn't believe this had worked. He was in the same room as Solomon, the man behind not only Peter's death, but O'Connell's blackmail too. He pulled slightly at his bonds. They held fast. He tried to temper his anger. A clear head was vital if he and O'Connell were going to survive.

"You must be the infamous Solomon," Erik said. "I'd shake your hand, but I'm kind of tied up right now."

"A necessary precaution, as I'm sure you'll agree," he said. "You've been quite persistent. I must say, it's admirable. Any other agent would have given up by now. But not you. You've determinedly pursued Clarissa for months. Tell me, Mr. Langston. Do you think you'll be able to sleep at night once you kill her?"

Erik stiffened. "I was never going to kill her. That might be your way, but not mine."

"My apologies. Arrest her then, correct? To avenge your partner."

"Why don't we talk about how you've used her, lied to her, pretending that you'd actually get her brother out of prison if she did this for you? When you and I both know there's not a damn thing you can do about Danny O'Connell rotting in a jail cell."

Solomon laughed, but it was without humor. "Clarissa is a bit naive," he said. "But, as I'm sure you know, extremely loyal to her brother, which in turn, has been extremely useful to me."

Erik's fists clenched and he struggled to not show his anger. Best to let Solomon think he didn't care about O'Connell. If he knew Erik cared, he'd use O'Connell against him just like he'd used Danny against her.

"Tell me more about you, Mr. Langston. Coming here tonight was a very brave, or very stupid, move. Your plan may very well backfire."

"What do you know of my plan?" Erik's palms began to sweat.

"I know how you think, Mr. Langston. I know all about you. You think you're the only one to make a study of your enemies? You've had quite the driven career. Driven by what, exactly? Oh yes, a father who abandoned you and your mother when you were just fifteen. A thief, wasn't he?"

"My father was a sonofabitch who left us to pay his debts and suffer for what he'd done," Erik seethed.

"And you were so angry with him that you disowned him, changed your name, told your friends he was dead."

"You bet I did," Erik growled. "And you're just like him. Using people without a care for how it ruins their lives. You've used Clarissa for nothing but your own gain, and when you're through with her, you'll kill her and toss her aside. I'm not going to let that happen."

"You might be right," Solomon mused. "But not for the reasons you think."

The blindfold was pulled off and Erik blinked in the sudden light. When his eyes focused on the man in front of him, the blood drained from his face.

"Hello, son."

EPISODE NINE

CHAPTER SEVENTEEN

"It's been a long time," the man who was Erik's father, who now went by Solomon, said. He sat back in his chair, his eyes narrowing as he watched Erik.

Erik struggled to regain his bearings, his mind reeling in shock. This couldn't be happening. The notorious mobster known only as Solomon was, in reality, his…dad?

"You seem to be at a loss for words," Solomon said.

"Do you blame me?" Erik replied. "I'd assumed, hoped really, that you were dead by now."

"After all these years, you're still so angry?"

"Why the hell wouldn't I be? You left us, Mom and me, to take the fall for you." Erik struggled not to yell, to stay in control. "We lost everything. Because of you."

"It wasn't just my fault, Erik. I wanted to take you both with me, you and your mother, but she refused."

"Living a life on the run didn't appeal to her? How strange," Erik mocked.

"I had no choice—"

"You had every choice!"

Solomon stopped talking, his face unreadable.

Erik took a breath before continuing, his voice low and clotted with rage and betrayal. "You chose to break the law. You chose to run. You chose to continue a life of crime and murder. Everything Mom and I dealt with—that was the fall-out from your choices."

"Everything, including your chosen career path," Solomon said.

Erik's lipped pressed into a thin line.

"I believe, even in absentia, I've influenced what you've chosen to do with your life, isn't that right, Erik?"

"If by 'influence' you mean every day I pray I'll get what I need to take you down, then yeah. I guess you're right."

"I see your foolishness is outweighed only by your ideal-ism," Solomon said. "And it was extremely foolish of you to come here tonight. The men who work for me are no fonder of federal agents than I am."

"I can see that," Erik said, pointedly jerking at his tied wrists. "For a reunion, this one really sucks, Pops."

"Do you blame me? I wasn't one hundred percent sure you wouldn't try to kill me on sight."

"Honestly, I can't say whether I wouldn't," Erik retorted.

"What's your connection to this woman, Clarissa?" Solomon asked. "You seem to have put yourself at an awful risk for her."

"That's none of your business," Erik gritted out.

"What affects you is my business."

"Since when?"

"Always," Solomon said. "You don't think I've been watching you? Keeping tabs on you? You think I didn't see how well you've done?"

Erik couldn't believe it. Was that...pride in Solomon's voice?

"I don't want you keeping tabs on me," Erik said in dis-gust. "You're no more a father to me than any other crimi-nal I arrest."

"And yet, at the moment, I hold your life in my hands." Solomon seemed completely unperturbed by Erik's animosity.

"It's not *my* life you should be worried about," Erik said.

"Then tell me the truth about Ms. O'Connell," Solomon bit out.

"Ms. O'Connell is a person," Erik said. "With a past and present, and hopefully, a future. She's not a bad person, but you've turned her into one. And now she's on the run for her life. Because of you."

"I didn't make her into what she is. You can thank her brother for that. I wouldn't even know about her if it wasn't for him."

Erik stared at Solomon in confusion. "What are you talking about?"

"Danny O'Connell was a hotheaded thief with an ego unmatched by his prowess," Solomon said dryly. "Despite my misgivings, I hired him for a job, thought I'd give him a chance." He paused. "You know how that turned out."

Erik didn't reply; images of his partner bleeding to death in his arms ran through his mind.

"Danny was desperate to get out of prison," Solomon continued. "But there was nothing that could be done. As you well know, there's only one fate that awaits you when you kill an FBI agent."

"Life in prison was too good for him," Erik said.

"Incidentally, I agree. But Danny was determined to get out. He sent a message to me. Had to speak to me. Said he wanted to make a deal. When I agreed, he told me about his sister, Clarissa. How...talented she was. How they were very close. How she'd do anything to get him out of prison."

Erik stared, aghast, at Solomon. "Are you telling me Danny offered up his own sister to you?"

"Danny not only offered up his sister, he told me exactly how to contact her, details as to what she could do, and how to appeal to her sense of loyalty for him." Solomon shrugged. "What else was I supposed to do with the information except find her?"

Erik clenched his jaw. "Well, she showed you, didn't she?" he said, twisting his lips into a smirk. "You fucked with the wrong woman, Dad. A hundred million dollars is a lot of money."

Solomon frowned. "Yes, I admit I underestimated her. A costly mistake. But you say you can get her to give me back the money. That she trusts you."

Erik laughed, a sound devoid of humor. "Now why would I do that, knowing who you are? Hell, I'm going to tell her to keep it and you can go fuck yourself."

"Because if she does, I'll let this little incident go and call it good." Solomon leaned forward. "But if she doesn't, I will never stop hunting her. And I will find her. And when I do, I'm going to kill her."

"If Clarissa doesn't want to be found, then you're not going to find her." Of that, Erik was certain.

"Ah yes, but you forget about her brother. He isn't one to live the quiet life, staying off the radar and out of sight. No, his ego couldn't handle that. He'll start taking jobs, small ones at first, but eventually larger ones, until his pride leads me right to them."

"Danny's going right back to prison tonight," Erik said, praying he was right. "Clarke double-crossed you. He wants the money for himself."

"Clarke is a greedy man, but not very smart," Solomon replied, relaxing back in his chair again. "I allowed him to go about thinking he's playing me, but in reality, I'm the one playing him."

Erik just stared, his mind jumping ahead to a conclusion that made the blood ice in his veins. "It's Danny, isn't it?" he asked. "The only way you could get Danny out was by using Clarke, so you dangled the hundred million in front of Clarke, daring him to double-cross you, and he did exactly what you expected him to."

Solomon smiled. "I always said you got your brains from me, kid."

"So what's supposed to happen now?" Erik asked. "Danny will kill Clarke and then tell Clarissa to give the money back?"

Solomon laughed. "I doubt Danny will be that smart. He'll kill Clarke all right, but then he'll want to keep the money. Greed is in his blood, and his overconfidence will let him think they can get away with it." He motioned to Erik. "This is where you come in. I'll let you go, so you can convince Clarissa to give me back the money. I've told you what the consequences are if she doesn't." His face hardened. "You've got one shot at this. If she trusts you, like you say, then it shouldn't be a problem."

"And if I don't?"

"Then she'll no doubt do what her brother says." He studied Erik. "So which will it be? Do you hate me enough to sacrifice Clarissa just so I don't get my money returned? Or do you care enough about her to try and save her?"

"I don't—"

"Oh please." Solomon interrupted him with a snort of disgust. "It's written all over you, plain as day. What did you do? Sleep with her?"

Erik kept his mouth stubbornly closed, his eyes staring daggers at his father.

"Clarissa O'Connell is dangerous," Solomon said. "Getting involved with her will only lead nowhere good. You can do better, son."

"Don't call me son," Erik bit out.

"Deny it all you will, it's what you are." Solomon walked to a nearby desk and pushed a button on the phone that sat on its surface. "It's been good to see you, Erik. Talk to you."

"Wish I could say the same."

Two men came in the room, one carrying a black hood. Erik could do nothing as they placed it over his head.

"I'm sure we'll meet again, Erik," was the last thing he heard before something was pressed against the back of his neck. A jolt of pain went through him, then his world went dark.

∼

The sky was just beginning to lighten when Kaminski pulled off the road about a quarter mile from the plantation and turned off the car.

"This is it," he said unnecessarily. "We'll split up and hike in from here so he thinks you're alone." He checked that his gun was loaded.

"What's our plan?" Clarissa asked. "He's going to assume I didn't come alone."

"Convince him you did. I'll circle 'round, try to sneak in from the back."

"And if you get caught?"

"You have a gun, don't you? And my knife? Or you can just pull some of that ninja shit on him," Kaminski scoffed.

"I'd prefer not to break a nail," Clarissa sneered. God, no wonder Langston had kicked Kaminski to the curb. What a smart-ass.

Speaking of Langston…"Do you think they'll hurt him?" Clarissa asked. She didn't have to explain whom she was asking about.

"Not if you give them their money back," Kaminski said. "You ready?"

Clarissa nodded. Kaminski started walking and she traveled perpendicular to him. Within moments, she was alone.

She thought about what Kaminski had said in the car, how surprised he'd been to think Langston might be helping her. So surprised, he didn't even believe it.

Was she acting the fool? Believing that Langston loved her just because she wanted it to be true?

What if Kaminski was able to capture Clarke and she returned the money to Solomon? Would Solomon release Langston unharmed? Would he then arrest her? There'd be no escaping prison this time, not with all Langston had seen her do with his own eyes. His testimony alone would send her away for years.

And then there was Danny.

Clarissa was nervous to see him again and dreading it, which only made her feel guilty. She should be glad he was out, that they would be reunited, but all she could think about was Langston's dead partner and fatherless child.

The house came into view much too soon, a grand white structure with soaring columns that reached to the roof of the two-story mansion. The air was heavy with fog this morning, making the house appear otherworldly, shrouded as it was with mist. The oak trees for which the plantation was named graced the drive leading to the front, two rows of huge trees creating an arbor of intertwined branches and a canopy of green. The heavy boughs rested on the ground with majestic ease, the gnarled roots grasping the earth with the tenacity of centuries.

It was beautiful and momentarily took Clarissa's breath away. Time seemed to have turned backward, flinging her into decades past.

Shaking herself from her reverie, Clarissa walked between the rows of oaks toward the still and silent house. Clarke would be waiting for her there with the building at his back. Sure enough, when she drew close, she could see a man sitting in one of the old-fashioned wooden rocking chairs gracing the porch. The chair gently rocked back and forth, as though the occupant were just enjoying the breaking dawn.

Clarissa glanced around, but saw no sign of Danny. Her eyes settled on Clarke.

He was slighter than she'd expected, his build making her guess he didn't reach six feet. Brown hair and eyes on an average face that she guessed was late forties to early fifties. Clarke was dressed incongruously in business casual with khakis and a white button-down shirt. He could have been a southern gentleman at his leisure, if not for the gun in his hand.

"Where's Danny?" Clarissa asked without preamble.

Clarke smiled. "Around. Wouldn't want you to get any ideas about double-crossing me. I'm not an idiot like Solomon. I know perfectly well what you're capable of, regardless of how much you've snowed Agent Langston with your supposed amnesia.

"Speaking of Agent Langston," he continued. "Where is he? I'd be quite surprised if he wasn't here."

Clarissa raised an eyebrow. "Why would I keep a Fed around?"

"Agent Langston is more than a Fed," Clarke warned. "But perhaps you know that already."

"What are you talking about?"

Clarke's smile was enigmatic. "Or maybe you don't. Do you have the transfer ready?"

Clarissa pulled out Langston's cell phone, wondering what Clarke had meant about Langston. "Just need the account you want it transferred to."

Clarke gave a sharp whistle, and Clarissa turned to see Danny emerge from the trees, a man holding a gun on him as they walked toward the house.

It was a shock, seeing him again after all this time. He was bigger, like he'd bulked up while in prison. His even gaze stayed locked on hers as they approached, finally stopping at the foot of the stairs leading up to the porch.

"There you are," Clarke said. "And now for my account number, I believe." He rattled off a list of numbers.

"And you think I'm just going to transfer the money and think you're going to let us go?" Clarissa asked, entering the numbers into the phone.

"I don't see that you have a choice." Clarke pointed the gun at her.

Where the hell was Kaminski? Clarissa caught Danny's eye. If they just had a distraction, just for a moment...

The sound of breaking glass startled Clarissa, but she checked her impulse to turn toward the sound. Instead, she pulled her gun. In her peripheral vision, she saw Danny had also taken advantage and was wrestling with his captor.

Clarke's attention returned to her in time for him to see the gun in her hand.

A gunshot rang out. Clarke jerked in his chair, red blooming on his pristine white shirt, then slumped to the ground.

Clarissa turned to see Danny had won his struggle. The gun he held was still smoking and the man who'd held him was lying unmoving on the ground.

"Is someone with ya?" Danny asked, not lowering the gun as he looked around.

Before Clarissa could answer, Kaminski stepped around the corner. His gun was pointed at Danny.

"Don't shoot!" Clarissa said to Danny. That's the last thing she needed, Kaminski and Danny killing each other. "He's with us."

Hurrying to Clarke, she turned him over onto his back. He was still breathing, but barely. Blood was everywhere. He wasn't going to make it. Clarissa felt a pang of remorse, not that she necessarily regretted Clarke's death, it just seemed like where she went, dead bodies followed. She sat back on her haunches with a sigh.

"Wait—" Clarke startled her, grabbing her wrist in a surprisingly strong grip. His voice was a rasp of sound. "Listen…" he said.

Clarissa leaned down so she could hear him better. A dying man's last words? This was a first.

"I've been…Solomon…for years…" he gasped out, his face creasing in pain. "…gotta know…Langston…his son…"

Clarissa's hands turned to ice as she stared at Clarke. "Are you saying that Langston is related to Solomon?" she asked in disbelief.

"His…son," Clarke managed. "Known for…long time… gotta know…careful…" Then his eyes went glassy and his grip loosened. His arm fell limply to the ground.

Clarissa's mind reeled, trying to reconcile what Clarke had told her. She had no idea why he would bother telling her that if it wasn't true. That must be why he had expected Langston to be with her. Solomon wasn't going to let that money be transferred to Clarke, and Langston had been his insurance.

Langston had lied when he said he was "collateral." He wasn't in danger, had never been. Solomon wouldn't hurt his own son.

What better way to get her to give back the money than for her to think someone she trusted was in danger? Someone she believed cared about her? Was in love with her?

Pain twisted like a knife in her gut. She'd been such a fool. So gullible. Believing his lies while the whole time he'd been laughing at her. What a stroke of luck the amnesia had been for him, making her even more willing to trust him and let him "help" her.

"Is he dead?" Kaminski asked, crouching down next to her.

No doubt he'd been in on it as well.

Clarissa didn't think, she just acted. She attacked Kaminski, knocking the gun from his hand and holding the knife to his throat as he backed up to the wall.

"What the fuck is your problem?" Kaminski spluttered.

"Thought he was with us?" Danny asked, not very concerned.

"I was wrong," Clarissa replied through gritted teeth. She narrowed her eyes. "So how long have you known, Kaminski?" she asked.

"Known what? I don't know what you're talking about."

"Known that Langston is a fraud and liar."

"I don't—"

Clarissa pressed her knife against his skin, nicking him slightly to get his attention. "He's made a fool of me," she hissed. Rage and humiliation burned in her belly. "You tell him that if I ever see him again, I'll kill him. Got that?"

Kaminski swallowed hard, his eyes glued to hers. "Yeah. I got it," he said.

Danny had picked up the dropped weapons and now stood behind Clarissa. "Probably shouldn't fuck with me sister, mate."

"Get Clarke's keys, Danny," Clarissa said. "We're leaving." She kept her eyes on Kaminski as Danny did as he'd been told, then she slowly backed away.

The ringing of a cell phone broke the tense silence. Clarissa fished Langston's cell out of her pocket.

"Yeah," she answered, watching to make sure Kaminski didn't make a move.

"Thank God," Langston said. "Are you okay?"

～

When Erik had woken up, he'd had a massive headache and been slumped behind the wheel of a car.

He groaned. Being Solomon's son certainly hadn't earned him any favors. That was twice now he'd been hit with a stun gun, and he hadn't enjoyed the second time any more than the first.

The first. O'Connell. Shit.

The car keys were in the ignition and he hurriedly started it, glancing around to get his bearings. He'd been to Oak Alley with his mother and still remembered the way, though he hoped he wasn't too late.

Erik was speeding down the empty road when he noticed a cell phone sitting on the empty seat beside him. He snatched it up and dialed, exhaling in relief when O'Connell's voice came on the line.

"Thank God," he said. "Are you okay?"

"So what's going on, Langston," O'Connell said. "Solomon going to kill you now?"

Her voice was cold, giving Erik pause, but he shrugged it off. "No, he let me go," he said. "Listen, did Kaminski catch Clarke?"

"Clarke's dead."

Erik winced. That meant things hadn't gone smoothly, and she still hadn't answered him if she was okay.

"But he did have something very interesting to say before he died," she continued.

"What?"

"He just happened to mention who you really are, Langston. Or should I say, Solomon, Jr.?"

Erik sucked in a breath. How had Clarke known when Erik himself hadn't? And now, knowing O'Connell, she was going to think the worst.

"Listen to me," he said urgently. "I didn't know—"

Her laugh could have cut glass. "Do you really think I'm that stupid? Though, I have to hand it to you, getting me to trust you, making me think that what happened between us was real, that was a stroke of genius."

Erik started to panic; the cold fury in her voice cut like a razor.

"I have the money. I have my brother. And you can tell Solomon to go fuck himself," she spat.

"O'Connell, please, just listen to me—"

"If you ever come near me again, it'll be the last thing you do."

The line went dead.

"Fuck!" Erik exploded, flinging the cell phone. His hands gripped the steering wheel. He drove faster but knew she'd be long gone by the time he got there. It had taken him a year and a huge dose of luck to find her the first time; how the hell would he find her again? What if he couldn't? Would Solomon find her and kill her?

By the time he got to Oak Alley, the sun was up. Erik sped up the drive, skidding to a stop in front of the porch. Kaminski stood at the top of the stairs, while another man was cuffed to a chair. Erik leaped out of the car.

"Where is she?"

Kaminski shook his head. "Gone, man. Can't even say what they were driving."

"What happened?"

"Her brother shot Clarke, but he whispered something to her before he died. Pissed her off at you something fierce."

Shit. Erik shoved a hand through his hair, thinking desperately. Where would they go?

"What'd he tell her?" Kaminski said. "She asked me if I knew you were a fraud and liar. What the hell was she talking about?"

Erik looked at Kaminski. His gut was telling him not to trust him, to keep the secret. But he was his partner. Even when Erik had blown him off, Kaminski had tracked him down when he'd disappeared.

Maybe Erik had been too hard on him. Maybe the death of Peter had blinded him to anyone that would have taken his place.

Maybe Kaminski deserved a second chance.

"Tonight, I met Solomon," Erik said.

Kaminski's brows flew upward. "You're kidding me."

Erik shook his head. "And it gets worse. He's my father." He waited, wondering what Kaminski would say.

Kaminski let out a low whistle. "And you didn't know?"

Erik shook his head. "I haven't seen or heard from my dad since he walked out on me and my mom when I was fifteen."

"This is like a whole…Star Wars kind of thing," Kaminski said with a wave of his hand.

Erik grimaced. "You're telling me."

333

"So, what, O'Connell thought you were hiding this all along?"

"Yeah." Erik scrutinized Kaminski. "Aren't you wondering that?"

Kaminski shook his head. "Nah. You're too much of a straight arrow with a stick up your ass for that, and you ain't that good an actor." He laughed good-naturedly, clapping Erik on the shoulder.

Erik didn't take offense. Kaminski was right and was just being honest. It surprised him how well Kaminski knew him.

Kaminski tossed Erik his phone. "Call it in. It's going to take some time to clean up this mess, and the tourists are going to start arriving in a couple of hours."

Kaminski was right. As much as Erik wanted to go after O'Connell, he had no idea which way they'd gone. Chasing after her would be pointless. His job now was to cordon off the crime scene and notify his superiors about Clarke. He did so on autopilot, his mind elsewhere.

Where was O'Connell? Why had she immediately jumped to the wrong conclusion, even after all they'd been through together?

She thought exactly what her experience has taught her, his conscience whispered to him. *No one can be trusted.*

If he reasoned with his head instead of his heart, Erik could understand her assumption. But it hurt that she hadn't trusted him. Had believed he'd been lying, deceiving her the entire time, just to get the money back.

He was in love with her, and it didn't matter what she'd done or how angry she was, Erik wasn't going to lose her.

Even if it took ten years to find her again.

CHAPTER EIGHTEEN

Clarissa's fingers clattered over the keyboard as she worked. Light from the street filtered into the apartment through the open blinds, breaking up the darkness. She hadn't bothered to turn on any lights since it had gotten dark, and she worked by the glow of her computer monitors.

Danny was still out, and for that she was grateful. They'd come back east because Danny had wanted to; he'd refused to live down south. Though he wanted New York, Clarissa couldn't stand the thought of living with so many people again. They'd compromised on Baltimore.

She missed her house, her things. Once she got Danny settled in, she promised herself she would go back to Louisiana. Obviously she couldn't go back to her house, but she could find another. The south was riddled with old homes nestled in the backcountry.

Once she got Danny settled in.

Clarissa sighed. She stopped typing and rested her head in her hands. Who was she kidding? She couldn't leave Danny alone. Despite the fact that they had money, he'd started thieving again. Little things, here and there, but Clarissa knew what would happen. Eventually, he'd start taking jobs, small ones at first. But it would give him a taste, and that would be all it would take. If he wasn't careful, he'd wind up right back in jail.

And Clarissa wasn't sure that wasn't exactly where he should be.

Her thoughts drifted to Langston. Was he looking for her? Did he intend to catch and kill her? Or maybe he'd forgotten all about her by now.

Was he sleeping with someone else?

Clarissa abruptly stood, her chair scraping against the wooden floor. She couldn't think like that. Yes, it had occurred to her that maybe he'd been telling the truth, maybe he hadn't known about the connection to Solomon. But it just seemed like too much of a coincidence that the one agent chasing her just happened to be Solomon's long-lost son.

"Whatever," she muttered to herself, going into the kitchen to pour a glass of wine.

Despite her anger and feelings of betrayal, Clarissa couldn't deny that she missed him. It didn't seem to matter what he'd done or how he'd lied. She missed being around him, teasing him, making his ears turn red. Making love.

"You're turning into a sentimental, angsty teenager, Clarissa," she mumbled. "Who talks to herself." She sighed.

She needed a distraction. Going back to her computer, she logged on to a chat room she hadn't visited in months. Probably not the smartest thing, but she was lonely. Danny wasn't the best company.

A couple dozen people were in the chat and a few names she recognized. They were talking about a recent operating system vulnerability one of them had stumbled across and the best way to exploit it. Clarissa offered a couple ideas, sipping her wine while she read the conversation.

A while later, her computer dinged. Someone was sending her an invite to a private chat. His name was Whiskey. Or she.

Curious, Clarissa accepted the invitation, waiting to see what Whiskey had to say.

Hey, Calamity.

Whiskey.

Hoping you could help me.

What's up? Clarissa wasn't much for hacking at the moment, but if Whiskey just needed some advice, she didn't mind offering it.

Looking for a woman.

Okay, that was different.

Hacking chat rooms maybe not the best place for that, she typed in. *Suggest needtogetlaid.com.* Clarissa grinned at her own smart-assery and took another sip of wine.

Not just any woman. Very specific. Red hair. Green eyes.

Clarissa's pulse sped up. Shit! What was this? Did Whiskey know who she was? Best to disappear fast. But before she could kill her Internet connection, another line came on the screen.

Likes chocolate chip pancakes.

Clarissa froze, her hand inches from the mouse. She stared at the screen. It couldn't be...could it?

Her fingers hovered over the keyboard while she tried to think. Her head was throwing a fit, but she couldn't help replying. *Who is this?*

The answer came back quickly.

Captain America.

Oh God. The poster on the wall of his room. It was Langston in the chat room with her. But how had he found her? He knew her screen name, yes, but there were thousands of chat rooms just like this one scattered throughout the Internet.

Unless Andy had squealed on her.

Clarissa sighed. She knew she should be mad, but how could she blame the poor kid? Langston had probably threatened to arrest him if Andy didn't tell him what he wanted to know.

As she stared at the screen, another line came up.

Don't leave. Please. Just talk to me.

She shouldn't. Clarissa knew she should just leave the room and disconnect. But her IP was masked so he couldn't trace her. Maybe she could stay for a few minutes…

What's there to talk about?

I miss you.

The cursor blinked at her. The line of text grew blurry in Clarissa's vision. Damn him.

That's too bad.

Do you miss me?

She swallowed, then slowly typed the letters, knowing she shouldn't.

Yes

Clarissa felt like she'd just taken a step out onto a high wire, so she took a gulp of wine, staring at the blinking cursor on the screen.

I didn't know. I swear to you. Had no idea of the truth.

Why should I believe you?

Because I love you and I'd never do anything to hurt you.

The words blurred on the screen again. Clarissa couldn't decide what she should say. She knew what she *should* say, but that wasn't what she *wanted* to say. More text appeared.

I need to see you. Will you meet me?

Alarm bells started going off in her head now. Was this a trap?

Why would I do that? She typed. *You could kill me. Or worse, arrest me.*

I'm not going to do either. Tell me what I have to do for you to trust me again.

Clarissa stared at the screen. Her stomach was in knots, her hand clenched around her wineglass. There was no way out of this, no happy ending, not for them. Too much was at risk for her to trust him, the stakes too high. She typed one word.

Nothing.

Before she could think twice about it, she unplugged her network cable from the computer.

She stared at the screen for a very long time.

≈

"Dammit!" Erik exploded, slamming his fist onto the surface of the desk where he sat.

[Calamity has left private chat.]

The text mocked him with its finality.

He'd been so relieved to talk to her, hoping beyond hope that she would believe him, agree to meet him somewhere. But O'Connell was a survivor, and she hadn't gotten this far by being stupid. Unfortunately, for O'Connell, trusting him fell into that category.

Erik turned to the guy sitting at the desk behind him. "Anything?" he asked.

Steve shook his head. "Her IP was bouncing around all over the place. She's good, and it would take more time than that to track her down."

Shit. "Well, thanks anyway," Erik said.

"Sure, no problem."

Erik had befriended one of the headquarters' third-shift IT guys, Steve, a couple of weeks ago. He'd gotten the idea to find O'Connell on the Internet when he'd remembered that's how Andy had communicated with her. And it hadn't taken much for Andy to show him the places to hang out and wait for her.

"Come back tomorrow night, same time," Steve said.

Erik glanced at him, hopeful.

Steve shrugged. "Hackers are creatures of habit, as much as they say they're not. She'll come back."

"Thanks. I'll do that."

Erik stopped at the liquor store on the way home. A shot of whiskey sounded just the thing.

His apartment was cold and dark when he opened the door. Erik flipped on the kitchen light and emptied his pockets on the counter. His gun and holster were deposited there too, and he stripped off his shirt as he walked through the apartment to take a shower.

It had been weeks and he hadn't been able to stop thinking about her. He'd scoured her files like a man possessed, staying up far into the night, trying to find anyplace she might have returned, any clue he had missed that might point to her whereabouts. He'd found nothing.

Kaminski had even helped, once he'd seen what it was doing to Erik. He knew O'Connell would stay with her brother, so Kaminski had focused the search on any information that popped on the grid about Danny O'Connell.

So far, nothing, but Erik wasn't going to give up and Kaminski hadn't said a word about doing so either. Erik had to find her, if for nothing else than to warn her about Solomon, though he assumed she already knew he'd be looking for her too.

Erik sat on his sofa, the bare skin of his back pressed against the soft leather, staring into space as he tossed back a shot of whiskey. He refilled his glass and drank the second shot slower, thinking.

If she did return to the chat room tomorrow night, what was he going to say? He'd already laid everything on the line tonight and she hadn't budged.

Though she did say she missed you.

That thought gave him renewed determination. He had to get her to come out of hiding, meet him somewhere. Only when they were face-to-face would he be able to convince her that he was telling the truth. But how?

Two more shots and the answer came to him. O'Connell was a fighter and loved a challenge. She hated to be viewed as incompetent or as if she couldn't take care of herself.

"That's it," he mused to himself. It had to be. He had nothing else to try and nothing more to lose.

The next night, Erik was back with Steve, logging on to the same website. He waited impatiently. Would she come? The hands of the clock seemed to crawl by. The hour she'd appeared last night came…and went.

"She's not coming," he said to Steve, his voice flat with disappointment.

"Chill. She'll come," Steve reassured him.

Nearly forty-five minutes later, he saw her.

[Calamity has entered the room.]

"She's here," he said excitedly.

"Invite her to a private chat," Steve reminded him.

Erik clicked the mouse a couple times and waited.

[Calamity has accepted your invitation.]

Erik's palms were sweaty as he typed.

I'm glad you came back.

Shouldn't have. Don't know why I did.

Okay, time to put his plan into action before she bolted.

Aren't you afraid I'll track you down?

Please.

Her disdain came through loud and clear, and Erik couldn't help grinning.

Is that why you won't meet me? Afraid I'll trap you?

Whiskey, you couldn't trap a goldfish.

Such a smart-ass. *Then it shouldn't be a problem. Meet me. I dare you.*

The cursor blinked, and Erik waited, holding his breath.

Gordon's. Baltimore. Tomorrow night. Third floor.

[Calamity has left private chat.]

∽

Erik sat nursing a whiskey on the rocks in a corner of the bar, the third floor, as she'd specified. She hadn't said a time, so he'd arrived at six. Hell, he'd sit here all damn night if he had to.

O'Connell had been in Baltimore this whole time. Less than an hour from him. He couldn't believe it. So close...

Hours passed, and still he sat. Waiting. His gut growing heavier with each passing hour. Maybe she'd changed her mind and wasn't going to show after all.

No. That wasn't her. She'd show. She had to.

The waitress came by yet again and Erik shook his head. If he kept drinking, he'd end up shit-faced probably about the time O'Connell showed up, and wouldn't that make a fantastic impression?

Erik studied the bar, trying to see into its dark corners. It was busy, but not overly crowded. The music from the floor below could be felt through the floor, but the patrons up on this level were here for the excellent booze and upper-class ambiance. Velvet padded sofas and chairs littered the space, while muted lighting gave it a classy feel.

A glass with another round of whiskey was sat in front of him. "I said I didn't want another round," he said, turning to the waitress. To his surprise, she slid into the chair across from him.

"You *are* really bad at this," she said. "I must say, Langston, I'm a little surprised."

Erik stared. The Boston accent that had colored her words earlier was gone, though the straight blonde wig remained, along with the heavily made-up brown eyes and lip piercing. The tight, black sleeveless shirt and silk shorts that hadn't even made an impression earlier now captivated his attention. The deep *V* of the plunging neckline made his mouth go dry.

"I knew it was you all along," he said.

Clarissa snorted. "Right. Whatever. If it helps you sleep at night." She shrugged.

Her eyes drank him in even as she pretended noncha-lance. She thought for sure he'd made her right away, but he hadn't said a word. It had taken hours of watching and waiting—to see if he'd been followed, to see if someone was with him, to see if he'd stay—before Clarissa had decided to approach him.

"Is the tongue piercing real?" he asked.

"Does it turn you on, Langston?" she asked innocently.

The look he gave her made the blood heat in her veins. Hoo boy. Clarissa grabbed his glass of cold whiskey and took a gulp. When she placed it back on the table, Langston picked it up. Never taking his gaze from hers, he turned the glass and took a drink, careful to place his lips where hers had been.

It was hard to breathe in here, Clarissa decided.

"What do you want?" she asked. Might as well get this show on the road.

He cleared his throat and looked down at the table before answering. "You know Solomon is still after you," he said, glancing up.

Clarissa shrugged. "You here to make a peace offering?"

Langston shook his head. "I don't work for him. He's my father, but one of these days, I'll have enough evidence to arrest and convict him." He paused. "I'm just here to warn you."

"I'll consider myself warned then." Clarissa stood to leave, but was stopped by Langston's hand closing on her arm. In one quick movement, he pulled her down onto his lap.

"Leaving so soon?" he asked. "What's the matter, O'Connell? Afraid you won't be able to control yourself around me?"

His teasing smirk made her lips twitch in amusement despite her resolve to remain detached. Langston's arms lightly imprisoned her, which should have pissed her off, but all she could think about was how good it was to be with him again.

"Is this any way for a Boy Scout to behave?" Clarissa said archly. "Manhandling me? I thought you were a gentleman."

"I'm not feeling much like a gentleman at the moment."

The low rasp of his voice sent a shiver through her. Then his hand curled possessively around the back of her neck and he was kissing her.

The weeks they'd spent apart faded away, along with the loneliness and persistent knot in the pit of her stomach. Clarissa kissed Langston back just as desperately, burying her fingers in his hair and pressing as close to him as she could possibly get while still clothed.

Langston tasted of whiskey and his own unique flavor and she couldn't get enough. The scent of his cologne brought back memories of their time together, and it felt like she'd finally found home.

What was she going to do with him? Well, she knew what she wanted to do right *now*, but what about later? Trust had never come easy to Clarissa, but was she going to throw away the best thing that had ever happened to her because she was too afraid to trust him?

It was time to take a leap of faith. If she didn't, Clarissa knew she'd regret it the rest of her life.

"Hey! I don't pay you to make out with the customers!"

The irritated voice came from behind her, and she didn't think Langston even heard. Or if he did, he certainly didn't seem to care. She pulled back but his mouth just moved to her neck. Clarissa glanced around and saw the bar's manager watching them, a livid expression on his face.

"Actually," she said, "you don't pay me at all."

Clarissa stood and took Langston's hand. "Let's go," she said, bypassing the manager and hustling down the stairs. A few moments later, they were climbing into the back of a cab. Clarissa barely had enough time to give the driver her address before Langston was all over her.

"God, I've missed you," he breathed against her lips.

Something warm expanded inside Clarissa's chest, melting the ice that had carefully guarded her heart. It didn't matter now if she was wrong about Langston; she loved him.

The ride to her apartment was mercifully short, though she thought they'd probably given the taxi driver quite a show. Alone in the elevator, it took only seconds for Langston to have her against the wall, tear several buttons off her shirt, and get his hand inside her shorts and between her legs. Clarissa's hands clutched his shoulders, and she moaned into his mouth as her blood thundered in her ears.

His tongue stroked hers to the same rhythm as his fingers. First one, then two thrusting inside her, faster and harder, pressing against her until her body shattered in a mind-blowing climax that Langston hadn't even needed the full eight-floor ride to achieve.

"I want you," he growled in her ear, the heat of his breath sending a tremor through her.

"Yeah, I get that," she said, her voice too breathy.

The elevator doors opened and thank God no one was around this late at night, for it took a few seconds for Clarissa's legs to work properly again.

She led him down the hall to her apartment, having problems unlocking the door with him against her, his erection pressing into her backside while he dragged off her wig and started sucking the back of her neck. His hands slid under her shirt to cup her breasts, and Clarissa forgot what she was doing.

Suddenly, the door was yanked open, startling her. It must have startled Langston too, because he yanked her back to his side. Then she saw who it was.

"Danny," she said nervously. "I thought you were out tonight." He'd told her he was going to Atlantic City with some buddies for the weekend.

Danny's eyes narrowed at her as he took in Langston standing behind her. "Changed me mind," he finally said. "Dinna realize you were havin' comp'ny tonight, Rissa."

He turned away from the door, and Clarissa breathed a silent sigh of relief. Danny hadn't recognized Langston in the dim hallway, plus she could tell from his bleary eyes and pronounced accent that he'd been drinking.

Clarissa turned around. "I didn't know he'd be here," she said in a low voice. "Let's go somewhere else, okay? There's a hotel on the next block."

But Langston looked much different now as he stood there, his expression cold and hard as he stared after Danny.

"So you're still with your brother," he said, and it wasn't a question.

Clarissa shrugged, the tone in Langston's voice sounding warning bells inside her head.

"I don't suppose he's told you the truth about Solomon, has he?"

Clarissa frowned. "What do you mean?"

Langston pushed past her into the apartment, heedless of her attempts to stop him. She hurried after him, skidding to a halt when he paused in the kitchen where Danny was getting another beer from the fridge.

"Don't you think it's time you told your sister the truth?" Langston said.

Danny squinted at him. "Who are you and what the hell are ya talkin' abou'?"

"I'm talking about how you used your own sister as a bargaining chip to get yourself out of prison."

The words hit Clarissa like a blow to the stomach, and she stumbled backward. Danny's eyes flicked to hers.

"Is that true?" she managed to ask.

"Danny here made a deal with Solomon, told all about you, what you could do, how to find you, everything," Langston bit out.

Clarissa just stared at Danny, who didn't say anything, just took a swig of his beer as he stared right back. She could tell he'd done just what Langston accused him of by the guilt in his eyes.

"How could you do that to me?" she asked, her mind still reeling from the idea that her own brother, her flesh and blood kin, had betrayed her. "You sold me out to someone who very nearly killed me, just to save yourself?"

"Wha' was I supposed to do?" Danny blustered, finally speaking. "Rot in that hell for the next twenty years? I thought you'd want to help your brother out, or does family mean nothin' to you?"

"I had no choice but to 'help out,'" Clarissa retorted, advancing on Danny until she stood toe-to-toe with him. "Solomon didn't give me a choice. And you deserved to rot in jail, Danny. You killed a man! I told you not to take that job, I told you it would go south, and I was right."

"Dinna be throwin' that up in me face again! The cop shot me first—I was just shootin' back!"

"That's a lie," Langston gritted out. "You shot first and without hesitation."

Danny studied Langston a moment before realization struck. "It's you!" he said. "You're the copper that arrested me." He twisted toward Clarissa. "What the fuck are you bringin' a copper here for? To send me back to prison?"

"Fuck you, Danny," she spat. "I'm leaving. I'm through with you. Since Dad left, you've brought me nothing but trouble, and I've had it."

"The hell ya are," Danny growled. "Ya think I'm just gonna let ya walk outta here and let him put me back in jail?"

"That's exactly what you're going to do," Langston interjected. "Or you and I are going to have a problem."

"I'll get my things," Clarissa said. "And once I'm gone, I don't ever want to hear from you again, Danny. What would Dad think if he knew you'd sold me out like that? We're through, you and me. From now on, you're on your own." Disgust was evident in her voice.

In a way, she was relieved. For years she'd lived a life not of her choosing, thinking that's all there was for her. But now Langston had shown her she could have more, she could have him, and she wanted it.

Clarissa turned away only to find her arm snatched by Danny as he yanked her back. She twisted to get away, then heard the smash of glass before he'd pulled her back to front against him, her neck in a choke hold.

"I'd hate to have to hurt ya, Rissa," Danny said evenly. "But I ain't goin' back to prison."

The cold glass of the broken beer bottle rested against her throat. Clarissa stared at the jagged edge in shock, then lifted her gaze to see Langston had drawn his gun and was pointing it at them.

They were frozen in the eerie tableau for several agonizing seconds, then Danny spoke to Langston.

"Here's what's gonna happen, copper. Me and Rissa are leaving. So you put your gun down and slide it real careful like over to me."

"And if I don't?"

Danny's grip tightened on Clarissa. "I'll start with her face before I move to her neck, mate."

O'Connell's expression was one of panic and terror, a combination Erik had never seen her wear before, and it only fueled his rage.

"You're going to torture Clarissa, Danny?" Erik asked, trying to keep his voice calm and reasonable. "She's spent the past year of her life trying to get you out of prison. You wouldn't even be here if it weren't for her."

"Rissa knows you gotta look out for yourself," Danny said. "Ain't nobody else gonna give a shit if you live or die. Now put down the gun." The panic in his eyes was one Erik had seen before, and it never boded well.

"She's your sister," Erik reminded him. "She's your family."

"Stop saying that!" Danny yelled.

Danny jerked and the glass scraped O'Connell's neck. Her hiss of pain made fear spike in Erik. He couldn't lose her. Not now that he'd found her again.

"Okay, okay," Erik said, letting loose of his gun so it dangled in his hand. "I'm going to put down the gun—"

A pounding at the door made Danny start, and Erik winced as he saw the glass jerk toward O'Connell's face. She pulled as far away as she could, but Danny's hold on her was tight. Her eyes landed on Erik, and they were filled with tears she refused to shed.

"Police! Open up!"

What the hell? How had they known? They couldn't have…but wait…

"Danny," Erik said urgently, "where were you tonight?"

The pounding on the door got louder. Danny's panicked gaze darted from Erik to the door and back. He didn't answer.

"Danny, in a second they're going to come through that door. And it won't go well for you, not holding a hostage. Listen to me, Danny."

Danny looked back at Erik.

"Think about what you're doing," Erik said. "All you have is a bottle, and they're going to come in with guns. You won't survive it. You know you won't."

He seemed to hesitate. Erik pressed his advantage.

"Look, Danny," he said, motioning with his head. "Look at what you're doing to her." Blood seeped from the cuts the bottle had made, the trails streaking O'Connell's white skin. Her hands clutched at his arm as she tried to stay beyond the bottle's touch.

Danny looked down, and he seemed to falter slightly as he saw O'Connell's wounds. Erik took his chance, bringing his gun up and firing. Danny cried out in pain, the bottle dropping from his hand. He released her and clutched his shoulder.

The door burst open at the sound of the gunshot and Erik raised his hands in surrender, knowing he had to stand still though everything in him wanted to go to O'Connell. She stood, seemingly in frozen shock.

"I'm FBI," Erik explained, handing over his gun to a cop and waiting while they searched him for his ID. As soon as they verified he was who he said, he rushed to O'Connell.

"Can we get some EMTs in here?" he snapped at an officer standing by. "She needs medical attention."

"They both do," the officer observed.

Erik wasn't in the mood at the moment to give a shit about Danny.

"Are you all right?" he asked O'Connell. She was shaking all over and staring at Danny, who lay on the floor, unconscious now.

She raised her eyes to his and Erik winced, her pain-filled gaze cutting him as surely as the glass had cut her. She didn't say anything, and Erik carefully folded her in his arms.

"Why would he do that?" she asked, her voice muffled by his chest.

"I don't know." Erik sighed. "Fear makes people do bad things sometimes."

The EMTs arrived then and began working on Danny. Erik reluctantly released O'Connell so they could see to her wounds as well.

"How'd you find him?" Erik asked the plainclothes detective standing nearby.

"He robbed a liquor store a few hours ago," the detective replied. "Surveillance footage gave us a facial recognition match, saw he was wanted for a prison escape. Used the traffic cameras and got lucky. Why are you here?"

"I'm with the girl," Erik said. No need for the cop to know O'Connell was wanted as well.

The detective raised his eyebrows. "Bad night for you, eh?"

"I've had better," Erik replied. It looked like the EMT was finishing up with O'Connell. "I'm going to take her someplace else for now." Best to get her out of here before someone took a closer look.

"Yeah, sure," the detective said. "Thanks for your help."

"Likewise."

A blanket was thrown over the couch and Erik snatched it up as he walked by, using it to wrap around O'Connell. "Let's go," he said. To his surprise, she allowed him to lead her out the door without asking any questions.

His car was parked a few blocks away, and soon they were heading out of the city.

"Where are we going?" she asked.

"Home."

It was less than an hour later that Erik was parking in the garage set aside for his apartment building. O'Connell had fallen asleep, and Erik took a moment to look at her. She looked very small and vulnerable in his passenger seat, the blanket tucked around her. The bandage on her neck was stark against her skin.

Erik didn't know if Danny would have hurt her any more than he had, but Erik didn't care to repeat the experience. He didn't want her disappearing again, and he couldn't handle the thought of not being with her, so he'd brought her here.

"Wake up," he said, gently brushing her cheek. "We're here."

Her eyes fluttered open. Erik gave her a small smile and tucked a strand of hair behind her ear.

"Thank you," she said.

"For what?"

"Opening my eyes. I don't know if I ever would have left him if you hadn't come."

"I'm sorry my telling you what he did made him panic like that." His fingers brushed the bandage on her neck. "I didn't intend for you to get hurt."

"It's not your fault Danny went bat-shit crazy."

"I shot him. Again."

"I know. He'll be all right." She paused. "He deserved it."

Erik relaxed slightly. She wasn't angry with him. He'd been afraid she would be, and he didn't think he could bring himself to regret shooting Danny.

"Come upstairs with me," he said. He really didn't want to talk about Danny anymore.

O'Connell sat up and pushed the blanket off. "You don't have to ask me twice," she said.

Erik took her hand and led her upstairs to his apartment.

It felt surreal, watching her walk inside. She was finally here, with him, in the flesh. Having her in his space, his domain, made his possessive streak rear its head again. Erik wanted to throw her down on the nearest flat surface and mark her as his. The image in his mind of her legs around his waist as he thrust between her thighs, her sighs and moans filling the room, was intoxicating.

The sight of an abandoned T-shirt flung over a chair quickly banished those thoughts. Erik hadn't cleaned up before he left to meet O'Connell, so he started grabbing discarded clothes that were lying around. Erik had been distracted the past few weeks and hadn't given a shit about the state of his apartment. Now, he was slightly embarrassed.

"Uh, sorry for the mess," he said, tossing the clothes behind a chair in the corner. He shoved some dirty dishes into the sink. "I'm usually much cleaner than this."

O'Connell shot him an amused glance before resuming her slow tour. "I'm sure," she said.

Erik abruptly remembered the state of his office and hurried to intercept her just as she reached the door.

"Don't go in there," he said, jerking the door shut.

She arched a brow. "Why not?"

"It's my office. It's a disaster."

O'Connell just looked at him, waiting.

Shit. Erik didn't know how she did that, but he found himself stepping aside.

She took two steps into the room and froze, her jaw falling open.

The entire room was dedicated to her. Photos, no matter how obscure, were plastered to the walls. A huge whiteboard took up an entire wall and was littered with scrawl. Clarissa recognized places she'd been, jobs she'd done, people she'd worked with.

"I, uh, haven't had time to clean things up," Langston said.

Clarissa turned around. He looked like a kid who'd gotten caught with his hand in the proverbial cookie jar. And as strange as it was, it was hard not to be flattered by his obsession with her. After all, without it, they would never have met.

"So long as you only used this room for work and not for…pleasure…I have no problem with it." She couldn't help grinning as his ears turned bright red.

"Of course not! I would never…do…that," he spluttered in protest at her insinuation.

Clarissa laughed lightly and decided to put him out of his misery.

"I'm here, Langston," she said, wrapping her arms around his neck. "And I'm not going anywhere. You're stuck with me now."

"That's all I wanted," he said. His hands were gentle as he cradled her face, kissing her as though she were made of spun glass.

When they parted, Langston was looking at her as though he could see into her soul…and that he liked what he saw.

"You know," she said, "you told me something once, and I wasn't ready to hear it, or say it back. But I am now." She could swear he was holding his breath at her words. "I trust you, with my past, my present, and my future. *Our* future." She paused. "I love you, Langston."

He lifted her off her feet in a bone-crushing hug, smashing his lips to hers. Langston's happiness was infectious. He still loved her. He hadn't forgotten her. He'd searched for her, come for her.

"Call me Erik."

She was suddenly scooped up in his arms, and he was carrying her to his bedroom and placing her carefully on his bed. He stripped off his shirt and joined her, covering her body with his.

"I can't believe you're here," he said, his voice nearly a whisper.

Clarissa cupped his jaw, the rough stubble abrading her skin. "I can't believe you still want me here."

Langston took her hand, placing a kiss to the palm. "Always."

EPILOGUE

"O'Connell, I'm home," Erik called out as he entered the apartment. He dropped his keys and cell on the table before removing his gun and holster.

"Are you still going to call me that when your mom is here?"

Erik turned to see her leaning against the doorjamb to the office.

"She's only visiting for a few days, just long enough for the wedding." He took her in his arms for a kiss.

O'Connell pulled back, "Wait a minute, what wedding?"

Erik looked at her strangely. "Ours," he said slowly.

"I don't remember saying I'd marry you." Her brow was creased in confusion.

Erik just looked at her. How could she not remember? Oh no, not again—

"Ha! You're so easy, Langston," O'Connell said with a grin, her green eyes twinkling with mischief.

Erik sighed with relief, then his eyes narrowed. "You're going to pay for that one."

"Promises, promises."

She kissed him again in such a way that he quickly forgot what they'd been talking about. When he finally pulled back, he scrambled to get his thoughts back in order and asked, "So did you get that code over to the DOD today?"

TIFFANY SNOW

"Of course," she said. "It's amazing how much they're will-ing to pay for me to show them how incompetent they are."

"Hey, just be glad they wanted to know how you hacked SWIFT more than they wanted to put you in jail for it."

"As if you had nothing to do with that," O'Connell said.

Erik started undoing his tie. "I might have helped them…see what was in their best interest."

"Let me do that," she said, pushing his hands aside. The tie was soon sliding out from under his collar.

"Heard that Danny had his hearing today," Erik said.

"Oh, yeah?"

"He's being moved to Chesapeake. Close enough for you to visit." Erik watched her face, but she gave nothing away.

"Maybe someday," she said noncommittally. Erik knew she still hadn't forgiven Danny for what he'd done. It would take time. "Anything more on Solomon?"

"No. After you transferred the money back, it disap-peared."

"I'll find him," she said. She'd moved on to the buttons of his shirt.

"I don't want you to find him," Erik said. "I want you to stay far, far away." It was an ongoing point of contention between them.

"I could say the same to you," she said. She pushed his shirt off his shoulders. "Now are you going to keep talking or are you going to 'make me pay?'"

The answer to that was patently obvious.

The End

ABOUT THE AUTHOR

 A native of St. Louis, Missouri, Tiffany A. Snow earned degrees in education and history from the University of Missouri–Columbia, before launching a career in information technology. After nearly fifteen years in IT, she switched careers to what she always dreamed of doing—writing. Tiffany is the author of romantic suspense novels such as the Kathleen Turner series, which includes *No Turning Back*, *Turn to Me*, and *Turning Point*. Since she's drawn to character-driven books herself, that's what she loves to write, and the guy always gets his girl. She feeds her love of books with avid reading, yet she manages to spare time and considerable affection for trivia, eighties hair bands, the St. Louis Cardinals, and Elvis. She and her husband have two daughters and one dog whose untimely demise Tiffany contemplates on a daily basis.

Kindle *Serials*

This book was originally released in episodes as a Kindle Serial. Kindle Serials launched in 2012 as a new way to experience serialized books. Kindle Serials allow readers to enjoy the story as the author creates it, purchasing once and receiving all existing episodes immediately, followed by future episodes as they are published. To find out more about Kindle Serials and to see the current selection of Serials titles, visit www.amazon.com/kindleserials.

Made in the USA
San Bernardino, CA
23 February 2015